I0613915

FOREVER IS ETERNITY

Kathleen R. Cuyler

Mocha Wave
Publishing

ISBN: 979-8-9880238-0-7
Library of Congress Control Number: 2023905623

The story, all names, characters, and incidents portrayed in this publication are fictitious. No identification with actual persons (living or deceased), places, buildings, and products is intended or should be inferred.

Book Cover and Illustrations by Story-First Marketing, support@story-firstmarketing.com

Forever is Eternity

Some stories must be stepped into backward

Words are spells.
Memory is the key.

Inter-Story Intercessor Codebook

Wonderland

Alsó-Világ

Portals align under moonlight

Neverland

The Jolly Roger

Nothando's Chart

Essence of Forgotten Tales

Scales from Vorever

*Whispers from
the Netherworld*

Not all relics were given.

Frieda's Lantern

PART ONE

ALSÓ VILÁG

CHAPTER 1
THE LODGE

Edmond Davidson wanted to reach the hunting lodge before nightfall. The sun's reddish glow clung to the black jagged jaws of the Carpathian peaks as his new 1936 blue Jaguar crawled up the winding mountain road.

Twenty-one, studying at Cambridge, member of the Royal Society, acclaimed author of "Mesopotamia: Key to Christian-Pagan Mythology" in the Royal Journal of Anthropology, Edmond was travelling on scholarship to further his research in the private collection of Count Vlad Tepov. "Religion and the Cultural Construction of Monsters" was the proposed name of his latest treatise. His mentor, Professor Millgrew, had corresponded with Tepov, and the count had invited Edmond to join him and his guests at his hunting lodge in the mountains for the season.

A pale gleam of twilight held back the gloom. The narrow margin between the Jaguar's tires and the crumbling precipice below veered Edmond's attention, but he clutched his steering wheel and focused on the climbing road before him.

It was night when he pulled into the dirt road before the lodge. The Jaguar purred to a stop, and the headlights darkened. The lodge was a restoration of a once derelict castle, surrounded by a spiked iron wall. Gray and rambling, its twin Persian-style towers were a shadow play back-dropped by the bleak orb of the harvest moon.

Edmond shivered. By the light of his electric torch, he rummaged in the boot for his luggage.

Balancing his bags, he was glad when an accented voice offered, "I take for you." He turned the torch to get a glimpse of the man beside him, a spare little man, whose green eyes darted under untidy brows and a cap of black fur.

"Edmond Davidson." Edmond touched the brim of his homburg with his gloved hand. "Count?"

The little man hit his own chest. "Miroslav. Come with me." He pried the luggage from Edmond and led the way towards the lodge.

Focusing the beam of his torch on his guide, Edmond followed. The drawbridge they crossed was fringed on either side with stalactites of ice. A gust of wintry air whistled past them, and Edmond raised the collar of his woolen overcoat about his face. Miroslav welcomed the blast bare faced.

A screech startled the night. Edmond lifted the beam towards a bird of prey circling the towers.

"Vulture," said Miroslav. "Many dead things in the fields. Gentlemen go hunting today. They hunt always this week."

Vulture? Edmond squinted at the winging creature. More like a small pterodactyl. Vultures have rounded heads. This creature has a large, diamond-shaped head. But it must be a vulture, a strange Carpathian variety, no doubt.

A door across the courtyard opened, emitting a pale light. A tall, big-boned woman, shawled and aproned, blocked all but a rim of the glow. Her long frown and protruding eyes were far from welcoming.

"Ilda," announced Miroslav. "Not pretty but good housekeeper." He jerked his head towards Ilda, signaling her to move aside.

She heaved to the left to allow them to be ingested into the doorway.

The vulture was alone with the moon. A yellow glow snapped on from an almond-shaped window in an upper chamber of the tower. Its jagged wings rustled past the frosted panes, and it roosted its splayed claws over the gable.

The creature craned its snaky neck down and cocked its diamond head as it leered in with one ruby eye. The windowpanes opened. An elegant loose-sleeved arm of a man reached out and unfolded, wrist upward. The scaly claws wrapped around the arm, and the arm drew the creature inside.

The front hall, though austere, had a chivalric splendor. Recent restoration had rid the place of cobwebs and crumbling stone and established clean, symmetric stone, polished wood, and fine feudal decor. From the balustrade guarding the second-floor landing hung a crimson banner bordered in gold, depicting a black clawing dragon.

An iron brazier commanded the center of the hall. The flames cast dark shapes upon the walls. As Edmond surveyed the hall, he slipped off his homburg and tossed his gloves into the hat. Ilda snatched his coat and hat, while Miroslav disappeared with the luggage.

Edmond stepped towards the fire to warm himself. "Edmond . . ." A woman's voice, like patchouli escaping from alabaster, rippled over the flames. He circled the brazier, towards the stairs. A form of a woman of ethereal beauty wisped in front of him. "Stop." She lifted the palm of her translucent hand towards him.

Intrigued, he moved forward. "Stop!" She pushed her open palm out and released an invisible force that rippled, hummed, and thrust him back. Her long, dark tresses floated about her as if she were in water.

"Madame. I beg your pardon. I come at the invitation of the count." He lifted his eyes with his charming smile. "What? Uh, who . . .?"

"You should not have come here." Her voice was a murmur of echoes. "Do not be deceived. Do not fall into temptation." The clip of approaching boot steps echoed from the second floor landing. She looked at the balustrade, then leaned towards Edmond. "I will see you in the garden by the well."

The count stood at the top of the stairs. Edmond glanced back at the fire, but the woman had vanished.

Count Vlad Tepov was a slender man, about thirty. He wore tall riding boots, country tweed, a silken ascot tucked into his vest and a suit jacket flung casually about his shoulders. One eye was darker than the other. His lashes were full and dark, his lips voluptuous and red, an eerie contrast to his pale, hollow face and blond hair. His eyebrows constantly frowned. He held a cigarette between his first two fingers and thumb.

"Davidson." The count tapped down the steps.

"Count?" Edmond nodded.

Tepov shot a perturbed glare at the kitchen, yelled for his servants, and the next instant bestowed a gracious countenance upon his guest. "How was your journey? Not too tiring, I hope." He was circling Edmond but paused to take a draught from his cigarette.

Edmond shifted, discomfited by the count's scrutiny. "Well, the journey was long, but I bought this Italian sports model, and those mountain roads were an excellent test for her engine."

"The blue machine you drove up in? She's a beauty. Miroslav." The little man crept forward. "Put Mr. Davidson's car away in the garage." Miroslav bowed and withdrew.

"I say," said Edmond, "it's excellent of you to invite me here. Your collection of books . . ."

The count had picked up a stack of letters from a side table and was barely listening anymore. "Not at all. I have some business to see to, but get settled and let Ilda or Miroslav know if you need anything. We have much to discuss. Your research fascinates me. Ilda, show Mr. Davidson to his room. Get him anything he needs."

"Yes, my lord." The maid barreled past Edmond.

Edmond followed, shooting a nervous glance to where the ghostly woman had been, but all else seemed as expected. And what of it if there was anything amiss? He was a clever enough fellow. He had nothing to fear.

CHAPTER 2
THE WEEPING LADY

Edmond woke, alarmed by two green eyes staring down at him. He backed deeper into the pillow, blinking at the morning light streaming through the window. It was Miroslav, one hand steadied on the bed post, who was watching Edmond.

Miroslav stepped back and gestured to the fireplace. "I bring coals, make fire warm, bring water to clean and shave." He pantomimed each announcement, keeping his eyes on Edmond as if waiting to be flogged for his trouble.

Edmond propped himself on his elbow. Bad dreams had haunted him all night, the usual nightmares of dark pits and locked doors. He groped for his cigarettes on the nightstand and lit one. "Miroslav, my man, is there anything like a bath around?"

Edmond returned to his room after the bath, robed and rubbing his full dark hair with a towel. Ilda arrived with a breakfast tray. Rolls, jam, and coffee. "Eat." She thrust the tray at him, rattling the cups and splattering the cream.

Once he had breakfasted and dressed, Edmond considered excavating the library, but he recalled his appointment in the garden with the mysterious woman.

"Miroslav." Edmond caught the servant crossing the front hall. "Is there a garden on the grounds?"

"Why, yes, outside kitchen." A wave of fear passed over the servant's face. "But no one goes there."

"Oh? Explain."

"The ghost. The ghost of the lady . . . She weeps. She sings and she weeps. By the old well she weeps."

"Ghost? Miroslav, are you a brave man?"

"Yes, sir."

"And a loyal man?"

"My family has served Tepov household faithfully for hundreds of years."

"Excellent. Worthy fellow. You are just the chap to guide me to this haunted garden."

Miroslav recoiled. "No, sir. It is evil place."

"Nonsense. You mean to tell me your family has served a line of heartless masters, hunting Gypsies for sport, boiling serfs in oil, watching Turks bleed to death on giant spikes, and you are afraid of evil? I will never trust your word again."

"You doubt the word of Miroslav?"

"I never doubt the word of the redoubtable Miroslav. I only suggest that, in honor of your loyal ancestors, you guide me to this garden."

Miroslav was confused but relented. "I show you. But the count will not like anything to happen to guest."

The servant led him into the kitchen, past Ilda cleaving cabbages with loud, steady thunks, to a back door wreathed in dried pungent herbs.

Miroslav pushed open the door, letting in a whoosh of autumn air. Leaving Miroslav behind, Edmond ventured into this garden and came upon a cobbled path over white-flecked winter grass. Along the sides ran a short stone wall tangled with brown, hibernating vines. Large, downy snowflakes drifted from the pale sky, a peep of yellow sunlight forming a mystic aura around the garden. Far from a place of evil, the nipping chill whispered of snow angels, plum pudding, buttered rum, and carols.

He heard the most beautiful voice. Like a nurse singing a sick child to sleep. As he followed the voice, a rabbit scampered across the snow-dusted path, halted and sniffed the air. Edmond pitied the creature and cursed the cracking shots from the hunting party that had driven it here. The singing continued, and he followed until he arrived at a fairytale well, its roof entwined with holly berries and ivy. Upon the well's broad circular base sat a maiden, her raven hair twisted in an elaborate braid with a mulberry-colored ribbon. She wore a white-trimmed mauve coat, her mittened hands tucked in a muff. Her eyes were sad swirls

of black and gold under full well-shaped brows. Her lips, the color of her coat, formed a pout that could drive men to duel dragons, defy fate, and descend into Hades. She slid her hand from the muff and held it out to him.

Go ahead. Touch me, she spoke with her eyes.

He touched the tips of her fingers. They felt like the frost that forms on windows and disembodies at the warm breath. His touch tingled through her immaterial hand. It sent a thrill of electricity through his body.

A ghost? his mind asked hers.

She shook her head and fixed his brown eyes with hers. You know who I am.

"What are you?"

That is not important. What matters is how to free you from this prison.

He laughed, and it startled him, because he laughed out loud. "I'm no prisoner. I'm here on scholarship. The count . . ."

Her eyes flashed.

"What is it?"

The count is evil.

"And you sing enchantments against him?"

"No," she said aloud, "I sing a prayer. A wish for you to find what your heart seeks, a light amid the darkness, a harbor amidst the storm, and a safe road home again." She shimmered and vanished.

A hunting rifle's shot exploded the white, still day, and Edmond started, wondering if he had been asleep and dreaming.

He retraced his steps towards the kitchen, but the snow-flakes had become a flurry and had covered the path. A set of imprints in the snow caught his eye, the paw prints of a large four-legged animal. They veered to the left, and Edmond saw where the prints skidded to an abrupt stop, pushing the snow into a disheveled heap of muddy slush. Beside the slush were scattered drops of blood. He followed the dragging paw prints up to a thicket. A howl of distress broke through the wintry air.

Kicking aside the bramble, he ventured into the thicket. He scratched his hand on the thorns and tripped on something that clanked like a chain. Huddled before him was a gray wolf, green soulful eyes piercing his own. Its shoulder had been ripped by a bullet, its paw caught in a trap.

Edmond pitied the beast. He reached forward, but the wolf growled a low warning. Edmond withdrew his hand. "I'm not a bad chap, really," he reassured the wolf. "Maybe not the best, but I know what traps are like." The wolf raised its chin a notch and pricked up one ear.

"I'd like to help if I may," said Edmond. The wolf bowed its head and tried to lift the paw clamped in the jaws of the trap. Again, Edmond reached forward. This time the wolf whined softly.

Edmond pulled with both hands to pry the trap's jaws open. The wolf's chin brushed against him, like moist prickly velvet. Once Edmond got it loose, the wolf yelped and sprang back. Its green eyes met his with gratitude. Then the creature drew back into the thicket. Its gleaming eyes were the last to be swallowed by the darkness.

Edmond spent the afternoon hunched over a desk in the library, studying a book borrowed from Tepov's famous collection. He wanted to ask someone about the ghost of the well, but

Ilda was stirring a sauce on the stove and Miroslav, she said, had gone for more firewood.

So, he focused on the books. The Book of Werewolves, An Account of the Principalities of Wallachia and Moldavia, and Hungarian Lore. According to Chapter VI of this last book, the dragon from their mythology was called Ordog, an evil god, and, according to pages cci - cciv, Alsó-Világ was a sort of under-world. Both Ordog and his underworld absorbed the souls of sinners when they died.

Not unlike Old English depictions of Hell Mouth. In Anglo-Saxon sermons, Hell Mouth was depicted as a giant wyrm or dragon in the bowels of which sinners were eternally digested "where the wyrm dieth not." Edmond clutched the wooden box which contained the relic he and his uncle had dug up on their expedition to the Middle East. The legends surrounding the relic claimed it was a fragment of a dragon's scale. Could it be . . . that in this box, I am carrying a fragment of hell?

He shook himself free of such musings and stood to stretch his tense back and shoulders. The room was stuffy, so he went to open the window.

At the window was a little girl, her breath forming a round white haze on the pane. As the steam cleared, he saw her fearful black eyes peering in and her turned up nose pressed against the glass. A servant? A child of one of the guests? The count's ward? The shiver along his spine sensed something supernatural about this child. She rapped on the pane. He stepped back. She rapped once more and threw an apprehensive glance behind herself.

Her index finger traced figures in the fog on the pane. The letters were in English, but backwards as in a mirror: NI EM TEL

He pressed his hand over his tired eyes, hoping this hallu-cination would vanish. He lifted the hand partway to find hers planted against the glass. The fog cleared around the area of her little hand. The circle of glass beneath it melted, and she reached through the glass. Her fingers had a bluish light around them as they stretched towards him. "Edmond, Edmond, let me in."

He grasped hold of the little icy hand, but it was not a hand of flesh but ectoplasmic, a viscous electricity through which his own hand passed. "What are you?" he asked.

A tear formed at the corner of her eye as she peered up into his face. Without warning, she evaporated.

Edmond had tried all his adult life to suppress his childhood fear of the dark and the unknown and had committed himself to disproving the supernatural, but the two encounters with phantasms had disquieted his resolve. Perhaps someone called Dracula did live here long ago, a nefarious vampire whose legacy of victims still haunts this place.

The dark impression of these apparitions vanished by the time his host returned with the hunting party that evening. The count looked the perfect picture of the 1930s European gentleman. He sported a fine hat, brim dipped below one eye, a cravat tucked into his suit, the collar of his overcoat stylishly raised. Despite his thinness, the count was attractive, the type Hollywood plastered across glam mags and cigarette billboards. Edmond's mentor, Professor Millgrew, had advised him to get in good with the count, that a man of his influence could open many doors for a clever, ambitious young chap.

Tepov set down his alpine stick, flung off his coat and hat, and tossed them to Ilda. He pushed back the stray blond lock from his forehead and joined Edmond by the fire. "Hallo. You should have seen the chamois scamper. Cajoled him into my scope and . . ." He raised his arms as if aiming a rifle and clicked his tongue to imitate firing, after which he sniggered a laugh through large grinning teeth and bright dazzling eyes.

The gruff huntsmen with him grumbled, patted him on the back, and sought the frothing brew Ilda was sloshing into their tankards.

Tepov held his long fingers out to the flames. He shot an approving glance at Edmond. "This, gentlemen, is the famous Professor Davidson, here to do research into the supernatural."

Edmond stepped forward to greet the guests, but they hung back in a huddle, muttering under the collars of their fur coats. They were dark whiskered with mistrustful amber eyes under black scowling brows.

Edmond frowned. "Not quite a professor," he corrected his host. "But I am rather keen on the concept of monsters. You see," he went on, his passion for the subject outweighing his annoyance, "there are many views on what a monster symbolizes. Some say they are the incarnation of the evil in a society, others that they are depictions of the mindless beast suppressed within each of us, the unsavory impulses of a less evolved stage."

One of the hunters, a taller man with a long face, snarled, "So. You believe in monsters . . . Professor Davidson?"

"Now, Dmitri," the count interjected, "be civil to our guest."

Edmond breathed out sharply but kept his temper. "I believe by explaining the origins of these myths we can enlighten the world to scientific reality as opposed to religious delusions."

"Tell them," said the count, "about what you keep in the box in the library . . . Tell them about your . . . interesting artifact."

"Yes, as he says, the artifact I uncovered has been suggested to be the scale of a dragon."

"A dragon scale?" Dmitri and the other guests chortled among themselves.

"Dragons," continued Edmond, "are referred to as supernatural beings in most folklore, your own included. This scale is evidence that perhaps all the monsters and gods of legend and myth were also mortal, made of fibers that shed and decay."

"Hrrumph," said one of the hunters. "What does an Englisher know about mortality? Or . . . immortality?" They turned their shoulders on Edmond, muttering among themselves.

The count shrugged and took a cigarette from his case. "Never mind these brutes." Edmond took a lighter from his pocket and lit the count's cigarette. The count's eyes caught on Edmond's hand. "What happened?" His eyebrows frowned as smoke sifted past his teeth.

Edmond glanced at the small cut on his hand. "Oh, I scratched myself on a thorn, out by the garden."

Tepov shifted. "Near the well. Hmm. You need to be careful out there." He pushed himself from the wall and moved into the midst of his guests to steer them towards the dining room.

Chapter 3
THROUGH THE LOOKING GLASS

Two weeks ago at Perlgate Manor in Bedfordshire, Edmond had packed his bags. Betty, his eighteen-year-old cousin, leaned against the bedpost, her black eyes fixed in disapproval as she unpocketed a book from the white apron of her housemaid uniform. "You know what's been said about that place?"

"About . . . the undead?" He blinked in amusement at the copy of *Dracula* by Bram Stoker she held.

Both wards of their uncle and aunt, Sir Eric and Lady Amelia Mallowan, Edmond and Betty were alike in their determination. However, while she continued in the station of a servant, he, who had begun as a stable hand, had managed to climb in favor so far as to rival their benefactors' own son, Leslie.

"Last year you objected to me doing field work with Uncle in Mesopotamia . . . afraid the curse of the tomb would claim me," Edmond reminded Betty. "And all of us got back all right . . . just a little heat exhaustion on poor Leslie's part." Their cousin Leslie was fair skinned and had a delicate constitution, and it had been up to Edmond to take Leslie's place as Uncle Eric's right-hand man on their last expedition.

"But Tepov is a vampire," she replied. "You know what vampires do to people."

"Rubbish. No doubt the historical Count Dracula resorted to cruel measures to punish his enemies and control his serfs, but so did most conquering warriors in those days. It doesn't mean he grew fangs, drank blood, or transformed into a bat. Anyway, I'm much cleverer than that Renfield chap. And I'm a good deal taller, too."

"Harker," she corrected. "You watched the Bela Lugosi movie. You need to read the book. Take it. At least you'll know what you're in for."

"I don't need any more books, and I don't need a crucifix either. Better put that back before Aunt Amelia sees it's missing from the library." He took up his bags and nudged her from the door. Leslie was in the hallway, looking pale and sleepy as usual.

"Thank goodness we're finally rid of old smarty pants." Leslie had resented Edmond ever since he had interloped into his world at age fourteen and had made him his scapegoat. Sweets missing from the kitchen? Leslie had said he could take them. A window smashed? Leslie shouldn't have been throwing so hard. He called down the stairs, "I hope you rot in those dreary old rat-infested castles. I hope you rot and never come back."

"And a good day to you too, Leslie," returned Edmond merrily, pausing at the foot of the stairs to swing his bag over one shoulder. "Stay out of trouble and away from draughts. Don't want you catching cold."

So Edmond departed, and Betty was left to wait. And to watch. At first, the watching happened subconsciously, when her mind drifted while reading a book or when she closed her eyes too tightly and ghosts of images played across the screen of her eyelids. But one day, she found herself consciously peering through the veil.

She was cleaning the ash out of the fireplace in the sitting room adjacent to Lady Mallowan's bedroom and accidentally knocked a hand mirror from a table. The glass shattered among the ashes, and something glinted in one of the shards. Betty, an avid reader of the classics, knew mirrors have a particular significance for authors. *Snow Queen, Snow White, Through the Looking Glass (And What Alice Found There), The Lady of Shalott, Dracula.* And a *broken* mirror was even more ominous. She snatched her magnifying glass from her apron pocket, where she kept it ever since reading *The Adventures of Sherlock Holmes*, and interjected it between her eye and the shard to examine the source of the glint.

Granted, she thought, *it could be the light from the window catching in the glass, but it's not exactly a light, more like a color.* She corrected the distance of the magnifying glass and was alarmed by what she saw.

It was an eye, an unblinking blue-irised eye, staring back at her. She jolted. A sharp edge of the shard pricked her finger. A drop of her blood obscured the glass. Numb, unable to move, she felt as though her mind belonged to some other entity.

Summoning her willpower, Betty flung the shard into the fireplace. She shoveled coal over the shard, grabbed a scrap of paper from a jar on the mantel and lit it on a candle. She threw the paper into the coal to get the embers burning.

The shard moved. It penetrated up through the coal, and, as if the shard were a film projector and the fireplace the screen, it revealed another place and time. She no longer felt controlled. She could see without being seen. Moving backward from an extreme close-up view was a white-sleeved arm with a miniature crimson dragon, about the size of a falcon, perched upon it. The back of the man's head had blondish-brown hair neatly clipped in the middle of a long, well-shaped neck. The head turned to the side, the longer strands of hair closer to his face falling across his forehead, past thick, frowning eyebrows, framing a pair of intense eyes, one blue and one brown. The man spoke to the dragon.

"What have you seen?"

"He is here, my love," responded the dragon in a smoky, brittle voice.

"Davidson? Excellent. Soon he will be our slave. And what he has will be ours. He is weak. He will not resist me." The man paused and knitted his eyebrows. "The only thing that could go wrong . . ."

The dragon cocked its head to one side and flicked its tongue. "What is it?"

The man let the dragon crawl off his arm onto a golden perch near a full-length mirror. He ran a hand through the hair fallen across his forehead, tossed it back, and faced Betty, but instead of looking at her, he peered into the mirror, searching for something. "Strange." The man tapped a cigarette on his wrist. "A while ago I dreamed." He lit the cigarette and turned from the mirror. "I *think* I was dreaming. It was different from my usual dreams. I was just beginning to stir, and the moist earth around me was so soothing, I could not be sure, but I believe I saw a woman observing me."

"*The* woman?" The dragon's eyes widened, its mouth open in anticipation.

"Yes, I'm sure it was her. She was here. In this room. Incredibly close. Her finger was so near my mouth. But, I assure you, it was just a little jab with the tip of my fangs."

"You tasted her? How much, my love?" asked the dragon.

"Just a drop. Half a drop at most."

The dragon drummed its claws against the golden perch in thought. Then, its red scales bristled as it fixated on the mirror, its eyes protruding right into Betty's.

"My love, my love!" squawked the dragon, flapping its wings in desperation. "The mirror. Destroy the mirror."

The man flung about to face the mirror and clutched up a cast iron poker. He hesitated, firming his mouth as if unwilling to comply.

"Destroy her, while you may," commanded the dragon.

And, cursing to himself, the man slammed the poker into the mirror.

Betty fell backwards to avoid the thrashing of the poker, and the ashes fell about her like splintered fragments of glass.

"What are you up to now?"

From where she was sprawled backwards on the floor, she strained her neck to see who it was. It was Leslie in the doorway of Lady Mallowan's sitting room, appearing upside down due to the backward tilt of her head.

"I thought you were supposed to tidy up the place, not play in the cinders." Leslie ran a finger along the dusty edge of the cherry wood armoire.

Betty growled and scrambled to her feet, adjusting her skirt and apron. "I wasn't playing." She thrust her magnifying glass into her pocket. The vision in the fireplace had vanished, and all that remained were embers, dust, and glass all over the hearth.

"Well, if you don't clean that mess soon, mother will not be happy. Especially if I tell her you were reading those trashy novels again instead of doing your chores." Leslie, who was nineteen, often behaved as if he were still thirteen. He was a little over six feet tall, although he slouched, and wore creased trousers with turned up cuffs and a brick red cardigan. His brown hair was parted to the left, and his dull brown eyes contemplated her under one uplifted eyebrow. He would have been handsome if he wasn't so annoying.

"Leslie," she asked as she stared into the fireplace, "do you ever see things? I mean, like faraway places and mysterious people?"

"Only at the cinema." Leslie flipped through a magazine rack. "Or when I get there by boat or train or automobile, like any *normal* person." He raised his eyebrows and snorted to indicate he doubted she would qualify as a normal person. "Say, you haven't thrown out my comic books, have you?"

"No. Aunt Amelia wanted me to, but I rescued your precious comic books. They're in your room."

"Oh. Well." Leslie, taken aback by Betty's thoughtfulness, turned to leave.

"Leslie . . ?"

He stopped and heaved an impatient sigh.

"When you were sick in Mesopotamia, you didn't have hallucinations?"

Leslie scowled. "I wasn't sick. The climate didn't agree with me, that's all. And Edmond the Almighty kept pushing me too hard. He pushed everyone too hard, but especially me. The worst decision mother and father ever made was taking you two in, him with his god-awful dimples and you with your eternal books."

"Books." Betty leapt to her feet. "That's it, thank you. I know what I need to do."

CHAPTER 4
HAMBERDEEN'S BOOKSHOP (1930S)

During her afternoon break, Betty borrowed the bicycle from the kitchen maid and wheeled the five miles down the path into town. Between Aunt Fanny's Antiques and Pennington's Confectionary shop was a shamrock-green shop with gold trim and letters in Old English font across the gabled doorway proclaiming it "Hamberdeen's Used Books." Betty leaned her bicycle against a lamppost, went in, and the door set off a bell to alert the shop to a new customer. She closed the door and breathed in the air of mildewing wood, dusty shelves, yellowing pages, and cracked leather spines. Between two avalanches of books on the front counter was a metal cash register, but no one was there.

"Mr. Hamberdeen," she called. She ripped the scarf from her head and wrung it as she looked around.

"Mr. Hamberdeen is out," called the warm voice of a woman from a back room.

Betty wound her way down a creaky wooden slope rumpled over with a faded rug, past a cavern of shelves and tables, around a corner, to an alcove labeled "Rare Books."

A woman of about forty, plump, with golden-blond hair in a bun, round rosy cheeks and a double chin, sat comfortably in an overstuffed chair torn in spots where it was losing its stuffing.

She wore spectacles on top her head, which she lowered to her nose as she peeped up from her paperback at Betty.

"I was looking for Mr. Hamberdeen," said Betty.

"Yes. I heard. But he's out right now. Had an errand to run. Asked if I would keep an ear open for customers, but this old place, no one bothers much, no one reads anymore, do they." She sighed and pushed her spectacles back on top of her head.

Betty slid a hand over the spines of old books, becoming dusty and cracked on the shelf. "I love reading."

"Me too. Sit down, fellow bibliophile." The woman patted the seat of a chair near hers. "And tell me what you're looking for. Maybe I can help."

"Well, I'm not sure."

"Catch your breath anyway. You've been running."

"Bicycling." Betty sat on the table between the two chairs and unbuttoned her coat. Her fingers fumbled on the buttons, and she jumped when a gust of wind banged the shutters.

The woman looked around to make sure no unsavory characters had invaded her sacred sphere. "Has someone been chasing you?"

"It's difficult to explain, and I don't have much time. I'm on break, you see."

"Oh yes, you're the little maid from Perlgate. You served me tea once when I called on your aunt, trying to get her to donate to something or other good cause. I'm Miss Fernsby." She put out her hand.

"Betty." Betty smiled and shook her hand.

"I know these books better than old Hamberdeen himself, I'll wager. I do most of my research here."

"You're a writer?"

"Not that I've published anything, mind you, except for those two poems in the local rag. But, one day." She sighed as one who expects little but hopes much. "Now. Most people who come into a rare books section are one of three types. Collector, seeker, or Intercessor."

"I've heard of collectors. And I suppose a seeker is someone who reads for knowledge." Betty put a contemplative finger on her chin. "But what is an Intercessor?"

"Few people are Intercessors. But I can usually recognize one. Intercessors don't simply read books. They *enter* them, take *part* in them, get to *know* the characters."

"I do love to read, and people always say I let my imagination get the better of me."

"What books have you read?"

"Fiction mostly. All the Sherlock Holmes stories, *Jane Eyre*, *Pride and Prejudice*, *Three Musketeers*, Verne, Dostoyevsky, Tolstoy, and *Dracula*."

"What happens when you read?"

Betty squeezed her upper arms as she contemplated the pile of books beside her. "When I read, I feel like I'm entering into their world. I can imagine myself right there with them, as if I, too, were a character in the story."

Miss Fernsby nodded, pleased. "And the books feel real to you, do they?"

"Yes, very. It's like they *are* real."

"That's not surprising. You see, books open portals, doorways to other dimensions, but not everyone can find their way in." Miss Fernsby closed her book.

"Could a mirror be a portal?"

"Lewis Carroll thought so. Most reflective surfaces or mysterious doorways *can* be a portal, but while these portals are the trains, the book is your ticket to your destination. Whatever your difficulty, my dear, if you find the right page of the right book at the right time, there is no telling what wondrous things you will accomplish."

"Am I an Intercessor?"

Miss Fernsby folded her arms across her full chest. "Let's try an experiment. I'll say a word, and you tell me what you see." She settled back and thought. At last she said, "Sherlock Holmes."

"A Persian slipper stuffed with tobacco, the scratched glossy wood of a Stradivarius, and a smoldering burn on the carpet from acid spilt from a test tube."

"*Jane Eyre.*"

"Paint smudge on the latch of a box, travel gloves wet with rain, the clatter of a carriage, the smell of mud, and the slippery stickiness of candle grease on a bed post."

"One more. Dracula."

"The crackle of a fire in the middle of a great hall with gray stone walls and a red tapestry with a picture of a black dragon. And Edmond." She jumped to her feet. "He's in danger."

Miss Fernsby clasped Betty's hands. "My dear, you are indeed an Intercessor. You have not just read of these things. You have been there and seen details only an Intercessor could see. I, too, am an Intercessor. That is how I know. If we are going to help this Edmond of yours, you will need to find the right page of the right book."

"You're going to help me?"

"Of course. You need someone who knows what they're doing." She heaved herself from her chair, emitting a slight moan, as from rheumatism. "The best place to discuss this is right around the corner at the teashop. I'll give your aunt a call and say you're assisting me with my research, so we'll have as much time as we need."

Betty was grateful to have at last found an ally. After calling Perlgate from the phone at the counter, Miss Fernsby borrowed a key from a brass hook near the front desk and locked the store as they left. She tucked the key under the door mat with the naturalness of habit, as if this were an agreed upon arrangement between her and Mr. Hamberdeen.

CHAPTER 5
A CUP OF TEA (1930S)

Betty had seen the teashop from outside but had never ventured in. Miss Fernsby gave the girl at the counter her hat and coat, kept her gloves, and led Betty to a table near the window. "I'm starving," said Miss Fernsby, "and a good cup of tea is just what we need, with a plate of scones, I think, or do you prefer cucumber sandwiches?"

"The sandwiches, please." Betty was quite hungry, having not had anything to eat since an early, meager breakfast.

"All right, Maggie," Miss Fernsby said to the hostess. "A pot of Jasmine tea, milk and sugar on the side, and some of your famous cucumber sandwiches. Just a hint of mint and lemon juice on the sandwiches, not so much pepper this time."

Soon the tea was ready to pour, and the sandwiches were stacked in perfect crustless white triangles on Wedgewood plates.

"Now." Miss Fernsby helped herself to a sandwich. "Tell me your adventure from the beginning. Do not omit a single detail, as our friend Mr. Holmes would say."

"My adventure. Hmm." Betty stirred her tea as her mind transported her back to her early childhood when she lived with her mother, a thin, tired woman who worked long hours at a shirt factory in London. A fire at the factory took her mother from her, and she was sent to live with her uncle, a merchant sailor, and his son Edmond. Uncle Mike was usually drunk, and Edmond helped her escape his tirades into the streets of London.

"We lived on the streets mostly," she explained to Miss Fernsby. "Edmond looked after me, protected me from the ruffians. Until Uncle Mike said he could no longer take care of us and sent us to charity school. Edmond went to a school for boys, and I went to a school for girls, where I learned to love reading. Four years later, Aunt Amelia came to take in an orphan over yuletide, and she chose me. I told her about my cousin Edmond, and so she took him in as well. At first it was just going to be a month or two, but we made ourselves so helpful she and Uncle Eric let us stay on as servants, Edmond as a stable hand and me as a maid. I was content as a maid, but Edmond . . ." Betty blushed. "He has always wanted a little more. He's clever, you see. He even managed to earn a scholarship to the university and made a name for himself. We were all so proud of him."

"Didn't he join Sir Eric on one of his digs?"

"Yes. And he uncovered some amazing finds. He told me he found a dragon scale from ancient Babylon." She thought back to the scale he had shown her, a bright scale of gold, so large she needed both hands to hold it.

"Well," said Miss Fernsby, "the Babylonians had all kinds of ideas, man-eating lions, kings turning into wild beasts. A dragon would not surprise me at all." She took a sip of tea. "Oh, and wasn't your cousin engaged? I don't usually pay attention to the society column, but there was a lovely photo of your cousin and . . . what's her name?"

Betty frowned. "Daphne Graham. Aunt Amelia gave her a debutante ball when Edmond came back from university. That's where they first announced their engagement."

Miss Fernsby set down her teacup. "What is it you don't like about Miss Graham?"

"Nothing. She's all right." Betty relented and met Miss Fernsby's discerning gaze. "I mean, I don't think she would know a book if it bit her, but she doesn't mean any harm."

Miss Fernsby raised her eyebrows in recognition of the type. "And what did you think of Edmond coming home?"

Betty blushed. "He had been gone a long time. He sometimes wrote letters, but he had gotten busy lately, so he stopped writing."

"Tell me the truth. What did he look like when he came home? Darcy? Rochester? Heathcliff? Or all three combined?"

"Miss Fernsby!"

"But he had eyes for only Daphne, right?"

"Well, he seemed happy about the engagement. Her father is a leading member of the Royal Society. He called it 'advantageous.' But we did have *one* dance."

Betty remembered that dance. She had always admired Edmond. He was different from most boys. Even on the London streets, with dirty face and hands, he was brave and rather gallant, not against stealing a bun from the bakery, but any ruffian who dared throw a clot of mud at Betty would face his wrath and eat mud from the gutter before begging forgiveness. His father had told him to look out for her, and he accepted the responsibility as a sacred duty. When they were separated into different schools, Betty worried about him. He was not the sort of boy who would do well under a system of rules and harsh discipline.

"One dance," prompted Miss Fernsby.

"He said no one looked as pretty as me. But Edmond always was a charmer. I've learned not to give credit to everything he says." She focused on the embroidery in the corner of the serviette.

"Ah, one of *those*. He makes our hearts swoon and our minds cringe."

"He just needs someone who understands him, I think. And Daphne . . . she may not be ready for someone like Edmond." Betty pitied Daphne, who expected Edmond to be the perfect

Prince Charming and reliable husband. Edmond, she knew, would inevitably disappoint Daphne as he had already disappointed Betty.

She remembered when they were children caught in a rainstorm. They had sat together on the steps in the shopfront, rain pouring on his head and down his neck as he shielded her from the brunt of the icy downpour. Then the Edmond she met after his stint in charity school, bitter and vengeful, unleashing his tirade of hate against do-gooder hypocrites. Then the Edmond who barely noticed her at all once he had been embraced by higher society.

Miss Fernsby sighed and sat back in her chair. "Is anyone ever ready for the Edmonds in this world?" She picked up one more sandwich. "Let's get to the important part. When was the first time you found yourself pulled into the pages of a book?"

"Hmm. I remember one time. I was reading *Through the Looking Glass*. Alice was going through the mirror, when my mind wandered, and I could see Edmond. I had just received a letter from him. He told me how cruel they were to him at school, how they beat him and left him in the cellar. I was so worried, I wished I could slip through the mirror and reach him. I looked into his world, but all I could see was a fireplace and books. And I felt so cold, as if I were outside. I tried to tell Edmond to let me in, but he was afraid of me."

"Now we are getting somewhere. That definitely sounds like a pilgrimage."

"Pilgrimage?"

"That's what we Intercessors call trips through the portals. Where is Edmond now?"

"That's why I'm so worried. I need to find a book on ancient vampire lore, or something. I need to know what I'm up against."

"Wait. Different books have different portals, and we need to choose them wisely. You may think you need a book on vampire lore, but that book may be a portal into a stuffy study somewhere to a professor who has nothing better to do with his time than dig up old legends and write about them in the

35

most uninteresting style possible. So, tell me, why do you think you need a book on vampire lore?"

Betty explained to Miss Fernsby about Edmond's correspondence with Vlad Tepov and his departure to the Carpathian Mountains. She also told her about the broken mirror, the drop of blood, and what she saw in the fireplace. By the time she finished her story, nothing but breadcrumbs were left on the sandwich plate and not a drop of tea left in the pot.

"Now to roll up our sleeves and get to work." Miss Fernsby snapped open her purse to pay. "The thing about portals is to get the time and place right. You go home for now while I do a little research."

CHAPTER 6
THE INTERCESSORS (1930S)

After dinner, Edmond withdrew from the company and occupied his mind with a solitary game of chess in the library. The hunters in the den were bellowing some riotous song, one heavy-handed fellow pounding away at a piano.

Edmond tapped the ashes of his cigarette into an ashtray as he leaned over the chess board, rubbing his forehead to dispel a headache. He was not thinking about chess. He was trying to shut out images of banshees, wolves, and phantom children.

"More coffee, sir?" It was Miroslav with a copper Turkish coffee pot. The after-dinner coffee Edmond had already sampled was nauseatingly sweet and rich.

"No, thanks, Miroslav. Where I'm from we're used to plain food and polite company. Why does Tepov put up with that boorish crew of nitwits?" He jerked a perturbed cigarette towards the clanking piano din.

Miroslav's eyes darted to the door. "You should not name them names."

"Oh, I have much nicer names than that to call them. If they . . ." Edmond glanced up from the chess board. Miroslav's forearm was wrapped mummy style in a long, tight bandage. Edmond set his hand on the servant's shoulder out of concern, but Miroslav flinched and concealed his arm behind his back.

"What's wrong? Did someone hurt you?"

"No. No." Miroslav backed away.

"Your arm . . ."

"I . . . I was bitten. Animal. Big, sharp teeth. "

"A . . . wolf?"

"No, no, not a wolf." Miroslav had backed himself into the corner, the firelight casting a grotesque, twisted, cringing shadow behind him on the wall.

"I saw a wolf today," said Edmond.

Miroslav's body sagged in surrender. He unhid his bandaged arm, rested it across his chest, and lowered his eyes in shame. "For many years we serve the family of Dracul. Many years." He looked up, his eyes wide and urgent. "Sir, you are wise, rich, important . . . good." His demeanor bespoke a tragic misery. "Please, don't listen to him. Don't do what he says. Leave this place."

"What do you mean? You said you were loyal to the count, your family, for generations."

"Such is the curse. But you . . ." Miroslav touched his bandaged arm, and his wild eyes softened. "You are kind to Miroslav."

They heard boot steps approaching the library. The servant skulked back into the shadowy hallway until his green eyes were swallowed by darkness.

Betty had no more "pilgrimages" or "visions" for the rest of the week. Focusing on laundry and scrubbing floors, she wished she had never told Miss Fernsby about any of it. What if she had imagined all those "pilgrimages"? What if Miss Fernsby was just humoring her and was now telling Lady Mallowan about her housemaid's "mental collapse"?

That weekend, Miss Fernsby called at Perlgate. Betty met her in the kitchen where Miss Fernsby sat at the wooden table used for dicing and slicing. Since it was market day, the cook and kitchen maid were away, so they had the kitchen to themselves.

"Sit down." Miss Fernsby plopped a wickerwork basket-purse onto the table. The purse had two or three old books poking out at the top.

Betty hesitated, remembering the rules for servants. "I'll stand if you please."

"Suit yourself. We won't be staying long anyway. Are you ready for an adventure?" Miss Fernsby looked at Betty over her spectacles as if to say the offer was genuine and she only needed to jump on board while the going was good.

"Where to?"

"A pilgrimage, of course, to rescue your cousin Edmond. I know some people who can show us the way."

"Who are they?"

"An eclectic group of esoteric eccentrics, but they are the experts in this type of enterprise. And, if you're wondering, yes, alliteration is a plus to join the Society of Inter-Story Intercessors."

"There's a society?"

"Of course. Amelia already gave me approval to whisk you away for the afternoon, so why are we dawdling? The others are waiting." Miss Fernsby gathered her purse and motioned her head towards the doorway. Betty drew on her coat and hat and followed her out the door.

Miss Fernsby had arrived in a rattley two-seater golf cart. She tossed her purse in the back storage area and gestured for Betty to hop in. Betty buttoned up her coat and climbed on board. Miss Fernsby adjusted a pair of pilot goggles over her eyes and started up the golf cart. They putted along at an even 15 miles per hour across the mown field towards a neighboring estate belonging to Edmond's professor and mentor, Dr. Millgrew.

It was not Dr. Millgrew they came to visit, however. They drove up in front of a small cottage on the far end of the grounds. The cottage was bordered by a well-pruned line of hedges and adjacent to a garden house garlanded by twisting pumpkin vines. Lurching to a stop, Miss Fernsby removed her goggles and clambered out of the cart with a little help from Betty.

"Hope I didn't dislocate your shoulder, dear, but thanks for the loan of it." Miss Fernsby knocked on the door, and it chirruped opened.

A little bald man with a meek, broad, wrinkled face peeked around the door. "Frieda. Good to see you. Um, what's the password?"

"But you know it's me."

"Yes, but Gregor insists. If I don't ask for a password, he'll think me remiss."

"You silly," said Miss Fernsby. "I've so much on my mind these days, I have no time for passwords. I have a hard enough time remembering my own name and where I set my spectacles. Now, for goodness' sake, let us in."

"That's close enough," shrugged the man at the door. "But we do need to be careful."

He let them pass, and with a sharp veering to the right, they entered a side room lit by table lamps and a crackling fireplace. The walls were all lined by bookshelves packed with old books. Betty peered in with anticipation, breathing in the atmosphere of brewed tea and tobacco. A tall, pale man with light-colored hair and piercing blue eyes, mid-fifties, stood in front of the mantelpiece, tapping the ashes from his cigar into the fireplace. The man who opened the door simpered in after Miss Fernsby and Betty. A dark gentleman was seated on the sofa, his arm draped around the back of it.

The austere scrutiny from the gentlemen in the room gave Betty pause, and she held back, clinging to Miss Fernsby's sleeve. But a familiar older gentleman with spectacles and gray hair stepped forward to welcome her. It was Mr. Hamberdeen who owned the bookshop. "Why, hello. How are you, my dear? And how's your aunt and uncle? Any word from Edmond?" he rambled, a sparkle in his eye. "Frieda, you didn't tell us the new Intercessor was young Betty." Betty managed a nervous smile, tugged at the floppy brim of her hat, and took the hand he extended to her.

"None of us were likely candidates to begin with." This came from a thin man with a dark mustache and beard. He emerged from the shadows and clapped the book in his hand shut.

"We don't need any interlopers," said the light-haired man by the fire. "The knowledge we possess is too vital to trust to just anybody."

"Please," said Miss Fernsby. "I know the ways better than most of you, and I would not be stupid enough to bring Betty here unless I was certain she was one of us."

The dark gentleman on the sofa leaned forward. He had kind eyes and a wise smile. "Girl," he said in a South African accent. "Come sit with us." He gestured to a chair across from him.

Betty hesitated. She looked to Miss Fernsby for guidance, but Miss Fernsby simply shrugged as if to say, "Don't look at me." So, Betty slipped onto the chair and tugged at her skirt to adjust it over her legs. She felt kindness from the dark gentleman, so she directed her tense chin in his direction. "I'm sorry. I don't know anything about Intercessors except what Miss Fernsby told me. It has something to do with books? And portals? I think I made one of those pilgrimage things, but not on purpose. Probably more than one. I'm confused."

"Do you wish to be unconfused?" the man asked her.

"Yes, sir."

"Well, then," sighed Hamberdeen. "First things first. Introductions. We, that is, all of us here, are the Inter-Story Intercessors. You know me, Thomas Hamberdeen, and you know Frieda. The gentleman by the fire is Dr. Gregor Macmillan, a mathematical genius, or that's what he tells me. At any rate, he teaches mathematics at the university and rents this cottage from Dr. Millgrew, the chair of Natural Science. We, in turn, use it as our headquarters. And the gentleman on the sofa finds no need to rise. He lives by the code of his tribe. His name is Daniel Khumalo, of the Zulus. And the gentleman who almost snapped your nose off with his book is Akira Yamada, descendent of the samurai, knights of old Japan. He has made more pilgrimages than any one of us and can recite the *Intercessor Code Book* from front to back in at least ten different languages. And there's Jeremy Spinderbeck, the chap who let you in. And now introductions are over, who would like to explain what we do?"

Khumalo unfolded a handkerchief from his breast pocket. "I will illustrate. Here I have a handkerchief, clean, new, unwrinkled. But, let us say this area in the middle did not like being part of the handkerchief. So, I cut it out." To Betty's surprise, he took a pair of scissors, creased the handkerchief in half, and cut a sizable hole in the middle. "What is left? My handkerchief is no longer complete. What can I do?"

"I could darn it," offered Betty.

"With such a hole missing from it?"

"I could use some fabric and patch the hole."

"Exactly. Now you understand the universe. It is a patch to fill the emptiness."

Macmillan snapped his cigar butt into the fire. "That's enough. You've told her too much."

Betty took this as a cue to rise and interject. "Gentlemen, I am not here to learn your secrets. Professor Macmillan is right. Some things are better left unknown. Frankly, I haven't slept well since I saw that vampire in the mirror, and I wish I could just call it a bad dream and go home. But if it's true, if what I have seen is a warning, and if you all have some secret power to stop this, I place myself at your service, and my hopes in your hands."

"A vampire, eh?" Macmillan massaged his chin.

"And The Carpathian Mountains?" asked Spinderbeck.

"Yes, my cousin is there. Can you help him?"

"Perhaps," said Hamberdeen, "it is we who are in need of help, and you who have the power to do so. Let's try this one more time, shall we? Imagine the universe as a large book, say, an encyclopedia, fit into a slot in a giant bookshelf. Within this volume are other books, and within those books are even more books, all microcosms of the book in which they reside.

Intercessors are characters in the universal novel who have, in times past, discovered portals that allow us to move through time and space, through fact and fiction, seeking to reunite the universe with its original author. The Intercessors of the past left a code book to guide us. Some of the codes are easy to decipher and others not so easy."

"It's a complex mathematical formula," insisted Macmillan.

"With so, so many variables," sighed Spinderbeck.

"Time," said Hamberdeen.

"Purpose," added Yamada.

"Location," said Khumalo.

"And, of course, the divergence and orientation of the portal," muttered Macmillan. "And now this vampire . . ."

"Vlad Tepov, descendent of Count Dracula," said Hamberdeen.

"And lieutenant among the ranks of the Accusers," added Khumalo.

"You see," Hamberdeen said, "there are Intercessors, who work to restore time and space to their original order, and there are Accusers, who work to establish a reign of chaos."

"And how does Edmond fit into all this?" asked Betty.

Yamada was already thumbing through an ancient book, and Macmillan was chalking formulas on the blackboard. After a few mutters, corrections, and a flurry of chalk powder, Macmillan announced, "Yes. That's it."

"Well, tell us all, Mack," prodded Hamberdeen.

"What we want is to get Betty to the place her cousin is so she can warn him of his danger. What we need are two books."

"*Snow White* and *The Secret Garden*," announced Yamada.

"Of course," said Miss Fernsby as she opened her purse and pulled out those exact books. "A wish. And a secret."

Macmillan read from Grimm's fairy tale, and Yamada read from the Frances Hodgson Burnett novel. Betty braced herself and whispered a nervous prayer that she would not let anyone down. She was drawn into a misty haze as if pulled into a snow globe where tiny sparks of white glistened down upon her as a bubbling gel buoyed her towards a dark world.

Later, she reappeared in the cottage, sprawled on the couch, her head propped against Khumalo's shoulder. The pilgrimage had stunned her nerves and depleted her energy. Miss Fernsby mopped Betty's forehead with a damp cloth. Khumalo held a pinch of sweet-scented leaves under her nostrils to revive her.

"*Umhlonyane*," he said. "It will calm you, help you to breathe."

"Edmond didn't recognize me," Betty said. "There was a garden and a well, but he looked at me as if I was a ghost."

"Hmm," said Yamada, "often the spirits people see are really Intercessors and Accusers moving between portals."

"But the place." Betty shivered. "I've seen it before."

"Yes," said Yamada, "Intercessors sometimes begin by making subconscious pilgrimages."

"But you saw your cousin?" prodded Spinderbeck. "You *were* able to warn him?"

"I tried." Betty heaved a sigh and pushed herself to her feet. "But Edmond can be so stupidly stubborn."

"Don't be discouraged," said Miss Fernsby, offering her a glass of water. "You are only beginning, my dear. Intercessors have been fighting the Accusers of that place for centuries."

CHAPTER 7
THE MASQUERADE (1930S)

Tepov entered the library in his vest and shirt sleeves, no tie. He lit his cigarette, ran a glimpse over Edmond's game of chess, and slumped into a chair, folding one leg over the arm of the chair and letting it dangle listlessly. "You're wondering why I invite those brutes to my house." He nodded towards the raucous singing from the hunters.

Edmond blinked and smiled. "No, I wouldn't . . ."

"No. *You* wouldn't be so bold, but I've sensed your judgement all through dinner." He pointed the cigarette at Edmond as if aiming a dart. "And you're right. They're boors. I crave civilized company. That's one of my selfish motives for inviting *you*, a gentleman and a scholar." He had been drinking and was a bit delayed in his coordination and sluggish in his speech. He flung his arms like a puppet. "Why shouldn't I choose my own company for a change? All *they* ever want to do is hunt and carouse and carry on like brutes."

"Don't you like the hunt?"

"Me? Oh, yes, I come from a long generation of warriors. I hunt. Yes. But I'm not like *them*." He pulled himself to his feet like a drunken ballet dancer coming up from an unbalanced grand plie and lunged towards the window. Tepov shoved back the drapes and held them grandly on either side. Edmond expected the ghostly girl to be revealed, but it was only the night with its wintry clouds besmirching the moon.

"I, sir, am Vlad Tepov. Son of Dracul, slave to no one." He bowed low and pulled up as if a puppeteer had yanked his head up by a string. "Tell me . . ." He slinked over to Edmond and draped himself around the back of his chair. "Who's the girl?"

"The girl?"

"The woman you love. Who is she? Why did you not bring her with you?"

"I am engaged to Daphne Graham."

"A sensible thing, to be engaged. Very sensible. Marriage, however, need not confine a man. There's another? A mistress, perhaps?" Tepov raised a knowing eyebrow.

"What makes you think . . ."

"Oh, a young man, virile, handsome, tall, intelligent, a man on his way to success, a man who has unearthed the Babylonian Dragon Scale, I would think such a man would have dozens of women paying him court. My father was such a man. He had so many women about the place, I'm not even sure which one was my mother."

"Do *you* have a mistress?" Edmond shifted the focus from himself.

"My father taught me many things. One of those was never love a woman, but rather, make them need you so badly, they think, breathe, and hope for nothing else. But, then, you have a gift that way yourself, don't you? You've got the world twisted around your little finger. You could easily manipulate this Betty any way you wanted."

Edmond vaulted to his feet, his face dark. "What do you know about Betty?"

A sneer curled up on the sides of Tepov's mouth. "She *is* the girl, isn't she?"

"Who told you about her?"

"Oh, I read newspapers, gossip columns." Here Tepov produced a scrapbook filled with articles. "She was a guest at Miss Graham's debutante party. Oh, and here's an article about you heading off on that archeological dig. Interesting that young Leslie was listed as the second in charge. I thought *you* were credited with that excavation?"

"Leslie has a weak constitution, and . . ."

"Never mind. I believe you. We all do what we must to get the power we need. A little something in his water canteen, and he would be flat on his back for weeks."

Edmond glared at the floor so Tepov would not see how nearly correct he was. He had *not* put anything in Leslie's water canteen, but he *had* goaded him on to overdo the work in the scorching midday sun.

"Yes, you *are* like me," noted Tepov. "Even as a boy you had practice at that sort of thing. What was his name? Little Barnaby Skeens? He so admired you, you could talk him into almost anything."

Edmond lurched forward, his hand poised to clench Tepov's throat, except Tepov grasped Edmond's forearm.

Tepov snickered. "We will have to do something about that conscience of yours. And I know just the thing. A party. A dance, a ball. Music . . . *good* music . . . with violins, woodwinds, tambourines, and guitars. A masque. Women with blood-red lips and black silk gowns. And my guest of honor, Professor Davidson."

Edmond was troubled by the count's sudden shifts in mood. Tepov had gone from depression to ecstasy in a second. "Don't go to any bother," said Edmond. "I came here to research, not to socialize."

"Oh, we must have a ball." Tepov stood before the window where the moon cast a blurred reflection of him dressed in formal attire and a black silk mask. The room reflected was not the library but a grand ballroom. The glimmers of moonlight converged into a whirl of masked guests dancing and twirling like sugar plum fairies. Edmond could hear soulful violins and tantalizing tambourines. He stood behind Tepov and saw himself in the reflection, dressed in his best attire, also wearing a mask and cape.

It was but a brief unpleasantness as they merged with their reflections into the window world, like being struck by a flurry of sharp-edged hail. The count swooped into the ballroom like a virtuoso conductor, using his walking stick as a baton, gesturing for the music to continue and the dancers to clear a path, and he laughed in triumph at the contrite guests swooning to the left and to the right.

Finding himself in this world within the window, Edmond thought, *Surely, I must have nodded off over my game of chess.*

But the sensual hand that slipped into his and yanked him towards her in an aggressive turn and the fiery eyes and scarlet lips that nearly collided with his were too tangible for a dream. "Good evening," the woman said, her luminous masked eyes fixed upon him. She was dressed in scarlet and black, fragrant with jasmine and spikenard, her gold necklace inlaid with rubies.

"Hello." He joined her in the dance. "You're not the woman from the garden?"

She laughed. "Beware of women from gardens, professor. Trees have branches, roots, and leaves, but what lies within the fruit of these?"

"Is *that* a riddle?"

"Perhaps. But a riddle with an answer is like an open door leading nowhere."

"I disagree. Each mystery opens the door to another mystery, and it is the ambitious man's task to open each door and discover knowledge wherever he may."

"I adore ambitious men." She arched an eyebrow. "Too bad you are not one of them."

"Clearly you know nothing about me."

She shrugged. "You know nothing of *me*, yet you would sell your soul for one kiss."

"Why on earth would I sell my soul? "

"Because. You do not believe it exists." She smirked. "Nothing for nothing, my love."

Edmond considered that a fair point and jogged his thoughts for a witty repartee. Something clutched his sleeve and made his blood run cold.

The walls were made of mirrors, and the guests appeared to be a legion of dancers whirling about like a giant puppet show. But the myriad of reflections was disrupted by a hand reaching out from the glass. The hand clung to Edmond's sleeve, tugging him towards the mirror.

"Back," snarled Tepov, and he slammed his stick down upon the fragile wrist. The reflection of the chandelier lights dinged off the mirror making the count's eyes blaze. A pitiable cry from a woman, and the bruised hand withdrew, but Tepov clutched her wrist to drag her out of the mirror. The glass of the mirror gleamed with a metallic luster and converted into elastic glop, stretching and clinging to the woman's body as if to ingest her. Edmond started. The woman was his own cousin Betty. Betty grimaced as she struggled against the brutal efforts of the count.

"Professor," urged the scarlet-clad woman. "Save her from the mirror. It will swallow her alive."

Alarmed, Edmond grabbed Betty's other arm. He aided Tepov in yanking her out of the mirror. With a loud *galurnk*, the mirror expelled Betty, and she tumbled into the room, a disheveled heap on the floor. She shot a reproaching glare at Edmond past the strands of hair hanging over her face.

"Ha!" The dancing woman stretched out her arms, dripping with scarlet tassels, and transformed into a falcon-sized dragon. "You have her, my love. You have her." The dragon circled the room in flight and came to roost on Tepov's arm.

"Yes, Avian." Tepov leered over his prey. "At last I bagged my quarry."

"What are you talking about?" Edmond demanded. "That's Betty, my cousin."

"The lovely Beatrice, eh?" Tepov gloated over her. "Are you quite sure? What would *she* be doing here?"

"What would any of us be doing here? We are all in a blasted mirror, for God's sake." Edmond knelt by Betty and looked her over with concern. "Are you all right?"

"She's the one who haunts my lodge," said Tepov. "She wants to destroy us. And now that she is here, she is under my power. Just as you are."

Edmond gazed at Betty, realizing that for years he had hardly noticed her at all. *She* was the woman by the fire and by the well. *She* had warned him away from this place from the beginning. The reality of the horror he was caught up in crashed in on his brain like a boulder.

Betty scrambled to her feet, pushed past Edmond, and stomped one foot defiantly at Tepov. "You do not have me. And you will not have *him.*"

Tepov caught her bruised wrist in his hand. "Flesh and blood. Only flesh and blood." He yanked her close to his body, pulsing with lust and rage.

She turned her face away to avoid his hot breath. Over her shoulder, she glimpsed through the mirror a book. It lay open on the desk in the library. If she could concentrate on the words, perhaps it would serve as a portal out of this entrapment.

The floor heaved and rocked. Gravity pulled her out of Tepov's grasp and she flailed backwards. There was a mighty rumbling.

Edmond wrapped one arm around Betty and with the other sought something along the wall to anchor them, to keep from sliding into the pit erupting in the middle of the ballroom.

Smoke hissed up from the pit, and the denizens of the ball clung to the edges of the room, like sailors heaved back and forth on the decks of a storm-tossed ship. Tepov's huntsmen entered, bearing chains. They stood upright, but their faces and ears and teeth had become savagely wolfish. They snarled and snapped.

Betty focused on the page on the desk. At last, she could discern the words from the pen of H. G. Wells: *"as men busied themselves . . . they were scrutinized and studied, perhaps almost as narrowly as a man with a microscope might scrutinize the transient creatures that swarm and multiply in a drop of water . . ."* As she read, she became one with the mirror.

Betty's hand slipped from Edmond's grasp. "Betty!" he cried over the roar of the convulsing room. A vague silver outline of her lingered in the mirror, and the glass of the mirror became a multitude of drops of water pouring over her, washing away her reflection like the rain obliterates the chalk on the sidewalk.

Tepov laughed at Edmond's panic. "Welcome to Alsó Világ, the land of nightmares. Allow me to introduce myself once more. I," he flung his cape back with flair, "am Vlad the third Dracul of Wallachia, heir to the Order of the Dragons."

An earthquake rocked the ballroom once more. The illusion of a masquerade dissipated, and Edmond found himself in an underground cave, billows of smoke issuing up through metal grates which covered the pits below. Sprawled across one of the grates was the nearly naked and twisted form of Miroslav. Lurking in the shadows were the glowing yellow eyes of wolves, standing upright, snarling and slathering through gleaming fangs.

Miroslav propped himself on one elbow, his hands spread in front, like an infant afraid to crawl. His back was streaked with red from a severe clawing. Edmond moved towards him but was yanked back by the wolf men.

In an alcove above, Tepov erupted from a burst of smoke, more monster than human, with enormous reptilian wings. He shrieked, and that shriek zigzagged down Edmond from his cranium to the base of his spine.

The grate in the middle of the floor rumbled, cracked, upheaved, and groaned. Crashing up through the grate was a giant flame-red fist with tufts of orange fur between each claw.

"Behold the dragon lord Ordog!" exclaimed Tepov.

"All hail the dragon lord," screeched the pet dragon that clung to Tepov's shoulder.

"*All hail the dragon lord,*" chanted the wolf men.

51

The dragon lord's clawed fingers wrapped around Miroslav. "Davidson. Help me," pleaded Miroslav. "Don't let them take me. Please, count. Please!"

Edmond strained against the grip of the werewolves as the dragon dragged the wailing manservant into the miasma of sulphur below, but Miroslav clutched at the grating, resisting his captor.

"Traitor," said Tepov. "You, Miroslav, will die the pitiful wretch you are."

"I have served you loyally! Count. Cou . . ." Miroslav's cries became a howl. His skin erupted into a coarse black mane. His face elongated into a wolfish muzzle.

The dragon fingers squeezed Miroslav and bore him down. Ordog unraveled his coils, lifting his crested crown to feast his flaming eyes upon Edmond, who appeared a mere toy compared to his immensity.

"Beeaatriice," rumbled the beast. "Pfash eenan?"

It was then Tepov realized the young Intercessor had disappeared. And he trembled.

CHAPTER 8
BETTY IN WONDERLAND (1880S)

The rain poured down in proverbial buckets, and Betty did not have an umbrella. Cold and wet, she felt a failure. The words she had read had opened a portal, but not to Intercessor headquarters. She was outside a dreary-looking apartment building, and a horse-drawn carriage clattered past, splattering her in mud.

"I say," said a middle-aged gentleman with a mustache, carrying an umbrella in one hand and a folded newspaper under his arm.

"Mr. Wells?" she presumed, shivering.

"Wells? No, I'm afraid not, miss, but dash it all, you're soaked through." He positioned his umbrella over her. "As a Dr. I must prescribe getting you out of this beastly weather. Shall I call a cab?"

"Wait. Is that 221 B?" Betty noticed the address plaque on the wall of the brown brick building before them.

The wind picked up, and the rain cascaded into the puddles. "Never mind the cab," decided the gentleman. "You must get out of this gale."

The gentleman guided her towards the doors of 221 B Baker Street. The inside hall was musty and lit by gaslight. The efficient, white-haired landlady gasped at the sight of Betty.

Betty was about to explain her modern attire, but then looked down at herself. The portal had provided her with the clothing of an honest working girl from the late 1880s. The landlady's gasp had been at the state the rain and mud had left her in.

"You poor dear," she said. "Come with me this instant. You can leave her with me, Dr.. What she needs is a change of clothes and some nice hot tea."

As the landlady tugged her away, Betty glanced towards the banister that led upstairs to catch a glimpse of the resident, but she could not even hear the scraping of his violin.

Reluctantly, Betty followed the landlady to a sitting room at the back. The corner stove and a strong cup of tea soon warmed her up and gave her time to assess her situation.

So real had the Sherlock Holmes stories seemed to her that last year she had run away from Perlgate, intent on reaching the country abode of a much older Sherlock Holmes. Once the constable had brought her home, Uncle Eric had reprimanded her, insisting in no uncertain terms that Sherlock Holmes was a fictional character and any further escapades in search of made-up people would be met with firm discipline.

"Feeling better, my dear?" asked the landlady.

"Yes, thank you. But the person I really came to see was . . ."

"I know, I know," sighed the landlady. "You came to see Mr. Holmes. You are in terrible danger. You haven't any money, but as soon as you marry, your husband's fortune will more than compensate him for his fee."

Betty pressed her lips wryly at the familiar lines.

"I am sorry," said the landlady, "but Mr. Holmes is not seeing anyone right now. He is in the middle of some horrific experiment, and he'll bite my head off if I so much as pass his door on my way up the stairs."

Betty set down her teacup and squared her shoulders. "But I *will* see him. I must." And she could not resist adding the cliché that usually worked in the stories, "It's of the utmost importance, I assure you."

"Well," said the landlady with a sparkle of admiration, "you are a determined, well-spoken young lady. We can try, but don't say I didn't warn you."

The landlady guided Betty down the hallway and up the stairs. As they approached the door, Betty braced herself.

"Ah, Mrs. Hudson," called the gentleman inside before they had even knocked.

"Mr. Holmes . . ." began Mrs. Hudson, opening the door.

"Indeed, indeed," he interrupted, as he scratched out some blotchy notes.

Holmes was a tall, slender middle-aged man with chestnut hair, piercing gray eyes, sharp nose, and a nervous mouth. His mouse-colored dressing gown was worn carelessly over his clothing, and he smelled of a mixture of strong tobacco, soap, and chemicals.

"Watson," he called out.

The gentleman Betty had met outside looked up over his newspaper. He was about to respond to Holmes when he noticed Betty waiting.

"I say, Holmes!" the Dr. announced, tossing the paper onto the floor, pulling on his jacket, and adjusting his tie. "We have company."

"Not now." Holmes was engrossed in what he was writing, double checking the results of his experiment through the lens of a microscope.

"Forgive him," said Dr. Watson. "And please do sit down and tell me what we can do to help."

Watson conducted Betty to a chair, and she seated herself, smiling shyly at the Dr., as she supposed most Victorian women would do in this situation.

"Well, to begin with, my name is Beatrice Talbin . . ."

"Beatrice? Talbin?" Holmes, suddenly attentive, returned the test tube to the rack and leapt over the back of the sofa by way of a shortcut. He took her hand in his. "My dear Miss Talbin, it is a pleasure to meet you at last."

Betty exchanged amazed looks with the Dr..

"You know this young lady?" asked the Dr..

"Of course. She sent letters in the post, requesting my assistance. Unfortunately, whenever I tried to send a response, the letters returned with 'no such person exists at this address.' And now at last the mystery of the non-existent client is solved, for here you are."

Betty jogged her memory. Yes, she had scribbled some letters to him to escape moments of youthful frustration, but they had ended up crumpled in the wastebasket. Perhaps this, too, was a power Intercessors possessed? To send messages via portals? She blushed, for she recalled one of the letters was a love letter, and she hoped that had not been one of the letters he had received. The twinkle in his eyes suggested it was. She wanted to disappear.

"My dear chap," said the Dr.. "You might at least have mentioned the letters to me. I could have been of some assistance."

Holmes pulled up a chair and sat across from Betty. "Yes, of *course* you might. But it was one of those absorbing conundrums I preferred decoding on my own, something to do on those dreary days when no interesting case presented itself. Pray, Miss Talbin. Tell us about this cursed archaeological excavation of your uncle's."

"They made it back safely, after all."

"Then, *what*," his eyebrow twitched with a hint of annoyance, "can we do for you?" He leaned back in his chair and closed his eyes wearily.

She was not surprised by his irritable manner, but it did irritate her. "Mr. Holmes. I am not some silly schoolgirl who's misplaced her fiancé and has nothing better to contemplate than a hairpin or curling tong."

Holmes's eyes snapped open. The Dr. smirked.

"I, sir, am your equal," Betty asserted, though shaking inside, "if not in deduction, at least in mind and will."

Holmes smiled. "Good. Excellent! But," after appraising her, his smile melted into serious concern, "tell us who it is that has used you so cruelly." He took the liberty of pushing her sleeve away from her wrist to reveal the blackened bruise around her wrist and the red marks on her forearm. "Not that cousin of yours. Nor your uncle. No, this ruffian has nails, *sharp* nails, and a grip of steel and no qualms about using a cane."

"The blackguard!" declared Watson.

Betty lifted her eyes to Holmes as he hovered over her arm with scientific interest. "My story is too fantastic, really," she said.

"Try us," said Watson.

Holmes reseated himself and gestured for her to continue.

"His name is Vlad Tepov, a count in Eastern Europe. He is keeping my cousin prisoner."

"Tepov, you say? In Eastern Europe? Tepov, Tepov, the name means something to me. Watson, my file catalogued under the letter T."

Watson dug through the files in a catalog drawer.

As he waited, Holmes stuffed his cherry wood pipe with tobacco from a Persian slipper. "While my list of M's is a fine one, the letter T is rather scarce. Therefore, the few that inhabit that section are indelibly inscribed in my brain."

Watson brought a folder with newspaper clippings and other notes to his colleague, and Holmes perused the contents with interest. "Ah, yes, Vlad Tepov. A vicious fiend indeed. He was rumored to be in Sussex last. Here's the bit about him aiding Sebastian Moran, and aha!" He rested his finger on a specific note. "Henchman to the nefarious Professor Moriarty, and member of that cryptic order that call themselves The Accusers. Miss Talbin," he continued, sucking on the pipe with energetic enthusiasm, "your case intrigues me. Tell us the entire story."

Betty was astonished. "You know of the Accusers?"

Holmes flicked a dismissive hand. "Rumors, you might say. My brother Mycroft knows more than I do. He keeps his finger on the pulse of the subversive elements. I do know that The Accusers attract the most diabolical minds of the criminal underworld. I suspect Moriarty himself of being a member. I also am aware of another organization loosely connected with the Diogenes Club, a society dedicated to thwarting The Accusers."

"The Inter-Story Intercessors," said Betty.

"I believe that *was* the name Mycroft mentioned. Now, tell us the part you play, Miss Talbin, in this conflict. You're an Intercessor, I take it."

"I am," she confided. "And . . ."

"Sh!" Holmes raised his index finger abruptly. His ear homed in on a sound from the hall. He crept to the door, finger still lifted. Betty and the Dr. held their breath to keep from making the slightest sound.

Holmes listened a second or two more, then threw open the door. "Ahh. Do come in. What-ho, Watson. Another Intercessor has made port."

Miss Fernsby stood in the doorway, dressed in the style of an imposing Victorian matron, complete with bustle, veiled hat, and kid gloves.

"Why, thank you. I knew you would recognize my footstep."

"I live for nothing else." He dipped into a gallant bow.

"Nonsense. Your showcase chivalry doesn't fool me." Miss Fernsby adjusted her spectacles as she surveyed the room.

"After your inestimable assistance in that matter of the Shipping Clerk's Toupee – remind me to tell you about that one sometime, Watson – no service is too great, Madame."

"All I need today is," her eyes rested on Betty, "the return of my ward."

"Miss Talbin has been corresponding with Mr. Holmes for years, it seems," explained the Dr., an amused sparkle in his eyes.

Holmes shot Watson a reproaching frown, noting Miss Fernsby's maternally censuring look aimed at Betty.

Betty lowered her eyes, cheeks tinged with embarrassment.

"Correspondence?" Miss Fernsby asked.

Holmes' eyebrows lifted in sympathy at Betty's predicament. "Madame, I assure you that while some foolish young girls are apt to compromise their reputations by following the dictates of their passions, the letters Miss Talbin sent were most discreet and contained only information that might be helpful in my investigations on her behalf."

Miss Fernsby looked doubtful, not because she thought Betty silly, but because she herself had once been an imaginative teenager.

"She was just about to tell us about her connection with the same society you belong to," explained Watson.

"Yes, she is one of our youngest, but also one of the bravest." Miss Fernsby gazed at Betty with the glow of a proud parent.

"Brave indeed," said Holmes. "Already she has taken on your arch enemy, as the bruises on her wrist indicate. A bit young to be in the thick of things, even *you* must admit."

Betty sprang to her feet and clutched her wrist to hide the bruises. "I *asked* to be sent there. Not Miss Fernsby, nor Mr. Hamberdeen, nor any other being on the face of God's earth made me do anything. And if you, sir, can face up to the Roylotts, Milvertons, and Moriartys of this world, the least I can do is work up enough nerve to confront the fiend who is out to destroy my cousin."

Betty's chest and neck were strained, and nervous tears wanted to escape, but she held her chin defiantly.

Rarely had Holmes been so impressed with a young lady. He raised a thoughtful finger to his lips. "You have a most remarkable ward, Miss Fernsby." Then, frowning, he added, "And I should not like any harm to come to her."

CHAPTER 9
THE ORDER OF THE DRAGON (1930S)

"Where is Beatrice Talbin? How can we find her? What is her plan?" A strong whiff of ammonia jolted Edmond from unconsciousness, but his vision was blurred. Shadows of wolf men crowded in on him. The interrogation stirred his sense of defiance. If the brutal headmaster at charity school could not break him, he knew he could withstand the relentless cross-examination in this hell.

"I don't know where she is," he insisted through clenched teeth, and that was the truth. Since he had left her at Perlgate, he had seen Betty at the lodge at least three times. Each time, she had vanished, and who knew where she could be now. Even if he did know, he would never betray a friend.

He tried to push himself to his feet, but the chains that bound him to the chair only cut deeper into his chest and arms. The stifling haze of sulphur mixed with a sickening opium-like smell beckoned him back to the dark, numb world of senselessness. An icy hand slammed across his face. "Talk!" Tepov's fully erupted fangs protruded close to Edmond's half-opened eyes.

"Grufen!" thundered a voice in a strange tongue Edmond had never heard before. *"Een mussen gevehthen sullen carpathan frie!"*

Tepov blanched. "Yes, I know," he protested, "but I thought he *would* give it to us once we had his cousin."

"*Beatrice bashan galunan. Lathan friegarnen, Tepov! Eenan crungaren wollen!*"

Edmond dipped back into blackness but had a vague sense of motion, like wreckage tossed upon surging waves. He started awake in bed. He was in the guest room at Tepov's lodge. A warm fire crackled in the fireplace, the aroma of coffee steamed from a Turkish pot on his bed stand, and morning light peered in at him through the window. He would have dismissed everything that had happened since the masquerade as another one of his terrible nightmares, except that a faint scent of sulphur still lingered on his sweat-drenched shirt, and the bruises on his chest and forearms ached when he tried to move.

He shoved aside the coverlet and scrambled out of bed. He was alone in the room.

If he could slip down the stairs unseen, he could escape through the garden to the garage, where Miroslav had parked his Jaguar. He turned towards the door and stopped in alarm. Tepov stood before him.

Tepov, dressed in his stylish hunting attire, greeted Edmond with a cold, affable grin. "Good. You're awake."

Edmond watched Tepov with a sidelong glare as the count walked casually past him into the room. Tepov pivoted to face him, and Edmond stiffened, on his guard, rubbing the side of his face where the count had slapped him.

One eyebrow arched and half of the mouth smirked on Tepov's thin, handsome face. He took a leather glove from the fold of the other and slapped it into his palm. "So now you know what's really at stake here. It's not just your pathetic research. Last night you met the mighty dragon lord Ordog."

"Yes," said Edmond, grimly. "Poor Miroslav." He watched for Tepov's response.

Tepov suppressed a derisive laugh and shook his head. "Miroslav was just one of a million specks of dust in an ancient quest that spans the eons and extends beyond the universe.

Long ago, my ancestor saved the people of this land from the Ottoman Turks. He was a knight of the Order of the Dragon, the *Draculae*. It was the dragons who ensured his victory. As per their agreement, the order vowed an oath of loyalty to Ordog, a vow we have kept for centuries. When Professor Millgrew wrote to me of your interest in dragons, I knew you would be a prime candidate for our order. Few can meet the requirements to join the *Draculae*. The conditions are quite stringent. First," he slapped the glove in his hand, "you must be of good family, good breeding. Second," another slap of the glove, "you must be well-educated. Third, you must desire knowledge, the secret knowledge only the Order can reveal. The Order promises to protect and avenge you, to lead you into full knowledge of the mysteries of the past, the future, things both worldly and otherworldly. We enable you to climb to the highest positions, to gain whatever it is you desire."

Flashbacks throbbed in Edmond's brain. His child-self defiantly glaring at the sanctimonious headmaster over a back raw from a caning, vowing vengeance. Leslie mocking him with, "You'll never be good for anything but raking up manure, *stable boy*." The classmate at Cambridge he overheard saying, "It's impossible to please old Millgrew, but if you get on his good side, it's a ticket to the top."

Tepov studied Edmond's expression and read his hesitation. "I see you need proof. Am I not living proof? Riches, power, immortality. Consider your own Professor Millgrew. He started life as a poor, ignorant Welsh boy working in the mines. Soon as he joined our order, he became a respected leader of intellectual society across the Western world."

Edmond pushed his knuckles across his dry lower lip as he weighed the argument. On one hand he had a chance to attain the power and knowledge he needed to get back at those who had persecuted him. On the other hand, there was poor Miroslav, who had dared to refuse the dragon lord's commands and had met a horrifying fate. The balance weighed heavily in favor of accepting Tepov's offer. And yet the prospect of aligning himself with an order of fiends sent a chill down his spine.

Tepov's hypnotic eyes glimmered as he beckoned for Edmond to follow him. Edmond felt like a man with a sheer wall on one side and a precarious precipice on the other while ahead of him waited a mound of gold and silver. He allowed Tepov to guide him down the winding stone stairs, past the brazier, down more steps into a dark, damp dungeon where every sound reverberated. Edmond swallowed hard as he peered tensely into the darkness. A heavy door groaned open, and from it issued a tiny dragon. The dragon reared and spewed a match flame from its tiny jaws.

"Yes, it's a dragon, a descendent of Ordog," said Tepov.

"That's not a dragon. That's an insect."

"Harmless enough, eh? But once dragons ruled the Earth. They were titans. But dragons require a certain form of energy. Without it . . . Well." He gestured towards the three-inch monster growling in a pathetic treble. He took the creature into his hand and stroked it.

"So the dragon scale I have . . ."

"Dates back to a time before the dragons fell. Ordog it was who led the dragons from the beginning. Ordog knows everything. He wishes to share that knowledge with you." Tepov let the tiny dragon free to scamper down the hall. He put an arm around Edmond's shoulders. "You are a fortunate man indeed. You discovered the golden scale. You triggered something cataclysmic, and you impressed the great one. He sees you as mightier than all humans. You rose up from nothing, using your wits. You have the potential to rule, and Ordog knows that."

"What does he want from me?"

"All you must do is perform three simple tasks. First, that golden scale you found. Turn it over to us. Second, Beatrice. Find her and stop her from interfering with our objective. And third . . ." He stared into Edmond's eyes. "You must give him your soul."

"Why didn't you tell me you knew Sherlock Holmes?" Betty asked Miss Fernsby as they browsed a bookstore on Baker Street.

"I did tell you I had made a pilgrimage or two, didn't I?" Miss Fernsby studied the spine of a book. "No, this one won't do."

"We could certainly use his help." Betty blew the dust from the shelf in front of her. "He's not the sort of man I would want on my track if *I* were an Accuser."

Miss Fernsby sneezed from the dust, and gave Betty a tolerant look. "No doubt he has a part to play. But now we must get back to headquarters to consult the code book."

"But how will we know which book will get us back?" Betty leaned against the bookshelf and folded her arms across her chest.

"Hamberdeen suggested I locate a work by his great uncle."

Betty fidgeted with her fingers on her elbows, her lips pressed suspiciously. She gave Miss Fernsby a narrow, sidelong glance. "Were you in love with him?"

"With Mr. Hamberdeen?" Miss Fernsby made an incredulous face.

"No. Sherlock Holmes. He was quite interested in you."

"Stuff and nonsense. I merely assisted him on a case or two. I think *you* are the one with romantic notions. Writing love letters to Sherlock Holmes, indeed." She clicked her tongue in reproach as she shelved another inadequate book.

"They were *not really* love letters." Betty blushed. "More like . . . fan mail."

"Oh, is that what you modern girls call it? A word of advice, my dear. Mr. Holmes wrote the textbook on confirmed bachelorhood, just as I am the perfect picture of spinsterhood. Now, no more tittle tattle. Count Tepov must not get the scale Edmond has. If Edmond willingly hands the scale over to the enemy . . . well, let's just say we do not want that to happen."

"What *would* happen?"

"Ah. This should do it." Miss Fernsby opened a book titled *Guide to English Country Estates* by Rudolph Hamberdeen. "If anything can get us to headquarters, this should do it. Now, I want you to concentrate on where we want to go, open to a page, then read." Miss Fernsby thrust the book into Betty's hands.

"Just like that?" Betty thought about Millgrew's cottage, about Edmond, about Tepov, and about 221 B Baker Street.

Her head hurt as she tried to focus her thoughts. Instead, she fixed her senses on the book. She breathed in the scent of ink and freshly cut pages. She allowed her hands to relax, and the pages fanned out like a peacock's feathers. She put her finger on the middle hinge of the book, and flattened out the page it had landed on.

She read aloud. *"The most wondrous ritual is spring cleaning. This is the time of year when the owners of the estate fly off to Bath while the domestic staff busies itself with whisking the black soot from wallpapered walls, cleaning out chimneys, and airing out rooms that have long lain shrouded in ghostly sheets."* Betty, who had often aided in the tasks, envisioned the flurry of dusting rags, the scrubbing of sponges, the unlatching of windows, the billowing of sheets. The bookstore whirled before her eyes and disappeared, and, when the blur refocused, she and Miss Fernsby were not in Dr. Millgrew's cottage, as they had hoped, but someplace quite different.

CHAPTER 10
WHERE THE WOLFSBANE BLOOMS (1930S)

Edmond followed Tepov down the dark passage. The walls were clammy, and scuttling things flitted over Edmond's hand as he steadied himself.

They came to a stone archway surrounding a rot-wood door. In the center stone of the arch was an engraving in symbols much older than hieroglyphics or runes. Tepov withdrew a ring of keys from inside his shirt and unlocked the door. Inside was a 12 x 12 chamber, heavy shackles built into the wall. While the room was not large in width or breadth, the ceiling was quite high. Near the top was a barred opening letting in the moonlight.

Two wolf men loomed up behind Edmond. Another came in through the doorway. "I have it." He presented the box that contained the dragon scale to Tepov.

"Well done, Dmitri." Tepov took the box and held it in front of Edmond. "Edmond Davidson," he commenced the ritual. "Do you willingly grant us this relic, one of five, stolen by infidels, rightfully belonging to the great dragon lord Ordog?"

The wolf man nearest Edmond snarled, baring his fangs. Edmond breathed in a deep, decisive breath and relented. "Yes."

"Open the box," Tepov ordered him.

Edmond took the box and unlatched it.

"Speak to it."

"*Speak* to it?" repeated Edmond. "Speak to the *box*?"

"Speak to the scale. Speak in the ancient tongue of the Fallen Dragons."

"I know Latin, German, Old English," listed Edmond.

"Touch the scale, and the words will come to you."

Edmond let his finger rest on the scale. It glowed with such a golden aura it was nearly white. Something burned his fingers and shot up through his wrist. The golden hues of the scale twisted up his arm like serpents, constricting his arm, and hissing into his mouth. He spoke the words the scale told him to speak. "*Iri plentis forboden fie / winthem curi plentis nie.*" The burning subsided. The golden serpents dissipated like smoke.

Tepov was then able to lift the scale into his own hands. "We have the Golden Scale."

A low rumbling responded.

Tepov nodded to the hunters. They yanked Edmond back against the wall and clamped the shackles around his wrists.

"Wait. Haven't I done what you asked?" Edmond struggled to free himself.

"I'm sorry we must bind you," shrugged Tepov. "Your mind may be willing, but the corporeal form will rebel against the next part of the ritual."

"What is the next part?"

"We take something your body in its natural form is unwilling to give up."

"What?"

"Your soul."

One of the werewolves spread out his claws and dragged them across Edmond's chest, digging five incisions that bled. Edmond grimaced in pain.

There was a tapping at the door.

Dmitri opened the door to Avian, in dragon form, who winged in and settled on Tepov's outstretched arm.

"Take the scale," said Tepov. "Place it in position."

Avian took the scale into her mouth and soared up towards the barred opening in the wall. She held the scale to reflect the moonlight down in a steady stream onto Edmond.

"The autumn moon," reveled Tepov. "Drink in the fullness of its rays. First, you will feel weak, for you are mortal. After that, you will feel pain, claws digging from the inside out, struggling to free the beast that has long lain dormant within you. Finally, you will want to scream, but, instead, you will howl in anguish, as if your heart has been wrenched out, but it will not be your heart. It will be your soul. And for a while, you will look upon it. It will wander, destitute and homeless, until our great dragon lord erupts and swallows your soul."

Betty stooped to avoid hitting her head on a ceiling of packed earth. She twisted to face Miss Fernsby, who was similarly inconvenienced. The scent of moist dirt filled her nostrils. They were in a burrow underground, the fat, knotty roots of old trees wound about the ceiling.

Miss Fernsby shook her head at the unkempt furniture, unmade beds, scattered twigs and rocks, and a fireplace filled with pinecones and soot. "Spring cleaning. I should have known."

"Look. Our clothes have changed." Betty wore a long, white nightgown with full sleeves and a blue lace shawl draped over her shoulders, and Miss Fernsby wore a Gibson Girl dress and straw hat with a burgundy ribbon around its brim. Her glasses had a thin, gold rim that complemented her ruddy complexion.

A lithe shadow crept in, casing the hideout. The shadow was followed by a youth dressed Robin-Hood-style, garlanded with greenery and leaves, piping on a pan pipe. The youth stopped short. "Oh. Hallo." He gave the two ladies a half wave of his hand and continued to pipe away as if they were not there at all.

"Peter," said Miss Fernsby. "Mind if we sit down?"

He shrugged and hopped up on the twisted garlands of leaves that formed a hammock. "Suit yourself," he said, and swung casually back and forth.

Miss Fernsby stomped the ground with the point of her buttoned shoe, and up grew a mushroom, the size of an ottoman. She sat and leaned primly on the handle of her parasol. Betty followed her example. For her, a large Hibiscus plant burst through the wall, forming an armchair.

Peter Pan sat up, resting his elbows on his lap. "What shall we play now?"

Miss Fernsby smiled fondly at Peter. "It's been a long time, Peter, but I suppose you haven't noticed the time go by at all."

"Of course I noticed. I notice *everything.*"

"It's been many years since my last visit to Neverland."

"Aw, it can't have been that long," said Peter, suspecting she was teasing him. "If it had been *that* long, you would be all grown-up, and you're *not.*"

"Why thank you, Peter, that's quite kind of you."

"Oh, I can always spot a grown-up," he announced, arms folded and chin raised. "Why, if you were a grown-up, you wouldn't even *be* in Neverland. You *couldn't* be here. You have to *believe* in something to get somewhere. And grown-ups don't believe in *anything* anymore."

"We have Betty to thank for us being here," said Miss Fernsby.

"Thanks, Betty." Peter tipped his hat to her and settled back in the hammock, piping a whimsical tune.

"Oh!" The realization of where they were lit Betty's face with delight. "Spring cleaning, Wendy Darling, Peter Pan, *Neverland.*"

Miss Fernsby tapped her parasol as she reflected. "I thought the author and similar location would get us a bit closer to home, but it's all for the best. I'm sure Peter can help us somehow."

"But how?" asked Betty. "We have no books here."

"Oh, yes, we do," insisted Peter. "We have books. Lots of books. All the books you want. Right on that shelf." And he waved his hand towards an airy section of the underground home, an airy section full of nothing.

"That," Miss Fernsby informed Betty, "is the imaginary bookshelf with the imaginary books. Peter and I built that when I was here last."

"You wouldn't happen to really be Wendy Darling, would you?" Betty asked.

"Why, of course not. Wendy traveled to Neverland long *before* Mr. Barrie wrote the play. Otherwise, he wouldn't have been able to write about her. I was about twelve or thirteen when I experienced my first pilgrimage. One minute I was looking out my window, thinking about the play, and the next I was off to Neverland, where I met Peter. He told me Wendy used to tell him and the Lost Boys stories all the time, and, since the Lost Boys had flown off to London and were all grown-up now, Peter had no one to tell him stories, so I said I would, but that I was the type who needed to *read* them. So, we went to work creating imaginary books, with imaginary stories, on imaginary paper, with imaginary pictures."

Betty puzzled. "Do imaginary books work?"

Peter bounded through the air to join the ladies. "Of course they work. Better than real ones. But if you're looking for a way to get somewhere, I know a lot better ways than books, *lots* of ways." He motioned his arm through the air to demonstrate the great expanse of ways. "Why, there's a pirate ship, a hollow tree, a puddle in the ground . . ."

"We need to get back to headquarters," said Miss Fernsby, glancing from Peter to Betty as she explained the situation. "Ordog may have the golden scale, which means it's only a matter of time before the Accusers find the other scales hidden by the ancient Intercessors, and if the scales fall into the wrong hands, all worlds, including Neverland, will no longer be safe. The codebook back at headquarters may give us a clue where to look for the scales."

Betty's eyes widened and her heartbeat quickened.

Peter grinned. "You always did come up with good games, Frieda. It's finders, keepers. The Accusers won't keep the scales if we find them first! I bet the mermaids know something about the dragon scales. I can take you to the lagoon. On *one* condition."

"What condition?" asked Miss Fernsby.

"Why, that I, Peter Pan, get to come with you, and finish the dragon myself." He dueled his shadow, but, while Peter used a make-believe sword, his shadow used a shadow sword, which made the duel much more dangerous, and Peter lunged and parried in earnest.

"Isn't he magnificent," beamed Miss Fernsby like a mother in proud amazement at the accomplishments of her own child.

CHAPTER 11
THE SHIFTING (1930S)

The hunger gnawed at Edmond. He thrashed through the thicket, his gray, pointed ears set back and his shaggy tail dragging through the cold, wet sludge.

His mind was clouded, but his senses were keen. The amber gleam in his eyes focused with the accuracy of a gun's sights and targeted a linnet on a pine tree from a hundred meters away. He could smell a rabbit's fear as it trembled in the brush. He could taste the sediment that drifted in the stream at the edge of the woods. His sharp ears flicked when a peasant who lived halfway down the mountain opened a cottage door.

Edmond tore across the moonlit mist of the field on all fours, his front claws digging through the clods of dirt, catapulting with huge bounds towards the earthen wall ahead, skidding across with his back claws and scampering back around.

He ran because he *could* run, because the momentum he gained sang strength and power and awoke his tight, supple sinew to action as something immortal coursed like rapids through his veins. He leapt, stretched, attained ten feet into the night sky, clawing up into the moon, his coarse gray fur standing on end as he howled. Exultant. Unstoppable. Alone.

The pit of his stomach tightened in an acute pang of hunger. His tail lashed, and he crouched in the tall grass as the smell of the red blood in the peasant's veins aroused his instinct to kill. Saliva trailed down his large, sharp canine teeth and off his long, slimy tongue. He growled, and raising his muzzle into the brisk air, his large black nostrils drew in the living scents of the night. *Tonight, I will feed!* And he crept down the slope towards the shack.

Edmond awoke in the dungeon, drenched with sweat, the taste of blood in his mouth. The lead huntsman, Dmitri, filled the doorway. "So, *Professor* Davidson," he sneered. "What do you say about gods and monsters *now*?"

Disgusted, Edmond sat up on the side of the cot, his half-naked body covered in a shabby blanket, his head hanging in exhaustion and shame.

"Here." Dmitri tossed a bundle of clothes at him. "Get dressed. The count wants to have a chat with you."

Edmond hesitated. His hands were quivering. Pulsing blue veins bulged from the strain. Cold, wet dirt crusted under his nails.

Dmitri laughed. "It feels good, don't it? A rush of power. It's like being god and all the other puny creatures are at the mercy of your strength and desire. You could crush them into dust." He scooped up his arm and made a fist. "Or you could let them grovel in the dirt just a little longer." He gloated over his imagined prey and jabbed his booted foot into the air as if kicking his victim in the jaw.

"But," Edmond shuddered as he remembered, "that man. I didn't want to *kill* him."

"Pshaw. Who cares? You gave up your soul, remember? So you might as well drink your fill, eh? Enjoy it. After a while, you won't give it another thought. In fact, you will get where you can't wait for the next shifting."

A while later, Edmond, dressed, not as a gentleman, but as one of the huntsmen, reported to the front hall. Dmitri had lent him a checkered long-sleeved flannel shirt, a kerchief about his neck, and over long trousers that he stuffed into work boots. Tepov, chin upon his chest, raised his eyes from where he sprawled in a tall-backed medieval throne next to a suit of armor. Avian was perched on the back of the throne, her snaky neck arched downward, her mouth hovering close to Tepov's ear. Tepov held the armor's mace and tested its weight in his hand.

"So, now that you have my soul, when do I collect my reward? Or do I need to grovel and call you *master*?" asked Edmond.

Tepov heaved a sigh. "Why do they never thank me?" he asked Avian, who responded with a hiss. "Souls are such a burden to carry around. They weigh so much and never stop nagging."

"Millgrew convinced me that the soul did not exist, and I believed him. I never realized how empty I would feel without it."

"Come now." Tepov pushed himself up by the iron-clawed arms of the chair. "It was useless to you. You threw a penny in the well, and now all your wishes come true."

"My wish was to no longer be at the mercy of my betters, and now . . . I'm no better than Miroslav."

"Miroslav was a slave, but he had ideas of his own. He refused to turn you as we ordered. That angered Ordog. But you are not a slave. You are my henchman. The mere fact that you retrieved the golden scale makes you legendary. The great Ordog has requested your presence. Imagine it. An audience with one of the mighty beings who once ruled the Earth."

Ordog's throne room lay in the heart of the Carpathian Mountains. The room was immense, with six gigantic pillars of onyx and gold holding up ancient archways on either side. At the front was the imposing throne upon which presided the crimson dragon. Tepov and Edmond were each the size of one of the dragon's claws. "*Ish brigthan vishin feelan?*" roared the dragon.

"*Immin vishtha Davidson so felth theen pfylt,*" replied Tepov.

Ordog curved his long neck down to bring his eyes on level with Edmond. The eyes were flaming orbs under heavy lids.

"*Hathan een fortunan?*"

"*Een hathan.*"

"*Hathan een sovoolan?*"

"*Een hathan.*"

As he listened, Edmond began to understand as if the language were part of his own history. "Yes." He fell on his knees before the dragon. "I have forsaken my soul. I have tasted blood."

"You will taste more. Always more," rumbled Ordog, settling back on his throne. "You have chosen the path of wisdom. Let me reveal to you a mystery." He cupped his talons and a spinning sphere erupted in his palm. Ordog narrated what the sphere revealed. "Long before this temporal world, long before time itself, the Golden Dragon was all. But the Golden Dragon was a cruel tyrant, determined to destroy any who opposed him. Yet I, Ordog, like you, sought to better myself. To use my wisdom to work my way up the ranks, until I became so wise and powerful, the Golden Dragon feared I would replace him.

"To understand what follows, you must know each scale of a dragon is a potential child of that dragon. Once removed from its host, the scale can, in the right circumstances, develop into an entirely new dragon. I persuaded many scales that their host was preventing them from attaining their full greatness. As they imbibed my philosophy, they changed. No longer did they share their host's golden hue but turned the colors of their own inner aura.

"But the Golden Dragon was angered by my ambition. He wrenched these scales from his being, and where those scales had been now existed an abyss of despair. And into this abyss, he hurled our remains down into a molten void.

"He stomped his foot and the scales were dispersed across the void, to lie dormant. There came a day when humans walked the Earth, sent by the Golden Dragon to replace us. When the first humans told stories to their kin, creating their own realities out of the energy and chaos in their little minds, they sparked something dangerous. They had created worlds of their own, and portals into those worlds, portals that were shut to me and my followers. Some of these humans gathered the remaining dragon scales and hid them in diverse and secret places, in portals within portals. Until now. We have recovered the first dragon scale, the first key to reviving an army of my followers and manifesting my destiny."

PART TWO

INTO THE STORY WORLDS

Chapter 12
AN AWFULLY BIG ADVENTURE

Peter led Miss Fernsby and Betty down a path in the woods. They came to a narrow stream. Peter followed the stream, walking bent, face to the ground, hiding behind the tall reeds and cattails. He popped his head up to get his bearing. He looked to the right, to the left, then ducked down.

"Are we nearly to the lagoon?" asked Betty.

"Sh." Peter held up his hand for them to stop as they came to steppingstones leading across the stream. He signaled them to come closer, and they hunched together in a semicircle. Peter used a stick from the ground to sketch the plan in the mud. "This is us." Peter drew three small circles. "And this," he added, dragging the stick to form wavy lines, "is Crocodile Creek. Here," he dropped pebbles across the squiggly lines, "is where we need to cross. Any questions?"

Betty lifted her hand.

"Yes, Betty?"

"So, all we need to do is skip across the water on those steppingstones?"

Peter scowled. "It's not that easy. *That* is *Crocodile Creek*."

Miss Fernsby turned to Betty. "You see, those steppingstones are actually crocodiles, half covered by the water and reeds.

Right now, they are taking their afternoon naps in the sun, but we must step *very* softly, or we could wake them up."

"And besides the crocodiles, there are *other* things," said Peter, "*lots* of other things. We must not make a sound or the *other things* will pounce on us and cut our throats." A hollow moan rose above the twitter and hoots of the wilderness.

Betty shivered and felt her throat.

"Have faith in me," Peter winked. "Now follow your captain, single file, and *quietly."*

Betty and Miss Fernsby filed in behind Peter. Miss Fernsby closed her parasol and shouldered it like a rifle. Betty wrapped her shawl about her and tied the ends in a knot.

Reaching the embankment, Peter hopped over two feet of stream onto the first crocodile's back, swung backwards while he balanced on one foot, regained his position, and gingerly extended his raised toe towards the next crocodile. Once Peter had made it to the second crocodile, he waved for the ladies to join him.

The crocodiles, though asleep, were floating with the current, and now there was an even wider space between the bank where the ladies stood and the first "steppingstone." Miss Fernsby hiked up her skirt and leapt to the first crocodile. "Why," she muttered to Betty, "did the portal give *me* the impossible girdle, and *you* the easy to navigate nighty?" She landed on crocodile back number one and tottered. She stretched out her arms to afford some balance and would have fallen if Betty had not caught hold of the end of the parasol and steadied her.

"That's it," said Miss Fernsby. "You hold on. And don't let go." It was a good thing Betty was holding to the parasol, for when she took Miss Fernsby's place on the first crocodile, she tripped onto the crocodile's head, and the creature groaned awake. The crocodile's eyes converged on Betty's naked ankle and its massive jaw creaked open. Miss Fernsby cried out, and, using her parasol, she yanked Betty to safety onto the next crocodile.

Unfortunately, when the first crocodile let out a grunting roar, it aroused its cohorts. Peter, who had almost made it to the other side of the stream, hopped back to protect the ladies, his dagger unsheathed and ready.

The crocodiles zeroed in on Peter. Miss Fernsby and Betty balanced on top of one crocodile, which increased speed and skimmed in circles, flailing about as it tried to snatch the prey just out of reach on its own back. Meanwhile, the jaws of a large crocodile loomed up behind Peter, preparing to snap shut upon him.

"Peter!" cried Miss Fernsby. And as they were skiing past, she swung her parasol and stunned the predator with a firm wallop to the noggin.

Peter nodded in satisfaction at the timely blow. "Let me try," he called to her. She tossed her parasol to Peter, and he jumped and nimbly caught it. Another crocodile was approaching Betty with wide open jaws. Peter shoved the parasol between the upper and lower jaw as a wedge to prevent the teeth from clamping shut.

"That's the way," cheered Miss Fernsby. "Now how do we get out of here?" Just as she said that, she lost her balance and flopped backwards into the water, taking Betty with her. The water was deeper than it looked, and the current was strong. It took every ounce of strength Betty had to keep her and Miss Fernsby's heads above water as the crocodiles swooshed towards them with sinister intent.

Peter's eyes and mouth widened in alarm. Then, he brightened and snapped his fingers as one inspired. He used the snout of one of the crocodiles as a springboard and leapt into the sky, hovering above the beasts in midair. As he took flight, he grabbed the waving arms of Miss Fernsby and Betty and helped them up into the air with him, just in time to avoid being chomped.

"You might have thought of this before," Miss Fernsby scolded him.

"Ah, where's the fun in that," he retorted, zooming through the sky for the opposite embankment, his two friends in tow.

"All ashore!" he called out as he released them onto the ground. And he let out an exultant rooster crow.

But before he could finish the crow, a knife struck him in the heart. He cringed in surprise and plummeted to the ground. Miss Fernsby crawled to where Peter lay wounded, his head tossed backwards, and his eyes shut, blood saturating his jerkin. "Peter!" sobbed Miss Fernsby, holding his head in her lap. "What has happened?"

The reeds swayed and bent and were slashed by a horde of mindless pirates staring straight ahead and encircling the three with a shuffling gait. They waved cutlasses, flintlocks, and blunderbusses as they raised a groaning chorus of "Kill the intruders. Slay Peter Pan."

"The monsters! The brutes!" Miss Fernsby's tear-filled eyes flared at the pirates.

The pirates were upon them. One wild-eyed man with a tangled beard and rotting teeth was about to plunge his knife into Betty's heart. Betty raised her hand before her like a traffic cop and shouted, "I command you to stop."

They stopped.

The pirates did not budge from their position. They stared and swayed where they stood.

"What ho there," called a voice from behind the pirates. "Excuse me, will you?" said the man who approached, squeezing between the shoulders of two brawny villains. It was Thomas Hamberdeen, in the garb of a jungle explorer, khaki shorts, pith helmet, and all. Along with him, similarly dressed, were Spinderbeck, swatting away flies and mosquitos with a leafy branch, and Khumalo, who waved to the ladies.

"Hamberdeen, thank goodness," Miss Fernsby sighed.

"Oh dear me," said Spinderbeck, seeing Peter's body twisted on the ground.

Khumalo knelt on one knee by Peter, and lifted him to a sitting position, leaning Peter's back against his raised thigh. He loosed the cloth from around his own neck and used it to apply pressure on either side of the knife. "We must get him to the lagoon. The mermaids may be able to help him."

"And what about them?" Betty indicated the dazed pirates.

"*Umthakathi*," noted Khumalo. "The evil one is upon them. Their minds are under the control of another, but your powers have weakened them."

"Yes," said Hamberdeen, "but let's not press our luck. Where is that lagoon?"

"Right beyond that hill," answered Miss Fernsby. "Follow me."

Khumalo lifted the limp body of Peter Pan in his arms and followed Miss Fernsby with the others past the dazed pirates and through a cluster of reeds.

Ordog had the golden scale. Four scales remained to be found, the emerald, the onyx, the sapphire, and the diamond scale. Whispering in the archaic tongue of the ancient dragons, Ordog persuaded the golden scale to speak to him. The scale spoke this riddle.

Inthem feggin corseesh
Nae inthem feggin saa
Inthem feggin norsish
Ba, fa, rinthem thaa

Tepov knelt before the throne in the gigantic shadow of the dragon. "What does it mean, O mighty one?"

Ordog scratched his chin with his front claw and let the lids of his eyes droop. "The literal translation is simple enough. *Literally*, it translates, 'Within the fire beautiful, no one within the fire lives, within the fire deed, sing, find, beyond the door.'"

"Shall I send in Davidson? Perhaps he . . ."

"No!" The pillars of the hall quaked. "I am wisdom. I shall solve this riddle, mark my word." He drummed his claws over the arm of his throne and closed his eyes in thought. At last, enlightened rings of smoke rose from his nostrils, and a sneer formed on either side of his muzzle.

"You have solved it, my lord?"

"I am wisdom, Tepov, I am wisdom indeed. *We* don't need to solve the riddle. We will wait and let the Intercessors solve the mystery for us. We will call on the aid of our brother Accuser."

"Which one, my lord?"

"The one in *Neverland*, of course," leered Ordog. "The one whose heart still beats to the ancient song of *time*."

CHAPTER 13
THE MERMAID LAGOON

The mermaid lagoon was the most beautiful place Betty had ever seen. A waterfall cascaded down from an emerald, mist-encircled summit into the bluest water, a dazzling rainbow weaving in and out of the falls. The jungle blossoms, pink, red, and orange, spread their petals in glorious array, breezing the steamy area with a refreshing fragrance. Verdant lily pads floated in the lagoon amid water ringlets as colorful dragonflies darted and danced about. In the midst of the lagoon was a large gray rock upon which lounged the mermaids, combing their hair with starfish and clam shells as they sang an entrancing siren song about star-crossed lovers.

Miss Fernsby put a finger to her lips as she and her colleagues peered through the camouflage of ferns upon the enchanting scene. A raven-tressed mermaid sensed their presence and stiffened to alert. She signed to the other mermaids, and they dove under the water.

"The merfolk don't trust humans as a rule," said Miss Fernsby.

"Is there any hope for Peter?" asked Betty.

"He is dying," replied Khumalo. "The spirits of death almost have him, but," he gave her a look of compassionate confidence, "we will do what we can." He adjusted the weight of the boy in his arms and turned to Miss Fernsby. "Legend speaks of a mermaid shaman with the wisdom to heal. Is there a way to reach her?"

"Only one way I know of," said Miss Fernsby, and she hiked up her skirts, sloshed through the muddy bank, and hunched down beside a moss-covered rock. Scraping aside the moss, she unburied a conch with a pink spiral shell. She spoke into the conch. "We beg forgiveness for this intrusion. Peter Pan is wounded. He needs your help."

Silence followed. Betty wondered if Miss Fernsby's action was a fruitless gesture. However, a few moments later, the waters stirred, and a large mermaid arose, her coarse black hair streaked with white. Her bronzed skin glowed in the sun, and her arms were thick with the firm muscles of strength and hard work. She wore seaweed and a coral necklace over her maternal bosom. The scales from her waist down were golden and worn. "Bring the boy to me."

"Yes, *Sangoma*." Khumalo took Peter's body in his arms and waded into the lagoon up to the mer-shaman.

Khumalo's eyes met the golden-brown eyes of the mer-shaman, eyes of wisdom and mystery. He released the body into her arms. She let Peter's drooping head fall back on her strong forearm and balanced his knees with her opposite arm.

Without warning, the mer-shaman plunged under the water, bearing Peter's body down with her.

Miss Fernsby gasped in alarm. "Peter!"

Khumalo watched the waters, praying he had not sent the boy to his death.

Betty threw off her shawl, and before anyone could stop her, she dove under the surface of the lagoon. She was a good swimmer, having practiced in her spare time in the lake close to Perlgate. Still, it was difficult to keep her eyes open under the water as sharp blades of underwater flora and wriggling creatures swayed and darted before her, stirring up clouds of bubbles and sediment, besides her own long dark hair pressing over her eyes.

Betty plowed in the direction where the mer-shaman had been. She held her breath as best she could, but her need for oxygen was about to force her to resurface. A red-haired mermaid caught hold of her and dragged her into an underwater cave. In the cave, the water was shallow and there was a pocket of air that allowed Betty to come up and refill her lungs. The mermaid leaned against the wall of the cave and narrowed her green eyes at Betty.

"Where is Peter?" asked Betty. "What are they going to do to him?"

The mermaid stroked her hair as she stared at Betty.

"Is he already dead?" asked Betty.

The mermaid gestured for Betty to follow her. With reservations, Betty waded through the shallow water, following the mermaid. The underwater tunnel led to a cave with a stalactite-lined ceiling and walls that shimmered with reflected light. Betty ascended from the water onto a limestone formation intruding into the flow of water.

She was startled by a splash and splutter behind her. She turned around. Frieda Fernsby was splashing through the water, muttering under her breath as she wiped the hair from her face and yanked out the drooping ribbon that had given up holding her hair in place.

"Don't look as if I did something astounding," snapped Miss Fernsby. "I would have been the first one down here if I hadn't been in shock. Daniel says we should have faith in the shaman, but Peter is a child, and he needs someone to look after him."

Betty extended her hand to help Miss Fernsby onto the incline.

The mermaid tossed a shell against the cave wall to get their attention. She gestured for them to follow her.

They came to an opening in the wall overhung with mossy flora. The mermaid drew the curtain of moss aside. At the end of the inner chamber was a rock-hewn daïs with three cathedral-style arch-shaped niches molded into the wall, each frescoed with a scene from the mermaid religion. In front of the wall upon the daïs was what looked like a sacrificial stone slab, upon which Peter's lifeless body was sprawled. The blood seeped from his chest, down his arm, past his limp pointer finger and splatted into the water.

The mermaids were gathered in the water around the daïs, singing a Gregorian-like chant and flinging garlands of flowers upon Peter. Nothando, the mer-shaman, was poised in front, her arms raised, chanting in a mysterious tongue as one proclaiming a eulogy.

Miss Fernsby cried out in grief, and Betty lent her the support of her arms.

Nothando's fierce eyes opened. "Land-dwellers have entered our sacred chamber." The singing mermaids fell into a stone-chill silence.

"We brought Peter to you for healing, not to bury him," Miss Fernsby flung back.

The raven-haired mermaid tossed her head in scorn. "Why should *you* have anything to do with *Peter Pan?*"

"Peter Pan was the son of a land-dweller," replied Miss Fernsby. "And he was my friend."

Nothando softened. "Come. Mourn his passing with us. Peter Pan was a great protector of the mermaids of Neverland."

Miss Fernsby and Betty joined Nothando on the daïs. Peter's face was pale.

"Tell me, please, is there nothing we can do to save him?" begged Miss Fernsby.

"There is only one hope for Peter," said Nothando. "But the cost may be too much. There must be one who loves him with all the power of a mother and with all the strength of a friend." Nothando lowered her eyes. "Someone willing to give her life for his."

Miss Fernsby stepped forward resolutely.

"Oh no." Betty clutched Miss Fernsby's arm. "You can't."

Miss Fernsby pulled herself free and took Peter's cold hand in hers. "He has lived so long, but hasn't really lived at all. The poor child." A tear streamed from her eye. "Always looking for a mother to heal the loneliness, one who would never abandon him." She raised her eyes from Peter to Nothando. "He *must* be allowed to live a little longer. Take my life, not his." Miss Fernsby knelt by the stone slab and flung her head over Peter's chest.

"So be it," said Nothando.

Betty lurched forward to stop Miss Fernsby, but the mer-shaman shot a force field of water out from her hands that threw Betty back and barred anyone from interfering. The mer-shaman put both of her hands on Miss Fernsby's head and chanted in the tongue of the merfolk. Out of her fingers flowed blue virtue, and, as the blue light wrapped and radiated around Frieda Fernsby, it moved through her to wrap and radiate around Peter.

Betty wiped tears from her eyes. She missed her own mother very much, and, in the short time she had known Miss Fernsby, she had become much like a mother to her.

Nothando's eyes closed, and the force field dissolved. "Betty," she called. Betty approached the daïs. "Your friend will not die. Every good mother sacrifices her life for her child, and when she does, it is a beautiful thing. Yet it comes at a cost. She must be strong when her child is weak. She must smile when she feels like crying. She must stay awake when her body aches to sleep. She must give of herself every day to teach the child what it means to love others.

"Long ago, a little girl named Frieda was happy to stay in Neverland, but she promised Peter she would return to her world and search for his mother. Sadly, she never found her. So, Miss Fernsby took the place of the mother Peter needed. Every night she put a lantern in the window, said her nightly prayers, kept a room ready, worried over his safety, kept his clothes clean and pressed, just in case he ever returned he would find a place where he belonged and was loved. Now, her sacrifice will be rewarded."

As the blue glow rippled down and disappeared into the water, Miss Fernsby raised her head. Peter opened his eyes. The color of vitality returned to his face. "Frieda," he said. "Peter."

Frieda's voice was higher and her hair blonder, for she had given her years of life to Peter, and, as the years washed away from her and into Peter, she kept the years she had when she had first visited Neverland as a girl of twelve wearing a light blue frock and white apron with a garland of daisies about her hair.

There had always been something youthful about Miss Fernsby, but looking down at the rosy-cheeked little girl who once was her matronly mentor took Betty some getting used to. Peter hardly noticed the change, for he had always seen Frieda exactly as she had been when he first met her. Frieda's nature, however, had not changed. She pushed the bridge of her now oversized spectacles back up her snub nose as she examined the religious frescoes around the daïs. "Nothando. This painting," she said. "The mermaid with the nimbus, what is she holding in each of her hands?"

Nothando joined Frieda and placed a motherly hand on her shoulder. "Those are the two scales once entrusted by the ancient Intercessors to the keeping of the merfolk. We guarded them well for centuries upon centuries."

Peter, who now bore a world of care upon his once unbothered mind, stared urgently up at Nothando over his white knuckles pressed against his lower lip. "Do you still have them? Are they safe?"

"Sad to say, they were stolen years ago. Captain Hook and his pirates discovered the hiding place and stole them away. We have not been able to retrieve them since."

"The pirates," inserted Betty. "They should know where the scales are."

"Those pirates?" sniffed Frieda. "They can't even blow their own noses without someone giving them a direct order. How would they know anything?"

Peter's eyes lit with the glimmer of a plan. "Exactly!" He snapped his fingers. "They wouldn't know what to do unless *someone* gave them an order."

"But Captain Hook is dead," said Frieda, pushing her glasses on top of her head and blinking up at Peter.

Peter smiled gently at Frieda. "At least we *thought* he was dead. But I suspect he's the one who ordered the attack, and the only ones who would attack Intercessors are the Accusers. Hook must be alive and in league with Ordog. He would know what became of the scales."

"But how on earth will we find him if he is still alive?" asked Frieda.

Betty tapped a finger on her lips. "From what I have read, the little fishes will lead you to the big ones. Follow the pirates, and I'll wager we'll find Captain Hook."

CHAPTER 14
THE HEART OF THE CROCODILE

The horde of pirates remained standing statue still, soaked by a recent rainfall, staring stupidly in front of them. Since Betty had issued the order to stop, they awaited her return to tell them what to do next.

Khumalo nudged Betty forward. "It's up to you."

Betty approached the slouching pirates. She tied her scarf around her waist and adopted a seaworthy swagger. "A' right me hearties," she said. "Stand to attention when your captain talks, or I'll make ye walk the plank."

The pirates looked worried and strove to attention, one going so far as to slam his hand into his eye in a clumsy effort to salute.

"Stop poking yer eyes out, blast you," Betty snapped sharper than Blackbeard.

"A-aye, c-captain."

"Now." Betty swaggered down the line of pirates as if inspecting the crew on deck. "You there. Take the front of the line and lead the way to where the blazes you came from before you tried to kill me and me mates."

"A-aye, c-captain," saluted the lead pirate, and he galumphed into the jungle, leading the way for the rest of the pirates and the Intercessors.

It was a long, humid trek through the dripping, squawking jungle. Peter was attentive to Frieda, slipping now and then away from the others to find her a drink of water or a piece of jungle fruit. Khumalo let Betty have the last drop from his canteen, and Hamberdeen requested a rest to catch his breath. Spinderbeck regretted that at sixty years old it would sound silly to ask someone to carry him.

Khumalo wiped the sweat from his face with his sleeve and peered into the steaming tangles of vines, branches, and palm fronds. "I hear water flowing from a mountain."

"Well?" demanded Betty of the pirates. "How long before we're there?"

"There it is, captain." The lead pirate pointed forward.

Before them were a range of tepui mountains, their flat tabletops crowned by low hanging clouds. From the top of one of the tepui flowed a grand waterfall, roaring above the jungle noises. The mindless pirates guided the travelers through a hidden passage behind the waterfall into an underground cavern.

The travelers proceeded down the thin, slippery rock path into the dark cave. The back nook of the cave was enlightened by an eerie green glow.

"One of the dragon scales?" wondered Frieda.

"It does not have the look of a scale," said Khumalo.

"More like a phosphorescent rock of some kind," Hamberdeen observed through his binoculars.

"Rocks don't pulse, though, do they?" Spinderbeck also had a pair of binoculars and remembered to use them when he saw Hamberdeen do so.

"Pulse?" asked Betty.

They proceeded with caution into the glow. Upon a pedestal of a petrified tree trunk resided a yellowish-green glob of stone, ellipsoid with folds of rock over each side and decaying fossilized tubes crumbling on one end. The object thumped, and, whenever the glow pulsed the brightest, a shadow within the core of the object was revealed.

The plunking of water dripping from stalactites was interrupted by a groan from the object. The pirates encircled the pedestal and stared without blinking upon the object, their faces reflecting its greenish light.

"Speak to us, oh Captain," they chanted in unison.

"Blast you, bilge-rats. Where have ye been?" came a voice from the object.

"It's Hook," gasped Peter.

"Is that . . . Peter Pan?"

"Yes." With his usual bravado, Peter moved in front, ushering his friends to stand behind him. "I am Peter Pan. And what doodle-doo does now?"

"Alas," wailed the voice. "I sent out my bravest men to kill that blasted Pan once and for all, and still my infernal foe thwarts me."

"Speak, thing," ordered Peter, drawing his dagger. "Tell us where you stashed the scales. Or I'll sink you into Davey Jones' locker and leave you for the crocodiles to swallow."

The voice from the object laughed maniacally. "Bi-carbonate of soda. *That* would be poetic justice indeed. For, *I* am the ghost of Hook, and I be trapped in this loathsome object you see before ye. And the object you see is not vegetable nor mineral, but the vile heart of the very crocodile who swallowed me gizzards and digested me soul. The rest of the croc is dead and decayed, but the black heart remains, now petrified, and continues to beat, not with life, but with revenge. And I will get you yet, Peter confounded Pan. Men. Kill them."

The pirates snarled and drew their weapons.

"Men. Stand at attention," snapped Betty.

The men stood at attention.

"What manner of mischief be this?" came the voice within the glowing crocodile heart. "Two captains?"

"Haha to you Hook," exulted Peter. "Beaten at your own game, are you? Methinks your crew has found another pirate captain to follow."

"This can't be . . ." screeched Hook.

"Oh, but it is," replied Hamberdeen.

"And she is much tougher than you ever were," put in Spinderbeck, poking his head out from behind Frieda with a ferocity that surprised even himself.

"And now that you have been bested," said Frieda, "you know what you must do."

"No!" wailed Hook. "Ordog will roast me on a spit and boil me in me own oil."

"How can he do that to a ghost?" asked Frieda.

"There are worse things awaiting the dead than becoming glowing lights within the heart of the crocodile that ate them for lunch, you know," retorted Hook.

The Intercessors exchanged questioning looks. Frieda raised a decisive finger and said to Hook, "One moment while I confer with my colleagues." Frieda and the other Intercessors went into a huddle a few meters away.

Hamberdeen adjusted his spectacles. "So, my friends, how do we persuade a green glowing lump to do anything?"

"We could try very low vibrations."

The rest of the team turned to Spinderbeck, dumbfounded.

"Vibrations?" asked Hamberdeen, not sure whether to laugh or tell Spinderbeck to stop talking nonsense.

"I've read a great deal about crocodiles," replied Spinderbeck. "And it has been noted on more than one occasion that sounds like thunder or a jackhammer or a volcanic eruption will create havoc among the old nest. Presumably they take it as an alpha crocodile threatening their territory. Not being sure what made the noise, they lash out at each other."

"And how would that help us persuade Hook's ghost?" asked Hamberdeen.

"Well," continued Spinderbeck, "we are so focused on Hook, we forget who his constant nemesis was. Perhaps we should concentrate our efforts on the crocodile."

Frieda looked at Betty. Betty looked at Khumalo. Khumalo looked at Hamberdeen, and Hamberdeen looked at Peter. They all looked back at Spinderbeck, much impressed.

"That's it," said Peter. "We'll persuade the crocodile."

Spinderbeck was so pleased one of his ideas made sense for once, he clapped and asked, "With low, loud vibrations?"

"Exactly," said Peter. "We'll stir up the old flint-hearted beast, and he'll turn on the ghost that has haunted him, and Hook will be so scared he'll tell us whatever we want to know. Spinderbeck, you are a genius."

They conferred on how they would make a loud, low vibration. Betty suggested singing in a hollow area of the cavern, and Peter offered to do a spot-on imitation of a full-grown crocodile on the prowl. However, neither of these ideas were accepted with much enthusiasm by the rest of the team.

"I'm waiting," called out Hook.

"I've got it," said Frieda. "Peter, do you remember how to signal Tiger Lily for help?"

"Of course. It was a special smoke signal," said Peter.

"That's right," said Frieda. "Go signal Tiger Lily. Ask her to bring her tribe."

It did not take Tiger Lily's tribe long to arrive, for they had been following the Intercessors to keep an eye on them ever since they started this expedition. The tribe members agreed that it was to all of their best interests to thwart Captain Hook. So they sat near the mouth of the cave and drummed as loud and low as they could with a constant war-like beat, which echoed throughout the cave as if there were a hundred drums or more.

As the echoes of the drums vibrated throughout the cave, the green glow pulsed more rapidly and with greater intensity. The center glowed yellow, then white, then an antagonistic red.

"Help!" cried Hook in agony. "He's squeezing the last bit of energy out of me very being."

"Tell us what we need to know," demanded Peter. "Where can we find the dragon scales?"

"I'll tell you, I'll tell you!" screeched Hook. "Just make it stop!"

"Agreed," said Peter.

"Long ago I was on the track of the scales. I was promised eternal life and all that blah blah blah," said Hook. "Then I got trapped in this miserable place, this cursed *Neverland*."

"But where are they now?" demanded Peter.

"There's one here in Neverland, the sapphire scale, safely hidden. And another, the emerald scale, in Algiers. I sold the emerald scale to bandits a long time ago, and rumor has it they buried it with the rest of their loot near some oasis. According to legend, it is still there to this day, only no one can find it. Many sandstorms have come and gone since the bandits buried it there. And that is the truth. So help me. Now make it *stop*."

Frieda nodded. Peter gave Betty the all clear signal. Betty signaled to Khumalo, who tapped Hamberdeen on the shoulder, who waved to Spinderbeck, and Spinderbeck cleared his throat and politely asked Tiger Lily to let her friends know they could stop drumming. The tom-toms were silent.

The light coming from the crocodile heart glowed calm and steady.

"You've been cooperative, Captain." said Peter, "And we will be sure to do all we can to save you from the wrath of Ordog."

However, everything Hook had said had been heard in the magical sphere Ordog held in his outstretched claw.

"*Algierss*," hissed the dragon lord, smiling with satisfaction. "Of course. That explains the riddle. *Beautiful, deed.* It's that loathsome novel *Beau Geste* that holds the key."

CHAPTER 15
THE LEGION

Dmitri threw open the door. Edmond, in human form, lay on the bed, books, maps, cigarette butts strewn about him, as he gazed miserably at the ceiling.

"The master wants you," snarled Dmitri.

Edmond did not rise. His eyes sharpened with a flinty gleam. "The *master*."

"Oh, pardon me," sneered Dmitri with an exaggerated bow. "I forgot that *you* were the fortunate *favored* one."

"Stand aside," ordered Tepov.

Dmitri reluctantly sidled out of the way to allow Tepov to enter. Edmond sat up cautiously, for his wolfish instincts could smell both prey and aggressor on the vampire.

"Ordog has summoned you."

"I will not be *summoned*."

"*Enough games, Davidson.* Slave or henchman, we are all dragon fodder any time Ordog desires. When he summons, we obey." Tepov's dual-colored eyes intensified.

"Very well. I will accept the invitation." Edmond pushed Dmitri out of his way and accompanied Tepov down to the throne room of the dragon lord.

Ordog revealed his plan. The objective, to obtain the emerald scale before the Intercessors could retrieve it. The portal was the novel *Beau Geste* and the means of transportation an ancient French saber from Tepov's collection. The plan was threefold. Find the buried treasure at the oasis. Retrieve the dragon scale. Kill anyone who tried to stop him. If at any time danger threatened his retrieval of the scale, Edmond was to send up the *howl of assemble*, and a pack of werewolves would arrive to reinforce him.

Ordog reflected the light of the golden scale upon the saber Edmond held as Tepov read the passage. *"Have you heard of our little post in Zinderneuf... North of your Nigeria? No? Well you hear of it now, and it is where this incomprehensible tragedy took place..."*

Passing into the saber stung at first, like a thousand sharp-edged pieces of metal sticking into his skin, then a cold, clinging sensation as the metallic semi-liquid substance seemed undecided whether to suck him in or spurt him out. Edmond had expected to materialize at the oasis. Instead, he emerged in the armory of the French legion's Algerian fortress.

A legionnaire entered the armory, whistling as he restocked his bandolier with bullets. He was a bright-eyed young man, who was not at all surprised to clap eyes on Edmond standing in front of the saber collection. "Why, it's *you*," he said in a delighted, ragged voice. "Thought you bought it in that last skirmish. Glad some of you chaps made it through after all. Come along, now. The sergeant will want your report." The young man ushered him into the main courtyard, where soldiers, weary and wounded, huddled against the battlements, gearing up for the onslaught. He brought Edmond to the sergeant's quarters.

"Sergeant," sang out the young man. "One of the relief made it past the enemy line, sir."

"Excellent," said the sergeant, a sharp-faced middle-aged man with cold blue eyes and a stern mouth. He was worn to his last nerve, but his uniform was still up to regulations, and he had recently shaved. "Have a cigarette, corporal." He held out a case with a few straggling cigarettes. Edmond was reluctant to accept, but the sergeant insisted. Clearly, the sergeant found it a point of honor to provide the survivor at least one cigarette.

Edmond accepted. The legionnaire stepped forward smartly and lit the cigarette with a match.

"Now." The sergeant slapped his own face to dispose of a mosquito. "Tell me. Are the reinforcements on the way? How soon will they arrive?"

Edmond hesitated, then answered. "They are sending an entire battalion to reinforce our position." It was a half-truth. A pack of werewolves *was* on standby with Ordog.

The glimmer of hope dancing in the sergeant's cold eyes made Edmond regret his prevarication. "Fetch the good wine."

"Yes, sir," saluted the young man, and he took the ring of keys handed him by the sergeant and unlocked the cupboard.

"Mon Dieu," said the sergeant, "don't mind telling you we were wondering if we could hold out another day. Supplies are low and morale is even lower, but they'll fight if I ask them to. If I ask them, they'll fight all the way to Hell."

After a few more toasts, the sergeant ordered the legionnaire to take Edmond to his new quarters, which he would be sharing with three other legionnaires.

"Gentlemen," announced the young legionnaire to the current residents, "I'd like you to meet Corporal . . . uh, what was your name?"

Edmond decided to give a different name. "Jones."

"Really? You too? I'm a Jones myself," said the young legionnaire with delight. "Well, that is, I used to have another name, but I left it behind in England. In fact, I believe half the regiment is from England. There's Jimmy here and there's Jack. But that tall, dark man with the turban goes by Ram Dass. He's from India's sunny clime. Good news, men, Corporal Jones here tells us we're soon to have reinforcements."

Jimmy looked up from where he lounged, nursing his wound, unenthused. "Laudable. Commendable. Did you bring the good cigars and a bottle of port?"

"Ah, don't mind Jimmy there," said Jones, giving Edmond a friendly jab with his elbow. "He comes from high society, he does, and he's not used to this kind of action. Now me, I've seen *lots* of action. More than most, I might add." Jones sat at the table where the others were playing cards. "Deal me in."

"Don't get started with that," said the large and somber Jack, who was chewing on a toothpick as he gathered the cards and shuffled the deck.

"You think these devils that got us pinned down are something," continued young Jones as Jack dealt the cards. "It's nothing to what I seen near Woking. That's when I served in the artillery, and . . ."

"Please," said Ram Dass. "Let the corporal speak. Are reinforcements really on the way?"

Edmond crushed his cigarette in a tin ashtray on the table, unable to meet the Indian's gaze. "Yes."

"But, how in God's name can they manage to get through?" asked Jack. "It would take a miracle for them to run the barricade."

"Easy," interrupted young Jones, as he assessed his hand of cards. "I've started a tunnel. We just dig and dig and dig until we can get past them. *Underground.*"

"Don't listen to *him*," said Jimmy. "He's barmy, I'm afraid. He saw some horrific action near Woking, and he's never quite recovered. He had to leave England or they would have slammed him into the loopy bin."

Jones scowled at Jimmy then turned back to Edmond. "Oh, *I'm* not as crazy as they think. They just don't understand genius. We geniuses need to stick together. I could tell *you* were a right one from the start."

Edmond felt at home with this group of outcasts. They reminded him of the ragtag group of boys at school who had looked to him to protect them from the bullies. "The reinforcements are coming, but they may need a little help."

"We're down to our last nerve and our last bullet," said Jack. "What help can we be?"

"Not the regiment," said Edmond, "but a small patrol. We could slip out and create a distraction, make the enemy think the reinforcements are already here. We'll swoop down from the hills. They will turn their attention on us and give the real reinforcements a chance to break through."

"What does the sergeant say?" asked Jack.

Edmond lied. "He likes the plan. In fact, he already gave me the go ahead to put together a patrol and slip over the wall while it's still dark."

"What plan?" asked a voice from behind him. It was the sergeant.

The legionnaires came to attention.

"Well, corporal? If you have a plan, I think we should *all* hear of it." There was something of the headmaster in the sergeant that rankled Edmond.

"I was going to discuss it with you, of course, sir," Edmond assured him. "I just wanted to first determine if the men were up for it."

"And when you told them I had already approved the plan?" challenged the sergeant.

"I said '*he*' liked the plan. I meant the lieutenant. He was shot down on his way past the siege," Edmond lied through his teeth.

The sergeant nodded. "I certainly hope that is the truth, for *your* sake. You and I, we must set the example for the ranks. And upholding the honor of France means . . . no lies."

"Of course, sergeant."

"What happens to men who lie, legionnaire?" the sergeant demanded of Jimmy.

Jimmy gave the sergeant a look that said he had experienced firsthand what happens to men who lie. "He's spread-eagled and flogged," he spat back.

"And that's the lucky ones," said the sergeant. "You see, corporal, the French legion recruits its men from the riffraff of society, so we must maintain a code of honor and discipline. Even in the midst of a siege, we must have discipline."

"I agree, sir," said Edmond.

"I did not ask you to agree, but for now, we will *assume* you were *not* lying. We will *assume* that you were going to tell me the plan back when we were in my quarters. And we will *assume* that your plan involved some sort of ruse where we send out a patrol, pack their horses with corpses and empty rifles, and send them out over the ridge during the night. And that we would prop them up to look like reinforcements, and the Tuaregs would think '*Mon Dieu!* Reinforcements are here.' And they would be so distracted the *real* reinforcements could march right into the fort playing a tune of victory."

Edmond cringed. The plan did not sound quite so clever in the retelling.

"It's been done, corporal," snapped the sergeant. "The rabble out there has seen it so often they would laugh themselves into a massacre if we tried it. No, we will continue to take our regular watches and pray those reinforcements you promised get through."

Edmond was allowed to forego the first watch and get some sleep. But he could not sleep. Since his plan to persuade the men to join him on patrol had been thwarted by the sergeant, he needed to think of something else, quickly. He sensed Ordog watching him, felt his hot, impatient breath on his neck. Tobacco was at a premium, so he chewed on the stem of a pipe he found in his pocket as he lay awake tracing ideas across the stucco ceiling.

"Psst," said Jones, ducking his head to avoid hitting the upper birth as he sat on the edge of the bed. "Can't sleep, eh?"

Edmond shook his head.

"Me neither. It's the nightmares. Have 'em all the time. Thought I would forget all about it, but you can't forget something like *that*, can you?"

"Nightmares. Yes," said Edmond.

"Were you there? At Horsell Commons, I mean? When *they* came?"

"They?"

"They thought they had us, didn't they," said the young man. "Them with their tripods and black smoke. But we showed them. You can't stop an Englishman, can you, sir."

The door opened and the silhouette of the sergeant loomed in the light of his candle.

"Corporal Jones," he whispered.

Edmond propped himself on his elbow. "Sergeant."

The sergeant gestured for Edmond to join him. Edmond stood, drew his suspenders up over his shoulders, and followed the sergeant, who led him to his quarters. The wine bottle on the desk was three-fourths empty. The sergeant's eyes were bleary and bloodshot.

The sergeant slammed down a tin cup and poured the rest of the wine into it, splattering some onto the maps and correspondence strewn across his desk. "We're not going to last much longer," he said. "And we both know those reinforcements aren't coming."

"But the . . ."

"I'm not a stupid man, corporal. I have a brain sharp and finely tuned." The sergeant pointed clumsily at his head. "Luck is what we need, and luck is what I never have. Only one time was I ever lucky. And since you are a gentleman, I will tell you about it. Just wait. Sit there." The sergeant moved over to a drawer, drew a key from a chain around his neck, and fumbled with the key until the lock gave way. He shuffled though papers, and, from the bottom of the drawer, he drew a sealed scroll. "Do you know what this is?" The sergeant waved the scroll under Edmond's nose. Edmond could smell blood on the scroll.

"I got it off Jimmy. Jimmy, pah! There's a rogue if ever there was one. Seduced a girl back in England, ruined her life, even framed her brother for a bank heist he had planned. What kind of man does a thing like that? I'll tell you. The same kind of man who would swipe this scroll from the hands of an orphan who had hoped to sell it to support his poor, starving family. That's the miserable kind of wretch this swine is."

"What is it, sir?"

"A map. Ages ago some filthy bandits buried a sacred treasure, and this map shows us the way."

"A treasure map, sir?"

"For twenty years I have fought in this hell for the honor of France. What has France given me? A few pennies a day and a medal for bravery. I'm a brave man, but I'm not stupid. When death knocks at the door, I don't fling open the gate. This treasure will be enough for both you and me." The sergeant's eyes burned with gold lust. "Enough for us to get lost in some faraway place and live a long and comfortable life. But I need a patrol to get me past the siege and dig up the treasure."

Edmond could barely believe his luck. "Count me in, sir."

"Good. Get together a small patrol. Feel out the men and only tell the ones you trust about the treasure. But leave Jimmy out of it."

"Of course, sergeant."

CHAPTER 16
INTO THE VALLEY

Edmond met one at a time with Jones, Jack, and Ram Dass. He confirmed that not one of them wanted to die a horrible death in the name of honor. Each agreed that a portion of the treasure would more than make up for the pension they would give up and the chance they took of being shot as deserters.

Jones agreed to it, not just because of the treasure, but because he thought it all part of the plan to slip one over on the enemy and put the Western World on top again.

Jack did not like the plan at all. He had seen what happened to men who fell behind or deserted. "Not a quick, painless death either." His tense fingers switched open the different tools of his multiplex knife. "We could be exiled to the Saharan desert, where we'd burn to death in the sun, or we could end up in the silo to be buried alive in a hole with no food or water, unable to move out of a painful hunched position while the sun beats down on your flesh and the cold mist eats you alive. Or maybe the *crapaudine*. To be trussed up like a bird with your arms and legs behind your back, enduring wrenching pain."

"But if we do not play along, the sergeant could report us for whatever trumped up charges he invents, and we'd suffer all of that anyway," pointed out Edmond. "Might as well take a chance at the treasure."

Jack could not argue with Edmond's logic. Besides, he had a girl waiting for him at home. He had dispatched her abusive husband and had promised to return to her with money enough to support her in the manner to which she was accustomed.

Ram Dass joined with them because it was the will of the fates.

Edmond reported back to the sergeant that he had a patrol ready and waiting for their purposes. The sergeant ensured that Jimmy was conveniently posted for a second shift on the wall, where, in all likelihood, he would be picked off by enemy sharpshooters prior to the imminent storming of the defenses.

That night, Jack managed to knock out the legionnaires standing watch and truss them up with rope, using good strong sailor knots. One by one, the members of the patrol helped each other slip over the low part of the wall, keeping down as to not attract the attention of the enemy lying in wait beyond the dunes.

"We'll need horses and supplies," the sergeant told Edmond after each of the patrol had made it over the wall and behind a shelter of rocks. "The mess was down to watery soup, and we sent out the last of the horses with the patrol that never returned."

"Leave it to me," said Edmond. "I know where I can find horses."

"Jack. Go with him," ordered the sergeant.

"No," said Edmond. "I'll do this alone."

Edmond could smell the horses and hear them swatting the flies with their tails from several miles away. He crawled through the gritty sand and brush. Reaching a large dune, he climbed to the top in the broad glare of the full moon against the purple night sky. He let the moonlight shower over him, fixed his eyes on its glow. The pain, like a thousand knives digging into his flesh, an unyielding rack pulling his tendons and cracking his bones. The sharpening of his senses and the clouding of his mind. He grabbed for the moon with jagged, angry claws.

Half a minute later, he was crouched on all fours, his pointed ears twitching to the tune of horses rattling their reins at their posts in the enemy's camp. He bolted across an expanse of sand and lingered at the edge of the camp, panting and glaring. A lookout was singing a traditional song of his people. The next moment his throat had been

ripped open. A shadow of a wolf man prowled past the tents in the glow of the campfire. One man saw but was dead before he could ready his gun. The others, too, soon were slaughtered. The horses neighed in panic and pulled desperately upon the tethers. The black clouds of night drifted across the face of the moon, and Edmond was human again. He patted the horses and whispered reassurance to them as he gathered supplies from the camp.

The morning sun spread long shadows through the valley as the patrol rode their packed horses towards the oasis.

"We are indeed most fortunate of men," said Ram Dass. "While our brothers at the fort are starving to death and giving their last drop of blood for the legion, we are here, well-fed, on strong horses, with a pleasant path before us, on our way to a most glorious reward."

"What will you do with your part of the treasure?" asked Jack.

"A friend of mine, an Englishman I served with, has fallen upon misfortune. I would like to use my portion to help him," Ram Dass said.

"Very noble," replied Jack.

"Me," added young Jones, "I'd like to make sure what happened near Woking never happens again. We can stockpile food and ammunition and hide them in tunnels underground, and I'll start a training camp to accustom people to living in the sewers and such, so that if anything invades our world again, we can pop out like moles in the night, and that'll surprise 'em." The others exchanged looks that agreed Jones was not quite right in the head. Jones rode along, smiling, oblivious to the looks. "What about you, corporal?"

Edmond fixed his eyes gloomily ahead. "I owe someone a lot of money."

No one asked the sergeant what he wanted. He rode in front with a saturnine expression and now and then, his eyes twitched as he addressed some invisible companion with cryptic mutterings. "Sorry, men. I had to do it. You understand, of course. The treasure. We had to get the treasure away from the enemy. You do understand, don't you."

The sun was climbing in the sky over the *Haute Plaines*, an arid region lying between the mountain ranges, when a bullet whizzed past the sergeant.

"Dismount," ordered the sergeant. The men slid from their saddles and forced their horses down to serve as barricades as they prepared their rifles. Jack used the sight on his rifle to survey the area. He glimpsed a metal object reflecting a gleam of light at the top of a ridge on the plateau directly in front of them.

"There," said Jack.

"How many?" asked Ram Dass.

"Twenty," said Edmond. "Here they come." He pointed in the opposite direction where twenty Tuaregs on horseback, in response to the signal, were pressing over the slope of the dune towards them, firing their rifles, and shouting for revenge.

"Return fire," ordered the sergeant.

"What I wouldn't do for a good ol' Gatling," said Jones over the mêlée.

"We're sitting ducks out here." The sergeant gritted his teeth against the stock of his rifle and squinted past the sweat.

Edmond considered the *howl of assemble*. The pack would arrive and make short work of these assailants, but, he reminded himself, those huntsmen did not discriminate once on the scent for blood, and the legionnaires themselves could fall prey.

"I'll get over the ridge and distract them," offered Ram Dass.

"No, stay down. I've got this." Edmond stood to take better aim, and his instincts could sense where the next volley would come from, giving him a chance to pick the riders off one by one with perfect aim. When he ran out of ammunition, Jones, in awe, handed up his own rifle, and Edmond continued his barrage of fire upon the charging horsemen. The oncoming bullets of the assailants hit their marks more than once, in his shoulder, his chest, his head, and his heart. They ripped his flesh and ricocheted against his bones, but he was immortal, so the pain passed.

"He's an idiot," said the sergeant.

"He's not human," said Ram Dass.

In a matter of minutes, Edmond had dispatched each rider.

"Now that's what I call a crack shot," cheered Jones.

Edmond slammed down the empty rifle and squeezed his eyes shut in anguish. The scent of blood was provoking his wolfish instincts, and he fought against shifting. He despised himself for how easy it had been to dispatch the men who were only seeking retribution for his slaughter of their comrades in the encampment. Ram Dass offered to tend to his wounds, but to his amazement, there was not even a scratch.

"Gather the horses, men," said the sergeant. "At least, the ones that are still alive, and let's get on to the treasure."

Jones handed Edmond the canteen of water and grinned. "Here's to you, chum," he said with a wink.

"I tell you," said Ram Dass to Jack, "he's not human."

They reached the oasis by midday. The sun was blistering hot, and their canteens had gone dry. They slid off their worn-out horses and refilled their canteens in the gritty water sheltered by brown-tinged palms.

The sergeant stood apart and unrolled the map, studying it by the light that glistened through the leaves. "The old well was buried years ago," he said, "but according to this map, it should be . . ." and he stepped out the paces. "One, two, three, four, five, six, seven, eight, nine, ten, eleven, twelve. Right here."

Once the men had cooled off in the water, they went to work digging in the dirt. It was arduous work in the desert sun, but the thought of the treasure kept their spirits high.

"You should see my Mary," said Jack as he worked his impressive muscles, scraping away the dirt with a spade. "She's an angel. Her husband were a monster, but she is the loveliest, kindest creature on earth."

"Let's put our backs into it," said Jones. "Each minute brings us closer to a brighter future where *I'll* be in charge, and cricket every Sunday!"

After two or three hours of the patrol taking shifts, the spade clanged against metal.

"It's the treasure. Hoist it up, men," said the sergeant.

They heaved a large chest out of the well and onto the mound of newly-dug earth beside it. The chest was locked.

"Well? Shoot it off," ordered the sergeant.

"But, sergeant," said Ram Dass, "We have only one bullet left."

"Are you *sure* of that?" The sergeant sneered.

"Yes, sergeant, Ram Dass is sure."

"Go ahead. We're in no danger *here*."

Ram Dass hesitated but loaded his pistol with their last bullet and took careful aim at the lock. He pulled the trigger, and the lock shattered.

Young Jones grinned as he vaulted over the chest and threw back the lid. "There it is, my friends. Enough gold, jewels, and relics to make each of us a very rich man."

Edmond stared at the treasure, hoping to glimpse the emerald scale. His ears caught the sound of an automatic rifle being loaded.

The sergeant had crept back to a higher slope overlooking the oasis. He aimed his automatic rifle at the men gathered eagerly around the treasure. "Enough to make *me* a rich man. And a hero, after I put a stop to this cowardly party of deserters."

Jack led the others as they scrambled to get out of range, but the automatic fired several well-aimed clips. Jack, young Jones, and Ram Dass, they all were dead. Edmond, too, had been shot. The bullets bore into his flesh and ripped his insides. He howled a long, bitter cry at the vultures circling above.

The sergeant, who had been chuckling sadistically, now turned pale. The threat of death had shifted Edmond, and the sight of a towering wolf man with razor claws, teeth sharp as scimitars, and eyes that glowed blood red sent the sergeant into a panic. He staggered backwards as Edmond stalked up to him.

"Back, you devil. Back!" cried the sergeant.

Edmond lumbered forward. The sergeant fired into Edmond until the rifle made empty, pathetic clicking sounds. Edmond's flesh was mutilated by bullets. He bled, but the wounds healed. The rage set his brain on fire and made him feel more powerful. He grabbed the sergeant by the throat and yanked his pale, contorted nose up to his own bristling muzzle.

"I smell your fear," growled Edmond.

"I – I –I," squeaked the sergeant.

Edmond shook him by his throat, rattling his bones, shook him so hard that the sergeant's mouth frothed, and his eyes bulged, and his neck snapped. Edmond cast aside the worthless rag of a man.

The rest of the pack had heard the howl. Their shadows fell over Edmond.

"Did you get it?" asked Dmitri.

Edmond did not answer right away. He passed a grim gaze over the bodies of Jack, Ram Dass, and poor young Jones, pathetic men who would be spared the cruelty of a court-martial but would never enjoy a single piece of gold.

CHAPTER 17
THE GHOST SHIP

Betty ordered the mindless pirates to lead the way to where Hook had hidden the scale in Neverland. The pirates shambled out of the cave and past the curtain of water flowing down from the tepui mountains.

As they rounded the mountains, Khumalo inhaled deeply. "Salt air. We are nearing the ocean."

"You're right," said Peter. "This is the trail that leads to the cove. Where the *Jolly Roger* has been anchored for over a hundred years."

Frieda set her fists on her hips. "A hundred years?"

Peter blushed. "Well, an awful long time. They say it's *haunted.*"

"Well, then. We shall unhaunt it," declared Spinderbeck, emboldened by the fact that his plan had worked back in the crocodile cave.

The ship was moored near Skull Rock. The beams and timbers creaked and moaned. The ropes were frayed, and many boards were rotting or missing. It was a skeleton ship. The Intercessors paused at the ramp, and Peter ordered his shadow to board the ship first to scout out for ghosts. But before they could board, Nothando and two of her mermaids splashed up like dolphins near the ship's anchor.

"*Sangoma*," acknowledged Khumalo, stepping up to the incoming tide on the shore's edge to greet the mermaids.

Nothando's eyes burned and her frown deepened. The mermaids with her bobbed sullenly, half-submerged, their wet hair drooping limply about their ears.

"The crocodile heart has betrayed us all," Nothando announced. "Before you leave Neverland, Ordog will already have the emerald scale. Our only hope is that you can find the three remaining scales before the Accusers get them."

A chill gust blew in from the sea. Betty untied her shawl from her waist and draped it about her shivering shoulders. She joined Khumalo at the shore's edge, the foamy tide sudsing her bare ankles. "Hook said there is one hidden here in Neverland. The pirates led us to the ship."

Nothando bent her glare upon the pirates. "Yes, the traitors who tried to murder Peter Pan. We will tend to them, be assured. And to aid in your quest, I have something for each of you." She gestured to the two mermaids. They lifted their arms from beneath the waves to reveal the parcels they carried.

The mermaids held out the various gifts, while Nothando described them. "For Daniel Khumalo, this magic potion. For Thomas Hamberdeen, this key. For Jeremy Spinderbeck, this sword. For Peter Pan, these boots. For Frieda Fernsby, this lantern. And for Beatrice Talbin, this chart."

The bottle for Khumalo had the words "drink me" printed on the label. The tag tied around the neck of the key given to Hamberdeen read "To open the door that is shut and to shut the door that is open." At first the sword was too heavy for Spinderbeck to lift without toppling to one side or the other, but once he read the inscription on the sword, "Courage," it became lighter and his grip firmer. Frieda's lantern was made of gold and there were words etched into the base of it. "To light the darkest places."

Peter tried on the boots, but they were several sizes too big for him. They were ugly, plain, dark brown boots, the sort one would wear for a dull working day on rough terrain. He wanted to toss them away, but Frieda stopped him. "No, Peter. Nothando gave you these boots. She must have a reason."

Betty's gift was a chart, partly complete. The star marking the starting point was near an ink drawing of a grand ship, with the name of the ship in beautiful calligraphy. "The *Jolly Roger*."

"That chart," explained Nothando, "will take you where you must go to find the remaining scale. But it will only show you the first step. To find out what to do second, you must complete the first. You, Beatrice Talbin, must sail forth on the *Jolly Roger*, and you must sail alone."

"What?" Betty nearly dropped the chart.

Frieda stomped her foot. "But she is so young. She needs our help."

"If anyone's going to sail the *Jolly Roger*, it'll be me," insisted Peter.

"Why should we not all go?" asked Khumalo.

"Only Betty can guide it," said Nothando. "The Accusers are gathering from all directions, and all of you must take your posts and defend your ground if we are to keep the remaining scales safe. You will know where you must go and what you must do with your gifts at the proper time." Nothando submerged herself under the waves, and her mermaid companions followed suit, their tails swooshing up and down in Nothando's wake, into the rusty orange horizon.

"We may not be able to sail with you," said Frieda to Betty, "but at least we can get you situated." The Intercessors accompanied Betty onto the deck of the *Jolly Roger*. Khumalo spread the chart over the helm and studied it with Betty. "According to this chart, you must steer a course due east, through that mist rolling in. After that," he looked close at the map and frowned. "After that, you will need to consult the chart again."

"Have you explored your ship, Captain?" Hamberdeen asked Betty. All agreed that was an excellent suggestion, and they went on a tour of the ship. The door to Captain Hook's cabin was locked, but Hamberdeen's key managed to unlock it. Once inside, Betty discovered a dashing feathered broad-brimmed hat and a brass-buckled belt with a long seventeenth-century rapier boasting a narrow shiny metal blade guard and a cup made of finely engraved gold. She tried on the hat and the belt and found they fit as if made for her, which was extraordinary, for Betty was much smaller than Captain Hook. Her friends voiced their admiration for how gallant and seaworthy she looked.

The helm was in good shape, though dusty and draped in cobwebs. The galley was crawling with scampering, squealing rats, and rolling with empty barrels filled with rotten apple cores. Neither magazine held any gunpowder, and the forecastle was empty, except for a skeleton hanging from a berth, sword still clutched in its bony phalanges.

"Not a merry prospect," admitted Hamberdeen.

"But certainly an adventure," said Betty.

Frieda gave Betty a hug. "I will miss you."

"But we *will* meet again," said Betty.

The *Jolly Roger* steered on its own, as if it knew the way. Betty rested her hand on the helm, just to lend herself more confidence, and waved her hat bravely to her comrades who had gone ashore. They looked so sad, and that made Betty happy, for she had never realized before how much she meant to them. She wondered which path each of them would take, as the bow of the ship dove into the ghostly mist, and gradually the light of Frieda's lantern on shore was swallowed in the fog.

The fog did not lift. The creaking of the masts sounded like the dead turning in their graves. An albatross landed on a beam and fixed Betty with red eyes.

"Water, water, everywhere," quoted Betty, watching the albatross.

Not far behind the albatross, a pale blue light pierced the mist and descended upon the deck like a falling star. The beams of the four points stretched broader into the shape of a giant bat. The bottom tip of the star lit on the deck like a dancer performing a *Brisé Volé*. Blue and silver wings unfolded to reveal Count Vlad Tepov. He fixed his eyes on Betty, brows arched and mouth turned up in a sneer. He drew the wings apart from his body and tucked them behind his shoulders to form a cloak. "And, instead of a cross, the albatross about my neck was hung."

The albatross flapped its wings and perched on Tepov's outstretched forearm, where it transformed into his pet dragon.

"So, my love, what now?" squawked Avian.

Tepov stroked the dragon's neck. "Now, we take what belongs to us."

Betty placed her hand on the hilt of Hook's rapier. "Where is Edmond?"

"Edmond." Tepov adjusted his blue-silver gloves. "Pathetic Edmond." He approached her through the mist. "His vanity cost him his soul. And you, Beatrice? Like Dante's *Inferno*, will you intercede for him and save his soul from Hell? It's no good, no good at all."

Betty matched his hauteur as best she could. "If all I do will be of no avail, why does the great Count Tepov bother to board my ship?"

He took a moment to assess her. "Why would I not come? Such a beautiful champion. Yet Edmond chose Miss Daphne Graham. Such a stupid man." He noted with sadistic pleasure he had hit home. Betty's shoulders sagged, her eyes saddened, but her chin remained defiant, though it quivered. He *échappéd* up to her. In a theatrical style, he proclaimed, "I have not come to harm you, lovely Beatrice, but to warn you. The undead call out. Do you hear them? There. A gremlin lurks. And there. Behind the mast. A goblin who will devour your soul soon as you fall asleep. And up there among the sheets the ghosts appear here, then there, until they swoop and pull you down."

As he spoke, she spied the creatures he described. A gremlin gurgled and ducked behind the mizzen. A goblin peered with glowing saucer-shaped eyes through a partly opened hatchway in the deck. The white, luminescent spirits whirled and wailed through the masts, sails, and lofts.

Tepov spun her about to face him. "Look in my eyes." He met her reluctant dark eyes with his own powerful stare. "When I first saw you, I desired you, more than any other

human I have known. And now I have risked the wrath of the dragon lord to come and take you from this ship and make you my own." His voice shook, and she felt a rapid pounding in his chest, but she knew not to trust his histrionics.

She pushed him back. "I don't need you."

He recoiled as if hurt. "I have traversed time and space. I have braved the storms of the universe. Why would I do that unless I really wanted you?"

"You want me the way you wanted Edmond, to be a slave for you and your so-called dragon lord. But," Betty drew her rapier and readied it, "I am not *your* slave or anybody else's. I am an Intercessor. The ghosts, the goblins, and even *you* cannot harm me."

"And you would do all this . . . for . . . Edmond?"

She aimed the point of her rapier at his throat. "I do this . . . because this is what I must do. If I lose Edmond, so be it, but I will not lose my world to the likes of you."

"Then," the count's face clouded over, "so be it." His wings once more covered his face. He flung them open, one at a time, to reveal sinister glowing eyes. He overlapped his arms across his chest as one who knew the immenseness of his strength. He lifted his arms, his long, claw-like fingers straining towards the darkness above. "Spirits of the undead," he rumbled. "Obey your master's voice. In the name of Ordog, smite my adversary."

All the goblins, gremlins, ghouls, and ghosts came to attention and joined together as one giant, reeking tidal wave of leering muck. Betty backed against the railing, her sword raised, but her heart was sinking.

The tidal wave, though a conglomerate of all the vicious fiends that had been lurking about the ship, had individual eyes, exchanging narrow, conspiring looks with one another and individual sneers that snickered to see their great advantage over one pitiful girl who had nothing but a human sword to defend herself.

Betty was tempted to find a portal and escape. She glanced at her chart to catch any bit of writing that could possibly send her someplace else. However, the words on the map at the spot where the ship was currently drifting flared up in flaming gold ink that jumped off the paper at her. "Stand firm. You are not alone." The brightness of the words lit her face like the warm glow from a campfire, granting her strength and courage.

Several dots of golden light hovered in the mist. *More vampires?* But the tiny golden orbs fluttered about and made rippling bell-like music. One of the lights glided onto her shoulder. "Don't worry," sang a tiny voice. "We are here."

"Who are you?" asked Betty.

"We're the pixies," sang a chorus of the golden lights. "Peter sent us."

Tondor Char, a gallant red-haired pixie, was armed with sword in its sheath, crossbow at her back, and a scabbarded dagger at each hip. "Pixies," she called, "unite!"

All of the pixies gathered together and formed a circle of light around Betty. Tepov drew back and shielded his eyes with one of his wings. The tidal wave of filth turned into splotches of gunk as they approached the light and splattered to the deck.

"Thank you, my friends," said Betty to the pixies.

"The battle isn't over yet," declared Tondor. "We had the element of surprise. Now that they know we are here, they will conjure even more darkness to overcome our light."

Tepov reached once more into the dark mist, and his arms became elongated shadows that slithered across the deck towards the pixies like sinister cobras. The shadows reared and struck at the light with full force.

"Hold fast, pixies," ordered Tondor. The pixies raised their shields.

But each time the shadows hit, the pixies' shields weakened, and the light around Betty flickered unsteadily. The ghostly goblin crew glowered in triumph.

"Creatures of the undead," called Tepov, "strike them now."

The goblins came slinking up like splotches of goo with saucer eyes and hungry mouths. Betty struck at them, but once she chopped a splotch in two, each side of the splotch formed new goblins, so that she had twice as many goblins as before.

Tondor blew pixie dust onto Betty's sword, and the sword glowed and sizzled as it moved. Betty struck at the goblins, and they sputtered and sparked and burnt into cinders.

The gremlins sprang from the masts and clutched at Betty, scratching her skin. The pixies pounced upon the gremlins and struggled to pry their claws off Betty. The pixies were gaining the upper hand, since every time the gremlins got too close to the pixie light they shrank back in fear.

But then the ghosts whirled in, bringing with them a gale force wind and sheets of rain. The pixies clung to the ship any way they could to keep from blowing away, but the winds were too powerful for them, and they found themselves being swept away from the ship.

"Lana!" called Tondor to a young pixie clinging to a shred of sail.

"Tondor!" said Lana. "I can't hold on much longer."

"Yes, you can!"

Tondor gasped as the wind pried Lana's tiny fingers from the sail, and they heard her cry fade as she was whipped off to sea.

Tepov marched up to Betty with his wings spread out to engulf her.

A figure leapt over the railing onto the ship. He raised both his hands in front of him, fight ready, the wind and rain assailing his face. "Vlad Tepov. I command you to stop."

The wind died, the ghosts shivered and flew back to the lofts, the gremlins stared with bulging bloodshot eyes at this bold newcomer.

Tepov confronted the new foe. "Who are you? What right have you to interfere?"

The rain subsided, and Betty could see past the jagged black hair the weather had edged around his face, Akira Yamada, from Intercessor headquarters. He wore samurai robes and flourished a formidable sword. "You and I have met before, many times," he said to Tepov. "You know this sword." He wielded the sword in graceful cuts in the air before him.

Tepov reared back. "Perhaps, but that was before I possessed two of the dragon scales. The balance does not shift in your favor *this* time, Akira Yamada."

Yamada touched his hand purposefully to the flat of his blade. He gave Betty and Tondor a knowing look, and from his pocket he withdrew a tiny sparkle of light, little Lana, whom he had caught as he came on board. He held Lana to his lips and whispered, "Little one. Light up my blade."

Lana cheerfully zigzagged around the samurai sword, setting it ablaze with light.

"The darker the night," said Yamada, "the stronger the light." He lunged at Tepov, crying out, "Now, let us dispatch this fiend once and for all."

Betty ripped the remaining gremlins from her neck and shoulders and powered towards Yamada to join him against Tepov.

Tondor sounded the battle cry on her trumpet and drew her crossbow from her back. The pixies reunited their forces and shone with a bright light around the two Intercessors.

Tepov drew his own blade and warded off several blows from both Yamada and Betty. Using his wing as a shield, he ducked behind a mast.

"So, count, you hide from a fight?" chided Yamada.

"I have other matters that await. It was good to cross blades with you again, Yamada. And it was a pleasure, my beautiful Beatrice. But for now . . ." He unfolded his wings and raised them high. He disappeared into a blue light that collapsed upon itself.

Without their leader, the creatures of the undead screeched in fear and scrambled about, bumping into one another. They fled to the rails and jumped overboard, hurried along by the arrows and swords of the pixies.

Betty gazed in admiration at Yamada. "How did you know to come here?"

"The code book," he answered.

"Long live Akira Yamada!" declared Tondor Char. "And long live Beatrice Talbin. You passed the test. You displayed faith and courage. For that, you are worthy of this."

The pixies flitted to the door to Captain Hook's cabin. They came out bearing a golden chest. Together, they carried it to Betty.

"Open it," said Tondor. Betty pried it open with her sword.

There, inside the chest, was the sapphire scale, shimmering like the waves of the calm sea in the moonlight.

"It was here all this time?" asked Betty.

"Yes," replied Tondor. "Captain Hook was never able to open the chest, nor were the lost boys, not even Peter Pan. Only you, Beatrice Talbin, Dispeller of Evil." The pixies bowed before Betty.

Betty blushed. "Please, *you* are the ones who rescued *me*."

"You have brought hope back to Neverland," said Lana.

The mist cleared, and the sun shone upon the sea before them. Betty set her hand to the helm and consulted her chart. The words on the map cheered her greatly. "Homeward."

CHAPTER 18
THE BLACKMAILER

The Intercessors returned with the sapphire scale to the cottage. That is, all of them except Frieda, who stayed with Peter in Neverland to maintain a vigil against invasion by Ordog's forces. Though time was short, the returning Intercessors agreed they had worked long and hard and needed respite before continuing in pursuit of the remaining scales. Macmillan put the sapphire scale into a safe with a combination lock, hidden in a secret panel behind the revolving bookcase. He vowed to guard it night and day.

"Where were you yesterday?" Leslie asked Betty the next day while she tidied the upstairs sitting room. He was relaxing in a comfortable chair, his feet up on a table, flipping through the latest adventure of some comic book agent of Scotland Yard.

"Aunt Amelia gave me the day off," she answered. "Now, please put your feet down. I just polished that table."

He frowned his annoyance and defiantly confirmed his feet's position on the table. "It's *my* table," he retorted. "*You're* just the upstairs maid."

Betty rolled her eyes. "And *you're* just annoying."

"Shouldn't let mum hear you say that. She would give you the sack like that." He snapped his fingers.

"What sack?" asked Lady Mallowan, entering the room. She raised a perturbed eyebrow at Leslie's feet. "Leslie dear, do put your feet down."

Leslie sheepishly moved his feet from the table.

Lady Mallowan was a tall, thin column of a woman with supercilious eyebrows and an unhappy mouth. She wore her hair on top in a pretentious bun, and a pair of pince nez dangled from a button on her blouse. She spread out an armful of freshly cut blue rambling roses to Betty. "Be a dear and put these in a vase, will you."

The butler heaved into the room, out of breath from climbing the stairs. "Ma'am." He mopped his balding brow and tucked the handkerchief into his sleeve. "There is a person here asking to see Mr. Edmond."

"A person?" asked Lady Mallowan, as if such a thing were too extraordinary to believe.

"Yes, ma'am. He says he went to school with him."

"Edmond is not here, Meades."

"I realize that, ma'am. I tried to tell him, but he said he was willing to wait. He is," and here Meades discreetly cleared his throat, "quite a *common* person. He insisted on letting himself in and making himself at home."

"Now, Meades," said Leslie, standing up and clasping his hands behind his back, "that's what we pay you for, to give unwanted intruders the fffft out the door."

"Of course, Master Leslie," said Meades, "but he mentioned something about it being worth your while to let him stay. He had a most unsavory look when he mentioned that, I might add."

"Sounds like a matter for the police," decided Lady Mallowan.

"I'll call Scotland Yard," offered Leslie.

"All that talk about Intercessors and dragon scales, I would, perhaps, recommend the loony bin, ma'am," said Meades.

Betty had been busy placing the roses stem by stem into the vase. However, when she heard the words "Intercessors" and "dragon scales," her ears became attuned. "I beg your pardon, but did you say 'Intercessors'?"

"Yes, that is what I said," he replied as if it was beneath him to even address Betty.

"Ma'am," said Betty, "I think I can handle this situation. Let me give it a try."

"Oh, very well," sighed Lady Mallowan, "but if he makes a nuisance of himself, do let us know. I'll send Eric down with his hunting rifle."

Betty had met a couple of Edmond's college mates, but they had been respectful and of good families. She was not prepared to run into a complete stranger ascending the stairs as she was coming down. The thin stranger had a smug, poorly shaven face and pale hair parted in the middle. He wore a disheveled dinner suit with collar open and cuffs frayed. The boutonniere on his jacket must have smelled his breath and died.

"Well, well," said the stranger, not moving his hand from the bannister, his arm blocking Betty's progress. "Who do we have here?"

"You first," said Betty.

"Me first what?" he asked with a drunken slur.

"Tell me who you are."

"Well, how do I know you are the party I should confide such intimate information to?" asked the stranger.

"I am the upstairs maid. I toss out trash every day. You are no exception, sir."

"Well, I see," he said, faking being impressed, but he did back down the stairs. "Shall we retire to the drawing room and discuss a little business matter then?"

"Whatever you want to say can be said right here. And if you try anything, Uncle Eric has a hunting rifle."

"Ooooh." He pretended to shiver in fear. "Spare me from Uncle Eric's hunting rifle. Ye Gods. Anything but that."

Betty lifted a finger in front of his nose. "Look here. Focus. Do you think you can manage that for a few seconds?"

He tried to focus, which was not easy after the amount of alcohol he had consumed to gear himself up to come to Perlgate.

"How do you know Edmond, and what do you know of the Intercessors?" she asked.

"Edmond? Oh, he and I go waaaaay back. We both were at the same charitable institution. Did he never mention Little Barnaby Skeens, the skinny tyke what went without porridge so that poor Ed could get a little more?"

"Actually, he never mentioned anyone from that place, except the headmaster. Now, what was his name?" wondered Betty out loud.

"Aw. I see what you're at, girlie," said the stranger. "Trying to test me, are you. Well, the headmaster was Bickerstaff, and no one had a *bigger staff* than he, for the purpose of caning, that is. He caned Edmond more times than I can count. Edmond was a plucky lad, always getting into mischief."

"Well, you got the name right, anyway."

"Of course." Barnaby spread out his arms. "All of us had reason to fear ol' Bickerstaff. But, listen, girlie, he ain't half as frightening as the things I've seen lately."

"Perhaps," Betty glanced nervously upstairs, "we *should* go to the drawing room."

"Right you are, my lass, after you."

Once in the drawing room, Betty remained standing, but Barnaby sprawled out on a chaise longue and put his hands behind his head. "This here's more like it. Where's the ol' decanter of port?"

"First, tell me what you know."

"First, I know that Edmond found one of them dragon scales on his fancy escapade. Second, I know Edmond is in league with folks what call themselves '*the Accusers*'. And third, I know that both the Intercessors and the Accusers are very much interested in something, and *I* know where it is." He sat up and looked her in the eye. "Interested?"

"So, *Barnaby*, where did you hear these stories?" she asked.

He smiled with pretended panache. "I'm just lucky that way. I seem to be a magnet for information. I just happen to be in the right place under the right circumstances."

"What if I said everything you heard is complete rot," dared Betty.

"Don't bother me none," he sighed as he stood and brushed off his sleeves. "I'm sure there's a certain count somewhere who would offer me double what the old battleax of Perlgate could scrounge up."

He turned to sashay on his way but stopped, for Lady Mallowan was standing in the doorway, looking unamused. "The 'old battleax' doesn't *scrounge* anything," she enunciated. She peered past him over at Betty. "Is this *person* annoying you?"

"No, ma'am," replied Betty, anxious.

"Your ladyship, please do not misunderstand," Barnaby poured it on. "I meant battleax in a good way, as in a force to be reckoned with, the right hand of the gods, the . . ."

"Shut up and sit down," ordered Lady Mallowan.

Leslie, who followed his mother into the drawing room, grinned, for he had never heard his mother tell anyone other than himself to shut up and sit down before.

"Stop grinning, Leslie, and fetch your father," Lady Mallowan ordered her son.

Leslie stopped grinning and did as he was told.

Barnaby sat on a wooden chair at a writing desk and turned pale at the mention of Sir Eric. He had seen pictures of Sir Eric in the newspaper and knew he was a formidable gentleman, one of those hardy, red-faced pickaxe-wielding adventurers.

"The butler told me Sir Eric was away," squeaked Barnaby.

"Oh?" Lady Mallowan sniffed in disdain. "The butler has been told to tell everyone that. Sir Eric dislikes being bothered."

"Then, by all means, let's not bother the poor gent."

"Nonsense, I think when the word blackmail is bandied about, it's a good idea to have all parties concerned in on the details," said Lady Mallowan.

"Blackmail? I never said blackmail," said Barnaby.

"Blackmail? What's this all about here?" Sir Eric entered, scowling under bushy eyebrows, sizing up the situation.

Barnaby gulped. Sir Eric was enormous, and he *did* have a hunting rifle over his arm.

"My dear," said Lady Mallowan, "this person claims to be acquainted with Edmond."

"Is that so?" asked Sir Eric, one eyebrow raised. "Highly debatable. Our Edmond would never associate with a blackmailer."

"Oh, I don't know, guvnor. You'd be surprised who Edmond would associate with." Barnaby tapped a few steps back from Sir Eric, who reminded him of a rampaging elephant.

"Betty," called Lady Mallowan.

"Yes, ma'am."

"Fetch us the decanter with the good brandy."

Barnaby was on the verge of reminding her that he had requested port, but one more glance at the hunting rifle affirmed it was not important enough to make a fuss over.

Betty left to fetch the brandy from the dining room. She muttered to herself as she went because she hated missing out on what was being said about the Intercessors, the dragon scales, and all. She flew back with the brandy and snifters just as they were getting down to "brass tacks."

"So," blustered Sir Eric as he wobbled his brandy glass to slosh it a bit, "I knew that scale Edmond found was going to be important. And you say there is a whole set of them? A map, bring me a map."

Betty unlocked the desk drawer, unrolled a world map, and handed it to Sir Eric.

"I can tell you the location of at least one of them," said Barnaby, "but I'm taking quite a risk. There are other parties who have expressed interest in finding this scale, and they are not the types who would play fair, if you get my meaning, guvnor."

"Excuse me, Sir Eric," said Betty, "but isn't it strange that someone like him would know where a relic like that is?"

"True," acknowledged Sir Eric. "She's got a good point there. How do you know about this scale?"

"I knew you'd want to hear me out." Barnaby raised his chin. "Well, sir, I gets by as I can, see? A little job here, a little job there. Might say how's I depend on circumstances, being in the right place at the right time. Well, I happened to be in one of them circumstances outside one of them posh nightclubs when I overheard two toffs talking. They were all quiet and sly, but me being on the other side of the lamppost and me being skinny as one, they didn't notice I was there. One of them was a count, I think. The other one *called* him 'count' anyway."

"Would that be Count Vlad Tepov?" asked Betty.

Barnaby was miffed that she would dare interrupt him. "Ahem, I wouldn't know, miss. I didn't hear that part."

"Did he have one blue eye and one brown eye?"

"I'm not sure. His hat covered his eyes. But the other one was someone I think you all know. The count called him *Professor Macmillan*."

Lady Mallowan, who did not startle easily, sat a bit straighter. "Gregor Macmillan?"

"The same," confirmed Barnaby.

"Wait a minute," interrupted Leslie. "What would ol' Drybones Macmillan know about relics? He's just my old mathematics professor."

Barnaby poured himself another brandy. "Seems your old Drybones belongs to some secret cult called the Inter-Story Intercessors."

"That's true," said Lady Mallowan, to Betty's surprise. "He tried to tell me about it years ago when he was courting me, but I didn't pay much attention."

"Mother!" said Leslie. "You never told me you dated old Drybones."

Sir Eric stirred impatiently. "Of course not. No business of yours, is it? After all, old Macmillan didn't stand a chance after

I came along, did he, my dear? Anyway, we seem to be getting off track here. Get to the point, man."

"I think that part is worth a little something, don't you, guvnor?"

"I suppose it might be worth not telling the yard about your attempted *blackmail*."

"Come, guvnor. You wouldn't deny me a little something to keep the lights turned on in the ol' digs and food in the ol' larder, would you?"

"Don't give him anything, father." Leslie assumed a comic book hero stance.

"Well. . ." Sir Eric thought it over, and generosity won out. He took a few crisp, unwrinkled bills from his wallet and handed them to Barnaby.

"Thank you, thank you, sir, you are generosity itself."

"Now. The information," insisted Sir Eric.

"Oh, yes, well, here's what they said. The count says, 'I can meet your terms if you tell me one thing.' The professor says, 'What would that be?' The count says, 'Tell me the location of the onyx scale, the mate to the one Sir Eric found in Mesopotamia.' And the professor says, 'I couldn't do that. The Intercessors will know. I've already taken a risk meeting you like this.' And the count, 'The Intercessors *will* know everything if you do not tell me now.' And the professor, 'What if Lady Mallowan finds out? Edmond *is* her nephew, you know.' And the count says, 'She won't learn anything from *me*.' And the professor gave in and said, 'Try Jack Stapleton, *Baskerville Hall*, the Grimpen Mire.' And the count thanked him and paid him a lot of money. And I thinks to myself, since they want to keep something from Lady Mallowan, it's my duty as a gentleman to come and tell you what I heard."

Betty was steaming. *Gregor Macmillan. That traitor.* She clenched her fists at her side.

CHAPTER 19
THE GAME IS AFOOT

Barnaby left, snickering and counting his money. Betty wanted to call Hamberdeen to warn him about Macmillan, but she did not yet have absolute proof, just the doubtful word of a blackmailer. She decided instead to try to get to the onyx scale before Tepov.

She emptied the ashtrays, cleaned the snifters, brushed off the furniture, and polished the table where the uninvited guest had propped his huge, dirty shoes. After all that, she retired to her room. It was a small room on the lower level of the house, more like a cupboard, with just space enough for a washstand, a narrow bed, and a trunk at the foot of the bed. She washed, let her hair down, and changed into her night clothes. From her trunk, she retrieved her collection of Sherlock Holmes books and was about to sink into her covers and turn on her torch to examine the books, when someone knocked on her door.

"Coming." Betty scrambled to climb out of bed, but Lady Mallowan let herself in. "No need to get up, Betty. I know you're tired." Lady Mallowan looked over the tiny room. "Not much of a room, is it." She touched the cracked basin on the washstand and sighed. "Edmond had spirit, even as a boy. He would dress up, join our guests, and get them to talking in such an engaging manner that it would be inconvenient to remind him of his station. Before we knew it, he was part of the family and off to college. But you, you were content to sit in your little reading nook and do the mending while catching up on one of those ridiculous novels you loved."

"I was happy to have a place at all, to have someone to look after me."

Lady Mallowan responded with an incredulous sniff. "No, you weren't happy. I know. You escaped into your books, into your dreams, much like I did when I was a girl. I wanted to go to college, but my parents wouldn't have it. Finishing school was enough for me, they said. Gregor would meet me secretly in the garden. He was beneath my station, my father said. Both my sisters had fallen in love with men beneath their station, Elizabeth with a sickly, poverty-stricken poet from America, Lawrence Talbin, your father, and Margaret with that drunken brute of a sailor, Mike Davidson, who gave her nothing but misery and little Edmond. That's all my family needed to say to convince me I should listen to them rather than my heart. But when my father kicked Gregor out of the house and threatened to horsewhip him, Gregor swore he would show them all. He would one day be rich and powerful, he said, and it appears he is still chasing that dream. And now you and Edmond are in this mess too. And there's no point in hiding it from me."

"What do you mean, ma'am?"

"You *are* an Intercessor, aren't you?"

Betty hesitated. She had no reason to not trust Lady Mallowan, but she also knew that the Intercessors were a secret society, and she did not want to betray their confidence.

"You don't have to tell me anything. I know. With Frieda Fernsby taking you off on adventures, I know."

"Oh, Aunt Amelia," cried Betty, "I am so worried for Edmond. And Gregor . . . how can I warn the others that he has betrayed them?"

"You need to be careful, my dear. Bad things always happen to the people who say 'I know who the traitor is'. And that blackmailer doesn't have the wits to know not to meet Jack the

Ripper in a dark alley with all the proof in his back pocket. But what did he mean? Baskerville? Stapleton?"

"I know what it means." Betty opened her book and turned to a page that showed an illustration by Sidney Paget of Sherlock Holmes and Watson peering from behind a rock on the moors at a monstrous, glowing hound about to pounce upon its prey.

"That," said Betty, smiling, "is *The Hound of the Baskervilles*, one of those 'trashy' novels I like to read."

"But how do we get there? It's just a story."

"First of all, we have to stop thinking of it as *just* a story. Remember, we all have our own stories, our own parts to play in this world. We make the same choices with our own lives that authors make for their characters. We are the authors of our own story."

"Then what can we do?"

"We can check what the chart says." Betty took her chart from under her pillow where she had hidden it.

"What kind of chart is that?"

"Please don't laugh at me," hesitated Betty, "but a mermaid in Neverland gave it to me." Lady Mallowan stared back at Betty in complete denial of what she had heard.

Betty consulted the chart. It said, "Use the book."

Betty pushed back the covers and set the book on her knees. She hesitated. "I don't call myself a hero. I know I'm just one person, but I'm going to do whatever one person can do to stand for what is right."

Lady Mallowan smiled sadly at the young girl she might have been. "All right, then, my dear. Lead the way."

Betty turned the pages of the novel. "The clue was Baskervilles, and we have Stapleton, so we need to look for a passage in *The Hound of the Baskervilles* where Stapleton is at Baskerville Hall, and I think . . ."

"Just a minute," said Lady Mallowan, "I seem to have dropped my pince nez. I can't read without my pince nez."

"You set them on the writing table in the drawing room," Betty told her.

"Let's get them. And bring the book."

Betty threw her robe over her shoulders, stepped into her slippers, and followed Lady Mallowan upstairs to the drawing room. They were just in time to catch Leslie trying to use a screwdriver to break into the liquor cabinet.

Lady Mallowan put out her hand. "Give that to me this instant."

Leslie started. "Mother, I was just trying to fix this hinge here. It was getting a little loose, you see, and . . ."

"Never mind that," snapped Lady Mallowan. "Where are my pince nez?"

"How should I know?" shrugged Leslie.

"Here they are, ma'am." Betty handed them to her.

Leslie stuck his tongue out at Betty behind his mother's back. Betty stuck her tongue out back at him.

"All right, then." Lady Mallowan adjusted her pince nez on the bridge of her nose. "Which passage did we need to study?"

Lady Mallowan gestured for Betty to sit on the sofa, and she sat next to her. Leslie, being nosy, sat on the arm of the sofa and looked over their shoulders.

Betty opened the book on her lap, flipping to the part where Dr. Watson traveled to Baskerville Hall with Sir Henry while supposedly leaving Holmes in London to tie up the loose ends on a different case. She slowed at the part where Watson first met Stapleton and read the words aloud. "*I prayed, as I walked back along the gray, lonely road, that my friend might soon be freed from his preoccupations and able to come down to take this heavy burden of responsibility from my shoulders.*"

Betty stopped reading, for she felt the familiar sensation of being pulled away by a strong and sudden force. She grasped Aunt Mallowan's hand. Lady Mallowan wailed in fright as she clutched the arm of the sofa. "Mother!" cried Leslie. "What's happening to you?" He reached out to catch her.

"I say!" said Sir Eric, who was looking for his wife, but he was just in time to see his wife, his son, and his maid vanish into a cloud of sparkles. "By thunder," he said. "Perhaps I *should* visit that eye Dr. after all."

CHAPTER 20
THE BASKERVILLES

They reappeared in a burst of light, arriving in the large dining room of a Jacobean-style estate. The portrait over the mantel was of a man in a cavalier hat, an unstarched ruff over a soft doublet with vertical slashes in the sleeves. His dark mustache curled upward on the ends. The gold label read "Hugo Baskerville."

"Aunt Amelia, Leslie." Betty's eyes sparkled as she spread out her arms and twirled to present the amazing transformation of location. "Welcome to Baskerville Hall."

Leslie turned green. Lady Mallowan paled and dropped her pince nez. "How in the world did we get here?"

"Maybe," Leslie threw aside a curtain to make sure no hob-goblins were hiding there, "the curse of the tomb exists after all, and we've gone to the underworld to pay for our desecration." He stopped before a mirror and gasped a hiccup as he noticed his clothes had changed. Betty retrieved Lady Mallowan's pince nez and joined her and Leslie at the mirror.

Leslie looked the typical nineteenth century country gentle-man in light trousers and cloth cap, leaning on a walking stick. Betty wore an eggshell jacket over a heather blue floor-length dress, her hair in a roll at the back of her neck. Lady Mallowan wore a long black skirt with a slim waist, a slight bustle, and a stiff collar.

A tall, grim, bearded butler entered the room. "Excuse me, sir, Mesdames, but is Sir Henry expecting you?"

"Oh, Barrymore," said Betty. "I hope your wife is well."

"I'm afraid not, madam. She had a severe shock."

"I'm so sorry." Betty realized they had entered the narrative not long after the escaped inmate had fallen to his death, attacked by the hound because he was wearing Sir Henry's hand-me-downs, which had been used to accustom the hound to the scent of its intended victim. The escaped inmate had been Mrs. Barrymore's wayward brother.

"It was the hound?" Betty asked gingerly.

"A hound? More like a demon. More like Sir Hugo himself come back as a cursed devil from Hell. I saw his hideous shape against the moonlight, a thing that stood on two legs and howled." Barrymore's hands were trembling.

"Is Mr. Holmes here?"

"Yes, madam, he has retired to the billiard room with Sir Henry and Dr. Watson. Shall I announce you?"

"Yes. Please tell Mr. Holmes that Beatrice Talbin is here with relatives."

Once he had received the news, Holmes hastened into the dining room. He met Betty in front of the fireplace and doffed his deerstalker cap to her. "Beatrice, Beatrice Talbin. How on earth did you get here?" He placed one booted foot on the hearth, one arm leaning against the elegant surround of the fireplace.

"I'm here on a special assignment from Frieda Fernsby."

"Ah, how *is* Miss Fernsby, by the way?" asked Holmes.

"She's . . . feeling younger than ever. Oh, and this is my Aunt Amelia and my cousin Leslie. Leslie, Aunt Amelia, I'd like you to meet Mr. Sherlock Holmes."

"Sherlock Holmes?" Leslie nearly fell over the walking stick he had been leaning on.

"Delighted to meet you, Madame." Holmes nodded to Lady Mallowan. "And, you as well, young man."

"Oh, just call me Buck Rogers," said Leslie, still not quite believing his senses.

"If you like," replied Holmes, puzzled as to why someone named Leslie would prefer a name like Buck.

Lady Mallowan marched to the fireplace. "All right. We are done with formalities, I hope. If I'm going to be zipping here and there into story books, I at least want to get the job done as quickly as possible."

"Aunt Amelia," Betty said behind the gloves in her hand, "it's not a story book to *them*."

"I say, Holmes, is that young Beatrice?" asked Watson. He took her fingertips in his hand. "Delighted, my dear."

"And her cousin . . . *Buck*," Holmes added, gesturing towards Leslie.

"We've been through all that," said Lady Mallowan. "I want to know where is my nephew."

"Maybe," Leslie suggested, "he is on a rocket to the moon, or perhaps he decided to stay in the jungle with Tarzan."

"Watson," said Holmes, perturbed. "I believe this condition may be more in your line than in mine."

"Elementary," sang out Leslie as he pretended to play croquet with his walking stick. "I think I'll jump through that painting and have tea with the Mad Hatter."

"Leslie," scolded Betty.

But Holmes was no longer paying attention to Leslie or Buck or whatever his name was. He shifted his weight from one leg to the other as he contemplated the paintings, one painting in particular. "Never mind cousin Leslie. He just revealed the key to the whole mystery." And, without removing his eyes from the painting, he walked past Betty and moved to the rows of portraits hanging on the wall.

Betty followed him, smiling to herself, for she knew what it was Holmes noticed. After all, it was clearly described in the exposition near the end of *The Hound of the Baskervilles*. "Quite a striking resemblance, wouldn't you say?"

"Yes," murmured Holmes. "The eyes." He placed one arm over Hugo's hat and the other over his chin. "Yes, unquestionably the eyes."

"The same gleam of greed you've seen in Stapleton's eyes?" she whispered, so as not to give the whole thing away to their attentive audience.

"Mr. Jack Stapleton to see you, sir," announced Barrymore.

Holmes and Betty exchanged alert expressions.

"Thank you, Barrymore," replied Sir Henry. "His sister isn't with him, is she?"

"No, sir," said the butler.

Stapleton entered, handing his cap and walking stick to Barrymore. "Sir Henry. We were worried. Did you hear about that poor man on the moors? Oh, you have guests, I see."

Betty could not help comparing Stapleton's facial features to those in the painting, but Holmes made a subtle gesture for her not to give the game away.

Stapleton fell silent when he saw Holmes by the fireplace casually lighting a cigarette. "Dr. Watson," said Stapleton, "you didn't tell me your distinguished associate had made it out to the Hall."

"Yes," said Watson, "it was quite a surprise for all of us."

Holmes nodded once politely and continued to smoke.

"And you have company, too," added Stapleton, noting Betty and her family, "so I won't infringe on your time. Just wanted to invite you to dinner tomorrow. Beryl would love to see you."

"Why, of course, but . . ." Sir Henry turned to Holmes.

"Oh, you all are invited." But even as Stapleton smiled his eyes fixed on Betty in a fiendish glare. Betty noticed he had one blue eye and one brown.

"Where are my manners," said Sir Henry. "It's been a long day. Please, everyone, sit down and help yourselves to the port."

"Very generous, I'm sure," replied Stapleton through his teeth.

"Mr. Stapleton?" said Betty. "Won't you sit here by me? I've heard so much about you. You're a naturalist, they say. I'd like to hear all about your butterflies." She pulled out a chair across from a mirror. Stapleton hesitated, as if he knew what she was trying to do, but stalling only made him more suspicious, so he smoothed his mustache and relented. He rounded the table. As he moved up to her, Betty glanced towards the mirror across from him. In the mirror, she saw the reflection of *Vlad Tepov*. Holmes was not at an angle to see the reflection, but he caught Betty's alarm. He moved closer to her, keeping a watchful eye on Stapleton.

Stapleton backed out of range of the mirror and distracted their attention by staring at the windows behind the table. "I say! The hound!"

A large, dark form was standing upright at the floor-length window. The twilight was turning to night, so Sir Henry turned up the oil lamp and moved closer to the window to see. At the window was the brutish face of a huge wolf up on his hind legs. His claws scraped down the glass, etching out a short message: "dE sti ni em tel."

"My God, Mr. Holmes!" said Sir Henry, shaken and pale.

"Stand back," ordered Holmes. Sir Henry backed away from the window.

"It's Edmond," said Betty.

Stapleton flattened against the wall near the paintings.

The werewolf sunk back into the shadows, away from the window, growling and panting. Stapleton relaxed, and Sir Henry wiped his forehead with his handkerchief.

The werewolf crashed through the window in a hail of shattered glass. He caught himself with his forepaws on the rug, his fierce amber eyes darting about the room, his chest heaving. Beyond the fierceness, Betty detected sorrow and pain. He hauled himself to his full height of at least seven feet, and extended a claw towards Betty with a desperate moan, as one pleading for salvation.

Holmes had snatched up a poker from the fireplace and hid it at his side. Watson reached for his army revolver.

Betty approached the werewolf with caution. "Is it really you, Edmond? What have they done to you?"

Edmond could barely meet her eyes, and when he did, he winced in pain and regret.

Leslie stared in horror. "*That's* Edmond?" Lady Mallowan fainted to the floor.

The werewolf watched the other life forms in the room, his ears on alert. "Betty," he said, "Take Aunt Amelia and Leslie away from this place. It's too late for me. I have . . . killed . . . this night, on the moor." He looked out the window in despair. "The onyx scale . . . Grimpen . . . grrim . . . grrrr . . ." A sharp beam of moonlight pierced the shattered window and hit his eyes directly, clouding them over with an inhuman glare. He bared his teeth and his ears flicked, lowered back against his head in aggression.

Holmes had crept closer to Betty, and now pushed her behind him, as the beast sprang at her with unbridled violence. Holmes whipped the poker up and lashed at the beast with steady command. "Back, back!"

Betty clung to Holmes' shoulder. He outstretched his free arm at his side to shield her from harm.

"I've brought the rifle, sir." Barrymore had returned, his weapon aimed at the beast, the spark of revenge in his eyes.

"Wait," cried Betty. "That's my cousin!"

The wolf man glared and growled, assessing the threats surrounding him. Poker, revolver, rifle, Stapleton. His instincts detected zero threat, as the elixir of immortality rushed through his veins and set his brain on fire with the lust for blood. He sprang for Holmes, swiping out at him with his razor-sharp claws. Holmes pushed Betty to the ground and blocked the attack with the poker. He summoned his full strength to impede the claws. Edmond growled and pushed back against the poker, bending the iron with his weight. Betty scrambled under the dining room table, her heart racing in her throat.

Watson aimed the revolver to save Holmes, but Barrymore fired his rifle and the bullet ripped through the beast's chest. The beast let out a piercing yelp. Betty screamed.

"Murderer!" cried Barrymore.

Bloodied and momentarily deterred, the werewolf raised his arm to shield his face and turned his powerful shoulder towards the direction the bullet came from.

"Silver bullets, that's what does the trick," said Leslie, from behind a chair.

The werewolf glowered and snarled. Holmes held the poker poised to strike again if need be. "Stay back!" he commanded, ready to ward off an attack, though in bulk and strength, he was hardly a match for the beast.

As the werewolf lumbered forward, he was distracted by movement in the mirror. He growled in surprise at recognizing a form of himself. He peered into the mirror, mesmerized.

Barrymore reloaded his rifle, and Watson took aim with his revolver. Holmes held up his hand to signal them to wait.

The wolf man's eyes were more sorrowful than hostile now, and he whimpered at his reflection. He let out a long howl of despair and smashed the mirror with his fist.

Holmes moved forward, the poker ready. The werewolf snarled and swung a heavy claw in contempt at Holmes and leapt for the window, bounding off into the mist.

Holmes sprang to the window to watch the beast disappear into the night. He helped Betty to her feet. "Are you all right?"

"Yes," said Betty.

"*That*," said Leslie in disbelief, "was *Edmond?*"

"Is that what killed my uncle?" asked Sir Henry.

"Whatever it is, I know who is behind it." Holmes looked towards the paintings. "Stapleton. He's gone. But not for long, by God!" The light that danced in his eyes foretold the doom of wicked men. "Watson. Coats, hats, lantern. Hurry! Before the trail goes cold."

CHAPTER 21
THE GRIMPEN MIRE

Lady Mallowan recovered with the aid of smelling salts. "Was *that* . . . really Edmond?"

"He's under the power of the vampire." Betty cradled her aunt's head on her lap.

"Oh, yes, of course there *would* be a vampire," said Leslie. "I mean, if we have a make-believe detective and a werewolf cousin, we might as well add a vampire in the mix."

"Barrymore." Betty turned to the butler. "Is there a coat and pair of boots I can use?"

"You're not going out there," protested Leslie.

"I am an Intercessor. I know how to deal with these forces better than Mr. Holmes or Dr. Watson. You both stay here."

"I'm not letting you out of my sight," said Lady Mallowan, who had fully recovered. "And Leslie, you're coming too."

A thick mist was settling, and the air was chill. The beam of Watson's lantern served as a beacon in the night. Holmes followed Edmond's tracks from the Hall across the moor, taking powerful strides from one huge paw print to the next.

"There." He pointed towards the blurry glow coming from Merripit House. "That's Stapleton's lair."

In Merripit House, Vlad Tepov tore off the guise of the naturalist, with cloth cap and spectacles, and resumed his own form. Edmond stood nearby, in wolf form, head ducked against the low ceiling, his muscular arms folded across his broad, pelted chest.

The vampire glared at Edmond. "You tried to warn Beatrice. I ordered you to distract them, not to *help* them. Fortunately, Sir Hugo had the key. It was hidden in the frame, just as the late Roger Baskerville aka Jack Stapleton confessed before his demise. This is your last chance to prove yourself. Destroy Betty and Holmes tonight while I use the key to retrieve the scale. If you fail, remember what happened to Miroslav."

Out the window, across the sloping moors, Edmond could detect the body heat of humans approaching the cottage, one with a high degree of nervous energy and authoritative strength. The heartbeat pattern matched that of the man who had defended Betty at the Hall.

Tepov threw open the windowpanes and spread his blue reptilian wings behind him. He darted out the window and up into the green-black skies.

Once Tepov was out of view, Edmond sprang upstairs to the back bedroom. It was lined with pinned butterflies and jars of samples. Mrs. Stapleton was bound with twisted sheets to an old beam. She was badly battered, bruised, and terrified. When she saw the werewolf, she swooned. Edmond removed the gag from her mouth and clawed through the bonds to free her. He gathered her in his arms and lay her gently upon the bed. "You are now free from the man who cruelly used you," he said. And reluctantly, but with compulsion, he turned from the young lady. The hunt instinct was surging inside him. He tore off into the night, desperate to outrun the beast that was choking out his humanity.

As Holmes and Watson approached Stapleton's residence, the light from the lantern fell upon a large form lurking beyond the mist, backlit by the light from the open cottage door. The werewolf burst through the mist, raving and clawing in fury.

The beast was in full possession of Edmond. An anvil in his brain beat the command to hunt and destroy. His long, upright ear flicked at the sound of the heartbeats before him. Edmond heaved deep grunting breaths as he fought against the beast. He scratched his claws across his chest in agony, wanting to rip out the beast, but the beast responded with a threatening growl, coercing Edmond back into submission.

The werewolf sensed one powerful form, the alpha, he who had struck him before. At the sight of this, the hammer in his brain ignited against the anvil, and rage permeated his body. With a terrifying roar, he came crashing from the top of the slope. He landed, haunches bent and claws splayed out in front of him on the ground. With muzzle lowered and nostrils flaring, he glared at Holmes.

Holmes readied himself for the confrontation.

Watson was at Holmes' side in an instant. He aimed his revolver, stalwart veteran that he was, and fired at Edmond's head. The bullets ripped into the werewolf's forehead, past fur, flesh, and bone, but only served to intensify his rage. Edmond sprang forward and barreled at Holmes with the full weight of his monstrous strength, throwing the detective off balance.

"Holmes!" cried Watson.

Holmes felt the stifling heat of the wolf's raw breath upon his face and a splatter of wolf saliva caught him near the eye. Watson grabbed the beast from behind, struggling to pull the ears and neck back away from Holmes.

The amber eyes of the beast burned as they bore into the eyes of his opponent. Holmes met the glare without fear, unwavering, with full as much intensity and far more control than the beast had of relentless aggression.

"Edmond. You don't want this," Holmes enunciated each syllable. "You are *not* a monster."

The steadfastness of his opponent disarmed Edmond. He shook his head against the confused buzzing that assaulted his brain. He clutched Holmes by the collar and yanked his face closer to his. "Who are you?" he snarled.

"I am a gentleman." Holmes, on his back in the mud, pushed his boot into the beast's gut with as much force as he could muster in an attempt to hoist the weight of the beast off of him.

Watson clasped his hands around the beast's large throat and pulled backward, but Edmond shook him off. Watson fell backward with tufts of wolf fur clutched in his fists.

The werewolf was unmoved. He sneered at Holmes. "I will tear you to shreds, *gentleman*."

"Edmond. Think," commanded Holmes, the werewolf's claws at his throat. "You, too, are a gentleman. A man of honor. If you are anything like Betty, you know this to be true." He watched, waiting to see if his words would hit their mark.

The hold on Holmes' collar let up. "Betty. Where."

"Safe," Holmes assured him.

Edmond shook his head. The throbbing of the beast would not be silent. He shook his mane again, even more vigorously and scratched at his ears. He snorted in frustration.

Holmes took the chance to scramble out of the grip of the beast and back to his feet. Watson reloaded his revolver.

"Edmond, think," repeated Holmes. "You know this isn't you."

Edmond hung his head in despair. "Ordog is my master. I serve Ordog."

The detective stood behind him and placed a steady hand on Edmond's shoulder. "Do you believe in Providence?" Holmes watched him keenly.

"Providence," Edmond snorted. "I am a beast. I have no soul. There's no 'Providence' for *me*."

"*I* believe in justice. And if there is justice, there must be a just judge. And if there is a just judge, then no one can take your soul unless He so rules. Edmond, look at me. You still have a choice. You still can choose to do what is right." Holmes' tone left no room for doubt.

Edmond backed away from Holmes, guilt-ridden and confused. "Tell her . . . tell them . . . the scales, they are dragons, they're all dragons. Ordog must not have them!" In despair, he turned and fled into the mist across the moors.

"Look." Betty pointed upward with her lantern. They had lost their way in the fog. The light of the lantern could barely penetrate the thick mist that had gathered on the moors, but it did reveal a vague form of a large-winged bat gliding past. "*That's* how Tepov is crossing the Grimpen Mires."

"Wonderful," shivered Leslie, wrapping his muffler more closely about his face and rubbing his gloved hands together briskly. "Do we have a pair of wings? It would be suicide to try to cross by foot, especially on such a night."

"I'm afraid Leslie is right, my dear," said Lady Mallowan. "There's no point in going any further."

Frustrated, Betty pursed her lips. With one hand, she held the chart, and with the other, she shined the light of the lantern upon it. The chart showed a dotted line leading forward three paces to the right, then four paces forward, then ten sharp paces to the left. "Follow me," said Betty.

She followed the chart, turning exactly where it said to turn and taking just as many paces as it showed. As she stepped, her feet found a firm footing on a row of stones. Lady Mallowan and Leslie clung close to her and followed in her footsteps.

"A-ha!" squawked a voice, and something leathery swooshed past Betty's face. Betty turned from her path and looked to where the voice came from. She stepped forward. Whatever it was cackled in glee as the Grimpen Mire sucked Betty's feet into its swampy bog with a loud, disgusting slurp. Betty gasped and dropped the chart, but Leslie grabbed her one arm, and Lady Mallowan grabbed the other.

"No," said Betty. "Let go. It will just pull you both in too."

Leslie held her arm more firmly. With his free arm, he removed his muffler. "Good thinking, Leslie," said Lady

Mallowan. She helped him make a sling with the muffler and put it around the part of Betty still above the mire, though the rest of her was sinking fast.

Leslie held to his mother with one arm, and pulled Betty as hard as he could, gritting his teeth. He was not the strongest man, but he had worked hard at the digs, so he had some muscle to speak of, and that served him well right now. He gave her a yank, and his mother kept him from falling back away from their foothold. She helped him pull Betty the rest of the way out of the mire.

"Thank heavens you both were here," said Betty, as Leslie held her until she could stable herself. "But I lost the chart."

"We still have the lantern at least," said Lady Mallowan. "And we have our voices. I suggest we send out a strong chorus of help at the top of our lungs until some brave idiot comes along to get us out of this."

"I should never have gotten you both into this."

"It's a good thing you did, though," said Leslie. "Or you'd be Betty of Bog-bottom by now."

"Ugh, Leslie, must you," Betty groaned.

"Children," scolded Lady Mallowan. "Now, one- two – three – Hel — "

Before she could finish her call of help, however, the sound of steady, deliberate sloshing approached them.

"What could that be?" Lady Mallowan shined the lantern about them.

"The werewolf?" asked Leslie, fearing that Edmond would have remembered all the times he had teased him.

"The vampire?" asked Lady Mallowan.

"The dragons?" wondered Betty.

"Nope," came a cheery, youthful voice. "It's me." A little nose emerged from the mist, followed by a spritely face wearing a green hat with a red feather through it.

"It's Peter Pan," said Betty.

Lady Mallowan and Leslie exchanged looks that said in stunned silence, "Who else?"

"It's a good thing Frieda made me wear these boots," said Peter, holding up one of his feet encased in the large, ugly boots. "They're actually quite handy. Look. Wherever I walk, the boots clear the way."

As Betty and her family followed Peter through the Grimpen Mire, the boots created a dry and firm footing for them to follow. The mist, too, cleared as they proceeded with as little effort as walking through the park on a fine day.

"I thought," mentioned Peter, "that the boots were too big for me. But they fit just fine now." In fact, Peter was a little bit taller and a little older than when last they met. "Guess they shrunk, huh."

"No, I think you've grown into them," noticed Betty. "But, how did you know where to find us?"

"Easy," said Peter, hopping on a rock to demonstrate. "I was balancing on a log across this old swamp near Pirate's Cove, and Frieda said, 'Oh Peter. Do be careful.' And I said, 'Look. I can balance on one foot.' Then 'Whoops!' down I fell and the next second I was here, following wherever the boots took me."

"Well, we are certainly glad you followed your boots, young man," said Lady Mallowan.

Once they reached a rocky island in the midst of the mire, Leslie looked around with the lantern. The light revealed dilapidated cottages that had long since been abandoned and a filled-in shaft to an old mine. The night was shaken by the barking of a hound and the rattling of a chain. Betty pitied the hound, but she also was glad it was on a chain, since it had been trained to kill.

Leslie caught sight of something gleaming behind a rock. He used his cap to wipe away the layer of mud and moss that disguised a large black chest with golden bands and a rusty lock. The others gathered around the chest.

"Pixie dust is the best way to get through locks," offered Peter. "But maybe my dagger will do." He lifted his dagger to pry off the lock. A screech invaded the misty night and Avian darted down, clutching at Peter's arm with her claws, clenching his wrists and forcing the dagger from his hand.

Tepov bent his knees as he descended from the sky, like a dancer returning to the stage after a magnificent leap.

Avian had Peter's arms locked behind him, and the boy writhed indignantly to free himself. Leslie lifted his lantern and aimed its beacon upon the vampire's face. "They hate the light!" Lady Mallowan and Betty clung to Leslie, hoping his wild idea had some merit.

Tepov sighed and narrowed his eyes with exasperation into the glare of the light. "The day light, young man, the day light." He sauntered up to them.

He set his glimmering scrutiny upon Betty and clutched her chin in his long, hot hands. "Victorian fashion suits you, Beatrice. Almost as much as a pirate hat. Too bad you don't have your sword with you now." He spread his wings and let his fangs fully erupt on either side of his mouth.

Peter glared his recrimination at Tepov as he continued to twist his shoulders to the left and right to work himself free of the dragon's clutches. "You are an evil, no-good cheat. You couldn't win in a *fair* fight."

Tepov allowed a smile to twitch on the corners of his mouth. "That would be amusing, a duel in flight between the undead and the undying."

"No," retorted Peter, "A duel between a gentleman and a filthy walrus." And he chanted relentlessly, "Tepov is a walrus! Tepov is a walrus!"

Tepov snarled and pounced at Peter, claws ready to slash.

Lady Mallowan, scared speechless, threw herself in front of Peter and the others. "Don't you dare hurt him! Don't you hurt any of them! If you come one step closer, I'll have my butler toss you out on your ear."

Tepov threw his head back and laughed. He shoved her out of the way, and she tumbled onto the ground. Betty and Leslie rushed to her side to help her from the rock and mud. Betty threw a dark glare up at Tepov.

From his waistcoat, he drew the key he had stolen from the Hall and inserted it into the lock. He flung back the lid of the chest, and his eyes widened greedily at the black glow that emanated from within. "Ah! The onyx scale, and, what's this? Another copy of the *Intercessor Code Book*. This should prove useful for Lord Ordog." He held them up, one in each hand.

Betty confronted the vampire, armed only with her outstretched hand. "Drop them."

Tepov laughed in mockery of her threat.

However, he did not laugh for long, for as he laughed, the chain that restrained the undernourished but overwrought mastiff snapped. Once free, the hound, glowing in phosphorescent green, leapt for the throat of Tepov, snarling viciously through bared teeth, the broken length of chain whipping about from its spiked collar.

Tepov cursed as he fought off the hound, losing the scale and the book in his struggle. Avian tossed Peter aside and winged to Tepov's aid.

Peter scrambled to his feet and glared at the dragon as she flew away from him to join her master against the hound. "Two against one, eh?" he challenged in disgust.

Lady Mallowan stopped him from charging into the fray. "My dear boy, as unfair as it is, we must save ourselves. How do we get out of here?"

A piteous yipe pierced the night as Tepov tossed the hound aside by the throat. The hound cowered close to the ground, whimpering and shaking in fear. Behind the hound loomed a wall of rock and before him the vampire leering over him with glowing red eyes and sadistic sneer. The hound's ears fell flat, and he whined, trapped and doomed to perish. Peter pushed past Betty and leapt towards the hound.

From behind the rock rose a large wolf. His eyes glowed amber. The werewolf growled low past slathering jaws, as he scaled the rock and climbed steadily forward on gripping claws, eyes fixed on the vampire.

The hound slunk away to nurse its wounds as the werewolf sprang at Tepov.

"Davidson! No!" Tepov slashed at the beast with his nails. The werewolf clutched Tepov's throat, and the vampire choked and gasped like a dog straining against a chain. He tossed Tepov aside and grappled with him across the bog.

Tepov shielded his face from the wolven claws with his wing. Avian squawked like a siren wailing for reinforcements, snatching at the werewolf to distract him.

A cyclone rose up and encircled the rugged island in the moor, a wind that whipped through the scraggly trees and tore them up by the roots. It carried off Leslie's hat and yanked at Betty and Lady Mallowan's hair.

Edmond pinned the vampire with his claw, and with the other he gestured towards Betty. "Leave! Get away from here!" he told her, over the screaming wind.

"No!" Betty pushed back her long hair. "I won't leave you!"

"He's called the pack! This place will be overrun with fiends! Leave now!" His commanding eyes prevailed over her desire to stay.

"Over here," called Betty to the others, and grabbing the scale and the code book where they had been blown into a rocky crevice, she tucked them under her arm and took hold of Leslie's and Lady Mallowan's hands and pulled them close to her. The last she glimpsed of Edmond, he was thrashing Tepov over and over with merciless claws.

Betty recited out loud as fast as she could from memory. "*The fog had lifted and we were guided by Mrs. Stapleton to the point where they had found a pathway through the bog.*" The rocks blocking the mine shaft crumbled away and the opening sucked them towards its mouth like a mighty whirlpool, dragging them away from danger.

Soon, they were all four standing safely in front of Merripit Place, where Holmes and Watson had found Mrs. Stapleton. Dr. Watson was administering a physician's care. and Sir Henry was assisting with the gravest concern.

Lady Mallowan held onto the doorframe to steady her wobbly legs. "Dr. . . ." Her face drained of color and she fell into a faint. Thankfully, Watson was there to catch her.

"Betty," said Holmes. "Thank Heavens you're safe." He caught her two hands in his own mud-encased leather-gloved hands and looked her over. She was disheveled and covered in the filth of the bog. "And a near escape too," he noted.

"Stapleton is not really Stapleton," she told him.

"I know. We found the *real* Jack Stapleton aka Roger Baskerville. He was hung by the rafters with his throat cut. Two deep puncture wounds."

"Vlad Tepov," said Betty.

"Elementary," declared a youthful voice. Holmes and Betty turned to find Peter lounging comfortably before the fireplace, Holmes' deerstalker cap set jauntily on his head and Holmes' long-stemmed pipe in his cupped hand.

"How's Wiggins these days?" Peter asked Holmes as if they had been chatting for hours. "You know, he was one of the best lost boys, but, once he heard about Sherlock Holmes, he had to go back to London to meet you. There was a time *all* of the lost boys wanted to play at Baker Street Irregulars, but *I* was always Sherlock Holmes!"

Holmes was a bit surprised. "Watson," he said as the Dr. passed through to fetch a glass of brandy for his patients. "What do you make of this?"

Watson, exhausted, was still amused by the youth. "Egad, Holmes, is that a miniature Robin Hood? Or an elf? With all that's happened tonight, nothing would surprise me."

"Dr. Watson, Mr. Holmes, this," said Betty, "is Peter Pan."

Peter leapt to his feet and took a majestic bow. "And a lucky day for you, Mr. Holmes. I can smell a clue from fifty fathoms and never fail to bring the villains to justice."

"His confidence doesn't suffer at any rate," chuckled Watson, shaking his head and returning to his patients.

Holmes observed the boy with amused wonder. "So, you know Wiggins?"

"Sure, do you know baritsu?" asked Peter.

"As a matter of fact . . ." began Holmes.

"Play the fiddle?"

"Why . . ."

"Fly over London?"

"Now that could be useful."

"Dance with the pixies? Kiss a mermaid? Cremate a cannibal?" Peter shot out the questions so fast, Holmes was unable to get a word in.

"How about following a logical line of reasoning?" Holmes' amused eyes met Betty's. He placed his hand on the boy's shoulder to hold him still. "Now come. This buzzing about will *not* do. Please desist."

"Ever lose your shadow? Your mother tell you stories?"

"My mother?" Holmes reflected with a puzzled look.

"I bet we had the same mother," said Peter out of the blue. "That's why we're both so clever. Blood brothers, at any rate."

"Well, I hardly think so, but . . ." Holmes stopped, for Peter had dropped into a dejected mood.

"Actually," said Peter settling on the hearth and resting the pipe on his upraised knee as he gazed forlornly into the flames, "My mother never told me stories. Soon as I was born, she took one look at me and screamed, 'Gadzooks!' and threw me out the window, out into the gutter with the rubbish and the rats. I tried to get back in, but the door was locked. I climbed up to the window, but that was locked too. So, I went away to Neverland. And I never saw my mother again."

Holmes sat beside Peter and gently took the pipe from the boy's hand. "At least I saw my mother now and then . . . during holidays."

"Did she tell you stories?" asked Peter.

Holmes reflected on those days. "No, but we had a nurse, you see, and she would sometimes read to us."

"I've got it!" said Peter, delighted at his own plan. "Betty can be your mother."

Betty blushed when Holmes glanced up at her with interest.

"Nonsense, young man," said Lady Mallowan, who had come to in time to hear the discussion of mothers. "If anyone is going to be the mother around here, it's me. And as the self-appointed mother, I insist we return to the Hall and get a good night's sleep."

157

PART THREE

INTO THE CAVE

CHAPTER 22
THE CODE BOOK

Safely back at the Hall, Lady Mallowan made sure each guest was assigned a suitable room. Holmes said he would stay up a bit and smoke, so Betty said good night and retired upstairs. She had the codebook and scale in her arms and her hand on the doorknob to her room, when she was distracted by Peter chatting away with Leslie in the room across from hers. Not a bit sleepy and not wanting to be left out, she tapped on their door and entered. She found Leslie, in his shirt sleeves and slacks, lying across the bed, his head dangling over the other side and Peter perched on the top of the bedpost. "In Neverland there's no such thing as bedtime," said Peter. "No grown-ups to tell you to stop your silly nonsense and go to sleep this instant."

Leslie moaned. "Why do I feel so ancient?"

Betty sat on a tasseled stool near the vanity. "I wish I could go to sleep. But I can't."

Leslie sat up and winced as he felt his head. "My one regret is that I missed Holmes and Watson beating up old Edmond. It would be nice to see old smarty pants bested for once."

"Leslie!"

"Stop saying 'Leslie!' and fetch me an aspirin and a glass of water, will you?"

Betty scowled. "You can fetch your own aspirin and water, Mr. Mallowan." Leslie nearly choked on his shock.

"Anyway, we got the scale and the code book." Betty placed the two items on the bed to examine them. "I wish I understood the portals thing, how they really work. Macmillan says only a genius can figure out how to get in and out of them, but how does that account for me always getting where I need to be?"

"Oh, I don't think he's such a genius." Leslie snatched up the book and thumbed through it. "Look at these chapters. 'Accusers and how to recognize them.' Sounds pretty simple to me."

"When I read aloud at the Baker Street bookstore, we miraculously ended up in Neverland, not where we were trying to go, but where we needed to be to find the sapphire scale." Betty rested her chin on her fists and frowned. "But Macmillan says there's all kinds of variables to consider."

"What's a variable?" asked Peter, scratching his head.

"Something no one knows that could be anything," answered Betty.

"Oh that," said Peter. "Like stories. You never know how they're gonna end. But they all work out somehow, because that's what stories do."

"Hold on," said Leslie, "I think Peter has something. Read this. 'The door awaits the one who believes. Let your will and mind be sure and let your heart be pure.' It's not a code book. It's a ruddy instructions manual."

Betty was skeptical. "But Macmillan's methods worked. He calculated the exact formula for getting me to the lodge, down to the precise decimal point."

"Oh, I've taken a mathematics course or two in my time," said Leslie, sitting up a bit straighter, his nose a notch higher. "You can turn anything into a mathematical formula. Inspector Farnsworth of Scotland Yard discovered a code that used mathematics, and all the message said was 'The man you're looking for is . . .' The rest of the note had been burnt."

Peter was listening in suspense, his mouth wide open. "What happened after that?"

"Oh, you know. Crime doesn't pay and all that."

"Brilliant!" Peter was in awe.

"But what does Macmillan accomplish?" asked Betty. "Why try to fool us into thinking it's so impossible?"

"Oh grown-ups always want to make things complicated," retorted Peter. "That Macmillan sounds like the most grown-up-ish person of all. Grown-ups always are saying stuff like," here Peter deepened his voice and drew down his eyebrows to look extra grown-upish, 'imagination is all well and good, but if you don't work for it, it isn't going to happen.'" Betty could not help but laugh at the apt portrayal.

"It could be a way to make himself feel important," guessed Leslie. "Or maybe he just wanted to delay you all, giving the other side the upper hand."

"When all along, you just need to follow your heart," concluded Peter.

"I see." Betty felt a cloud lift from her mind. She thought about her childhood, alone, huddled in a corner, reading her book, finding a way to traverse space and time to reach her cousin. "It's . . . faith."

After breakfast, Peter said goodbye. Betty opened the large front doors of Baskerville Hall and stood with him on the porch. The late morning light had chased away the mist of the night before, and the moors, though still rugged, exuded a wild beauty.

"Do you know your way back?" asked Betty.

"Yep," he replied, planting his hat more jauntily on his head. "Frieda's waiting for me in Neverland with her lantern shining." And he whistled a robust tune as he tramped through the gate and across the moors.

He emerged from a curtain of moss hanging over the end of an old hollow tree. He came out upon the Neverland scene he had left, except before it was morning with buzzing dragonflies skipping across the stream, pausing to dip their feet in the water as they skimmed along.

It was now a soft twilight with wisps of purple drifting over a pink sky and moths fluttering about the lantern Frieda had hung from a twig. She was asleep, a half-plucked daisy in her hand and spectacles askew on her little nose. Peter leaned over and gently adjusted her spectacles. He took the lantern to light his way as he climbed the old, gnarly vines that twisted around the tree.

He crawled out on an overhanging limb and handed the lantern to his shadow to hoist on a branch. The moths darted about, disturbed that the light had been moved. Finally, the moths settled on the glass panes of the brass lantern. Peter leaned his back against the tree trunk and lifted one knee, upon which he rested his arm. His shadow, meanwhile, dangled by his legs down from a branch just a little higher up and swung back and forth as he watched the stars open their eyes in the darkening skies.

"Hello!" Peter saluted the stars. "Did you miss me?"

Frieda joined Peter on the branch. "Yes, Peter, I missed you. But I lit the lantern so you'd find your way home."

They sat side by side, Frieda resting her head on Peter's shoulder as the nightlights in the sky, like good mothers, watched over the children.

"Dr.," said Betty, meeting Watson at the foot of the stairs. "Have you seen Mr. Holmes?"

"I left him in the sitting room."

Betty wound her way to the sitting room, where she pushed open the door. The room was heavy with smoke. At the far end, perched in a chair, arms wrapped around his raised knees, his pensive eyes bent upon the embers, was Sherlock Holmes, smoking his pipe. Betty hesitated to disturb him. She knew his acerbic temper was inclined to lash out at anyone who dared to trespass on his thoughts at such moments.

However, Betty, being Betty, dared. She opened a window to let in the fresh air and the singing of a bird. Holmes growled and shifted his position, letting his long legs down from the chair. Betty joined him at the hearth, kneeling in front of him, focusing upon the smoldering log, matching the intensity of his silence.

At last he spoke. "I've had a notable career, and I've seen my share of horrors. A serpent turning on its master, ghosts of the past frightening strong men to their deaths. But the sight of your cousin coming at me with such ferocity . . . and the look of torment in his eyes." He held his pipe pensively. "I don't know what I would do if I were in his place. I pray God he finds peace."

Betty, grateful for these words of kindness towards Edmond, rested a hand on Holmes' knee. She felt his body become tense and withdrawn under her touch.

He lifted her hand from his knee, patted it paternally, and returned it to her. "He told me something of the scales you mentioned. He said they're all dragons. The Accusers are gathering an army of dragons to destroy the world. This is the knowledge that has kept my mind from sleeping. And now I ask, where does my duty lie?"

"Why, with your fellow human beings, as always," said Betty.

"My duty lies with *justice*," he corrected her. "And, if the world is besieged by a force seeking its ultimate ruin, the problems of Scotland Yard seem quite minute in comparison. You must take me to these Intercessors and allow me to lend my abilities to their cause."

"Really? You'll join us?" In her joy, Betty threw her arms around him and kissed his cheek. His hands floundered behind her back. But, recovering his usual aplomb, he smiled just a bit and withdrew an inch for space.

Betty's enthusiasm subsided. She returned to the floor, her concerned eyes moving in rapid thought and her mouth frowning in serious review. "But what if Tepov comes back here? Ordog is already trying to invade Neverland. Now that Tepov has gotten through the portal to this place, he will spread his claws across *your* world as well. I would be selfish to take you with me now, right when *your* England may be facing a crisis."

Holmes had been watching Betty. Her black eyes had a glow of intelligence and empathy he had rarely discovered in anyone besides Watson. It was intriguing, how her brows knitted then twitched upward at the center to indicate mental contention.

Aside from the obvious facts that she had not slept well that night, that she had brushed her hair facing the north, and that she had been outside that morning, he saw something else, her spirit. And even if the spirit *was* willful and foolhardy, these were qualities he admired when motivated by intelligence and compassion. Feelings beyond a professional comradery he abruptly dismissed. Any deeper emotions would be like an annoying scratch in the lens of his mind, a scratch that would widen until it shattered that natural state of objectivity, and, without objectivity, his mind would be of little use to anyone.

He impassively removed the pipe from his mouth. "You know as well as I, Betty, that the problems we are experiencing here are merely the tremors along the radials of the web. Stop the spider at the center, and we take down the entire web."

Betty could not argue with this logic. She clasped his hands in hers. "Welcome to the Inter-Story Intercessors, Mr. Holmes."

He returned her clasp warmly. "Now then. How do we get to Perlgate?"

"Just think lovely thoughts . . ." She scrunched her nose and added with a laugh, ". . . about squashing the spider."

CHAPTER 23
LESLIE'S MISSION

Betty was confident in selecting the right book from the Baskerville library. She chose a well-read copy of *The Scarlet Letter* by Nathaniel Hawthorne. On the fly leaf, she found an inscription by the late Sir Charles Baskerville, Sir Henry's uncle who had fallen victim to Stapleton's hound. The note indicated the novel had had a strong influence on Sir Charles' sympathies for women such as Laura Lyons, whom he had supported after her husband deserted her.

Holmes explained to Watson why he needed to accompany Betty to Perlgate in the 1930s and asked his associate to remain with Sir Henry and keep watch over nineteenth century England until he returned. Watson vowed constant vigilance.

Lady Mallowan, Leslie, Holmes, and Betty gathered in the library. Betty turned to a random page and scanned the text until her eyes landed on the familiar passage describing the child's reflection in the brook.

It was strange, the way in which Pearl stood, looking so steadfastly at them through the dim medium of the forest-gloom; herself, meanwhile, all glorified with a ray of sunshine, that was attracted thitherward as by a certain sympathy. In the brook beneath stood another child, — another and the same . . .

When they materialized through the mirror in the drawing room, no time had passed at all for Perlgate. Sir Eric was still standing there, adjusting his monocle to make sure he wasn't hallucinating. He was put out by the fact that his wife and son had reappeared with a guest he was not expecting. To calm her flustered husband, Lady Mallowan ordered Betty to fetch some hot cocoa from the kitchen and to prepare a room for the guest. "Mr. Holmes can have Edmond's room," she decided, "and, Betty, make sure the other servants are informed that there will be a guest for breakfast."

When Lady Mallowan grouped her with "other servants," Betty cringed and turned away from Holmes. Her clothing had changed from Victorian finery to her usual maid's uniform. She understood from reading Doyle's stories that maids, to Sherlock Holmes, were merely witnesses to be questioned, highly strung females who conveniently listened at keyholes or screamed and dropped the tea tray upon discovering the corpse. Lady Mallowan, having waved her hands and given orders, helped her husband upstairs, muttering something about Leslie never being allowed to read trashy comic books again.

Betty kept her eyes away from Holmes as she hastened to fetch the hot cocoa as ordered. She paused in the doorway, her hand resting on the doorframe. She lowered her forehead to the back of her hand. "I . . . I suppose I should have told you," she whispered, and swallowed hard. "Here . . . in this world . . . I'm just . . . nobody."

Holmes came to stand behind her. "Betty." His eyes contemplated her maid uniform. She glanced back at him over her shoulder, eyebrows raised with apprehension.

He lifted a long finger and barely touched a strand of her hair before withdrawing his hand with a sense of respect. "I read *all* your letters," he told her. "I *know* who you are. And, believe me, you are *not* a nobody. You are the *leader* of the Intercessors." He reached into her apron pocket and withdrew the magnifying glass she kept there. He presented it to her as if it were a scepter. "So, lead."

Betty met his unwavering eyes and saw in them sincerity and esteem. She felt the warmth around her cheeks and held back a grateful tear. She accepted the magnifying glass.

"And," he added, rubbing his hands together, primed for action, "Someone else can fetch Uncle Eric's cocoa. Right now, we have work to do."

"Right," she said. "Time for strategy. Leslie, we'll need a map of the area. There's one in a light blue tube by the desk in Uncle Eric's study." Once Leslie brought the map, she unrolled it across the card table and surveyed the details through the glass.

"Leslie," said Holmes, "or was it Buck, I can't keep it straight . . . do you happen to have such a thing as a pipe or cigarette here in the future?"

"Of course. We're not savages, you know." Leslie, back in his 1930s evening attire, took his cigarette case from his pocket. He gave Holmes a cigarette and lit it for him. "Thank you," said Holmes. "Now then, this must be Perlgate." He marked it with a pencil.

"Yes," said Betty, "and this is Professor Millgrew's Estate. There's a small cottage on the edge of the estate where Gregor Macmillan lives. That's Intercessor headquarters."

"And what's that over there?"

"That's the town," she told Holmes. "This is Hamberdeen's bookshop. Hamberdeen is an Intercessor and a good friend. His shop may come in handy as an alternative headquarters."

"And on the other side of the estates?"

"Farmland, mostly," replied Betty. "If our information about Macmillan is correct, Macmillan told Tepov about the onyx scale being near Baskerville Hall. Tepov is not going to be happy he lost out on the promised prize." Betty set the onyx scale on top of the map. "Now, the Accusers have the gold and the emerald scale. We have the onyx and the sapph . . ." she stopped, and her eyes widened with horror. "No, we *don't* have the sapphire one. The sapphire scale was in a safe in the cottage. If Tepov is there, Macmillan will hand over the scale as recompense for not getting the one from Stapleton."

Holmes firmly crushed his cigarette in an ashtray. "We don't have much time. And it looks like we'll need the help of your friend Hamberdeen."

Leslie knocked on the door to the cottage on the Millgrew Estate. While at the bookshop planning the operation with Betty, Holmes, and Hamberdeen, Leslie mentioned, "I used to visit Ol' Drybones at his cottage to get help before exams. It never did much good. All he ever wanted to talk about was how poorly the college paid him and how ungrateful we students were."

"Tomorrow," said Holmes, "you will visit him again."

"Why?"

"To thank him, of course."

Macmillan answered the door, wearing an elaborate smoking jacket and smoking an expensive brand of cigar. Leslie was taken aback. He had always remembered "Old Drybones" in a seedy dressing gown, biting the stem of an old relic of a pipe.

"Oh, hallo." Leslie shuffled his feet and studied the frayed edges of the door mat.

Macmillan was perturbed. "What can I do for you, young man?"

"Oh, well, nothing, not much anyway. Just, you know, wanting to say, thanks." Leslie glimpsed up, smiled, but Macmillan was not smiling, so Leslie resumed his tired frown.

"I'm a bit busy right now and . . . do I know you at all?"

Leslie sulked. "Well, of course, sir, I was in your class two or three terms ago. You remember, Mallowan, from Perlgate, there across the way?"

"Oh, yes, you're Amelia's boy. How remiss of me not to remember. Do come in." Macmillan stepped aside to allow Leslie to pass into the cottage. "I can't visit for long. I have guests, but we can chat a bit in the dining room."

Leslie slid off his cloth cap as he stood in the hallway. He appeared tired and uninterested, but his mind was snapping photos of everything, following Betty's advice to be a good secret agent. He noted a fashionable black coat on a peg, a fancy walking stick with a gold handle leaning against the umbrella stand, and a sealed envelope on a silver tray on the side table. A tilt of his head allowed him a glimpse of the first line of the address scrawled across the envelope. Reykjavík, Iceland.

Macmillan scowled, pocketed the envelope, and pushed Leslie along by the elbow down a hall and into the dining room.

"Let me fetch you a drink. I'll let my guest know I will be a few minutes. Then we can chat." Macmillan poured Leslie a whiskey, topped it off with a splash of soda, and plopped in an ice cube for good measure. He handed it to Leslie with a sanguine smile. Leslie took the glass and assumed an air of sophistication.

"Help yourself to the cigars. I'll be right back." The professor ducked out of the room.

Leslie sat at the table, drink in hand, lightly clinking the ice cube against the sides of the glass. A rapping on the dining room window startled him out of his equanimity.

He set the drink down and pushed aside the drapes to see Hamberdeen peering over his spectacles from the other side of the window. The window was a sliding glass door, and Leslie lifted the latch and pulled the door open a few inches. Hamberdeen pushed his face into the opening. "Well?"

Leslie shrugged. "Nothing much so far. He has a guest, someone with expensive taste judging from the coat and walking stick. And there's an envelope addressed to Iceland."

"Iceland. I'm not surprised," said Hamberdeen.

"Be careful, Leslie." Betty joined Hamberdeen at the window. "The guest could be the vampire."

Leslie jolted. "The vampire? You didn't happen to bring a wooden stake . . . or a crucifix? Or a clove of garlic?"

"Now, Leslie, don't worry, we'll be right here," Hamberdeen reassured him. "You leave the door open a crack and cover it with the drapes. We'll be on the other side, listening. The point is to buy time for Mr. Holmes. Oh, and, Leslie . . ."

"What?"

"Do you know the call of the great white egret?" Hamberdeen blinked.

Leslie stared back, not registering.

"It's quite distinctive. It sounds rather like a lot of stray mothballs rolling around the bottom of the wardrobe. Anyway, once we have what we need, I'll scratch on the shutters in imitation of that call, like this," and Hamberdeen scratched against the shutters on the side of the door with a short-soft, long-hard pattern. "When you hear that, you get out of there. I don't want you risking more than you have to."

"I've handled worse." Leslie was offended they would doubt his aplomb after he saved Betty from the Grimpen Mire.

"Now, get back to the table. And, for heaven's sake, don't look over in this direction." Hamberdeen withdrew, and Leslie closed the door, leaving it open a crack, and returned the drapes to their original position.

Hamberdeen frowned as he turned to Betty. "I don't like this idea of pinning so much of our hopes on young Leslie."

"He's the only one Macmillan would let in without getting suspicious."

Hamberdeen sighed. "It sounds silly to say this, but I do hope Sherlock Holmes knows what he's doing."

CHAPTER 24
THE TRAITOR

Leslie returned to the table, stretched out his legs, and took a sip of the whiskey. His pulse had picked up after the mention of the vampire, but he forced himself to breathe as naturally as possible.

Macmillan returned, more nervous than before. "Now, young Mallowan." He sat to the right of Leslie and managed an attentive, interested expression. "You must tell me how things have been. The excavation was a success, they say. Even found a golden dragon scale."

"Well, yes. Yes, *we* did. Edmond-blasted-Davidson got all the credit, though."

"Davidson always was clever in school." Macmillan trained his eye on Leslie to catch his reaction. "While he struggled a bit with mathematics, Professors Millgrew and Stanford had nothing but praise for him."

Leslie leaned forward sullenly. "Everyone has nothing but praise for Edmond. I don't know why *he* should get all the hooplahoo. He finds a scale, is nutty enough to think it belonged to a dragon, and everyone bows to his every wish and whim. Fat lot of fools, if you ask me."

"Some people think there are more dragon scales out there, just waiting to be dug up by would-be geniuses like young Davidson."

"Well, I don't know anything about that." Leslie took a sip of the whiskey. "Betty blathered a bit about a scale she found. Something about a black one and a blue one." He chuckled. "Sounded rather like a boxing match."

"Now, this black scale . . ."

"Oh, it's a lot of nonsense. Can't pay any credit to what Betty will dream up. I only came to say thanks for helping me pass mathematics and to ask if you think there might be a scholarship for next term." Leslie yawned and eyed his old professor dully.

"A scholarship? Why, of course, a bright lad like yourself, from a good family, naturally there'll be one for you, but why would you want to waste your time in school?"

The truth was, Leslie had no intention of returning to university and, even if he did, the family fortune was sufficient to pay his way, but he congratulated himself on inventing a good excuse for showing up on Ol' Drybones' doorstep. He had not expected Macmillan to call school a waste of time. He blew out slowly as he restructured his narrative. "Well, you know, trying to keep up with Davidson. Mother hardly notices me anymore. Thinks Edmond the sun, moon, and stars. Me, I'm just the lazy chap who reads too many comic books, or so *she* thinks."

"Oh," Macmillan brushed lint off Leslie's lapel, "I think you have tons of potential. I've always thought you were capable of much more than mathematics."

"Is that why you let me see the answers to the exams?" Leslie shot him a knowing sideways glance.

Macmillan cleared his throat. "Well, I was just helping out the son of an old friend."

"Oh, yes, I think mother mentioned you."

Macmillan stood. "She hardly remembers me, I suppose."

Leslie pushed back his chair, and stood as well, bringing his drink. "What did she mean when she said you were an Intercessor? Do you work for the embassy?"

Macmillan's eyebrows twitched upward in disdain. "The Intercessors are an elite society, a top-secret society, that only the most intelligent, insightful, and gifted people can belong to. Your cousin Betty is an Intercessor."

"Well, if Betty belongs to it, they're probably just a lot of daydreamers."

"You're right, Leslie." Macmillan leaned in closer to Leslie, gripping his arm. "There is a group that is even more exclusive. Only those who can pass an incredibly difficult test of courage and will can join."

"And they give out scholarships?"

"They could get you untold wealth and power." Macmillan shot a nervous glance back at the dining room door, then scrutinized Leslie as if making up his mind if he could be trusted.

"Hmmm." Leslie examined his fingernails. "I've got wealth, or at least I will when father pops off, but the power sounds interesting."

"Power is always interesting," agreed Macmillan.

"Who are these people who could get me this power?"

"They're called the Accusers. One of their leaders is here now. He wants to meet you."

"Are you an Accuser too?" Leslie tried not to look too eager for the answer.

"Yes."

Leslie gulped. "Do," he cleared his throat to resume his normal, dull voice, "the Intercessors mind people belonging to more than one secret society?"

"What the Intercessors don't know won't harm them. And they are such pitiful fools, anyway."

"Yes, well, if *Betty* is an Intercessor, how great can it be?"

"Indeed. Hamberdeen, Yamada . . . Spinderbeck." Macmillan practically spat the last name. "Those fools need someone who can lead them to their true potential, someone with knowledge deeper than what they are willing to explore, someone like me who recognizes the benefits of working with both sides of the equation."

Leslie nodded, pretending to listen. He swallowed the last bit of whiskey and set down the glass. "When do I get to meet him? This leader of that group you mentioned?"

The door opened, and Tepov entered. He wore a black fedora with a silk band, a mask-like shadow angling across his eyes and nose. His black, silk-lined suit was perfectly pressed, and his black shoes gleamed. He looked more like a snazzy gangster than a vampire.

Tepov frowned and leaned against the wall. He took a silver cigarette case from the inside pocket of his suit jacket. He opened it, drew out a cigarette, which he held lightly between his first two fingers and his thumb. Macmillan nearly tripped over the oriental rug in his eagerness to light Tepov's cigarette for him.

Tepov drew in the smoke and let it stream out between his teeth. "We've met," he acknowledged Leslie, a smirk curling up on the corner of his mouth. He pushed himself away from the wall and walked up close to Leslie, breathing smoke into his face. "You're the one with the deadly lantern." He tilted back his head and laughed. The next instant, he resumed his poker-faced frown. "I want the onyx scale."

"Mallowan knows where it is, I'm sure of it," said Macmillan.

Tepov shrugged and sauntered past Leslie. "Also, young Mallowan," he continued in a soft voice, "I want to know what has happened to my favorite henchman." He allowed his fangs to show as he tested their sharpness with his little finger.

Leslie thought now would be an excellent moment for Hamberdeen to reproduce the sound of the great white egret.

Instead, the drapes ripped aside, and Hamberdeen and Betty were shoved into the dining room by two massive werewolves.

Tepov reached into the side pocket of his suit jacket and produced a pistol. He tossed it to Macmillan. "Keep them covered."

Hamberdeen looked sternly at Macmillan over his spectacles and shook his head. "So, Mack, falling for the same old lie, selling your soul for a pinch of power?"

Betty fixed Macmillan with a glare. "We trusted you."

Macmillan remained silent, keeping the pistol aimed at his former colleagues.

Tepov moved close to Betty. She turned from him in disgust. He used his index finger to push her chin up to him. "Hello, Beatrice." He grinned. Her glare intensified. He retaliated by clutching her wrist, the same wrist that still bore the bruises he had inflicted upon her in the ballroom. She winced in pain, which gave him cruel pleasure. "Dmitri, Mikhail," he said to his huntsmen, "lock those two in the cellar for later. I want to be alone with this wench." Betty worked to pull her wrist free, despite the pain.

"Tell them nothing," called Hamberdeen as the werewolves dragged him away. "That's the *key*."

"If you hurt her . . ." warned Leslie as the two huntsmen pushed him and Hamberdeen from the room.

Macmillan remained, gun aimed at Betty, but his breathing came quick and nervous.

Tepov's eyes gleamed as he examined Betty's chest, shoulders, and neck. He let his finger slide down her neck slowly, deliberately. She shirked away from him.

"I hate you," he told her. "Yes, it's true. I have hated you ever since I tasted that first drop of your Intercessor blood."

"Let the others go," she said.

"Yes," he breathed in, dreaming of that first drop, as his tongue slid over his fangs. "It wasn't enough. I want the rest of it, every last bit. You are feared, Beatrice. Even the greatest of the dragon lords hears your name and trembles." He noted her reaction with interest. "This surprises you. Aww. Little Betty. Poor Betty. Orphan and chambermaid. But the veins inside these delicate white arms burst with power. And I want to absorb that power. Then. The dragon lords, *all* of them, will fear *me*."

"Well?" snapped Macmillan. "Take it and be done."

Tepov turned on Macmillan in rage. "Don't. Ever. Tell me. What. To. Do." He slammed his hand to Macmillan's throat and rammed him up against the wall.

Macmillan gasped to breathe. "I - I'm sorry."

Tepov deliberated the sincerity of the response, exhaled in satisfaction, and reluctantly released his lackey and allowed him to regain his oxygen. "Very well," he conceded, smoothing his lapel and straightening his tie. He turned at a right angle to face Betty. She was inching towards the glass door. "You can't get out that way," he told her. "Czerny!"

Another werewolf moved into the doorway and folded his brawny arms across his broad chest. Tepov sneered. "At long last. No more pixies, no more hounds. Just you and me."

He grabbed her arm and spun her close to him. Now she was pressed against his chest. His sultry breath smelled of tobacco and blood. She met his penetrating eyes with angry resolution.

"Why did you capture Edmond?" she asked.

He scowled. "He was just a pawn," he shrugged. "We needed his scale, and we needed you. He was the lure, the bait, for *you*." With his free hand, he flicked her disheveled hair away from her throat.

"You have two of the scales, I believe?" said Betty.

He drew closer to her throat. "Not so. I have more."

She turned her face away from him. "I know where the onyx scale is hidden."

He stopped. Every fiber in his being longed to puncture her neck and infuse the powerful spirit coursing through her arteries, but the shadow of Ordog still hung over him like a guillotine. And Ordog wanted the scales.

In fury, he flung her to the floor and stood over her, one foot on either side of her body as he glowered down at her. "Where?"

She pushed herself up on her elbows. "First, tell me where Edmond is. Let Edmond go, and I'll give you the scale you want." She met his eyes force for force.

He laughed and stepped back from her. "You must know I haven't seen him since the Grimpen Mire. But even if I could grant you his werewolf-ridden body, his soul belongs to Ordog, *for eternity.*"

"Release his soul." Betty climbed to her feet.

"That is not within my power. No soul ever returns from Alsó-Világ."

"Then, take me with you to Iceland. Once you find the diamond scale, I'll tell you where we've hidden the onyx one."

He grinned widely. "Yes, yes." He rubbed his hands together. "That would please me very much. Czerny," he called the werewolf at the glass door. "Take her to the cellar with the others for now."

CHAPTER 25
CIRCUMSTANCES

Around the corner from Hamberdeen's Used Books was a pub frequented by the working class of Bedfordshire. Barnaby Skeens, though he rarely lifted a finger to honest labor, also frequented the pub. It was the ideal place for eavesdropping on the latest gossip. As he listened, he jiggled the beer in his mug and let the foam plaster his upper lip while he leaned against the bar, hoping to pick up some information of value.

Mostly the talk was about Millgrew's estate. According to Meg, the barmaid, her husband Tim's brother, who kept the grounds of the estate, had told her grandmother, who was now living with Meg and Tim since her bout with rheumatism, that there were weird things going on at the estate.

"The phantom, that's what it is," said Meg. "A great ghoulish phantom with wings and fangs, that's what he seen."

"You're barmy, you are," said a fat, rosy-nosed workman at a table.

"No. Jack never lies about ghosts," swore Meg, with a flick of her dirty washrag. "And there was somethin' not human lurking among the plants."

"Granny seen the phantom, did she?"

"Nooo. Jack seen it, he did. Fair gives me the chills to think of it."

Barnaby's eyes lit up when he spotted a young man seated in a corner pushing the bill of his cap down over his eyes and hunching over his beer. His collar was pulled up around his face, and all that was visible was part of the nose and the grim line of a mouth. Barnaby's instinct for people with something to hide was keen. So, Barnaby sidled over to the furtive young man in the corner and seated himself across from him. He slammed his beer down and grinned.

"New to our parts, are you? Looking for a spot of work, are you?" asked Barnaby in a warm, friendly manner.

The man in the cap looked down, but Barnaby peered closer. "Why, bless my beer, if it ain't Ed the almighty. I'd know that handsome blighter anywhere."

Edmond glanced up in alarm at being recognized. His eyes were bloodshot and dark-circled. His face was covered in black stubble, and his hair was matted to his forehead.

"I was right. It *is* you," said Barnaby.

Edmond glanced with anxious caution over his shoulder at the other customers.

"Here incognito, are you?" whispered Barnaby with a knowing glint, bending his head over his beer. "Don't worry. You can trust *me*."

Edmond breathed out, long and weary. He leaned back in the chair. "I don't know, Barnie. I'm so . . . tired."

"What? The Davidson boy I knew could take anything. You were tough as they came. Don't tell me the headmaster still has it out for you."

"I wish it was only that." Edmond twisted his glass around on the table, watching with fatalistic gloom the chain of circles the condensation made on the table. "My life has been a series of headmasters. And there's no escaping the last one."

"What now? In trouble again?" asked Barnaby. "Who is it this time? Sir Eric? Colonel Graham? Did you upset Daphne? *Don't tell me* you upset *Daphne*?"

"You wouldn't understand."

"Well, maybe not." Barnaby winked. "But that pretty maid over at Perlgate. I bet she'd understand."

At Barnaby's reference to Betty, Edmond knocked over his beer and the puddle spread across the table and dripped off the edge. He grabbed Barnaby's coat collar in his fists, stiff blue veins popping up at the knuckles. "You've been to Perlgate. Did you see Betty?"

Barnaby glanced down at Edmond's fists near his throat. "You mean the maid? Let go of the collar and I'll tell you."

Edmond winced. "I'm sorry, Barnie." He mentally commanded his hands to release him. They only tensed up further. Summoning his will, he forced his right hand to pry his left hand from Barnaby's coat. "I'm sorry."

"That's better." Barnaby readjusted his collar and felt his throat. "Yeh, I seen her. Sweet thing. She's got it for you, lad. Of course, don't all the girls."

Edmond covered his face with his hands. His shoulders shuddered. "What have I done?"

"What gives, mate?"

Edmond shook his head, eyes fixed on the door.

"Come on, ol' man, you can trust me. Wasn't I the one what smuggled you food when you were locked up in that cellar in the old days? Wasn't I the one what took the blame when you imitated Bickerstaff behind his back? Didn't I catch the blows for you that time? And never once did I tell, not once. I took each blow for you, ol' man, for you. Come on. What do you need? Maybe I can help you now."

Edmond looked Barnaby in the eyes. "I'm worried about Betty. She mustn't go near Macmillan's cottage. I've been watching the place, but I can't get close enough without being spotted by Tepov's guards. But you, you could see Betty, give her a message. Tell her to stay far away from the cottage. Vlad Tepov is there, lying in wait. Tell her I want to help, but I can't trust myself. I never know when I could . . . I might do something rash."

Barnaby leaned in closer to Edmond and whispered, "Something to do with them Intercessors, Accusers, and . . . dragon scales? Is that it?"

"You know?"

"Bits and pieces, bits and pieces. It was me what told your uncle about Tepov and what he was after. Say, what are you to Tepov, anyway?"

"Bait. I'm just the bait for Betty."

"If that's the case, you better not go anywhere near her . . . don't want to play into their hands now, do you. That would be just what Tepov wants. You leave it to ol' Barnie. I'll get yer message to Betty all right, and then we'll find a way to get you far away from this place."

A tired half smile made an attempt on Edmond's face. "Thanks, Barnie."

Barnaby shrugged as he mentally calculated how much Tepov would pay to know where Edmond was hiding. "What are friends for?"

In the cellar of the cottage, beetles scurried up and down the rock walls entwined with invading weeds and frayed wires. Earwigs followed the rusty pipes that twisted around the barred stairwell to the open junction from which trickles of icy water dripped down on the three captives.

Hamberdeen sat on the straw-strewn floor, his arms wrapped around himself for warmth. "Gregor. A traitor."

Leslie paced and slammed his cap into his palm. "I was doing splendidly myself, until someone got themselves captured by great hulking werewolves." He stopped pacing. "Are we going to just wait here for them to come back and gnaw our throats out, or are we going to think of a way out of this ratty hole?"

"Patience, young Leslie," said Hamberdeen. "We can leave any time we choose."

"What?"

Hamberdeen drew the key the mermaid gave him from his pocket. "I have a key."

Betty sat on the top step of a moldy wooden ladder. She leaned her elbow on her knee and rested her face in her cupped hand. "We need to wait for Sherlock's signal."

"Not more great white egrets, I hope." Leslie shoved his hands in his pockets and leaned his shoulder gloomily against the wall.

Holmes snuck into the den, wearing a black silk mask, the brim of his homburg pulled over his eyes. He found the safe where Betty had described, behind the revolving bookshelf. Using his burglary kit, Holmes did not take long to break into the safe. He found the sapphire scale, but the code book was missing. Once he had the scale, he put the room back the way it was. Keeping to the shadows, he slunk over to the dining room door, where he hid himself flat against the wall. He listened as Betty and Hamberdeen were captured. It had all been part of the plan. Holmes seethed as Tepov harassed Betty. It took great restraint not to rush in and wrap one of the more lethal metallic objects in his burglary kit around the vampire's neck.

After Betty, Hamberdeen, and Leslie were taken to the cellar, Holmes remained hidden, listening. As he had calculated, Tepov unraveled his plans to Macmillan, confident he had his enemy safely under lock and key.

"Give to me the sapphire scale," said Tepov. "All that will remain are the onyx and the diamond scales. You have the code book? You have worked out where the diamond scale can be found and how to get there?"

"Of course. This code book tells me all," Macmillan assured him. "It's exactly where one would expect to find a diamond dragon scale. Ironic that Haggard probably never realized there was a dragon hidden in his novel."

"Then that one is as good as found. Young Beatrice will soon tell me where to find the onyx scale. She will not be able to deny me. Then to Iceland to retrieve the instructions for restoring the scales to the mighty dragon warriors they once were."

Holmes had heard enough. He crept out of the house and around to the back. He threw himself on the ground and patted handfuls of dirt and loose grass over his clothing. Then, he crawled to the stairwell to the cellar. He put his gloved hand to the side of his mouth and hooted like the Tawny Owl.

That was the signal. Hamberdeen pushed his key against the stone wall of the cellar, and a golden light traced the outline of a doorway.

Leslie, wide-eyed, leapt to his feet. "Ooh! It works!"

Hamberdeen pressed on the outline of the door, and it pushed open with a gush of light. Leslie and Betty followed Hamberdeen out the door, across the lawn, to the large gnarly tree behind which Holmes was hiding.

"You got it?" Betty asked.

Holmes patted his coat where the scale was hidden. "Now quickly," he said. "Cover your clothing with dirt. That will disguise your scent from the werewolves. There are several of them patrolling the area."

The others did as Holmes instructed, though Leslie cried to himself a little as he sloshed the dirt onto his brand-new suit jacket and trousers. Betty was about to suggest they make a rush, but Holmes put his finger to his lips and gestured towards the cottage.

Someone was arriving at the front door a few meters away from where they were hidden. The new arrival had driven up in a rundown model that sputtered and backfired. The man leapt out of his car and sauntered to the door, whistling and swinging his umbrella. The porch light snapped on, and Betty saw his face. Barnaby Skeens.

"The swine," said Leslie. "Selling us out, I'll bet."

Holmes gestured for them to duck behind the shrubs while they watched the cottage. A side window lit up, revealing the silhouettes of Macmillan and Barnaby against the glass. Barnaby doffed his hat and tossed it aside. They talked.

Macmillan poured a drink for Barnaby. Barnaby downed the drink. They talked some more. Macmillan opened a billfold and was counting out bills and handing a wad of them to Barnaby. Another silhouette loomed up behind Barnaby, a great winged shadow with fangs. The fangs caught Barnaby by the throat, and the night was pierced by a blood-curdling scream. The scream ended in a choke and a rattle, and the silhouette of Skeens slumped to the floor.

Betty gripped Holmes' arm, her face drained of color. He clasped her hand at his arm.

"Come," said Hamberdeen. "It's time to get away from this wretched place."

Not far from the cottage stood a garden house draped and twisted with thick, snaky vines of pumpkins overrunning the garden. On the roof, a werewolf leaned forward on his haunches, keeping a lonely vigil. His amber eyes stood out against his gray-tinged mane, and his mouth at the end of his long muzzle was straight and grim. As Betty fled, guided by the gallant arm of Sherlock Holmes, the werewolf nodded, satisfied that she was safe.

Tepov resumed his human form. He licked the excess drops of the blackmailer's blood off the tip of his fangs, and the fangs retracted. He smirked at Macmillan's nauseated expression.

"Relax," commanded Tepov. "This greedy parasite will feed the worms in the garden. Does he think I would dig into my ancestor's reserves to meet his exorbitant demands? Pathetic creature. He tells me Beatrice Talbin is back at Perlgate, but I already have her in my power. He tells me Davidson has turned against me. This I already knew. But Davidson is on a short leash. His soul binds him to Ordog. And more, I have his cousin. He will return to me and beg me to forgive the error of his ways. Most importantly, through Davidson I have delivered two scales to my master. Now, the sapphire scale, as you promised." Tepov stretched his hand out to Macmillan.

"Of course." Macmillan led Tepov to the side room. He resumed his self-assurance, knowing he would soon win the favor of Ordog who could grant him power such as he had just witnessed. He smugly sprang the mechanism with the books. The shelf swung around. He worked the combination and pulled open the door of the safe.

"The sapphire scale," repeated Tepov impatiently.

"The safe . . . it's empty," gasped Macmillan. "I've been robbed."

Tepov's face turned dark as he spread out his wings, and his hands distorted into claws, while his eyes became two luminous orbs shooting fire. "Traitor!" roared Tepov. "Traitor!"

CHAPTER 26
SOLOMON'S MINES

Hamberdeen, Leslie, Betty and Holmes arrived in front of the old bookshop. The iron wrought porch lantern by the door welcomed them with a warm glow in the night. It seemed like ages since Betty had rushed here from her first encounter with Tepov in the shard of glass and had met Miss Fernsby.

Hamberdeen unpocketed his magical key, and with eager expectation he applied it to the lock of his shop. The key made a low hum of electrical resistance, and something pushed him back. "Well, I thought it *might* work." Hamberdeen sulked at the uncooperative key.

"Perhaps you should try the key that has been carelessly thrust under the doormat," suggested Holmes. Hamberdeen checked, and sure enough the shop key was there where Miss Fernsby had left it.

Inside, Hamberdeen prepared tea in a cozy nook. The familiar smell of dust and old books along with the warmth of a good cup of tea dispelled for a moment the fear of encroaching evil. Holmes slid the sapphire scale onto the table. Betty set the onyx scale next to it.

"We have two scales," observed Hamberdeen. "And the Accusers have two as well." He stirred his tea and settled in a tattered, overstuffed armchair.

"It's a stalemate, then," said Leslie. He helped himself to a biscuit from a box. "Except now we know about Iceland."

A strident clash made Leslie jump, but it was just the gong of the grandfather clock in the corner striking ten. "Ah!" said Hamberdeen. "It's time. They should be here now."

Before Leslie could ask "who," the beams of headlights rolled across the room through the front window, and the rumble of a car's engine came to a stop outside. Two car doors shut, and the doorbell rang at the front door. Hamberdeen put down his cup and opened the door a crack, leaving the chain bolted for safe keeping as he peeked through.

Two gentlemen stood on the porch, their faces in shadows. All he could make out was that one of them was a taller man with a sharply angled fedora and the other was a shorter, twitching man in a rounded derby. Hamberdeen turned on the porch light. As he expected, the taller man was Khumalo, and the shorter man was Spinderbeck.

"I trust we are on time," said Khumalo, consulting his watch.

"Yes, yes, come in, come in!" said Hamberdeen. "Betty is here along with reinforcements."

Betty hurried to the door to greet them. She stopped short and looked behind them.

"You are looking for Yamada," noted Khumalo. "He is not here. He said he needed to follow a clue, and away he went through a portal. But," he added warmly, "it is good to see you again." He took both her hands in his.

Holmes assumed a position at her side and placed a hand in the crook of her arm. "Another Intercessor," he observed, "recently from South Africa."

"Yes," said Betty, "this is Daniel Khumalo. Daniel, this is Sherlock Holmes."

Khumalo surprised Holmes by grasping the hand of the detective and shaking it with enthusiasm. "Mr. Holmes. I have read about you. You are one of my favorite characters. Brilliant! Absolutely brilliant! We are most fortunate to have so great a man on our side. I have learned much from studying your methods."

Holmes permitted himself a small, gratified smile as he shook Khumalo's hand. "Thank you. I'm sure you have done much to earn the respect of Miss Talbin."

The group gathered around the tea table, and Betty related what had occurred since they last met.

"Iceland is where Tepov will go next," said Leslie.

"To find the instructions for bringing the dragons to life," said Holmes. "But I overheard Macmillan also mention Haggard. I suspect he was referring to the recent best seller, *King Solomon's Mines* by H. Rider Haggard. Watson was reading parts of it to me last week."

"That's interesting." Khumalo stirred his tea. "I have been following a clue of my own in a book left to me by my great grandfather. He was ruler of a tribe in the Congo, people who later migrated south. The book is called The *Book of Ancestors*, and as I was reading, two names caught my eye. Ignosi and Twala. It seems I am related to these two men. Both are featured in Haggard's novel. I have a copy of it with me now." He set the novel on the table with the two scales. "Along with this." And he twisted the golden ring on his finger around to face outward, revealing a figure of a snake with a diamond eye. "This is the same symbol that Ignosi wore to identify himself as the rightful ruler of the Kukuana tribes. This ring has been passed down from Ignosi, to my grandfather, and to my own father, and, now, to me. According to the *Book of Ancestors*, he who shows this ring to the tribe will be received as a brother."

"Then, you and I must go there and bring back the diamond scale," said Betty. "And Spinderbeck, you will travel to Iceland."

"Me?" Spinderbeck paled. "But you said the *vampire* was going to Iceland."

"Exactly why you must go. He must not get those instructions," said Betty.

"But . . . the vampire!"

"You'll have your sword," she reminded him.

Spinderbeck found the reminder small comfort. "But how do I get to Iceland?"

Betty picked up a book and handed it to Spinderbeck. The book was *Journey to the Center of the Earth* by Jules Verne. "This will be your portal."

"Excellent," said Holmes, "and I'll go with Betty and Mr. Khumalo." He was snatching his hat and coat when Betty intervened. "Thank you," she said, "but you must stay here with Mr. Hamberdeen to guard the onyx and the sapphire scales. Tepov will be looking for them, and I trust no one but you two to keep them safe."

Holmes noted the intensity of her conviction, and he rested his hand on hers. "Then, so be it. I will remain, and the Accusers will not take the scales while I live."

She gazed up at him in gratitude.

"I hate to interrupt this moment," said Leslie, "but I think mother must be wondering where I am, and I . . ." He was heading towards the door, when Betty caught him by the arm. "Aunt Amelia will be fine," she told him. "You're coming with us." Before he could protest, she snatched up the copy of *King Solomon's Mines* Khumalo held out to her.

She threw it open to the page the bookmark indicated. She concentrated on the passage that caught her eye. "*It is far. But there is no journey upon this earth that a man may not make if he sets his heart to it. There is nothing . . . that he cannot do, there are no mountains he may not climb, there are no deserts he cannot cross.*"

"Things have a habit of slipping through your fingers, count," remarked Macmillan as they surveyed the empty cellar. The count frowned and paced the straw-strewn floor. He kicked a dead rat out of his path, flung about, and continued to pace. "Dmitri! Czerny!"

The two wolfish huntsmen descended the steps, lowered their heads, and moved in sideways so that they could pass through the cellar door, one at a time.

"My lord," bowed Dmitri.

"How did the prisoners escape? I put you in charge of them! Where are they?"

Dmitri looked over the cellar in dismay. "They were *here*, my lord, I swear. My men were on sentry duty all night. They could not have escaped."

"Unless they used a portal," said Macmillan. "This room is not portal proof, after all."

"*You* said they could not escape from here," growled Tepov.

"Under normal conditions, they couldn't," said Macmillan. "But the girl is learning the ways quickly. I thought I had her convinced that without my formulas she was powerless to use the portals. Someone has disabused her, it seems."

"That Sherlock Holmes, perhaps. It probably took him two minutes to see through your charade!"

"I did not factor Sherlock Holmes into the equation," confessed Macmillan.

Tepov shot a violent glare straight into Macmillan's eyes. Then, he turned from him sharply. "Dmitri! You and the others scour the countryside. Find Davidson. If we have him, we have the girl. I know Beatrice. She would sell her own soul to redeem her loved one. Bring him before Ordog in chains and on his knees. We will break him so abominably that she will hear his proud heart burst no matter which portal she may be hiding in."

"Yes, my lord." Dmitri and Czerny bowed and hastened to do his bidding.

Tepov pushed past Macmillan and dashed up the steps to the kitchen and out the side door. He put his gloved hand to his mouth and called in the tongue of the ancients, "*Avian! Ishata! Ishata! Aventiss!*"

A piercing cry rang back. Out of the pink streaks of morning hove the crimson dragon, Avian. She glided down to her master's outstretched arm.

"Avian, my love," said Tepov, stroking her neck and chin, "Our enemy has gone to fetch both the instructions and the final scale. You must not let them get the scale."

"Ay!" cawed the dragon. "And you? Will you find what our master seeks?"

"Yes, you can assure Ordog that before the moon is high in the mountains, he shall have all the scales and the secret to the ritual. And, he will have his dreaded rival Beatrice Talbin's soul to digest for eternity."

"This is well, my love, this is well," acknowledged the dragon with half-closed eyes.

Edmond, in the shadows behind the garden house, growled low as he watched with resolve.

The heat of the African sun glinted off the grasslands and plateaus. The rough grains of dirt and sharp blades of grass scraped Betty's sandaled feet. She wore a beaded shawl and a skirt made of soft animal hide. Eyes closed, she raised her face towards the sun, letting its warmth thaw out the chill of England. They were on a ridge in the mountains overlooking a wide grassy plain. Leslie and Khumalo were dressed in the khaki garb of late nineteenth century explorers, with pith helmets and boots.

"The moors were bad enough," groaned Leslie, surveying the long stretch of brush. But before he could complain further, the cold steel point of a spear jabbed the small of his sweaty back. He raised his hands and rolled his eyes.

Khumalo and Betty also raised their hands. Khumalo managed a cautious glance back over his shoulder at their captors, a retinue of warriors led by a tall, handsome man with the sign of the snake tattooed around his middle. The leader, whom Khumalo recognized as Ignosi from the novel's description, gestured for the others to draw back their spears.

Ignosi strode in front of the newcomers, assessing them. He stopped before Khumalo. "You have the look of a brother."

"Ignosi. My king." Khumalo bowed with respect.

"He bears the ring." Ignosi gestured to Khumalo's hand.

One of the warriors came forward, keeping guarded watch on the newcomers. He snatched the ring from Khumalo's finger and brought it to Ignosi. Ignosi held the ring up to the sun. The sun glinted through the diamond eye of the snake on the ring, and Ignosi nodded, satisfied. "Yes, it is true. You are the ones the prophecy foretold." He returned the ring to Khumalo. "The prophecy spoke of a brother, the son of the dead, who would come with the yet unborn. The prophecy says you know the one who can defeat Ordog."

"Ordog is powerful," admitted Khumalo. "We have come to retrieve the diamond scale and take it beyond his reach.

"Yes," said Ignosi. "The diamond scale. Gogool, a sorceress of our people, says she knows where it is hidden. The ancient one has seen much from the evil days. She has promised to guide us to the secret place. Come, our camp is this way."

Ignosi led the way around the ridge to where two of the Englishmen from the novel, Allan Quatermain and Captain John Good, were waiting, with the lovely Kukuana maiden, Foulata, and the ancient one, Gogool. Foulata, sitting next to Captain Good, wore a beaded halter over her breasts and a short animal hide skirt around her shapely hips and thighs. Her eyes gleamed with rapturous love when she looked upon Good. He wore a monocle in one eye and had shaved only one side of his beard. The Kukuana warriors had found him so and interpreted the monocle and half-shaved beard as a sign from the gods, so Good was obliged to maintain the aura.

Gogool hunched over her staff behind them. Her head was bald with a few straggles of white hair, her face wrinkled like a prune, and her gaunt skin stretched thin against her protruding bones. Her mouth hung open in a fiendish sneer.

Foulata's face brightened when she saw Betty, and she stood to offer her a canteen with water. "Welcome, sister. You have come at last."

"I don't understand," said Betty. "How do you know me?"

"I know the ways," replied Foulata. "I have seen you in my dreams. You are a mighty warrior maid. I have seen you walk with beasts and stand with dragons."

"I'm just a servant."

"The dreams do not lie," Foulata insisted. "Now come." She put down a shawl on a rock nearby. "Sit with me. We will talk."

"It's been a long time since I've talked with someone my own age," said Betty.

"We will be friends. My name is Foulata."

"I'm Betty."

"I see you, too, wear the beads of a promised woman. Is that handsome warrior with King Ignosi your man?" Foulata pointed boldly at Khumalo. Khumalo politely averted his eyes with a knowing smile as he spoke with Quatermain and Ignosi.

Betty glanced sidelong at Khumalo. "Actually, no." She twisted her hair as she allowed herself the luxury of contemplating his manly physique. "But Daniel *is* very handsome and kind."

Foulata nudged Betty's arm. "He likes you, I can tell. Imagine! You engaged and you don't even know!" Foulata leaned close to Betty. "My man is the god with the glass eye. And," she added in a whisper, "he has beautiful white legs." And the two girls both moved their eyes towards Captain Good. "He's a real catch, that one," said Foulata, and they both giggled. "I know your man will make you happy, just like my man makes me happy too." She clasped her hands at her heart and sighed.

"According to the ancient one," Quatermain told the group, lighting his pipe, "the treasure hidden here in the mountains contains the diamond dragon scale you seek."

"Not far, not far," cackled Gogool. "The treasure is not far. It lies in the halls of the dead. The dead possess the treasure."

Foulata shivered. "The place of the dead is forbidden to our people."

"You are right to be afraid." Betty remembered the tragedy that befell Foulata in the novel. "If you want to stay here, I'll stay with you."

194

Foulata frowned. "No, I worry for my man. I will not leave him. If he goes to the place of the dead, I will go too."

"Then we will go there together and look out for each other," said Betty.

Ignosi placed a hand on Khumalo's shoulder. "Brother, you will go in my stead. It is not fitting that the king should travel to the Place of the Dead."

"I will not allow dishonor to fall upon the hallowed place," Khumalo promised.

"This way, this way," screeched Gogool scrambling up the mountain ridge. "Hurry. Nice, precious diamonds await you."

No one appreciated Gogool's strident voice or her impatient manner, but all wished to find the treasure as soon as possible. They gathered their gear and followed.

CHAPTER 27
THE DIAMOND SCALE

All lights were off in the bookshop, and it was locked up for the night. There was a rattle of the lock breaking. The front door pushed open. A hulking shadow crouched into the shop, its wolf ears pricked up and forward. The bell on the door jangled, but one swipe of the claws and the bell was ripped from the door and clattered into silence on the floor.

The werewolf crept into a side corridor. The wooden panels in the floor groaned and he panted in regular, heavy surges. His eyes could detect in the darkness, outlined with yellow and blue lines, a settee in front of rows of bookshelves. His ears flicked at the unnerving hum radiating from behind the books. With a leap forward, he thrust down books in a chaotic cascade of paper and covers.

The light of an electric torch snapped on and encircled him like a spotlight. He turned, his eyes narrowed in the glare.

Sherlock Holmes slowly sat up from where he had been reclining on the settee, keeping the torch aimed at the werewolf, his free hand reaching for his pocket. He peered at the intruder. "Oh, it's you." He lifted his chin with interest then tilted his head. "I had hoped you had turned *against* Tepov."

Without warning, Edmond cringed and clutched at his head. "Kill it! Before it kills me!" He collapsed to his knees. He groaned and dug his claws over his ears, his face, his chest. His claws left long, red horizontal cuts across his chest. He roared in agony.

In disgust, Holmes watched Edmond gnaw at the fur of his arm as if tearing into his own flesh would end the agony. The werewolf opened his jaws, and a guttering sound rattled in his throat, and the shadow oozed out of his heart like black oil weaving upward and clinging to the wall, a grotesque silhouette of a wolf, expanding upward, filling the wall, and overlapping onto the ceiling. The shadow howled in a hollow, far away voice, like a nearly forgotten dream, and dispersed into smoke.

Edmond crumpled forward in his human form, dressed in tatters. Pale and clammy, he raised his eyes to the man who towered over him. "Mr. Holmes. Help me."

Holmes lowered the torch. "I can only help if you want to be helped."

Edmond's shoulders sagged as he used what little strength remained to push himself up. "I'm all in." With his wrist, he wiped the dirt and saliva from his chin. "I've been on the run all day, all night. Tepov's huntsmen have been on my heels, their howls in my ears. I've been hiding in gutters, ducking down alleys, scrambling across fields. I turned against Tepov, and he hates me for it."

Holmes knitted his brows. "So you came *here*? Leading them *here*!"

"No. I made sure they weren't following. I knew Tepov was looking for Betty, and I needed to see if she was safe."

"Hm," said Holmes. "So you break in here like a thief and pillage the bookshop." He ended the statement with a scornful lift of one eyebrow.

Edmond managed to sit up. He ran a hand through his shaggy black hair and looked down at his hands, crusted in mud. "You're right. I was looking for the scales. I thought if I found one of them, I could use that to bargain with Tepov. If I could convince him I could be of use to him again, I could be an agent for the Intercessors. I could learn the Accusers' plans and give them false leads, keep them away from Betty."

There was a click, and by the wavering light of the torch, Edmond saw Holmes was releasing the hammer on the gun he held. Edmond breathed more freely.

"Off the floor," Holmes ordered him, but more gently.

Edmond held onto the tea table as he pulled himself to his feet and collapsed backward onto the chair. Holmes noted that Edmond was shivering. He slipped off his own jacket and threw it at Edmond. "Put that over your shoulders, Mr. Davidson."

Edmond pulled the jacket about himself. Holmes, keeping a wary eye on the young man, pocketed his gun, returned to the settee, and crossed one leg over the other. He opened a cigarette case. "Do you smoke?"

Edmond accepted the cigarette, and Holmes lit it for him. Edmond closed his eyes and breathed in the tobacco to soothe his nerves. Holmes lit himself a cigarette and hung the arm of the hand that held it over the back of the settee. The two smoked, Holmes watching Edmond, Edmond avoiding the detective's scrutiny.

At last, Holmes spoke. "Do you love Betty?"

Edmond blinked in surprise. His mind grappled for the right answer. "She's my cousin." He ended his sentence by glancing at Holmes.

"That's not what I asked. Do you *love* her?"

Edmond lowered his eyes again. "My father told me it was my job to look out for her, see that no harm came to her. I tried my best to do that. And when we both went to Perlgate, I continued to look out for her." He allowed himself a reminiscent smile. "She used to bring me lunch in the stable. She would sit on a barrel and tell me about the books she was reading." He scratched the side of his nose. "Some of those stories were about *you*. But then," Edmond's smile faded, "I was a fool, a great, blasted fool. I never loved Daphne, but her father had title, position, wealth, and I thought that was what I needed, to prove to the world that I was *someone*. Now it's all so meaningless."

"But you still have Betty."

"No, she doesn't love *me*. She *couldn't* love me." Edmond leaned forward with his elbows hung on his legs.

"Don't be an idiot." Holmes touched his own head where it ached. "I've seen her put her own life in mortal danger for *you*. Girls like Betty do not do this for people they dislike."

"I read one of the letters Betty wrote to you."

"Mr. Davidson! Do you make it a habit to read the private correspondence of young ladies?" He tsked Edmond soundly.

"She had thrown it away, and I was curious."

Holmes shook his head. "Shameful."

"My point is *you* are the one Betty loves. When I saw you with her, back at the cottage, I was happy for her. Betty . . . has always wanted stability. *You* are the one who could give her that."

Holmes raised his eyebrows with amusement. "Stability? I would hardly call *my* line of work a stable one. By the same token, a werewolf is not known for being the most stable of creatures either. No, my dear Davidson, neither of us are suitable for fulfilling that particular role for Betty. But we *must* do what we can to assist her."

"Then, I will ask you for one of the scales."

"You'll need to kill me first."

"I must have it if I'm to rejoin Tepov and work from the inside."

"Tepov will never buy it. He is not a forgiving man. Once you cross him, your life is forfeit. The only way you will return to Vlad Tepov is as his prisoner. If he captures you, he will continue to use you as bait to lure Betty back to his lair."

"Then," decided Edmond, "let him take me. Let him think I am the bait, but I will really be the hook to catch The Accusers and thwart them every chance I can."

"And Betty? She would tell you to stay, to lend your powers to the Intercessors."

"You must tell Betty to forget about me. I'm going back, and, frankly, I don't expect to come out of it alive. It's the only way."

Holmes's eyes softened in sympathy for the young man. "Perhaps. I pray God, for Betty's sake, there *is* another way."

Leslie rubbed his hands together greedily. *A diamond mine, eh? Well, Edmond high-and-mighty Davidson, I guess this is one excavation you'll miss out on. Imagine the headlines. Leslie Mallowan, discoverer of the Lost Treasure City.* Chin high, he followed the expedition, led by Gogool, up the narrow mountain path, a sheer drop on one side and a rugged, bramble-strewn rock wall on the other.

The incline was steep with unexpected twists. The travelers kept close to the wall and clutched hold of the roots and tree branches jutting out from the rock. The red glow of dusk was settling. Gogool pushed into a tangle of vines hanging over the way ahead and vanished. Good followed her, pushing past the curtain of vines. Suddenly, he plunged off the ledge with a startled cry, for the vines had veiled a sharp precipice. Foulata gasped, but Quatermain caught Good by the belt and pulled him back to a firm footing. Quatermain shook his head and tossed a stone into the chasm to gauge its depth. A hollow cackle erupted, and Gogool called out, "Did poor white gentlemen have a fall?"

"That sounds like the echo of a cave," noted Betty. Khumalo searched the rock wall beside them. He unsheathed his knife and cut away the bramble. After close examination, he found a narrow opening hidden by an overlapping level of rock. He entered first, and Quatermain lit a lantern and followed.

Foulata froze before the entrance, her hands on either side of her anxious face. "I should wait here. It is the Place of the Dead."

"Nonsense, my dear. That's just superstition." Captain Good took her hand. She looked into his reassuring eyes and allowed him to guide her in.

Leslie glanced back at Betty, who was also hesitating. "Coming? We're almost to the diamonds, I can sense it."

Betty shook her head. "This is the part of the story where Gogool kills Foulata and traps everyone in the treasure room without food, water, or air."

Leslie stayed his foot. "Should I call them back?"

Betty closed her eyes, seeking a voice within to guide her. "No, if the diamond scale is in there, we must get it before the Accusers do. But," she fixed her eyes on her

cousin, "look out for Foulata. Do not let her go near Gogool."

Leslie swallowed hard and nodded. "I'll stay by her. I won't let anything happen to her," he vowed. He helped Betty over the vines and into the cave.

In the dark passageway, they were assailed by a torrent of flapping wings. Leslie raised his hands to guard himself from the onslaught. The winged creatures fluttered all along the passage, making high-pitched pinging calls. Quatermain lifted his lantern to reveal the passageway filled with bats. A flock struck past the group to join several more hanging from stalactites overhead.

"Hope that's not Tepov," shuddered Leslie as he inched past a bat sleeping in the blanket of its leathery wings. Betty followed Leslie past the bats, eying them with suspicion.

"It's lighter down this way," announced Captain Good, a few feet ahead of them. They caught up with Good, and Leslie positioned himself next to Foulata. Before them was an enormous marble archway. Quatermain put out his lantern, for a bright light emanated from the archway.

Khumalo passed onto a platform at the top of a long, broad marble stairway surrounding a sunken cathedral built within the cave. Betty joined him on the platform and gazed in awe around them, for she had never seen anything so majestic, not even in Neverland. Light as from a heavenly source streamed down from the lofty opening far above, lighting a natural temple large enough to accommodate many dragons. The temple was guarded by giant white pillars carved out of magnificent stone. The stillness was broken by the steady plink and plunk of water dropping from the stalactites above, nature carrying on her duty, carving out more rock for even larger, grander pillars of the future.

"Come. Come," called Gogool from a ledge. She tossed down a ladder of vines. Quatermain made sure the vines were sturdy and helped the others up.

"In here, in here," called Gogool. A door painted with Egyptian hieroglyphics slid up and revealed a dark niche. "The Place of Death. The Place of Death," cackled Gogool. They followed her inside.

As if by magic, the torches lining the walls lit in succession and cast flickering light, which revealed a giant headless skeleton, spear in one bony hand, seated on a throne of human bones. Its skull was clutched in its bony fingers and held upon its knee. The hollow sockets of the skull leered at the intruders.

"Twala," said Khumalo. "Just as the writings described."

Gogool tossed the skeleton king off its resting place.

Foulata gasped at the irreverence. Khumalo frowned in solidarity with her sentiment. "Twala may have been an evil king, but he was still one of our people," he admonished.

"Twala is dead as all men must die." The ancient one dug past the bones to disclose several chests. With a cackle, she threw open the chests to reveal more treasure than any of them had ever imagined, gold, ivory, and diamonds.

It was to the diamonds Khumalo made his way. "Help me look for the scale. It should be one to two feet long." Quatermain and Captain Good set about helping him dig through the mound of diamonds.

Betty was watching Foulata, who was glaring at Gogool.

"Hold Foulata here," said Betty to Leslie. He nodded, eying Gogool, and placed a hand on Foulata's shoulder to keep her close.

Gogool's blood-red eyes were alight with evil anticipation. "Bathe in it. Dance in it," she sang, leaning her bent and scrawny frame upon her gnarly staff.

"Here it is," called out Good, holding up the scale to Foulata. "That should make a nice bauble for you to wear at our wedding."

Foulata held it in the torchlight, and it sparkled with white iridescence.

"That is no bauble," Khumalo reminded him. "It is the scale of an ancient dragon. And that is the only thing I wish to take from this grim place."

"So beautiful," said Foulata. "Yet it has the coldness of death."

"Yes, yes." Gogool uncovered the tip of her walking stick to reveal a spear's head and flung the spear full force at Foulata. It caught the girl's chest. Foulata crumpled backward to the ground. "My God!" cried Good in despair. He fell to his knees beside the maiden.

The wrinkles and bones of the ancient one were replaced by the crimson wings and claws of Avian. Avian grinned and screeched, and, in a second, had clutched the diamond scale out of the dying Foulata's hands. Quatermain shouldered his rifle and fired at Avian, but the dragon cawed, cackled, and flapped out of the chamber. Quatermain cursed at missing the shot.

Khumalo chased after Avian, dark rage burning in his eyes, but the door slid shut after the dragon, trapping them in the chamber of death.

"Foulata, oh, Foulata," sobbed Good, holding her in his arms. "My dearest one." He fumbled for the medical kit he carried, but when he opened it, he saw the box was filled with empty bottles. He threw the worthless box at the mound of diamonds as tears streamed from his eyes.

Leslie's hands trembled as he looked helplessly to Betty. "I tried to watch her, I tried."

Betty was heartbroken. She reproached herself, for she had read the book, knew of the treachery, but had failed to prevent this tragedy.

Khumalo scraped at the door in vexation, and, leaning his back against it, slid down to the ground. "How? How did we not stop this thing? Now we are trapped, just as in the book. Foulata is dying, and so are we."

"Daniel. . ." said Betty, her lips pursed and her eyes darting in thought. She picked up one of the empty bottles that had rolled down the mound of diamonds. "The bottle the mermaid gave you. Do you still have it?"

"Yes." Khumalo unsnapped the leather pouch on his belt and retrieved the bottle.

"Do you know what it does?" asked Betty.

"I know what it *says* to do. It says to drink it," said Khumalo. Betty nodded and gestured to Foulata. Khumalo knelt by Foulata, who was drifting into death, put the bottle to her lips, and poured several drops into her mouth, but the light of life faded from her face.

In another minute, however, she sputtered, coughed, and opened her eyes. She inhaled deep and long. "Foulata!" cried Good in amazement.

Determination and strength permeated her body. With one powerful effort she yanked the spear out of her heart, and the flesh healed over. She rose, glowing like burnished gold, her arms and legs pulsating with increasing muscle and tightening sinew. She snapped the spear in half and tossed the two pieces aside. And she began to grow . . . and grow.

She grew over one hundred feet tall. She lifted her hands, and, with great strength, she pushed up the roof of the cave, creating an opening in the top of the mountain. Fresh air and sunshine flooded in. The dumbfounded expedition members breathed in the welcome air and shielded their eyes from the downpour of light.

Avian soared in triumph overhead, the scale in her mouth. Foulata reached for the dragon, like a child catching at a moth. She caught it, but the dragon squeezed out from between her fingers. Her eyebrows lowered upon the pesky creature. She grasped for it again and caught it between her index finger and thumb. It squirmed and screeched as she held it up for examination. The scale dropped from Avian's mouth and Foulata caught it in her free hand. "Don't kill me! Don't kill me!" begged Avian, staring with wide ruby eyes at her own reflection in the shining black mirror of Foulata's eye.

"I will not kill you, ancient one," Foulata told the pathetic creature. "Go back to your master. Tell him the people of Kukuana will not be beaten, chained, or trampled underfoot." She flicked the dragon away like a discarded piece of fuzz. Avian sped off, flapping her wings fast towards the setting sun.

Once Foulata was certain the dragon was gone, she reached down. "My darling, Captain Good," she called into the mountain below with the resounding voice of a goddess. "Step onto my hand." Good stared up at the giant hand of Foulata. "Yes, of course, my dear," he stammered. He stepped onto her hand, and she lifted him up. As he rose, his eyes widened and his monocle popped out of his eye, and he could not suppress a long cry for help.

Foulata gently set him down on a safe place at the foot of the mountain. She did the same for the others. Next, she pulled herself out of the mountaintop and stood with one foot on either side of the valley, like a Colossus guarding the expanse of a city.

"Well done!" said Khumalo. "What of the dragon?"

"Flown away. But I have the scale."

All the members of the expedition cheered for Foulata.

"Now that you're a goddess," said Good, "I hope you'll remember me, tiny and undeserving though I am."

Foulata gazed down at Good with beams of love. "My darling, perhaps you can drink from the bottle too?"

"Don't you dare," Quatermain said. "You're insufferable enough as it is. Just imagine you tripping around and accidentally stomping on us like ants. And 'Sorry, ol' chaps' won't quite do it in *that* instance."

However, the potion was short lived, and Foulata shrank back to her normal size.

"I'm glad to have you back, my dear," said Good. "You were lovely as a goddess, but I also want you to fit in my arms." She threw her arms around his neck and kissed him. Even Quatermain, who had his own Victorian views on such things, smiled in approval.

"I don't know," said Khumalo. "I like Foulata the Goddess. She would make a good ally in battle. And I think," he added to the Kukuana maiden, "that this bottle belongs to you. You will know when and how to use it."

Foulata took it, promising to use it only as needed by others. "And this belongs to you." She handed the diamond scale to Betty with reverence. "I trust no one else with the keeping of this relic."

Ignosi approached the expedition, followed by a patrol of his most trusted warriors. In their custody was a small man, tied and gagged. It was Jeremy Spinderbeck.

CHAPTER 28
THE BARGAIN

Ignosi's warriors had been patrolling the area when they had spied Spinderbeck splashing and sputtering across a lake up to the shore. Before he could set foot on the bank, the warriors had surrounded him to question him. Spinderbeck had drawn his sword, spitting lake water and screaming a stream of wild gibberish, which left them no choice but to apprehend him. Khumalo reassured Ignosi that Spinderbeck was one of them and meant no harm. Although Ignosi had his doubts, he relented with a gracious wave of his arm and ordered his warriors to release the prisoner.

Spinderbeck collapsed upon a large rock and wiped a handkerchief over his bald head.

"My friend," said Khumalo. "I thought you were in Iceland."

"Well, like Miss Talbin suggested I took up my sword and read the passage from *Journey to the Center of the Earth*," began Spinderbeck, wringing his nervous hands. "But it didn't bring me to Iceland at all. No, indeed. Instead, I found myself in France with none other than . . . you'll never guess . . . Jules Verne. An interesting gentleman, Jules. An Intercessor too, it turns out. He has traveled in and out of different portals so many times, it's no wonder his novels are so prophetic.

"Well, Mr. Verne gave me a copy of his book, *Carpathian Castle*, which he said holds great significance for us. I said I needed to find out what the vampire was up to in Iceland. Verne knew just the passage to read. Thank goodness, the passage did not lead us to the Carpathian Castle. Dear me, if I had ended up there with Ordog and his hordes of vampires and werewolves, I would have been at my wits' end! Thankfully, it led us to Iceland, which is where we were trying to get to in the first place.

"Jules said he always enjoyed visiting Iceland, and we toyed with the idea of testing his theory of the volcano leading to the center of the Earth, but we decided that could wait. Instead, we were distracted by a tall gentleman in a top hat and fur coat. The sleigh he rode up in was driven by someone who looked suspiciously like a werewolf.

"Of course, Jules and I are intelligent men, so we knew right away this was no *ordinary* gentleman. 'This must be Vlad Tepov,' I said to Jules. And Jules said, "I think you're right, Jeremy!' Once Tepov alighted from the sleigh, we followed him, cloak and dagger style. We were *very* sneaky! From building to building we crept, keeping always out of sight. We followed him to an old bookshop that looked as pretty as plum pudding. I remember thinking how at home Hamberdeen would feel there. Unfortunately, the windows were frosted over. It was quite impossible to see inside.

"Jules said he did not think Tepov knew him by sight, so he slipped inside pretending to be a customer, singing an old Icelandic song, just to throw them off the track. Later Tepov came out with a book under his arm. I kept my hand on the hilt of my sword, but, thankfully, I did not need it. Tepov was in such a hurry, he never noticed Jeremy Spinderbeck blending in with the window display. He shouted something to his driver, who snapped the whip, and the sleigh barreled away down the street.

"Jules came out soon after and told me he had heard Tepov asking the bookshop owner for a copy of *Makt Myrkranna* or *Power of Darkness*, a rare Icelandic translation of Bram Stoker's

Dracula. Jules thought this rare translation a key to regaining the lost dragon scales and preventing a most horrible deed.

"So, back we went into the shop, and Jules asked the owner if he had another copy. The owner at first said 'no' and was being most uncooperative, but Jules Verne recited all the scientific names of the flora and fauna native to Iceland, in several varieties, which ones made excellent dishes and which ones had medicinal value, at which point the bookshop owner begged Jules for pity's sake to stop and made a full confession. He had one more copy of the book, he said. It had been a gift from the translator, Valdimar Ásmundsson himself.

"He would not let us take the book, but he did let us examine it. I was wishing I had brought a camera with me, and Jules was for copying the most prominent passages with pencil when a slip of paper, a note in the translator's own handwriting, fell out of the jacket of the book.

"I've been an Intercessor long enough to know slips of paper can be important. I showed Jules the note, and he laughed in a *'c'est ça!'* way. He said it was not the book Tepov needed at all, but that very slip of paper. The note described some variations the translator found in Stoker's original drafts of *Dracula* and went into detail about a dark ritual that was something the final English version of the book left out because it was much too dark and sinister. The ritual, Verne said, is the thing the Accusers needed. Well, Tepov figured it out too. He came whipping his sleigh back to the bookshop. He crashed the sleigh into the side of the building and leapt out, cursing. He stormed into the bookshop, but the shop owner knew nothing of the note. We needed to get out of there quickly, so we focused on a book in the shop window. It was a book about 'Far Away Africa,' and so here we are. And I wonder where Jules has gotten to!"

Quatermain was all for forming a search party, and Ignosi was questioning his warriors, when a distinguished, older bearded Frenchman limped up from behind the foot of the mountain, carrying a plant with pink and white flowers in one hand, and reading from a guidebook he held before him in the other. He glowed as he announced, "Cinchona! From the family Rubiaceae. The bark of the plant is commonly referred to as Jesuit's bark, and it is the key ingredient in Quinine, and was first recorded as a cure for Malaria in 1663. Few people realize the plant also makes an excellent werewolf repellent."

Spinderbeck guided Verne to the rest of the expedition. "Fellow Intercessors, may I introduce Mr. Jules Verne!"

Betty was tongue-tied, not sure if she should ask for Verne's autograph, or if that would be awkward, since no one in her world would believe she actually met the famous author from the 1800s. Verne stopped when he saw Betty, and his face lit up with recognition. "Is this the famous Beatrice Talbin?"

Betty was stunned. She glanced over her shoulder expecting some other famous person to be standing behind her.

Verne handed his plant and book to Spinderbeck and gave Betty's hand an enthusiastic clasp. "Mademoiselle!" he beamed. "It is an honor and a privilege!"

"I don't understand," said Betty. "How do you know me?"

"C'est simple! We are both Intercessors, are we not? Perhaps in your world you have not yet inspired me with the loyalty of Aouda in *Le tour du monde en quatre-vingts jours*, or the kindness and courage of Nadia in *Michael Strogoff*. Past and present and future all become one when you portal here and portal there, but, believe me, in my world, you have become an important part of many of the novels I have written."

What could Betty say to that? Grateful tears were welling up in her eyes when Spinderbeck cleared his throat, reminding her of the urgency of their current mission.

"Mr. Verne?" asked Betty. "Do you still have that note?"

"Mais oui!" Verne took the note from his pocket and handed it to Betty. "Be careful with that. Evil men are seeking it! I would have destroyed it at once. Unfortunately, the note and the scales are parts of the infinite cosmos, and only the Golden Dragon can destroy them."

"Then we must go to the Golden Dragon," said Betty.

"That . . . I cannot help with, I'm afraid," said Verne. "No human contrivance can take you to the Golden Dragon. He must send for you himself."

Spinderbeck rubbed the back of his neck. "And no one has ever seen the Golden Dragon, not as far as we know."

"Not as far as we *know*," agreed Betty. "But what *do* we know? Daniel, remember the hole in the handkerchief? If we have the remains of the handkerchief, we can reconstruct what is missing."

Khumalo glowed, proud of her insight. "Excellent! So let us begin with what we do know and fill in the missing pieces."

Leslie withdrew the code book from his rucksack. "Would this help?"

"The ancient code book!" declared Verne in amazement. "Turn to the chapter on 'Summoning'."

Betty opened the book and scanned the table of contents. The chapter on Summoning started on page 333 and was broken down in sections, a section on summoning fellow Intercessors and a section on being summoned by Vorever. She flipped to the latter section.

Betty peered closely at a gold edged ink drawing of a dragon wrapped around the illuminated first letter of the chapter. "Vorever?"

"Some say," said Khumalo, "the Golden Dragon goes by the name Vorever."

"Look." Spinderbeck peered at the page over her shoulder. "The marginalia on that section."

"It's a note left by . . ." Khumalo angled the book and examined the Kanji characters in the margin. ". . . the three-pronged character pointing upward followed by a square with a cross inside it. Those are the characters for mountain and field. Yamada."

"And he sketched an arrow pointing to this part of the text," noted Betty. "It says, 'The lost must be found. The found will be lost. In the place of your greatest fear, the Golden Dragon will be near.'"

"So," asked Spinderbeck, "do we have the mathematical formula to work it out?"

"Let's follow Leslie's assumption that it is saying exactly what it means," said Betty.

Leslie stood a bit taller at the recognition, then reviewed the passage, puzzled. "But what *does* it mean?"

"First of all," replied Betty, "what has been lost?"

"We are trying to find the scales that were lost," offered Spinderbeck.

"Exactly. And what is the place of our greatest fear?"

Spinderbeck shivered. "Wherever that vampire and his dragon lord are lurking."

"Then that is where we need to go." Betty faced Jules Verne. "What passage in your novel will take us to the Carpathian Mountains?"

Verne opened the book to a passage marked with pencil. "*This old castle occupied on an isolated shoulder of the Vulkan range . . . In the bright light the castle stood out with the clearness displayed in stereoscopic views.*"

"Our greatest advantage," Betty said, "is that Ordog does not know how many of us there actually are. He thinks it would be easy to lure us into his trap."

"Hmph," said Quatermain, adjusting his rifle over his shoulder. "Many a time I have seen a wounded lion caught in a trap, only to spring out and maul its captors to death."

"And we will do the same," replied Betty. "Daniel, stay here with our new friends. We'll summon you when our trap is set."

"We will be ready," he assured her.

Foulata pushed past the others to stand by Betty. "No. I will not wait here. We said we would be friends. My man and I will go with you."

Betty's eyes moistened. "Thank you, Foulata. I admit, I will be glad to have you both at my side where we are going."

Smoke coiled up from Ordog's nostrils. He drummed his claws upon the floor, and the hammering echoed throughout the lower levels of the lodge. "Soon, soon," he reminded himself.

A gong clattered, and werewolves worked the wooden windlass to wind up the rope that drew open the immense portcullis-style door to the throne room. A huntsmen entered. He dropped on his knees before Ordog. "Great one."

"Speak, worm." Ordog did not deign to lower his eyes to the huntsman, whom he could easily crush in his claws.

"Your slave Count Vlad Tepov is here to report."

"Tepov . . . Tepov . . ." Ordog examined the orange fur between his claws, searching deep into his memory for a recollection of yet another insignificant being. "Oh, yes, Tepov. Yes, he feeds me many souls. Let him enter." He rested his chin upon his folded talons, yawned, and smacked his lips drowsily.

Tepov entered, dressed in his spotless country tweeds and knee-length riding boots, a horsewhip folded in his hand. He strode across the hall, his shoulders back, his chin high. He halted before the throne, bowed on one knee, face down. "My lord, I bring good news."

"The remaining scales?" Ordog brought a monstrous eye to a level with the tiny vampire.

"The weak Intercessor betrayed us. Gregor Macmillan. He was useful for a time, but in the end he failed. He allowed three of the scales to fall into the hands of our enemy. I brought you his soul as a gift."

"Send it to the pit for now," commanded Ordog with a flick of his tail. "I will begin digesting it when I am ready."

"It has been done, my lord."

"Now." Ordog blew a stream of smoke, which spiraled around Tepov, who covered his mouth to stifle a cough. "What about the scales?"

"I will soon retrieve the scales and the ritual. I have set a trap. And I have the bait." He raised his riding whip in a grand ringmaster gesture towards the doorway.

On cue, six huntsmen entered, struggling to restrain a seven-foot werewolf in fetters, shackles, and chains, a large metal restraint collar around his gray shaggy neck. The captive reared, and pulled, and roared, and it took all six of the huntsmen, each on their own length of chain, to control the beast.

"Edmond Davidson!" rumbled Ordog.

The huntsmen forced the captive down on his knees before the dragon lord. Edmond bared his teeth at his captors, his black nostrils flaring. Tepov snapped his whip across Edmond's chest. Edmond flinched and growled. "Your *precious* Davidson," said the count, "deserted me in the Grimpen Mire, but he was easy enough to find."

"He lies." Edmond pushed against the restraints. "He did not *find* me. I returned willingly. I would continue to serve you, mighty Ordog!"

Tepov darted an anxious glance up at Ordog.

Ordog contracted his flaming eyes at Edmond. "Fool! You have no will. Your soul is mine. Your will is mine. You returned because you had no choice."

Edmond raised his muzzle defiantly. "You once said you sought me out because you saw in me someone who would not be subjected. My will is my own. I challenged your slave Tepov on the moors because he imagined he could rival me as your henchman. I alone will have that honor."

Ordog stretched his lips into a sneer, impressed by Davidson's nerve.

"That isn't true," protested Tepov, clutching his whip. "He turned on me because he still loves that Beatrice woman."

Edmond snorted. "I have no soul. How can I love? I willingly gave my soul to only one, and that one is Ordog."

"Yes, we are alike in many ways, young Davidson. Your soul is most delicious." Ordog slid his tongue over his teeth. "It tastes of defiance and ambition."

"I delivered both the gold and the emerald scales to you. What has Tepov brought you?"

Edmond tossed Tepov a demeaning glance. "Tepov has promised much and has delivered nothing."

Ordog spread his talons towards the vampire.

"Not so, O great one." Tepov raised both hands in defense. Ordog stayed his grasp and listened, an ominous tilt to his head and furrow to his brow. "It was *I* who lured your precious Davidson here in the first place. Yes, your enemies have the scales, but I have a plan. Stake this pathetic wretch out in the garden by the well. Inflict him with tortures such as no mortal can bear. *She* will sense his pain. Her love for him is so strong, she will cross time and space to reach him and would gladly trade the scales for his life."

"Ordog is no fool, Tepov," said Edmond. "He has seen all. He knows Betty has no feelings for me. She loves the famous detective now. Torture me and she will pity me, yes, but her love for Sherlock Holmes will guide her, and he stands for the greater good. He will advise her to keep the scales at all costs."

"Yes, I have seen this," confirmed Ordog. "Tepov, you were there. You saw her admiration for this detective. Lure *him* here. Stake *him* out."

"The detective." A glimmer of a plan brightened Tepov's face. "Yes, she will do anything for *him*. I know what to do. Thank you, great one."

"Then go," said Ordog. "This is your last chance!"

Tepov bowed deeply and withdrew.

"Meanwhile . . ." Ordog turned his attention back to Edmond. He waved the huntsmen away, and with one stroke of a talon, cut Edmond loose from his chains. "What is *your* plan? How will *you* beat Tepov and prove your worth to me?"

Edmond rubbed his neck and wrists where the chains had gripped him. "Tepov is driven by his moods. He thinks Betty will come because she wants to save the man she loves. But the Intercessors are not fools. They have three of the scales, and they have the ritual. If they had the gold and emerald scales, they would have an army strong enough to challenge even one so mighty as yourself."

"That must not happen. *I* must be the one with the army. How will you get the scales back from them?"

"I will visit them as the repentant friend. I will pretend to tell them news that will help them in their fight against you. They are weak and forgiving. They will receive me as a long lost brother and will reveal to me where they keep the scales. While pretending to help guard the scales, I will steal them in the night and bring them back to you."

Ordog frowned, scratched his chin, then nodded once. "Yes. It could work. Go, Davidson. But remember." He leveled his brow with Edmond's face. "I will be watching!"

CHAPTER 29
THE LAST HOPE

From the throne room, Edmond scoured the underground corridors. Ordog had given Tepov charge to hide the gold and emerald scales somewhere in the lodge. Edmond's sharp ears stiffened as they caught the distant high-pitched hum radiating from the scales. His instincts homed in on the soundwaves, following them up the stairs that led to the front hall. Strings of moonlight, like the rays of a spider's web, splayed down from the cathedral windows above. Edmond blinked into the moonlight and let its energy infuse his wolven senses.

The brazier in the front hall was ablaze. He circled it, staring into the flames, his eyes wincing in regret as he recalled Betty's warning the first day he had arrived. He reached for the memory that quivered in the flames. The fire burnt his paw, and he flinched. His mouth firmed. He inclined his head to one side and concentrated all his acute senses on the humming of the scales.

The housekeeper, Ilda, emerged from the darkness into the lambent glare of the fire. Her mouth was set in a deep-carved grimace that weighed down her wrinkled, leathery visage. Her eyes locked with Edmond's, and she jerked her head towards the hallway behind her, signaling for him to follow. She pivoted and lumbered back down the hall.

Edmond stalked after her, one ear up, the other tentatively down. Ilda pushed open the door to the kitchen, where the moonlight filtered in through frosted windows. Edmond flattened his ears and squinted suspiciously as Ilda clutched up a chopping cleaver. His fur raised on his neck, and he snarled. She laughed and used the cleaver to clang the copper pots hung on pegs from the ceiling.

"Look!" She used the cleaver to direct his attention to one large pot. Edmond took a cautious step forward and peered at his bleary reflection in its copper base. His long snout cringed, and he drew back his lip from over his incisors in disgust.

"The charming Professor Davidson," chided Ilda. "The *handsome* Professor Davidson. *That* is what he has made you!" She hovered up behind him and scowled at her own reflection. "And *this* is what he has made me!" She used the flat of the cleaver to trace the wrinkles in her face and ended by dragging it through the split ends of her dry, grizzled hair. "Your Beatrice is beautiful. Young. Ilda was too. A young, happy maiden in the village. Then I met *Count Vlad Tepov.*" She spat the name in repugnance.

She reeled about to face Edmond, her eyes wide as she brandished the cleaver for emphasis. "But we can have our revenge. You must do everything Ilda says."

Edmond turned a rebuffing shoulder towards her.

"Ahh! You don't trust Ilda. But I know where the two dragon scales are. I know how you can save your beautiful Beatrice."

He looked back over his shoulder and breathed in through his nostrils. He smelled no deceit upon her, so, reluctantly, he lowered his chin in a nod.

A satisfied smirk twitched at the corner of her mouth. "Go to the garden. To the place where the lady weeps. There you will find what you seek."

Edmond headed out into the garden. He followed the familiar path, this time through a flurry of crackling, dead leaves and across patches of wilted grass and puddles of mud reflecting the dying moonlight. By the time he reached the wishing well, the birthing orange light of dawn awoke on the horizon. A voice was singing, echoing up from the depths of the well. The singing soothed and stung his heart. He recognized the voice as Betty's, and the realization weighed him down to his knees at the base of the well. He brushed away the leaves that had buried the place where Betty once had sat in her mauve cloak and black boots warning him of the fate that awaited him.

Up from the well echoed her words, "I wish for you to find what your heart seeks, a light amid the darkness, a harbor amidst the storm, and a safe way home again."

He buried his muzzle in his arm. "I wish I had listened to you." He opened his eyes and saw his own reflection in the waters at the bottom of the well. It was no longer the werewolf, but his human self, ashen, gaunt, and drawn, wearing his torn shirt and ragged trousers. He pushed the straggling strands back from his forehead and shivered from the chill. Beyond the reflection, something glittered green and gold beneath the murky waters. He used the pulley rope attached to the bucket to position the bucket under the glittering object and pulled it up from the well. It was a leather satchel bedraggled with briars and dead ivy, but the opened flap revealed both the golden and the emerald scales.

Ilda loomed over his kneeling form. "There. The scales. But they won't do you any good on their own. You promised Ordog you'd bring him all five scales."

"How did you find these?"

"No one notices Ilda. But I notice. Yes, I notice many things," she said. "I saw where Tepov hid the scales. I took them, kept them here. The one place Tepov fears to come." She patted the well with satisfaction and heaved herself down to sit upon the base. "But it's all five scales that Ordog demands, and it's all five scales you will give him."

Edmond jolted to his feet in burning defiance.

"You would never do such a thing, eh? Ah, but Ilda has a spell that creates synthetic scales that only the light of the full moon can expose. Even Ordog will think they are the true scales. These I will give you."

Edmond regained his composure and contemplated the scheme. "And from me? What do you want?"

"Sit down." Ilda pushed the dry leaves away from the base next to her.

Edmond hesitated but complied. Ilda grabbed Edmond by both sides of his face and her bloodshot eyes searched his. "You love the woman? You would do anything, give anything, to make things right for her?"

"Of course." Edmond pulled himself out of Ilda's grasp.

"Then you can help me. You and me, dead things. But one thing keeps us, day by day, night by night. Hate. Hate of Ordog. Hate of Tepov. That is the sap that feeds our veins." She drew a dagger from her pocket. "Many nights I dreamed of death. But the thought of grinding him to dust, *that* kept me alive."

The knife gleamed like silver ice. It smelled of blood, and of something lethal. "The blade is pure silver," she said, "dipped in a mixture of dragon blood and the essence of wolfsbane." Edmond shuddered and turned away from it.

Ilda chuckled. "In my youth, I was fond of collecting herbs. My mother kept a book of spells. It has taken many years, but now I have almost all the special ingredients to destroy Count Tepov. But I need one thing from you."

His apprehensive eyes regarded the tip of the knife. "What is your price?"

"Hear my plan." She wrapped her saggy arm about his shoulders and, dagger in hand, she drew her plan in the air before him. "Your friends will come soon. Beatrice will feel your sorrow, and she'll come. When they do, go to them. Take them the two scales. Do not allow them to enter the lodge. Ordog will crush them if they do. Instead, they must make their way to the village inn. The inn is run by an old friend of mine and is protected by spells and potions. There they can use the ritual to raise up from the scales an army of dragons to destroy Ordog. But tell them to leave Tepov to me."

"Yes, that *should* work," Edmond agreed still eying the knife warily.

"And in return, one thing." She touched the point of her dagger under his chin. The scent of wolfsbane made his stomach churn. "The one ingredient I lack is the last breath of hope from a werewolf as he shifts for the last time, never to be human again."

"*Never* to be human?"

Her eyes glimmered. "You will not die. You are cursed to wander the undying realms as long as Ordog has your soul. But for *her*, for the hope of saving *her*, you will make this trade, eh?"

Repentant tears rolled down as Edmond contemplated the flesh of his empty hands outstretched before him. For a fleeting moment he thought of Betty, what might have been. Then he thought of Ordog and Tepov and the army of dragons they would raise up to crush everything he cared about.

"Take it," he relented.

Ilda plunged the dagger into his heart. He breathed out a long stream of hope. She caught it in a bottle which she quickly stopped with a cork. From the knife wound, the blood ran black down his chest, and the wrenching pain shifted him back to his werewolf form. He howled. Long. Mournful. Resigned.

Tepov fitted on his gloves at the threshold of the lodge. Ilda smoothed the collar of his coat. "Anything else, my master?"

"Yes." He brushed a speck of lint from his sleeve. "What did Davidson tell you?" His blond lashes flicked up, and he stared into her eyes.

Her expression did not alter from its usual sullen frown. "That girl is coming."

Tepov's eyebrow twitched upward. "I knew she wouldn't stay away for long."

"She brings friends. They head for the village inn."

"Dmitri," Tepov called. His lead huntsman stepped forward, ready for orders. "Summon the pack. When the Intercessors come, draw them to the village. Let them enter. Then, when I give the signal, attack."

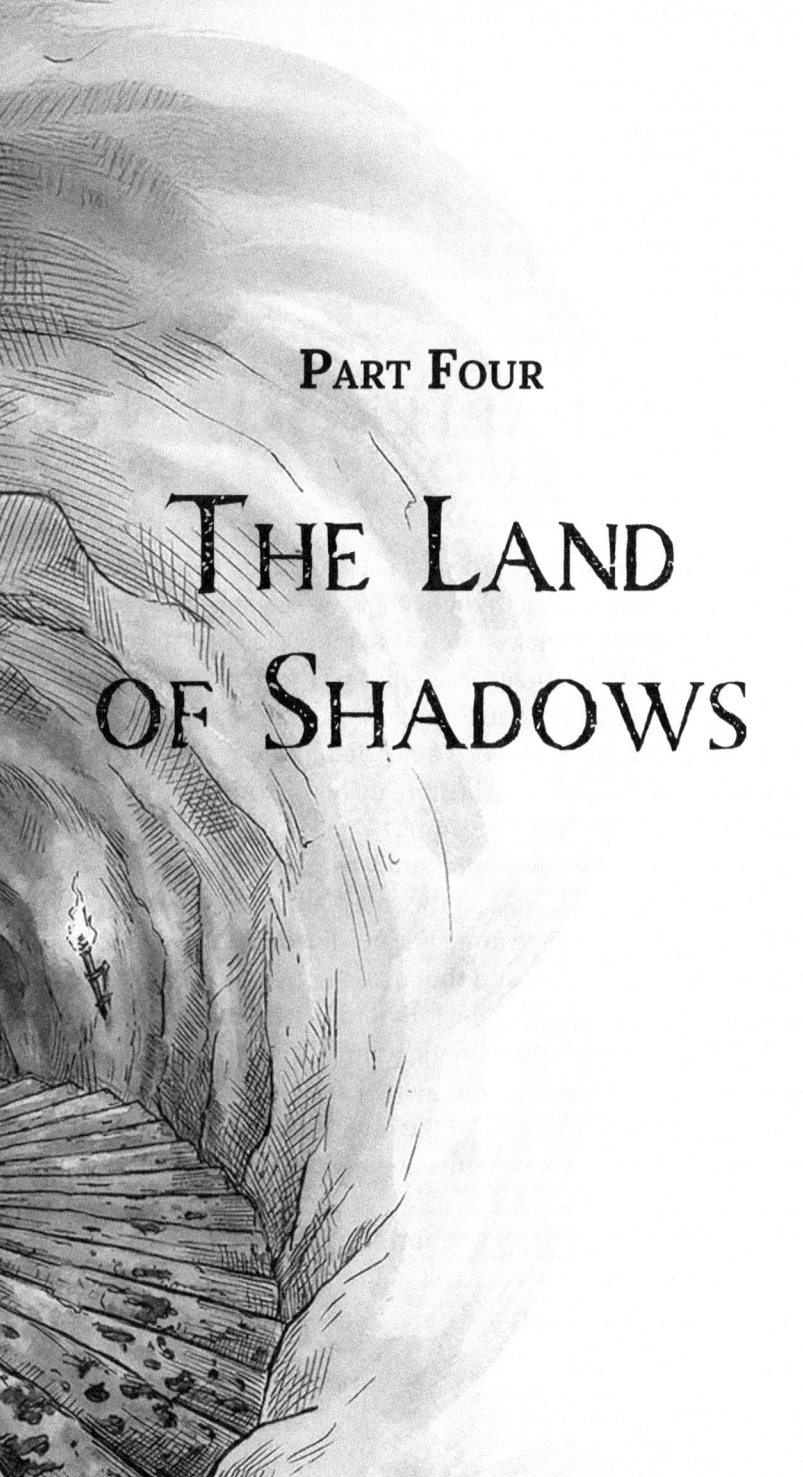

Part Four

The Land
of Shadows

CHAPTER 30
THE TRAP

A pink dusk was spreading across the pale sky above the Carpathian Mountains. A light snow was falling. The band of Intercessors found themselves on a ridge overlooking the village in the valley below. Since Verne had written his *Carpathian Castle* during the 1890s, the Intercessors arrived in Victorian-style clothes. Betty now wore a hooded mauve coat. Her feet were kept warm with black button-up boots, and her mittened hands were tucked into a fur muff.

Foulata, who had never seen snow before, reached out from under the warm cloak, and let the soft feathers of ice drift onto her fingertips. She smiled amid her fur-lined hood as the flakes lit on her long eyelashes and the tip of her nose. Captain Good, grateful to have long underwear under his woolen trousers and a pair of weather-resistant boots, wrapped his arm around the shoulders of his fiancée. As he wiped splats of snow from his monocle, he told her stories of the fun he used to have with his chums back in his boyhood home at Yuletide, sledding, snowball fights, and all.

Spinderbeck's teeth were chattering as he drew his scarf more closely about his neck and pulled the earflaps of his cap about his red-tinged ears.

"I apologize, mon ami," said Verne to Spinderbeck, "but I am afraid I cannot build a fire. The enemy would see the smoke. But I will concoct something that, even if it does not warm our stomachs, will at least provide some nutrition." Verne knelt in a clearing in the snow and rummaged through his rucksack. He took out a pot and mixed together cold rations, adding spices to lend it a more palatable taste. Betty hunched near Verne and observed his culinary efforts.

Verne glanced at her and shrugged. "Bien sur, it is not much. If it were July, we would find raspberries bursting from those branches over there. But I have added some mushrooms and a little of that cattail root for flavor. We hope it will not upset the digestion."

"You know so much about everything," said Betty. "I wish we had more time. I'd love to ask you about Captain Nemo, Michael Strogoff, and, of course, Passepartout."

"Passepartout, ahh! The acrobatic, foolhardy valet with a heart of gold. Well, in a way, you *have* met him. When I inserted that brave and resourceful Frenchman into *Le tour du monde en quatre-vingts jours* I really inserted myself. Captain Nemo is a fascinating character, oui, and Michael Strogoff is as good as he is strong and brave, but what you should be asking is why is that werewolf on that ridge behind you."

Startled, Betty turned to see what he was pointing at.

A large werewolf was crouched on the ledge, watching Betty as the snowflakes flecked his thick, gray fur. The werewolf blinked his doleful eyes.

Betty walked away from the others towards him.

"Betty."

Betty's heart caught in her throat. "Edmond!" She started up the side of the ledge. He reached down, and she grabbed hold of his arm with both of her hands as he lifted her to join him on the ridge. As she rose, her hood fell back. The white flakes of snow contrasted with her black braided hair. The glow of the setting sun created swirls of gold in her black eyes.

Landing on the ridge, she steadied herself against his shoulder.

"Tepov has ordered his huntsmen to occupy the village," Edmond told her. "It may look deserted now, but they are there, lying in wait for you. Once you are in the village, the gate will shut and you will be outnumbered. But there is a way to defeat them." He placed a paw on her back and guided her up the slope of the ridge to a vantage point that provided a good view of the village below, past, white-frosted branches of the evergreens.

"You see there?" He pointed. "That is the village inn. Built on a prominence. I have information that if your friends can make it to that inn, you can set up a command center from which you can see every move they are making. Once there, you must use the ritual."

Betty gasped and backed away from him. "Edmond. No. The ritual is evil."

"Ordog is too powerful for you and your friends. You saw him. He destroys life, he crushes souls. It would take an *army* of dragons to defeat him. Once you have all five scales, you will be powerful enough to destroy Ordog and all his forces."

"But the last two scales? How can we get them?"

From the satchel he wore across his shoulder, he withdrew the gold and the emerald scales to assure her of the contents. He replaced the scales and hung the strap of the satchel over her shoulder. She glanced into the satchel and knitted her eyebrows.

"I can never pay you back for all that you have done for me," he said. "I hope this makes everything . . . all right." A tear trickled down the side of his whiskered muzzle.

Betty reached up and caught the tear on her fingertip.

His eyes cringed. "Thank God, you have not abandoned me to my fate."

"I will never abandon you," she promised.

His lips tugged in a sad, reassuring smile, and he turned back towards the lodge.

"Stay." Betty clutched his wrist.

"I am bound to Ordog. As long as he has my soul, I will never be free. I must go back. I must do what I can."

"But Edmond . . ."

"I think Leslie is looking for you," he said, gazing past Betty.

Betty glanced over her shoulder to see Leslie below her talking with Verne. She turned back to tell Edmond that Leslie was fine, but he had vanished into the frosty woods.

From the ridge, Betty, Leslie, and Captain Good made a surveillance of the village in the valley below. The village was surrounded by a four-meter-high palisade-style fortification built of felled pine logs. The gate was tall and arched with two wooden panels locked firmly in the center.

Good used his binoculars to scan the village. "Ominous. Carts with no horses, shops with no shopkeepers, streets with no children. No lights in the windows, no smoke from the chimneys. Only one or two proverbial wooden signs rattling in the wind."

"Where did everybody go?" asked Leslie.

"It's not completely deserted," observed Betty.

"She's right. Look." Good handed the binoculars to Leslie and pointed.

Using the binoculars, Leslie spotted two surly werewolves lurking behind the side of a tavern. "Oh, yes. The doom squad. Right on schedule."

"That," Betty pointed towards the inn, "is our objective." The inn sprawled over a prominence behind the homes and the shops, with the slope of the mountain just beyond it. The first floor was built of rocks and mortar and the upper stories were made out of finely carved wood with at least eight wooden gables, brightly painted.

Good adjusted his rifle over his shoulder and made sure Betty and Foulata also had loaded rifles. He gave his old army revolver to Leslie. Spinderbeck waved away the gun offered to him, preferring his sword. Verne said he would rely on his wit and the skills of his friends for protection but that first everyone needed to try some of his delicious soup. The others took one sniff of the slop and politely refused. Verne sighed and shook his head, wondering if Passepartout ever felt like this.

The small band of Intercessors descended from the ridge and marched upon the village. As they passed through the front gate, Betty spied a werewolf stationed on each side, watching them. One of the werewolves spat on the snow and glowered at them but made no move to stop them.

In the village, a blacksmith was pounding an anvil in an open shelter. The blacksmith was a werewolf, forging a length of iron into a weapon of war. He paused, hammer held mid-way, and watched them with narrow, threatening eyes. Another werewolf was leaning against the tavern, using a dagger to whittle a piece of wood while his companion slogged down a tankard of beer. He chortled at the newcomers and muttered something to his comrade.

"We'll never get out of here alive." Leslie nervously handled the revolver, as he looked around.

"Eyes forward," said Good.

As the Intercessors converged upon the village center, the two panels of the gate scraped and squealed along the ground and slammed shut behind them. The werewolves closed in.

"Just 500 meters to the inn," said Good. "Briskly now."

Betty took a deep breath. Leslie cocked the hammer of his gun. They pressed forward.

The hair on the backs of the assembling werewolves spiked, their long sharp ears stiff, their teeth bared. Drums sounded, loud and steady. One werewolf leapt up on a thatched roof, waved a hatchet in the air and howled. He charged towards the Intercessors, and hundreds of werewolves yapped and barked as they fell in with the attack.

Spinderbeck whipped out his sword. Leslie fired into their midst, and a werewolf cried out. "Well done!" commended Good. Leslie beamed and held his gun at the ready.

"Back to back, everyone!" said Verne. "You can shoot these monsters, but you cannot kill them with mortal weapons!"

The Intercessors formed a moving circle, their backs up against their comrades' backs. "Is this a good time to drink?" asked Foulata, reaching for the magical bottle in her pocket. "Not yet," said Betty, aiming her rifle. "Save the last few drops for an emergency." A wolf pounced at Foulata, and Foulata screamed as the open jaws encompassed her face. She fired her rifle, and the werewolf fell back. "This isn't an emergency?"

Verne, who bore the supplies in the pack on his back, watched with fascination as he followed his friends. "The werewolves come in many varieties. Some are gray, some black, some brown. I wonder what determines the color of the fur."

Spinderbeck drew his sword out of the innards of the werewolf he had run through. Good noted the sword with approval. "Their fur may be different, but they all bleed the same."

"But hang it all!" Spinderbeck's sword hand quivered as he skirted along with the others. "These weapons are no good! The beasties won't stay down!"

"We need to make it to the inn," Betty replied over the shouts, yelps, and gunfire.

"Strangers! Here!" called a gruff woman's voice. An old peasant woman wearing a black scarf and shawl, hidden in the inn's empty stable yard, waved her arms above her head, motioning to them. "Hurry! The back way!"

The Intercessors slipped behind the fence and maneuvered to the back of the inn. "They can't get you here!" The woman's eyes protruded in her dark, wrinkled face. Her wry thin-lipped grin revealed several missing teeth. "The place is surrounded by wolfsbane! And fresh garlic on every window and doorway!"

"We are here to fight the Accusers," said Betty.

"Then ol' Maria fights with you," said the peasant woman.

CHAPTER 31
THE INN

The Intercessors slipped from the stable into the courtyard paved with medieval stones. Wooden shelters against each wall were hung with drying herbs. Maria gestured the group into the inn through the back door. The stone-floored front room was cold and bare. The large fireplace was unlit. An old relic of a crossbow hung over the mantel. The only other furniture in the room was a wooden-framed, floor-length mirror pushed into the corner.

Maria hurried them down the hall and into the kitchen. She warmed up the stove. "The beasts are building bonfires all around the village," she said, filling a pot full of water to boil. "Part of their ritual. One to the east, one to the north, one to the south, and one to the west. Next, they will build the great fire in the center of the village. They have taken everything in the front room that will burn. But now, ha, *now*, I have hung wolfsbane and garlic at the windows, across the eaves, and over the doorways. *Now*, they will leave us alone."

Verne held out the Jesuit's bark he had brought with him. "I suggest adding this to the collection. It makes an excellent repellent for werewolves, and, when ground into a fine powder, causes extreme discomfort to vampires as well."

Outside the drums continued to beat as the moon rose in the sky. Amid the drums were wild yelps and howls. Good stationed himself in a perch at the attic window. He watched the werewolves as they flung into the bonfires logs felled from the forest and furniture pillaged from the deserted homes. Other werewolves hunted outside the walls, scraping in the undergrowth for prey while others were pacing, leaping across the rooftops, impatient for the call to attack.

Betty joined Good in the loft. "Little use *this* is," Good said, patting his rifle.

"There are so many of them," agreed Betty.

"Well, they *are* the undead, you know. They have probably been undying for several centuries now." Good blew on his monocle and wiped it against his sleeve.

"There must be thousands," she said.

"And what of this Ordog chap? Ever get him in your sights? What's he like?"

Betty stared grimly upon the blazing bonfire in the center of the village. "I've never seen a volcano exalt itself from the depths of hell and spew destruction upon all living things, but I *have* seen Ordog, and that is the only thing I can compare him to."

Good sucked in his breath but tried to giggle it off nervously. "Well, then, I should say this is definitely the place of our greatest fear, like the code book says. I do wish the Golden Dragon would hop to it, though. Nice if he shows up *before* the massacre, what?" He winked to lessen the severity of his words.

Betty firmed her mouth and nodded. She patted Good's shoulder and left him to make her rounds, checking all the windows and doors and walking out into the courtyard to see that nothing was scaling the wall. The thatched roofs of the wooden shelters were black silhouettes against the fire-lit sky.

Maria joined Betty. "Come, child. I have warm coffee in the kitchen."

Betty hesitated, then allowed Maria to guide her back to the kitchen where Foulata was already pouring herself a cup of coffee. Betty propped her rifle in the corner and sat, tired and forlorn, at the wooden table. Foulata poured Betty a cup of coffee.

"Thank you," said Betty. "I'm glad *you're* here." Betty swallowed a mouthful of coffee. She closed her eyes as the warm brew slid down her throat.

"Each night, the werewolves chant." Maria sat on a stool in the corner and picked up where she left off weaving more garlic garlands. "They call to the dragon scales. Maria sees you have some of these scales. Legend says whoever has all five scales will be the most powerful being on Earth." She darted a meaningful look at Betty. Betty simply stared into her coffee. Maria washed her rough hands and wiped them down her apron. "Well, Maria must put these where they will be of use." She gathered up the garlands and left the kitchen.

Betty made sure the door to the kitchen was shut and that no one was on the other side listening. She leaned close to Foulata's ear. "I'm going to use the ritual."

"The ritual?" Foulata spilled her coffee in astonishment. "No! You must not do it! The ritual is forbidden, it's evil!"

"You heard Maria. It is the only way we can fight Ordog. Look. I have it." Betty extracted the folded piece of paper from her pocket.

Foulata shrank from the note. "You haven't told the others?"

"No," said Betty. "They would give me all the reasons I shouldn't use it. But we need to stop Ordog anyway we can. I'm just . . . afraid to try it on my own."

Foulata swallowed hard, firmed her resolve, and looked her friend in the eyes. "In my dreams I have seen you walking with dragons. I know you can do anything."

Betty smiled gratefully at her friend and sat beside her at the table. She unfolded the note onto the table, and her voice trembled as she read. "To bring to life the fallen dragons, place the scales in the pattern of a four-pointed compass, the golden scale in the middle, the blue scale facing the light of the rising sun, the onyx scale facing the rays of the full harvest moon as it sets, the diamond scale facing the last gleams of Polaris, and the emerald scale facing the southern light of Alpha Serpentis."

Betty took the two scales from her satchel. "I have the emerald and gold scales." She set them on the table.

Foulata drew the diamond scale from a rucksack. "And I have the one I took from the little dragon. Who has the other two?"

Betty slammed her hands on the table, annoyed with herself. "Of course! I left the sapphire and onyx scales at the bookshop with Sherlock. I was so excited about finally getting the gold and emerald scales, and so busy working up the nerve to try the ritual, I forgot."

Leslie sauntered in. "I smell coffee. It's beastly cold in the front room." He poured himself a cup. "Don't suppose there's anything like cream around here?"

Betty shifted, aggravated by the interruption. "Maybe the others want a cup too."

"Right-o!" He noticed that she was not budging from the table. "Oh, well," he said, "since you're not doing the maid thing anymore, I'll be a sport and serve. Ever ready to sacrifice, that's me." His eye caught the note in Betty's hand. "Is that the ritual everyone is talking about?" His eyes widened. "You're planning to use it! Capital! Just the thing I was going to suggest." He joined them at the table.

Betty and Foulata exchanged questioning glances. Foulata shrugged and nodded to say it was safe to confide in Leslie.

"Well, we *were* going to use the ritual," Betty replied. "But we need all five scales, and we left two of them at the bookshop."

Leslie frowned as he wrapped a hand over his chin and strained his brain. "Wait. Didn't the codebook have something on summoning friends? Perhaps it is a good time to summon the old gents."

"Mr. Holmes is *not* an old gent," Betty corrected him.

"Oh, that's right." He raised his eyebrows at Foulata. "Betty's absolutely loopy about Sherlock Holmes. Every time she sees him she's all blushes and fluttery eyelashes."

Betty shoved Leslie. "I do *not* flutter my eyelashes!"

233

Foulata laughed in delight. "Now I *must* meet this man! Is he better looking than Daniel Khumalo?"

Betty ignored the question. "Do you have the codebook?"

"Of course," said Leslie. "Mr. Verne told me to keep it on my person at all times." He took the codebook from inside his jacket and set it on the table.

Betty opened the book to the first few pages where the table of contents was inked in calligraphy. She scanned the titles of the chapters. "Pilgrimages," "Books as Portals," "Looking-glass Portals," "The First Dimension," "The Second Dimension," "The Third Dimension," "The Fourth Dimension," "The History of the Lost Scales," "Accusers, and How to Recognize Them," "The Unholy Rites," and "Summoning."

Betty intended to turn to the chapter on "Summoning," but her eyes would not leave the title "Unholy Rites." An undeniable desire welled up inside her, a compulsion to extract the knowledge that chapter offered, perhaps some little-known secret that would enable them to perform the ritual with the three scales they had. It was like an invisible hand clutched at her own, forcing her fingers to turn to that chapter. However, as soon as she turned the page, a scream ripped from the page and a dark cinnabar-colored ooze seeped up from the inner hinge and spread out across the facing pages, dripping towards her hands. Betty stared, unable to move. Before the ooze overflowed from the page, Foulata slammed the book shut.

"What the blazes was that all about?" Leslie was paler than usual.

"A warning." Verne entered the kitchen with Spinderbeck.

Verne snatched up the note and waved it for emphasis. "The unholy rites tempt us, but once we try them, we will never be free from their grasp." He gave Betty a stern look.

Betty and Foulata exchanged guilty expressions. Leslie took a gulp of coffee to hide his own chagrin.

Verne spoke in an earnest, fatherly tone. "Fear and curiosity make us think we can use this power, and we justify it with worthy motives, telling ourselves that we are different, that we have the strength to control the dark forces. But remember, my friends, these scales were once a part of the fallen dragons who regard us as their enemies. We would not control them, *they* would control us, and destroy us."

Seized with panic, Betty fled the room, retreating into the washroom to let tears of self-reproach burn down her face as her shoulders shook with sobs. She looked at herself in the cracked mirror that hung by a rusty nail over the wash basin, at her red eyes and straggled hair.

"Idiot," she hissed at her reflection. "The leader of the Intercessors indeed! You should have stayed at Perlgate, making beds and dusting furniture."

Foulata tapped on the washroom door. "Betty? Are you all right? Can we talk?"

Betty dabbed her tears with the back of her sleeve and pushed her hair from her face. She breathed in unsteadily. "Yes," she called back. "I'm fine."

Foulata opened the door and peered in at her friend. "We all were tempted to use the ritual. No one blames you."

"But how are we going to get out of this? I've brought all of you here . . . for what?"

Foulata put her arm around Betty. "You did not *bring* us here. We came. I want to stop the Accusers just as much as you do."

"I wish Sherlock were here. Not because I am in love with him, mind you . . ." She met Foulata's questioning eyes in the mirror's reflection and the tight sides of her mouth bent upward a little. "Well, all right, yes, I guess I *am* in love with him a little."

Foulata beamed and squeezed her friend. "I knew it!"

"I'm not sure how he feels about me, but for some reason, when he's around, I feel stronger, like I can handle anything."

"Betty," called Leslie from the front room. "The looking glass is doing something."

Betty and Foulata exchanged foreboding expressions and joined Leslie in the front room. Two silhouettes wavered in the glass of the floor-length mirror, undulating as when a pebble dropped in a lake forms rings in the water. Through the midst of the rings a long trembling hand and wrist emerged.

"It's the vampire!" Spinderbeck raised his sword to fell it upon the wrist.

"Stop!" cried Betty. "I know that hand!" She grabbed hold of the long-fingered hand and pulled. Leslie and Spinderbeck lent their strength to help her pull Sherlock Holmes the rest of the way through the mirror.

Once through, Holmes cleared his throat and adjusted his deerstalker cap. "Well, for myself, I am partial to the reading-a-passage-from-a-book method. Travel by looking glass is rather disorienting. Just a minute, we're missing one person."

He looked back at the mirror. Five short stubby fingers were reaching out from the glass. "All together now," said Holmes, and Leslie and Spinderbeck helped him pull Hamberdeen through. Hamberdeen adjusted his spectacles and blinked around at his friends. "Hello, everyone. And some new friends? Wonderful. Betty, my dear. Are you all right? Mr. Holmes said he heard you calling, and, as he tracked down the origin of the voice, the mirror in the back of my shop just pulled us both in."

Holmes lifted Betty's chin and studied her face. "Your eyes are red from crying. And you're pale as a ghost."

"I'm all right," she said, lowering her eyes, and her mind added, *now that you're here.*

Maria glanced up from sweeping the dust and cobwebs from a corner of the room. "Did the gentlemen bring the scales?"

Holmes scanned Maria. He observed her hands, worn and calloused from hard work, and her face, wrinkled with hardship and age. Her dark-circled, bloodshot eyes suggested sleepless nights, and the sneer lurking in the corner of her mouth indicated some dark intent. Her clothing was simple. A peasant scarf, shawl, and apron. But her belt buckle was ornate, engraved with the heraldry of a black dragon clawing upward against a red background. He felt sure he had seen that symbol before.

"Yes, of course we brought the scales," said Hamberdeen. "We kept them safe, just like we promised."

"And we will continue with even more vigilance." Holmes gave Maria a sharp look. He brushed past her, pushed the curtain aside, and peered out the window. "Those drums."

"It's the war dance," said Maria, following him to the window. "The pack will work itself up into a frenzy, and, once Ordog gives the word, they will lay siege."

"What's the plan?" asked Hamberdeen.

"Well," said Leslie, "we thought about using the ritual, but that turned out a bust, so now we're just sitting around hoping the Golden Dragon shows up out of some mythological handkerchief no one has ever seen, and if all else fails, we're going to end up chipped beef in Ordog's stewpot. I think that about sums it up."

"The Golden Dragon will come," said Foulata. "The code book said he would come when we find ourselves at the place of our greatest fear."

"Then he should be here any second now," said Spinderbeck, "because I am scared right out of my wits."

"But what if he doesn't come in time?" asked Maria. "What will the gentlemen do if the werewolves take the inn? We must not let them have the scales."

"They'll climb over my dead body first," declared Good, from the top of the stairs.

"But, if we do die, who will stop them from taking the scales?" asked Spinderbeck.

"They will never find the scales here." Maria pushed aside a throw rug and lifted one of the stone tiles on the floor. "Here they will be safe. The stone will keep them from burning in case they set the house on fire. And we will surround it with the Jesuit's bark, wolfsbane, and garlic, and they will never be able to touch it."

They placed the five scales in the crevice along with the code book and ritual. They added a layer of garlic, wolfsbane, and Jesuits' bark on top for good measure.

Leslie sighed as they lowered the tile and replaced the rug. "Don't suppose I would fit in there?"

"It would be stupidity not to recognize the danger," said Holmes, taking his pipe from his pocket. "But we must also take into account that all they have is an oaf of a dragon, an egotistic vampire, and some high-strung werewolves. We have the advantage." He lit his pipe. "We have brains!"

CHAPTER 32
WHEN THE AUTUMN MOON IS BRIGHT

Long into the night, the werewolves beat their drums and howled their vows of death to the red-tinged moon. The blaze of their bonfires reached such a height that it sent wavering reflections of orange and red across the walls of the inn.

Maria showed the Intercessors to their rooms upstairs. While the downstairs of the inn was bare, the rooms on the second floor were comfortably furnished. Lookout shifts were decided by drawing straws, and Captain Good had the first shift at the attic window. Maria stationed herself in a rocking chair facing the front door, a loaded rifle balanced across her lap.

In her room, Betty lay wide awake, clutching the top of the blanket in her tense hand. She stared through the window at the rampage of wolfish silhouettes against the light of the bonfire brandishing swords, axes, and bows.

There was a sharp tap at her door. The door creaked open, and the doorway was filled with the tall, lean stature of Sherlock Holmes. His chestnut hair was mussed, and his shirt was unbuttoned at the top and untucked at the waist, as if he had been aroused from sleep. "Are you all right?"

Betty pushed herself to a sitting position, adjusted the oversized nightgown she had borrowed from Maria, and punched her pillow to give it more bolster power behind her back. "I'm all right. But who can sleep with all that going on?"

"I thought I saw something beneath your window."

Betty moved to investigate.

"No-no." He gestured for her to stay put. "Allow me." He studied the window. "The latch is locked . . . and . . . garlic." He frowned and backed away from it.

"I'm glad you came." Betty hugged her knees and rested her chin on top of them.

"So am I." He sat on the side of the bed, and his eyes fixed her face with interest.

Betty shook her head. "I know better. All brain and no heart."

He clutched her hand. She started. His palm was hot and clammy. "But *you* have aroused something new and exciting in me," he told her. "Stimulation of the body can be just as exciting as the stimulation of the brain." There was a strange, energetic light in his eyes. "You are more than a woman to me. You are an *obsession*." He leaned closer and closer in, his mouth open and eager.

She raised her eyebrows skeptically, pulling away from him. "Obsession?"

"I'll prove to you it's true." He tore open his shirt, pulled her hand towards him, and flattened it against his taut chest. His chest, too, was hot and clammy, and she could feel the fervent, rapid beating in his breast. "Beatrice." He closed his eyes and licked his lips, relishing the sensual pleasure of her touch. "I must have you . . . have you entirely."

Her mind was conflicted, but her heart was surrendering. She had read and re-read the Doyle stories, imagining Holmes as the chivalrous knight in shining armor, vigilant to uphold the safety and honor of the widows and orphans. She had daydreamed what it would be like to be Holmes' friend and colleague, but she was not prepared for such passion. The throbbing of his heart against her hand tempted her to yield to his pleasure.

He closed his eyes, intoxicated by her surrender. "Your eyes, the depths of night. Your lips red as blood. Your skin soft as shadow." He pushed her sleeves down and massaged her bare shoulder erotically.

She leaned in and rested her lips against his chin. "Do you really love me?"

"Edmond has been a fool not to see what I see in you." He traced his long finger down her soft neck and over the curving flesh of her chest.

Her skin shivered under his touch, and she squirmed. "No." She pushed against his rigid chest.

"Why not? What could be more natural than the merging of our flesh and blood?" He held her neck in his hand. He covered her parted lips with his open mouth, his hot, smoky breath invading her own.

Pale and indignant, she thrust him away from her. "I *thought* you were a gentleman." She pulled up her sleeves and scrambled to escape the bed.

He grabbed her arm and yanked her back. "We are so close to discovering immortality. Let us pursue this magic together." She struggled against his strength, and he laughed, as he hoisted her thigh up and around his hip.

He put his mouth to her neck, sucking the supple flesh. He paused a moment as one who enjoys the scent of a good wine before indulging. He smothered her scream with his hand. She felt a sharp poke, followed by a numbing sensation spreading down her neck. Her vision blurred and her arms fell limp. He drew back from her, his fangs flecked with her blood. Then, he plunged towards her again.

But he stiffened and choked, his hand dropped from her mouth, and she screamed. There was a long stake sticking out of his heart, encased in dripping viscous material.

"Back to hell, fiend!" declared someone standing behind him. The white face of the impaled man corroded into the face of Vlad Tepov, staring straight ahead, lifeless. The man who had rescued her turned the light of the kerosene lamp up, and she could see the resolute face of the real Sherlock Holmes. Beside Holmes, his rifle ready, was the stalwart Captain Good. Betty collapsed back against her pillow.

Holmes knitted his brows at the limp figure of the vampire and ran his nervous hand over his pulse and hovered a palm over his mouth to check his breathing.

"Is he done for?" asked Good.

"Yes," replied Holmes. "I knew something was wrong when I saw myself sneaking around the hallway at this ungodly hour. Though, I must confess I expected to meet more resistance when hammering the stake through, more bone and cartilage." Holmes shrugged. "Luckily, I have had some practice with the foil on dummies. Speaking of which," he lifted the lifeless form of Tepov, "let's dispose of this one, shall we?"

Good assisted Holmes in dragging the body from the bed and over to the window. Propping the body against the bedpost, Good unlatched the window, pushed open the two panes, and with a "One! Two! Over you go!" they heaved the body over the ledge, sending Tepov hurtling down to the courtyard below.

Holmes drew a handkerchief from his pocket and pressed it against the puncture wounds on Betty's neck. "This has been a terrible ordeal for you." He asked Good to ring for Maria. No answer came. Holmes muttered a complaint under his breath and took it upon himself to guide Betty to a different room, one with secure shutters on the window and a firm lock on the door. Holmes assured Good he could return now to his post in the attic. Good saluted and left, but Holmes lingered to see that Betty was all right.

Betty's back curved wearily as she drew down the feather-bed. "If he had disguised himself as anyone else, I would have recognized him at once." She sank onto the bed.

Holmes pulled a chair to the bedside and sat down. "This villain has studied the art of deception well. He learns his victim's weakness and preys on that."

Betty cringed at the word "weakness." "You think I'm weak?"

"Not at all. Wise? Now, that . . ."

"Do you mean I am a foolish girl who has nothing better to do than fall in love with people who don't give a rap for her?"

"No. No. I think . . ." He weighed his words. "Were I young Edmond and had a woman like you, willing to risk her life for mine, I should consider myself quite fortunate indeed." He planted a kiss of reassurance upon her worried brow but abruptly broke off, his eyes sharp as flint.

"Confound my distracted brain!" He leapt to his feet and tore out of the room. Betty wrapped the blanket from the bed around her shoulders and hurried after him. "What is it?" she asked. "The black dragon!" he called back. "The symbol on her belt! It was under my file on Vlad Tepov. I *knew* we shouldn't trust her."

"Maria?" asked Betty

"Yes. She's one of *them*." He coursed around the wooden staircase and grabbed an oil lamp hung on a nail near the back door. He unbolted and threw open the back door and held the lamp up to survey the courtyard. In the distance, the drums and calls of the werewolves echoed through the misty darkness. On the ground below Betty's window there was not even a trace of blood.

Betty gasped as her eyes widened. Holmes clutched Betty's hand as the same horrible thought struck them both at once. "The scales!"

It was Maria who had invited Tepov in. Through the back window, she saw his body hurtle to the ground. She rushed outside and found the body twisted and rigid on the courtyard stones. She kicked him in the ribs hard with the point of her boot. His lifeless form was unresponsive. She nodded, satisfied. She ducked back into the inn, retrieved the scales from the hiding place in the floor, and bore them into the kitchen.

Using a sharp knife, she scraped a sliver off each scale, and, with a mortar and pestle, she ground up the slivers with the Jesuit's bark. She uncorked the stopper from a small brown bottle, let the steam that sighed mournfully out settle into the mixture, and tossed the bottle to the floor. She emptied the mixture into a pot of boiling liquid on the stove. She gave it thirteen stirs with a silver spoon, raised a spoonful to her nostrils and sniffed. She grinned in sadistic satisfaction and poured the brew into a brandy snifter. She shoved the scales into the leather satchel, flung the strap over her shoulder, and carried the snifter back to the courtyard.

She knelt over the body, held the vampire's head in the crook of her arm and poured the brew down his throat. She let his head fall back onto the ground, and with one horrible yank, she wrenched the stake out of his heart. He choked, gasped, his eyes flew open. "Ilda?"

"I am here, my master."

"You did not fail me." He grasped her hand. The warmth of the brew still tingled in his throat. His veins throbbed steadily stronger and stronger with a strange, invigorating rush of power.

"I cannot forget my husband," Ilda replied, observing his reactions with interest.

"Of all my wives, you have always been my favorite."

"That is why the master makes me a servant in his house?"

"I have been protecting you," he said. "The others have faded and turned into ghosts digesting over the centuries in the bowels of the dragon. I loved you too much to surrender you to such a fate. It was the only way."

She laughed bitterly. "And I am grateful. For all the years you forgot your love for me, I am grateful. For all the years you made me your slave, I am grateful. For the times I watched you with your other wives in your bed, I am grateful." She sneered as she offered him another sip from the snifter.

"Silence!" He brushed away the snifter, then, slamming his hand upon the cold stone tiles, he thrust his top half up into a sitting position, one eyebrow raised as he focused upon the topmost peak of the Carpathian Mountains. "After we finish this last task for the dragon lord, you and I will rule together in a kingdom he has promised me. I will restore your youth and beauty, and you will please me as you did long ago."

"And Ordog has always kept his promises," she snorted.

"Would you wish to challenge his word?"

"You are afraid of him, my master?"

"I fear nothing," said Tepov, leaping to his feet. "I am darkness. I am evil. What should I fear of dragons? Now, the scales as you promised."

"Of course, my lord," she said. "All five of them." She let the strap of the satchel slide off her shoulder and revealed the satchel's contents to the vampire.

"At last! And the ritual?"

"Here, my master." From tucked between her sagging breasts, she took the folded note she had filched from Verne's pocket. Tepov snatched it from her.

"A kiss for your bride?" she asked.

He grimaced in disgust. "Get away, hag! I have no need for you. It's Beatrice I desire. Not for her beauty, but for her power, the magic that flows through her veins. Now leave me before I send *your* soul to Alsó-Világ as well!" He thrust her to the ground. He glanced up at Betty's window, at the two silhouettes in close proximity with one another in the light from the kerosene lamp. His chest heaved in fury. He growled a curse. "Soon, Beatrice. I will be back soon. And your precious detective will pay dearly!"

He withdrew into the darkest shadows of the courtyard, closed his eyes as in sleep and crossed his arms across his chest as he transformed into a giant demonic bat. His heart throbbed with a wild vigor. His eyes glazed with a newfound elation. He beat his silver-blue wings and, leaping up, he took to the night sky.

Ilda pushed herself up on her hands and knees and lifted her scraped face to the black skies to watch Tepov dart among the black clouds. She laughed a toothless cackle as she listened to the clock tower in the village chime the midnight hour. It was only a matter of minutes now. The recipe she had followed for the potion had predicted ten minutes at the most. Heaving herself to her feet, she tugged her scarf about her face and clambered over the wall, keeping the winged figure in view.

The shadow of the winged figure slid up and down the snow-daubed hills and into the surrounding woods, mottled by the patchy moonlight between the grotesque branches. Ilda snapped past twigs and slopped through slush as she peered up beyond the bare, twisted branches overhead at the bat beating its wings through the gusty air.

A great gray werewolf pounced out of the bramble into her path. Ilda gasped and skidded on the ice. The werewolf caught her arm to stay her. "I have been waiting for you," the werewolf said, his amber eyes piercing into hers. "Where are the synthetic scales to deliver to Ordog?"

"There!" cried Ilda, jabbing her finger at the sky.

Above them, spiraling up towards the mountain peak, Tepov bore the satchel with the scales towards the lodge. But the wide reptilian wings were heavier than before. Each flap against the shrill wintry wind was like fighting the full pressure of the ocean depths. Tepov stroked a claw across his chest where the stake had been to reassure himself the wound had fully healed. The skin was thin but had filled in the gash left by the stake. *The sinew will restore. The strength will return.*

He sustained himself by ordering the steps he would take next. He would present the scales to Ordog and be hailed for his ingenuity and skill. "Well done, good and faithful Tepov!" Davidson would then be nothing to Ordog, only a forgotten soul long since consumed. Tepov, as Ordog's chief henchman, would be the one required to conduct the ritual, and he would agree on one condition, that Beatrice would be brought to him in chains. At last he would ingest her power and satisfy the hunger. And with this power he would turn the dragon army against Ordog and defeat the dragon lord once and for all. He would keep Beatrice around for a little while, as long as it amused him. She could take the place of that old hag of a housekeeper. As for her detective, he would break his will to bits and crush him into a pitiable wretch, like Miroslav.

As Tepov strained upward towards the lodge, circling the spiking peaks of the mountain, the air grew thinner and his breathing became more labored. The side of the peak was frozen over, and his reflection glinted back at him in the sheet of ice. He shrieked. It was not his own face he saw, but the reflection of a ghastly skeleton. A piercing squee whistled past him on the wind followed by the rush of familiar wings. Avian eddied down from the clouds to her master. "My love, my love!"

He clutched at his hair and pushed it back from his face in horror at the visage that gaped back at him in the ice. "Avian! What is happening to me?" His wings now felt like weights and his joints like rusted gears. He reached his long, bony arm out to his dragon pet.

Avian veered close to the winged skeleton and inhaled. "Smells of magic! Smells of treachery! Ilda has done for you at last!"

"Help me!" screamed Tepov.

"Give Avian the scales and Avian will help!"

Tepov could work his wings no more. He was about to plummet, but he clutched hold of a branch in the cliff wall. He held tight while his free hand drew off the satchel from over his shoulder and handed it up to Avian.

Avian took the strap of the satchel in her greedy mouth and grasped her talons around the branch. The weight of the dragon caused the branch to droop.

"Away! Avanti! Avanti!" cried Tepov.

Avian shrugged and pushed her weight off the branch with her claws and the movement snapped the branch, plunging Tepov down with a decrescendoing wail, down to the valley far below. Avian flew to the lodge, bearing the satchel away.

"She's taking the scales to Ordog!" Edmond pushed past Ilda and crashed out of the woods in pursuit of Avian.

Ilda clambered out of the woods and sloshed across the meadow to the base of the mountain where a heap of sepia bones clattered down at her feet. A hollow-eyed skull thumped down in the midst of them. Ilda stood over the pile of bones, a rush of icy wind thrust back her black scarf, revealing her wide eyes with pin-point pupils gleaming in a wild ecstasy and her gray straggles of hair whipping about her haggard face. She scraped back her boot through the sludge and kicked the bones into the mud. The skull rolled to a stop at her feet. She picked it up, pressing its anguished fangs against her mouth and whispered to it. "Master? Do you hear me? Will you kiss your bride *now*?" The skull did not answer her. She screamed with laughter, drew back her arm, and hurled the skull against the side of the mountain. Then she cantered away laughing and screaming until the gnarly limbs of the trees and the gusting flurries of snow buried her stooped figure from view.

Holmes twirled back the rug, threw himself on the floor like a tiger on the prowl, and homed in on the loose stone tile. He pried it open and found the cavity empty except for some garlic petals and Jesuit's bark crumbs. He snarled. Sitting up, he tapped his lip in thought, then scrambled back to his feet.

On the counter in the kitchen, he discovered a strange, iridescent residue at the bottom of the mortar, with flecks of green, red, blue, onyx, and gold. He scraped these into his handkerchief and folded it over to preserve the residue should he need it later. Next, he bent over, examining the floor, and in the corner, half hidden by a newly spun spider's web, was an empty brown bottle. He picked it up and sniffed the mouth of the bottle, noting a distinct bitter tang. Grimly, he tucked the bottle with the handkerchief into his pants pocket and returned to the front room. "She's gone," he reported.

"Listen," said Betty, head tilted to one side. "The drums have stopped." Betty and Holmes listened together to the oppressive stillness, watching the doors and windows.

A long unearthly howl ripped through the night sky.

Captain Good tore down the stairs, three steps at a stride. "Stations, everyone! They're surrounding the inn!"

Czerny, the werewolf quartermaster, distributed weapons to the other huntsmen as they filed past him and joined the rest of the horde that surged towards the sloping elevation upon which the inn was built. "Sword for you! Crossbow and quiver for you! Hatchet! Knife! Stop you! Take this!" Czerny handed a makeshift ladder to every third huntsman. "When you reach the top of the hill, throw it against the wall like Dmitri said!"

The wolfish huntsmen slid their knives into leather sheaths at their belts and in their baldrics. Three to a ladder, they bore them overhead to the inn, sloshing through the icy mud, breathing out heavy frosty air. As they passed the bonfire, one of the three ladder-bearers grabbed a burning brand from out of the flames and joined the rest of the besieging throng. Their long-eared silhouettes scampered up to the base of the hill, the brands they bore flickering like evil stars winking through a storm-shrouded sky.

Once they had scaled the hill, they threw the ladders up against the wall surrounding the inn. Knives in teeth and burning brands in hand, the werewolves clambered up the ladder, rung by rung, their eyes gleaming. As they reached the top of the ladder they sprang up on the wall and, pulling back their brawny arms for greater momentum, they tossed their torches at the inn to burn the residents out.

The Intercessors were at their stations. Good commanded from the loft, where he sprawled face forward, rifle tucked firmly into his upper arm. He aimed to pick off the werewolves before they made it over the wall. As his bullets struck their marks, the werewolves sent out piercing yelps, loosed their grasp of the ladder, and plummeted to the bottom of the slope. Then, still dazed, they gave their heads a shake to clear them, and started back up the slope. Leslie sat behind Captain Good, reloading rifles as quickly as Good finished a round.

Downstairs, Spinderbeck pranced about with large wet towels, smothering the fires as the brands hurtled into the inn.

Jules Verne came from the cellar bearing an armful of wine bottles. He stuffed cloths bound with wolfsbane into the bottle mouths and lit the cloths with matches borrowed from Holmes. He handed the Molotov cocktails to Betty and Foulata, who hurled them out the windows. The werewolves cried out and backed away as the baneful fumes from the bottles exploded into the air.

Hamberdeen stooped low to avoid the hail of arrows from the archers crouched on the wall. He crawled up to Verne. "Anything I can do?"

"The Jesuit's bark," replied Verne. "Take little pieces and put them at the tips of the arrows supplied by our wolfish adversaries." He gestured to the hail of arrows that had stuck in the walls. "You will find a crossbow on display over the mantel."

"Excellent! I did go in for archery in college," replied Hamberdeen.

Holmes pressed against the side of the doorway and waited for the werewolves to bound over the wall. Once he saw a clear target, he fired his revolver.

"We can't hold them back forever," Good called down to the others.

"This Jesuit's bark is keeping them at bay," replied Hamberdeen, impressed with the accuracy of his own crossbow skills.

"Listen!" said Holmes. "They're on the roof!"

Leslie heard the scampering claws on the tiles of the roof. "That's it. I'm all for Foulata using her giant goddess potion," he suggested between panicked breaths.

Betty called back. "No, we should save that for when the dragons attack."

Leslie groaned. "She had to remind me about the dragons!"

CHAPTER 33
THE DRAGONS AWAKE

Avian had disappeared into the clouds that shrouded the peaks of the mountains. Edmond, in pursuit, heaved his wolfish bulk up the side of the mountain, clinging with his claws to the crevices and hauling himself from one scraggly root to the next, pausing on the narrow ledges only long enough to catch his breath. He did not reach the lodge until the moon hovered in the west behind the silhouetted towers. His frame filled the gateway before the courtyard, his legs set wide apart and his arms hanging heavily on both sides. His claws clenched, as he huffed deep, ragged breaths. The amber crescents of his eyes darted across the courtyard, on alert. Avian was nowhere to be seen. Edmond snarled a curse, at himself for being too late, and at Ilda for breaking her word to him.

He crept across the empty courtyard and pushed open the door. The gray-stone front hall was cold and empty. The fire in the brazier had gone out and was wisping smoke from its dying coals. Edmond's loping footfalls echoed as he crossed the room. He paused at the top of the stairway that led down to Ordog's throne room. He sniffed the moldy air in the passage, but his wolfish wiles peered into the devious paths of the dragon's brain, and he realized Ordog would not conduct the ritual in the throne room.

He snorted into the cold passage and backed away, creeping along the wall to the library. The unconcluded solitary game of chess still stood on the table where he had left it. He swung his heavy hand across the board, knocking the pieces to the floor. He faced the window. In the window was his faded reflection, the reflection, not of the werewolf he now was, but of a bright-eyed, smiling young man. Beside his own reflection, the lingering reflection of Count Tepov still stood, beckoning the naïve young man to join him in the land of nightmares. Edmond's eyes burned at the memory.

On the floor near the window lay the count's walking stick. Edmond clutched it up and smashed the stick across the window, and splinters of glass flew from the gaping hole. He crawled through the broken window and came upon the ballroom, its floor still fallen open. He slid down the slanting floor, towards the gaping pit below.

He landed on his feet, bending his knees and crouching to retain his balance. He found himself in a dark corridor at the end of which an arched opening was guarded by iron bars. Staying in the shadows, he edged up to the bars and peered past them at the unholy inner sanctum of Alsó-Világ.

The cavernous hall was cobwebbed with stalactites and scarred with uneven crevices. Along the wall were ledges of stone sunk in natural alcoves that served as perches for miniature dragons. These curious creatures craned their scaly necks to witness the events transpiring in the colosseum below.

Werewolf huntsmen formed a circumference around an immense stone table set upon the iron grate from which intermittent streams of smoke would erupt. The huntsmen beat on drums made from the hides of chamois and roe slain in the hunt.

Edmond seethed, pressing his muzzle against the bars that blocked his progress. He was too late to stop the ritual.

As the drums reached the climax, Avian, in human form, scantily draped in scarlet silk, tasseled with feathers of various shades of rhodonite, rounded the table past the werewolves.

She inspected the five scales arranged exactly as the ritual described. The sapphire scale was placed on the furthest end facing the large arch shaped gates to the East in the light of the rising sun. The onyx scale was on the opposite side, facing West, in the rays of the setting harvest moon. The diamond scale was facing the north window, with the gleam of Polaris glinting in each facet of the scale. The emerald scale faced South, in the light of Alpha Serpentis. The golden scale, in the center of the table, spread its beams in an overlapping star shape to each of the other scales.

Once all the scales were aligned, the drums stopped. The silence was shaken by slow, thunderous footfalls of the approaching dragon lord. Each stomp triggered a quake that shook the walls and billowed clouds of dust from the unstable masonry. With a loud, low rumble, Ordog settled in his position in a formidable archway before the table and leered with pleasure at the arrangement. He gave a satisfied nod to Avian.

"I have brought them, my father." She swept down in a low bow with a flurry of feathers and silk. "The ritual is ready to begin."

"Well done. And the Intercessors?" Ordog asked Avian.

"The pack has them pinned down in the village."

"So be it. Soon we will deal with the Intercessors. For now, let the ritual begin!"

Avian waved her tasseled arm towards the werewolves, and they resumed their steady beating of the drums. Ordog bent his face over the round table and spoke in a low, commanding voice to the scales. *"Nuthan infantis eenam . . . beethen, wissan, fithu. Uren eenam. Erutham greefar. Dirthic, Hordin, Suthen, Ghulantan, mithin thonen beethen Vorever eeran ultina Ordog, gevuthan! Gevuthan!"* Ordog breathed a blast of fire upon the table.

The light of the setting moon hit the onyx scale, that of the rising sun hit the sapphire scale, that of the stars hit the diamond and the emerald scales, and all the light combined and reflected into the golden scale, and the golden scale burned to ashes. The werewolves sprinkled ash from the golden scale on each of the other scales.

And the scales evolved.

The sapphire scale bubbled with the pocks of multiple scales. Willowy fins burst forth on the sides, and a tail grew out from the end. As a round bulbous head erupted, two large protruding eyes boiled forth, each round, staring eye with a red pinpoint pupil in the center. In the middle of the bulbous head was a protrusible mouth, nasal cavities on either side, and curved fleshy barbels growing around the mouth. A shimmery blue gelatinous substance surrounded the shaping thing, and with tentacle like claws it burst through the substance and splatted the goo in all directions. This hideous sea creature grew to fill one side of the hall. It gargled and roared, spewing forth bilge water from a round, pulsing mouth. Water-Ghoul had awakened.

A golden film encrusted the onyx scale, until sharp pointed horns of black broke through and claws dug an opening and heaved a gigantic frame out of the scale. At first, all that could be seen was a dark, expanding shadow, but the shadow took shape, a towering shape like unto Anubis of the Egyptians. A long neck formed, and a head emerged with a canine-like face, and almond-shaped eyes of green surrounded by black kohl. Two fangs protruded from the front of the elongated mouth. The long neck was encircled by golden ornamental coils. The neck arched down into broad, muscular shoulders, and two sturdy arms, golden bands clasped around the upper and lower parts of the arms. The onyx dragon wore a belted wraparound skirt of linen that reached just below his muscular thighs. He roared, and from the sides of his canine mouth oozed blackened lava, heralding the arrival of the Death-Guardian.

The emerald scale turned into a slithering mass of hissing vipers, writhing among one another, rearing up and lashing out at one another. The most aggressive of the nest swallowed the others one by one, and as it did, it grew into an enormous serpentine dragon. He, too, had a human-like form with sloping shoulders and muscular chest and a long, snaky neck that rose into a triangular head. He had sharp, venomous fangs and indented pits above his mouth for nostrils. His eyes were narrow with vertical irises and an overarching brow. A forked tongue flicked in and out between the fangs. The mouth widened and the dragon breathed a shrill hiss. This dragon was aptly called Serpentine.

The last dragon to come into being was the diamond dragon. The diamond dragon was sheathed in a white crystalline substance. The substance crumbled and as it did it stacked up into a massive hill of diamond dust that clung together and formed the body of an ancient eastern lion god with upturned ears and wide mouth lined with glittering teeth. His rounded eyes glared like diamonds under thick lowered brows. He bore a mane of curled hair around his ears and under his chin and a tuft at the tip of his long tail. When he roared, a violent wind tore through the hall, stinging the inhabitants with sharp and violent granules of sand, and all knew that Diamond-Hoarder had been unleashed upon the world.

Ordog triumphed. "Behold! My children! The army of Ordog!"

Edmond groaned as he clutched the bars of the iron gate in dismay.

The werewolves clattered over the roof of the inn. Spinderbeck squeezed his eyes shut and crossed his fingers that the garlands of garlic, wolfsbane, and Jesuit's bark would prevent the assailants from entering, but the werewolves contrived to shoot the garlands off the windows with their arrows. The attic windows smashed and hatchets hacked into the barred shutters. Through the apertures screamed the jaws of a werewolf, followed by claws, ignoring the gashes from the sharp glass as they tore at it to widen the entrance. Good and Leslie fired the rifles, shooting the beasts down as soon as they crawled in, only to have them recover, clamber to their feet, and spring towards them.

"Betty, this would be an excellent time to summon help!" said Leslie.

"She's on it," called Holmes from the foot of the stairs.

Leslie, out of ammunition, used the barrel of the rifle to ward off the werewolves. "Tell her to hurry," he shouted back.

Betty had hoped the Golden Dragon would miraculously appear and wield his ancient magic and legendary power to save them. Yet, with swarms of their enemies overtaking the inn and still no sign of a rescue, she

admitted it was now up to the Intercessors themselves to unite and strike back with as many of their forces as she could summon. She dashed to the kitchen where she had last seen the code book. She pushed open the door, but, once inside, she was assailed by a glare of light. She shielded her eyes and pushed forward.

"Beatrice Talbin!"

The voice was like the crash of a stormy wave against a stark cliff wall. The sound was inside her mind but also reverberating in her ears.

"Beatrice Talbin!"

She opened her eyes to have them dazzled by a thousand sparkles. When her eyesight adjusted, she was seated on a rocking chair before a hearth, a kettle humming on the hob. On her lap, a fuzzy gray kitten was curled up and purring. The room was warm, comfortable, and peaceful.

"Hello, Beatrice," said the voice. "I've been waiting for you."

There was no one in the room with her besides the kitten until a golden swirl of light formed the shape of the gigantic golden-scaled forefoot of a dragon, with sharp pointed pearlescent talons. The foot filled the whole room. Looking up, she saw the entire dragon, gazing down at her with warm blue eyes that sparkled like a tropical sea. She trembled inside, not from fear but from a natural awe of the finite in the presence of the infinite. She set the kitten in a basket and fell to her knees in veneration.

"It's He. It's Vorever!" she heard herself saying.

"Yes, I am," replied the dragon through a haze of smoke. The haze smelled like the mist right after a refreshing spring rain. "All that you see, I am. All that you breathe, I am. All that you know, I am. All that has been or will be, I am."

Betty's tears welled up. "Forgive me, Vorever!" was all she could say.

"For your fears and doubt, I forgive you. But as you now see, wherever you have been, I have been there with you all along. For I have been preparing you from the beginning to be my special child."

"Why me? Who am I?"

"You are Betty. You love to read. And as you have read, you have absorbed the best of every character you love. You have the sense of justice of Sherlock Holmes. The adventurous nature of D'Artagnan. The free will of *Jane Eyre*. The curious mind of Alice. You have everything you need to set things right."

Edmond watched as the five fallen dragons assembled around the stone table to hold their council of war. In the ancient tongue, Ordog related what had passed since the dispersal of the scales. As he described his proposed plan of attack, he used his talon to etch across the table a map showing the position of the lodge in conjunction with the village and the inn. He slashed overlapping spheres across the map and labeled them with ancient hieroglyphics, one sphere for each of the portals in which enemies of the Accusers had been identified.

Water-Ghoul cleared his throat with a low gurgling sound. "It's too soon! We should not reveal ourselves so quickly! The Intercessors have access to the Golden Dragon, all the power of the universe and more!"

Death-Guardian slammed a fist on the table, causing the foundations to rattle. "Coward! We know the Golden Dragon is powerless against us! We defeated him once, and we can do so again! We'll slaughter him and all his followers! Blood shall flow, for all who will not serve us will die!"

Diamond-Hoarder roared. "Not all! We must not slay them all, but breed them, harvest them, feast on their souls!"

Serpentine hissed as he craned his neck forward to peer into the bronze gong hung against the side wall, mesmerized by his own snaky face. "Lissten, all of you," he said in a soft, slippery voice, "we musst be clever. We musst plan this out carefully!"

The Water-Ghoul trembled, jiggling each gelatinous bulge. "With Beatrice Talbin on their side, we are doomed! Let us hibernate until we are strong enough to face such a foe!"

The Death-Guardian clamped his fingers around the Water-Ghoul's throat to throttle him. "Weakling! They are puny! Mere specks! *We* are the mighty! *We* are the ones who will crush our foes underfoot!"

"But," inserted Serpentine, "we could alsso ssneak up to their hideout. Come upon them unawaress. Then sspew forth our venom and drown, burn, ssting, and sstrike!"

"Now is the time!" roared the Diamond-Hoarder. "Beatrice Talbin will be no match for the spirits of the sand!"

Ordog flexed his wings and shook the table with impatience. "You will keep Beatrice Talbin for me. Her soul is rich with the essence of the Golden Dragon. Now, hear me and obey! Water-Ghoul, from Neverland we have retrieved you. The portal is open. Go to Neverland and destroy all Intercessors you find there. Death-Guardian, your scale was found on Grimpen Mires, but it is Serpentine I will send there. Serpentine has the wisdom to wield the ancient curse that clings to that place to his advantage. Go, Serpentine, and confound our enemies. Diamond-Hoarder, your scale was discovered in King Solomon's secret hoard. Return to that place and defend the hoard with all your natural fury and greed. Death-Guardian, my favored one. For you I have the greatest task of all. Go down unto the village. Destroy all who would defend Beatrice Talbin, and bring the girl to me."

Time stood still for Betty in the warm, peaceful presence of Vorever. "I still don't understand how I am able to travel into all these different worlds," she confessed.

Vorever smiled. "It is my nature to create. I am the author of all the stories of all time, and your universe is one of my favorite stories, for I wrote it with the last remnants of my heart to replace the void left when a third of my own family turned against me. And, while many on earth choose to believe Ordog and his lie that their stories have no meaning, no infinite purpose, there are still those like you who make it all worth the many heartaches I have suffered on your universe's account."

"And the portals?"

"All the stories are intertwined, for just as I love stories, each person on Earth is a story and a creator of stories. And every time a life touches another, an intersection of the stories is created. Some of these stories are still in the mind of a would-be writer, waiting to be born. Others are a memory left over from a pilgrimage long forgotten. If you have the faith and determination, you can cross in and out of these stories where they intertwine. It's up to you to choose your story. For you, there are infinite possibilities. You could choose to become a part of Sherlock Holmes' stories, in which case you will become an inspiration in the mind of Sir Arthur Conan Doyle and the stories you now know will change. You could become a part of the world you were born into. In this case, you would become a vague memory in the mind of Sherlock Holmes, one he will reach for fondly whenever he senses what might have been had he loved a woman like you."

"What about you? Why have you taken so long to reveal yourself?"

"I've been waiting for you. It's taken you this long to realize I have been with you all the time. Meanwhile, I have been holding back the forces of evil, standing between the universe and total destruction. I have been preparing a handful of people who will be willing to stand with me."

"I will stand with you," said Betty. "But how do we stop Ordog?"

"That is up to you. I am not a tyrant. I would not force the beings on Earth to live the story I have written. They must become their own authors and choose their own stories. The story you choose will determine what happens to Ordog."

"What about Edmond?"

"He, too, must choose."

"But they took his soul."

"I am aware of all revisions Ordog has tried to make to my story, and I can restore them, if those at stake wish to be restored. What can be unwritten can be rewritten."

"And now?" Betty gazed past the golden aura into the gentle eyes of Vorever.

"Do not be afraid. Time is a tool, not a taskmaster," Vorever reassured her, lowering his chin to touch her upraised hand. "You will return to the time and place where you can do the most good, whichever story you choose. But you must make the choice."

The kitten rubbed her whiskers against Betty's ankles. She mewed and led Betty to a child-sized doorway. Betty ducked her head to peer into the room. Through the doorway, she beheld a vast and multilayered library with bookshelves as tall and wide as the Golden Dragon himself. Betty crawled through the doorway and climbed up the golden steps to the walkway that curved in a shining spiral all around the room, a golden banister on either side. Her awestruck eyes devoured the immensity of the room and the millions of books of every color adorning the shelves. For a lover of books, this was paradise.

Breathless with wonder, she strolled the red carpeted catwalk along the first shelf, and, as she passed each book, golden lettering appeared on the spine with the title of the book. *Jane Eyre*, *The Three Musketeers*, *The Adventures of Sherlock Holmes*, *Tale of Two Cities*, *The Christmas Carol*, *Pride and Prejudice*, *Lady of Perlgate*. Each book tugged at her a different way.

Her hand hovered over *The Adventures of Sherlock Holmes*. As she reached for it, she could see a glimpse of how the story would play out should she choose to enter that world. She saw Holmes and herself sitting together in his flat before a cozy fire, he in his dressing gown and slippers, perusing the news and smoking his clay pipe. She relaxed on the chaise lounge, jotting suggested edits in the margins of Watson's latest manuscript.

Holmes broke the silence without lifting his eyes from his paper. "I myself favor an afternoon wedding."

She raised her eyebrows. "Do you mean *our* wedding?"

He let the newspaper fold down. "My dear Betty, what else would I be referencing? Oh." He dipped two fingers into his waistcoat pocket and drew out a ring. He thrust it towards her, past the paper.

Betty took the ring and admired it by the firelight. "Did you pick it out yourself?"

"No. Mrs. Watson did. She and Watson have been badgering me about this for weeks."

"And you really want to marry me?"

The newspaper resumed its position before his face, and pipe smoke rose from behind it in calculated puffs. "Everything I have to say has already crossed your mind."

She smiled. "Then, no doubt, my answer has already crossed yours."

"A cottage in the country, then."

"Naturally. With three children, at least."

"John, Mary, and Irene," he decided. "None of those Anglo-Norman names that sound like places rather than people."

Betty glowed. She flew to her knees before his chair and took one of his hands in hers. But even as she held his hand to her heart, an uneasiness clouded her mind. "What about the cases you will never solve? The evil geniuses you will not be around to stop?"

He shrugged and laughed once. "They can all jump off Reichenbach Falls, for all I care. Let Scotland Yard handle their own problems for a change."

Betty let her hand fall away from the spine of that book and shuddered. The thought of no one being around to stop the likes of Moriarty, Moran, and Milverton, no one to balance the scales of justice or to defend the helpless was unbearable.

Next, her hand rested on the spine of the book titled *Lady of Perlgate*. She saw herself back at Daphne Graham's debutante party at Perlgate. The estate was thronging with the social elite, a twirling array of tuxedos and evening gowns. Betty wore a long, bronze backless gown. Edmond, in his tuxedo, whirled her across the ballroom floor. As the dance concluded, Betty grabbed his arm and coaxed him out onto the veranda. Daphne cut in between Betty and Edmond, but, with one shove, Betty sent her rival splashing into the fountain. Daphne screamed. Scrambling over the base of the fountain, she threatened to make sure Betty was fired and sloshed away on wobbly high heels.

Once alone on the veranda with Edmond, Betty caught his handsome, smiling face in her hands, and ensconced his lips in her seductive kiss. Looking deep into his dreamy brown eyes, she knew she had him within her power. "Edmond," she murmured, "how would you like it if you and I were lord and *lady of Perlgate?*"

"Why, darling," he leaned one arm on the stone balustrade and blinked into her eyes, "you read my mind."

"It's high time we got what we deserve." She tugged at his collar and stroked his dark hair. "It would not be difficult to work your way into the will. Leslie has been such a disappointment to the Mallowans, after all."

"I know I can manage it. I already have the right people eating out of my hand."

"You are so clever, Edmond." She scrunched her nose at him with a devious smile. "And we'll be charitable. We'll let Aunt Amelia remain at Perlgate as a maid, and Sir Eric could help Meades the butler."

"But first," said Edmond, a vengeful gleam in his eyes, "Bickerstaff!"

"Yes, we can lure him here on some pretense or other, then we will both give him the caning he so long has deserved."

Edmond's lips pressed in towards hers in a passionate kiss, but the kiss had the taste of poison, a poison that crept into her heart and twisted it with rot and decay. She thrust that book away.

The kitten, on the level just below hers, sat on its haunches and meowed, fixing her green eyes upon Betty. Betty walked down the golden steps to join the kitten. She scratched the kitten behind her ears and the kitten stretched out its paws against the books in the shelf, her paws kneading the spine of one book in particular. It was a black book with the golden words *The Legend of Blackwick* on the spine.

Betty held her hand over the spine, but she could see nothing in her mind's eye. She pulled the book out of its slot, and still she could see nothing. Determined, she took the book and squeezed her eyes shut, concentrating upon the aura exuding from the book. In her mind, a white curtain fell away and draped over the shoulders of a dark-haired woman. The woman wore a golden diadem with pearls suspended from it on golden tassels. She sat before a large gold candle. The flame that danced upon the long, black wick of the candle reflected in her dark eyes. From an open window, a multitude of voices called to her, cries of despair, pain, disillusionment, and grief. The woman tilted her head, focusing on each individual call.

She unlocked a wooden cabinet, from which she took a long white candle. She lit the candle on the wick of the larger golden candle. As the wax of the white candle melted, she tipped it over the melting wax of the large gold candle and chanted, "*Seven drips from the wick, and from the thick, is born . . . Blackwick.*" From the charred wick of the gold candle emerged a shadow that spun upward like a funnel of smoke. It took on a human form, but the shadowy face was hidden by the wide brim of a cavalier-style hat and the upturned collar of a black cloak. Betty was prepared to fear the shadow, but instead the shadow exuded a sense of sorrow and compassion, like a warm summer night after a storm-ridden day. The woman rested her hand upon the outstretched hand of the shadow, and a golden light radiated from that clasp. Warm, healing, comforting. Reaching into the darkest night and driving out despair.

"Do you recognize the woman?" asked the Golden Dragon, who was now standing behind Betty in the middle of the library.

Betty concentrated on the woman's features. "I wish I knew who she was."

"She is you. What you see is Beatrice Talbin, Keeper of the Golden Vigil, and her faithful henchman, Blackwick, ever ready to do her bidding. Together, they intercede on behalf of all people within all stories. She maintains strongholds for the Intercessors even in the darkest places."

Betty met the dragon's eyes, questioning if such a thing could truly be. His mouth firmed with steadfast assurance. "Then," said Betty, "I should like to be a part of that story."

"This is your choice?"

"Yes."

"So be it."

The pages of the book opened and out of the pages came particles of gold that spun around Betty. The gold particles formed a golden diadem wrapped around her head, a fur-lined cuirass with clasps at the shoulders for her long flowing cape. On both forearms were armbands inlaid with gems. The beige suede skirt was of a diagonal asymmetric cut, with the hem at her right knee above her fur-lined boots, and the hem on her left leg dropping past her calf.

"Kneel, Beatrice Talbin," said Vorever.

Betty knelt before the Golden Dragon and lowered her head humbly. Vorever brought his eyes on a level with her own. His eyes were both sad and joyous, like a mother who sees her baby take its first steps. He closed his eyes and inhaled deep and long, then exhaled his warm breath of golden light over Betty.

"Now rise, Beatrice Talbin, Keeper of the Golden Vigil."

The golden light filled her with strength and confidence. Her body surged with a new energy she had never felt before.

"What you feel," he explained, "is my spirit. I am in you just as you are in me. My power, strength, wisdom, courage, and compassion now are yours. You are ready to face the army of Ordog. But you will not do so alone."

"You're coming with me?"

Vorever laughed kindly. "Remember, dearest one, I will always be with you. But you will also be accompanied by a faithful and powerful Intercessor who has been here day and night interceding on your behalf. He understands the code book like no other, having sought to discover the deeper meaning it holds, using his knowledge of linguistics, mathematics, science, and history to aid him in his quest."

Akira Yamada entered from a side door and bowed to Betty with reverence. He wore a leather belted tunic over brown canvas pants tied at the knees, just above his boots. His samurai sword hung at his side from a leather baldric that spanned his chest. He rested one hand on the hilt of his sword and held out the other to take her hand. "Congratulations, Betty, Warrior Maid of Vandor."

"You have been here all this time?"

"Yes, I followed the clues in the codebook to find the Golden Dragon. He has been helping me guide you as you have traversed the portals to stop the threat of the Accusers. I have something for you." He handed her a small wooden box.

Betty lifted the latch and peered inside with wonder. "They're miniature books."

"Yes, and powerful weapons. In each of these books there is something you can use to face the coming foes."

She attached the box to the side of her belt and turned to Yamada. "Will you face them with me?"

He drew his sword and held it before him, the palm of his hand steadying the blade. "Indeed. I humbly dedicate my sword and my service to the Keeper of the Golden Vigil. I and the spirits of my ancestors who have used this sword before me will be with you to the end of all stories."

CHAPTER 34
THE EVE OF BATTLE

Every window in the inn had been smashed, every door splintered. The brands were hurtling through the apertures like fiery hail. Holmes' jacket, used to smother erupting fires, was now burnt tatters discarded in a heap upon the floor, a relic of the vanity of any further efforts to deter the flames.

The hallway to the right leading to the kitchen was blocked by a wall of fire. Holmes tried to pierce the smoke and flame with worried eyes. Still no sign of Betty. Face smeared with sweat and soot, his shirtsleeves rolled up to the elbows, Holmes checked his revolver. Just one more bullet. Breathing out, he slid down against the back wall to sit on the floor, next to Hamberdeen and Spinderbeck, who were equally spent. The detective's revolver rested on his raised knee, ready to dispatch one last fiend before his own inevitable demise.

Good and Leslie careened down the stairs. Good threw the wooden framed mirror across the foot of the staircase as a temporary barrier to the werewolves who were scuttling down after them. Werewolves were pushing in through the windows and crashing in through the doors, like flood waters pouring in through every crack of a sinking ship.

Even in this last desperate moment, the Intercessors turned to the tools they had on hand. Spinderbeck took up his sword.

Hamberdeen tossed Leslie his crossbow and hunted in his pocket for his key, hoping to open a magical escape in the back wall. Leslie fumbled with the crossbow, wondering if it had any purpose without arrows. Foulata hovered the top of her bottle labeled "drink me" over her lips. Verne was flipping through his novel to find the perfect passage for escape, and Holmes waited for the werewolves to pounce so he could go down fighting.

A flood of werewolves surged in upon the Intercessors huddled against the back wall. However, a sudden whoosh of gold particles flew into the midst of the werewolves and thrust them back, some to the left and some to the right, dividing the pack into two flanks, and clearing a path between them from the remnants of the doorway to the cornered Intercessors. As they were pushed back, the werewolves in front collided with those behind them, creating a confused tangle of snarling, growling, clawing beasts. Czerny spread wide his maw and roared into the faces of the werewolves who dared to jostle him. They shrank back from their leader, whimpering and snorting.

A long thin column of a shadow spread from the entrance across the stone floor between the two roiling flanks of werewolves. On the threshold stood the source of the shadow, Beatrice Talbin, arrayed in warrior-maid attire and backlit by the setting moon. The light from her diadem shone like a nebula around her. A gray kitten snuggled around her neck on her shoulder. The kitten opened one eye at the werewolves and prrowed at them with disdain.

Betty advanced, taking her position between the jumbled ranks of werewolves, fully absorbed in a page of the book she held open in front of her face. Just a step behind Betty strode Akira Yamada, arching his eyebrow at the werewolves as they passed them, like a sergeant inspecting a slovenly group of recruits.

"Yes, you're right, Sensei," said Betty. "The Parting of the Red Sea *was* a good choice. Now, let me see." She turned the page.

The werewolves, on either side of her, stood back, mouths hanging open, eyes narrowed, unsure what to make of this interloper. Mikhail scratched the back of his ear in confusion. Czerny lowered his muzzle suspiciously.

The kitten on Betty's shoulder mewed in her ear and waved a paw at a specific passage. "Ahh, yes, Portia," said Betty, finding what she sought in the book. "That *should* work." She stopped before her friends who stared at her in awe. Akira Yamada assumed his position at Betty's side, arms folded across his chest. He closed his eyes calmly. As he did, the fires in the inn abated as of their own accord.

Betty reached across to her left hip scabbard and drew her sword. She held it before her and from its tip rippled waves of light that formed a pavilion of energy around herself and the Intercessors before her, creating a barricade of light between them and their assailants. The golden light emanating from the sword was so bright and pure, the eyes of the werewolves turned stark white as they cringed in agony. Some howled while others threw their arms over their eyes to block the light. Some werewolves tried to storm past the light but were forcefully propelled back into their allotted space.

"Well done, my dear," exclaimed Hamberdeen. But his smile turned to alarm as the rafters shook and the floor rumbled from the crashing footfalls of something huge and foreboding closing in.

Czerny curled his lip in disdain. "The Death-Guardian approaches. Your pitiful magic is no match for the deities of old."

Betty did not flinch but held her sword with all the more confidence. "This is your last chance, slaves of Ordog. You can join us against the fallen dragons, or go to your Death-Guardian, and ensure your own destruction."

Czerny sent up a howl of laughter. "A handful of idiots and a magical sword? Against the raw unbridled power of the dragon lords? We swore our allegiance to the mighty ones!"

The horde of werewolves behind Czerny snarled and raised their fists to confirm.

"Then you have ten seconds," said Betty. "Go. Join your master while the truce still stands. We will be ready for you." Foulata placed a hand of solidarity upon Betty's shoulder. Captain Good held his empty rifle. Spinderbeck flourished his sword. Holmes raised a determined eyebrow.

Czerny's narrow eyes met the steadfast gaze of Betty. He twisted his head, incredulous, but the glint in her eyes and the firm press of her mouth convinced him he best obey. Disgruntled, he swung a vexed claw at the barricade of light, then jerked his muzzle towards the door. "Back!" he ordered, and the rest of the pack, fur drooping, shoulders sagging, ears lowered, loped back down their ladders away from the inn to join the approaching dragon.

As the werewolves retreated, the Intercessors gathered around Betty and Yamada. Betty sheathed her sword. Holmes wiped his brow and looked at Betty, impressed, his gray eyes dazzled by the light that glowed around her. His hand moved towards her face, but paused, as one hesitates before touching a holy relic in a church. "I think I can speak for us all," he said. "What you have done is truly remarkable."

Betty was grateful for his words, but the sound of rolling thunder echoed from the mountains and clumps of plaster and dust rained down upon the Intercessors from the shaking rafters. Portia covered her ears with her paws and squeezed her eyes shut. Betty looked up at the rattling ceiling anxiously. "We need time," she said. "And shelter."

"This way," said Verne, gesturing for the others to follow him to the stairway. He pushed away the debris that had piled up against the area beneath the stairway and revealed a wooden-planked doorway that led into the cubbyhole under the stairs. Crouching low, the Intercessors followed Verne into the cubbyhole. On the floor was a hatchway. Verne yanked it open. "The inn has an excellent wine cellar," he explained.

"Perfect," said Betty.

One by one, the Intercessors climbed down the moldy wooden ladder into the cellar below. Once all were through, Yamada closed the hatch over them and instructed the others to look for something they could use to brace the hatch, to deter the assailants for as long as possible. Leslie hunched over to scout out the damp, low-ceilinged cellar for something that would serve, when he nearly collided with amber eyes glaring back at him from the shadows. "Who . . . who's there?"

Heaving, ragged breaths replied, and a sharp-toothed muzzle with wet black nostrils emerged into the pale light. Leslie's heart caught in his throat, and he readied his empty crossbow before him.

A large gray werewolf stepped into the light. "It's me. Edmond."

Leslie regained his breath and lowered his crossbow. "Edmond. Thank goodness. That is, I *should* be thanking goodness, right? I mean, you *are* on our side now?"

"Yes. I come from the lodge. I know what Ordog is planning."

Betty and the others joined Leslie. Betty's eyes swam with tears as she gazed at her cousin trapped in this wolfish form. "Edmond." She put out her hand to him. Edmond fell on his knees, grasped her hand, and rested his forehead on the back of her fingers. She brushed her free hand gently over the raised fur on the back of his neck. As she did so, she could sense his thoughts.

"Why, Edmond, why?" she asked. "Give up your soul? Trade your last hope?"

Edmond could not bring himself to meet her gaze. He closed his eyes and lowered his chin against his chest.

"We'll have time for explanations later," interrupted Holmes, looking towards the hatch. "If we survive, that is. For now, tell us what you know about Ordog."

Edmond stood to face the others. "There are now four dragons besides Ordog, each more loathsome and terrifying than you can imagine. Water-Ghoul has been sent to Neverland. Diamond-Hoarder, to Kukuanaland. Serpentine, to Baskerville Hall, and Death-Guardian will be here any minute."

"There must be a way to stop them," said Verne.

Betty nodded as the strategy formed in her mind. "First, we must do as Yamada suggested. Leslie, Captain Good, brace the hatchway."

"This should do it," said Leslie, laying hands on some large empty wine racks.

Holmes, Yamada, and Captain Good assisted Leslie in moving the wine racks up against the hatch. Once the hatch was secured, Betty let Portia crawl down from her shoulder and placed her chin on her fist. "If only I had my chart." Portia mewed to second that.

Yamada reached into his vest. "You dropped this in the Grimpen Mire." He handed her the marsh-daubed chart. "I retrieved it and kept it safe for you."

"Thank you, my friend. Now." She spread the chart before her on the floor. Edmond and the Intercessors formed a circle around the chart.

On the chart, the regions of interest were indicated in different colors of ink. At the top of the chart was an area with the blue words Neverland written next to a star. To the west, were the words Dartmoor, Devonshire 1889 in dark green ink, with Baskerville Hall circled in red. On the east side of the map was Kukuanaland in the Congo with the mines, the village, and the plains indicated. To the east, the words The Carpathian Mountains 1936 were scrawled in black ink.

"Those are our objectives," said Betty. "And these," Betty took the box from her belt and opened it, "will be our weapons." She opened the box, and the glow from the miniature books lit her face. "All these regions are from different times. The *Time Machine* should serve us well." She plucked H. G. Wells' book from the box and twirled it on the surface of the chart, where it spun like a top, whirling around the map, faster and faster, until it had formed circular portals, one over each region marked. Then, the book disappeared in a puff.

The portal over Neverland was a swirl of ocean water. "Whom shall I send?" asked Betty. "Who will help Peter Pan and Miss Fernsby against the Water-Ghoul?"

Spinderbeck raised his sword. "I will go." He plunged the point of his sword into the water to cut a path and sallied in after it. "And I too!" said Jules Verne.

"Wait. Take these with you." Betty handed two miniature books to Verne. Verne held the tiny books up close to his eyes and read their titles. "Ah! *20,000 Leagues Under the Sea* and *Around the World in Eighty Days*! Two of my favorites."

"Good luck, and please look after Jeremy," said Hamberdeen. Verne pocketed the two books, shook hands all around, and plunged into the whirlpool.

The portal over Kukuanaland was a circle of diamond dust shifting and sifting continuously inward. Betty looked over her shoulder. "Foulata?"

Foulata squared her shoulders and raised her head high. "I am not afraid."

"And where she goes, I go," declared Captain Good.

"Your bottle will come in handy," Betty told Foulata. "But I also have these for you." She handed Foulata two of the miniature books. Captain Good adjusted his monocle and read aloud, "*Don Quixote* and *War of the Worlds*. I hope we get more than a delusional knight to come to our rescue."

"I don't need a knight to rescue me," said Foulata. "I have *you*!" And she pulled him along with her as she leapt into the circle of diamond dust.

The portal over Baskerville Hall was a dark and slimy mire that sloshed around in a sluggish circle. Sherlock Holmes unfolded his deerstalker cap from his belt, brushed it off, and placed it on his head. "I suppose it's into the mire for me." He smiled, though his eyebrows were sad as he glanced at Betty.

Betty held his arm to detain him. "I won't send you there alone. I commend to you my friend and colleague, Akira Yamada."

Yamada bowed his head.

"And," Betty added, "you'll need these. *Crime and Punishment* and *The Picture of Dorian Gray*."

Holmes took the books and attached them to his watch chain. He looked into her eyes. "When the battle is over, then?"

"When the battle is over," she promised him, but she looked down.

Holmes clasped his hand over hers on his arm. "Be brave."

"You too. And remember," Betty told him, "your greatest weapon against Serpentine will be your logic and reason."

"No, my greatest weapon is my hope to see you again." Holmes smiled faintly, then tunneled into the portal, accompanied by Yamada.

Meanwhile, in the cellar of the inn, Hamberdeen, Leslie, Edmond, and Betty exchanged apprehensive expressions. The rumbling outside the inn stopped, the dust had settled, and the only sound was a distant howl and the squeaking and scratching of the mice in the cellar walls.

CHAPTER 35
THE WATER-GHOUL

In the dark caverns of Neverland, set upon its stone pedestal, the petrified heart of the crocodile pulsed. The ghoulish green glow wavered against the wet walls, reflecting the dimly shimmering surge of the water inlet. The disembodied Captain Hook trapped within still had nerves enough to experience the painful pressure. "Blast ye!" snapped the voice of Hook. "It's bad form to pulse without announcing what the blazes you are pulsing about!"

The heart ignored the voice and pulsed even more powerfully to the tick tock rhythm of the clock that had become a fossilized assimilation within its core. With each pulse, the crocodile sought to convey to Hook the orders from Ordog.

"The Water-Ghoul?" replied Hook. "I need a little more to go on than simply the 'Water-Ghoul.'"

Now the heart glowed an angry orange, and the force of the pounding choked the remnants of Hook's being. "Argh! No! Enough! I'm with you! The Water-Ghoul, hooray! Yes, of course I'm on *your* side. Did ye think I'd be on the side of that impish prankster and his team of miserable little brats?"

Peter Pan's shadow stood poised on one foot on a ledge near the mouth of the cavern. Hand to ear, he listened in to the one-sided conversation of Captain Hook. Having heard all, he snapped his fingers and flew back as fast as he could to Peter and Frieda in their underground hideout, where they were starting to bake a cake.

"Ah, there you are." Peter tapped the mixing spoon in his free hand. "Now then, report. What's the news?"

His shadow used charades to convey the message to Peter. He put both his arms out in front of himself and used them to indicate large jaws clamping together.

"No need to clap, just report," said Peter.

"No." Frieda wiped her hands on her apron as she watched the shadow. "That's the crocodile's jaws. It's something about the crocodile."

Peter crooked his index finger under his lower lip and raised a quizzical eyebrow. "You must be right. You always are." Then, to the shadow, "So, what did the crocodile do?"

The shadow used his index finger to draw a valentine-shaped heart in the air in front of him and, pointing at the invisible heart, puffed his cheeks in and out to indicate pulsing.

"What is he saying, Peter?" asked Frieda.

"Heh, who knows." Peter shrugged and went back to the bowl to take a finger-full of strawberry frosting and pop it into his mouth.

The shadow raised his hands to heaven in frustration, pushed his hat firmly forward, and stalked up to Peter. He dragged Peter by the collar to the shelf where Frieda had left the colored chalks she had used to teach Peter how to play hopscotch. The shadow took the chalk and, on the ground next to the smudged hopscotch squares, spelled out the words "Hook" and "Ordog." He scraped a long, emphatic line under the word "Ordog."

"Peter!" Frieda took her spectacles from on top her head and moved them down to the bridge of her nose to examine the words. "Ordog must be on his way here, and Hook is working with him."

"Hmmm." Peter rested his chin in a ponderous fist. "Now where would I go if I were a Hook plotting with a dragon?"

The shadow sat on the ground and rowed himself across the room with invisible oars.

"His ship of course!" said Frieda.

"Say, Frieda. You're better at this than Sherlock Holmes. Come on. Off we go to the *Jolly Roger*, and, Shadow, you call Tondor Char and the rest of the pixies. We're going to need all the help we can get!"

Frieda and Peter found Hook's ship moored where Betty and the pixies had left it near the cove. They searched the ship from bowsprit to stern, from mizzen to main, and from forecastle to galley, but there was no sign of skullduggery, just a few rats chattering under the planks and cobwebs flapping in the corners. Pan's shadow came soaring back through the air surrounded by a whole regiment of pixies, led by Tondor Char, who lit on a peg in the helm and bowed to Peter. "The Neverland Pixies stand with the followers of Beatrice Talbin!"

"There'll be danger and mayhem enough to go around, I'll wager," replied Peter. He blew the boatswain whistle, and the pixies worked together to unfold the sails and sprinkle them with sparkling clouds of pixie dust. The ship took off skimming rapidly across the ocean surface towards the caverns. As the ship powered into the rising sun, Frieda, up in the crow's nest with Tondor Char, kept look out for any sign of danger.

As the ship rounded the coast and neared the Mermaid Lagoon, Frieda spied a large, unfamiliar shape looming across the horizon. "What in heaven's name is that?" Frieda adjusted the spyglass. "It looks like a giant octopus."

As the *Jolly Roger* pushed closer through the ocean spray, they could see the large mass was an immense coral reef shaped like an octopus with crusted red tentacles splayed out across the churning waves.

"Ahoy!" cried out Frieda. "Reef ahead! And methinks I see a landlubber atop."

"With a hook for a hand, I'll wager," said Peter from the bridge, wearing Hook's best topcoat.

"No, he doesn't have a hook, but he has a sword. He's waving the sword at us. Oh, wait, there are *two* people on the reef! They are both waving at us! Why, one of them is Mr. Spinderbeck! I don't recognize the other man, but I'm sure he's a good egg if he's with Jeremy."

"Right," replied Peter. "Pixies, steer a course for yonder reef!"

Stranded on the peak of the octopus-shaped reef, Spinderbeck and Verne shouted with joy to see the ship speeding towards them.

"They've seen us," said Spinderbeck.

"Oui, thank the bon Dieu!" said Verne.

Spinderbeck sheathed his sword and grinned. "I was afraid the portal would push us right into the midst of the fray, but so far things don't look so bad."

But he spoke too soon, for the reef heaved and lifted up on the crest of a crashing wave. Spinderbeck and Verne toppled back and forth as the reef veered to and fro. Up from the ocean beneath the reef emerged the colossal bulbous head of the Water-Ghoul.

The reef splintered as the Water-Ghoul erupted from the ocean with a gargling roar. The pinpoint pupils in the midst of the round, bulging orbs darted all around in search of prey as his fishlike mouth compressed open and closed, bilge water spilling down from the sides of the slimy lip down his scaly blue body. As the Water-Ghoul lunged for the ship, Spinderbeck and Verne lost their footing and plunged into the water.

"Oh, no!" exclaimed Frieda. "Faster, Tondor!"

The Water-Ghoul dipped one of his tentacle-like arms into the waves and retrieved the two squirming men.

"Fire the cannons!" ordered Peter.

The pixies worked together to load the cannon ball into the cannon and light the fuse. The cannon ball sailed through the air and crashed into the Water-Ghoul, leaving a gaping powder-burned hole in his scaled body. Next minute, the gelatinous folds of his wriggling body sealed the wound. Furious, the Water-Ghoul squeezed his two captives more tightly and threw them down into the ocean. He gurgled a roar, spewing forth a flood of bilge that spread across the ocean, changing the beautiful blue waves to a disgusting greenish brown.

Verne and Spinderbeck were drowning in the sludge, sputtering and choking on the foul water, but the under current buoyed them up. However, as soon as their heads bobbed up to the surface, the Water-Ghoul pushed them back down with a heavy tentacle. Verne, underwater, straining to hold his breath, struggled to reach inside his pocket for one of the miniature books. The tentacle lashed down into the water, knocking the book from his hand. As it billowed away from them, *20,000 Leagues Under the Sea* transformed into a giant shark that ducked down under them, tossed Verne and Spinderbeck onto its finned back and rushed them up to the surface where they gratefully inhaled the clean air.

"Merci, Monsieur Shark!" said Verne.

"Mais bien sur!" replied the shark. "Anything for you, Monsieur l'Auteur!"

The surges of brown sludge dragged across the entire Neverland Ocean, corrupting the water from the pirate's cove to the Mermaid Lagoon. Eyes aflame at what he beheld, Peter Pan leapt to the quarterdeck railing, his hot, sweaty fist clenching the ratline. "The dirty dog." He clutched his dagger in his free hand. "Frieda! Take the helm! I'm going to teach that oversized guppy!" He set the hilt of the dagger between his teeth and took off into flight, zeroing in on the Water-Ghoul. Tondor Char and five other pixies joined his squadron. Frieda shimmied down the rope ladder from the crow's nest and took her place at the helm, steering the ship towards the shark with its two passengers.

"Jeremy," cried out Frieda. "The mermaid sword. Dip it in the water."

Spinderbeck, on the back of the shark, unsheathed his sword and held it high. Though it was dripping with sludge, it glowed blue, and Spinderbeck felt imbued with courage. He plunged the tip of his sword into the filthy water that was roiling up around the shark, and from the sword a powerful vortex formed. The spinning water screamed like a siren wailing into a giant conch. Peter Pan lit on some wreckage from the discarded reef and held up his hand for the pixies to halt. The Water-Ghoul gurgled and moaned at the siren sound and, heaving himself up on three tentacle legs, maneuvered across the water towards the whirlpool.

From the whirlpool emerged Nothando, the mer-shaman, followed by a school of her mermaid daughters. The mermaids leapt into the air like flying fish to fill their lungs with oxygen, since the filthy water had clogged their gills. Nothando pushed up the gold bands that adorned her muscular arms and glared at the Water-Ghoul in fury. "Destroyer of Neverland! Be gone!" She raised her face to the crackling clouds above, and her voice swelled in the ancient tongue of the merfolk. "Ruler of the sea and sky, rid us of this thing once and for all!" At those words, a blue shaft of energy bolted down from a cloud all around Nothando, sparking about her arms and shooting out of her hands. The shaft of energy formed a vast blue wall of water to hold the Water-Ghoul at bay.

"That's it," exclaimed Peter. "Now we have a chance." Tondor, perched on his shoulder, readied her crossbow.

Meanwhile, in the cavern, the filthy sludge water steamed and stank into the darkest corner where the petrified crocodile's heart beat in readiness. The crocodile thrived on the sludge that streamed into the cavern where it had lain for countless years. The muck oozed of the swamps from which the crocodile had originated. The bilge water revived the heart, and the heart grew a thick crocodile hide, a long snout, a tail, and four squat legs.

"What be this?" demanded Hook from inside the crocodile. "Be we seaworthy once more?"

The crocodile ignored the voice, and, with a large hungry grin, dove into the slurrying water of the cavern in the direction of the Water-Ghoul.

The shark detected a shift in the currents made by a new form entering the waters. "Monsieur!" he exclaimed. "Something not good is coming." The shark shifted its weavings to avoid the currents made by the new form.

The Water-Ghoul was pressing his full weight against the blue energy of the mer-shaman, and Nothando was exerting her full strength to keep the shield in place. But the shield of energy was beginning to crack and give way. The mermaids held up the arms of Nothando to offer her support and sang. Their song was a powerful war-cry with dissonant tones that vexed the Water-Ghoul, causing it to gurgle and scream in torment.

The shark leapt up out of the water beside the hull of the *Jolly Roger*, and Verne and Spinderbeck hopped from his back onto the deck of the ship.

"Nothando is growing weaker," cried Frieda.

As she spoke, the Water-Ghoul thrust one of his tentacles through a crack in the energy shield. He used two tentacles to rip into the crevice made by the crack and tore the energy shield in two. He then lifted his bulge towards Nothando.

"Now, Tondor!" cried Peter.

Tondor let her arrow fly and it whizzed past Nothando and struck one of the Water-Ghoul's eyes. The Water-Ghoul let out a wail of pain and wobbled his head, disoriented.

"Oh, he didn't like that," crowed Peter in delight. "Now, let me at him!"

But just as Peter Pan took flight, dagger in hand to attack the Water-Ghoul, the giant crocodile came up behind him.

"Look out, Peter!" shouted Frieda.

Peter jolted to a stop and whirled about to face the crocodile in alarm. The crocodile's jaws were open around him.

"Avast, ye bilge-rat!" came the voice of Captain Hook from the crocodile. "If it isn't Peter blasted Pan! Looks like you're about to join me in crocodile hell!"

"You're still nothing but a codfish, Hook!" Peter flung back, his dagger ready.

"Monsieur Pan!" called Jules Verne from the deck of the ship. "Try this!" He waved the other miniature book he had with him.

"Tondor!" cried Peter, his voice echoing in the crocodile's maw. "Get the book!"

Tondor Char saluted with her sword and zipped back to the ship, grabbed the miniature book from Verne and zoomed back to Peter, whipping in between the great sharp jaws of the crocodile just as they clamped shut around them.

"Welcome, ye pitiful souls, to *my* kingdom," hailed the voice of Captain Hook.

Peter Pan frowned, slumped down onto the tongue of the crocodile, and hung his chin on his fist.

"Don't give up now!" said Tondor Char. "The book, the book!" She handed it to Peter.

"But I don't know how to read," protested Peter.

"Oh, Peter! If only Frieda were here. The crocodile is going to start chewing us to bits, and all because you don't know how to read."

"How many times Frieda offered to teach me," sighed Peter Pan. The jaws clanked and creaked into motion.

"Try! Maybe you know some of the little words."

By the light of Tondor's pixie glow, Peter studied the title of the book. "That's an A at the beginning."

"Such a smart young fellow, eh?" laughed Hook. "Didn't even go to school! I went to Eton myself!"

A sly smirk curled up on the side of Peter's mouth. He gave Tondor Char a wink, and she had to cover her mouth to hide a giggle.

"I don't believe it," Peter replied. "No pirate ever attended Eton."

"I assure you, it's true!" replied Hook. "I learned everything I needed to learn to be first and last an Englishman of good form and breeding. They teach you how to talk correctly, to walk correctly, to duel like a gentleman, and to sing 'Hail Britannia' and, most importantly of all, they taught me how to *read*."

"You'll never convince me of that," replied Peter. He reached up to hold back the pressure of the jaws lowering upon his head.

"Oh, I've done quite a bit of reading in my day."

"Bet you can't read this." Peter brandished the miniature book.

"I could if I had my spectacles," replied Hook.

"A voice needs spectacles?" asked Tondor Char.

"Oh, why did you remind me! I forgot that I was disembodied! But I suppose if I squint, mentally squint, that is, I can just make out the words. It says *Around the World in Eighty Days*! There! Mr. Know-everything Peter Pan!"

As he finished reading the title, out of the book came a gentleman's hand holding a large pocket watch. Tondor Char took the pocket watch, and the gentleman's hand waved and disappeared back into the book. The pocket watch ticked loudly and rhythmically. The crocodile stopped chewing and listened. His whole body bounced to the rhythm of the tick-tick-tick-tick as if he had been hypnotized.

"What's going on now?" demanded Hook. "What have I done?"

"Open up, Mr. Crocodile!" demanded Tondor Char. The crocodile mesmerized into obedience, opened his jaws, and Peter and Tondor sprang out. "Now back to the cave!" Peter ordered. The crocodile closed his jaws into a mellow smile and waved his little front leg drowsily as he continued to move in a tick-tick motion back towards the cavern. "Coward! Traitor! Turn around and fight, you scurvy knave!" shouted Captain Hook.

"Now for a crack at that big blue blob!" Peter Pan whizzed in the direction of the Water-Ghoul, who was grappling with Nothando. Peter darted around the tentacles as they flailed about trying to catch him. Tondor let her arrows fly, and Peter jabbed at the dragon with his dagger.

"Peter!" called Tondor in between firing her crossbow.

"What?" Peter darted and jabbed.

"After all this is over, promise me one thing!" said the pixie.

"What's that?"

"Learn how to read!"

The *Jolly Roger* loomed up behind the Water-Ghoul and Frieda called on the pixies aboard ship to bombard the dragon with cannon fire.

Nothando held the Water-Ghoul in a chokehold and gritted her teeth. "The cannon fire won't touch him!" she called to them. "Mr. Spinderbeck, you must use the sword!"

"Me?" gasped Spinderbeck, blinking timidly.

"Mon ami!" cried Jules Verne. "You must!"

Spinderbeck's hands were shaking as he drew the sword from its sheath. He was but a flea compared to the bulk of the water dragon. He held up the sword, and the blade was shaking like a leaf on a windy day.

"Throw the sword!" said Nothando.

"I can't! My hand won't let go!" cried Spinderbeck.

"You can, mon ami! We are all counting on you!" said Verne.

"Counting . . . on . . . *me*?"

"Yes!" said Frieda.

"En avant!" cried the shark.

Spinderbeck drew back his arm with all his might and flung the sword at the Water-Ghoul. It landed right between the Water-Ghoul's eyes and sank deep into the bulging scales. At first just a trickle of water oozed from the tiny puncture, like a drop of water from a leaking faucet. Then, like a dam unplugged, the insides of the Water-Ghoul came splashing forth and the dragon deflated into nothing.

CHAPTER 36
SERPENTINE

Thunder rumbled and lightning flared in the banks of charcoal clouds weighing over Devonshire, silhouetting the crenelated battlements of the seventeenth century hall. A whoosh of wind clanked the metal sign that hung from the lofty iron gate at the front of the estate. The raised moldy copper lettering on the sign proclaimed the estate as Baskerville Hall. The gate creaked as Yamada pushed it open, the wind whipping his black hair about his face. Holmes followed him in and made a sharp perusal of the grounds, staring down the long dirt drive that led from the gate to the Hall.

"Our adversary has been here." Holmes pushed aside a large branch the wind had blown across the path. Behind the branch, sunk in the dirt of the drive, was a large three-taloned print. Holmes and Yamada exchanged wary but determined expressions. They gingerly rounded the imprint and strode on to the front entrance of the Hall, surveying the bleak surroundings for any other sign of the dragon. At the front door, Holmes rang the bell. Yamada kept watch on the lower step, the lightning glinting in his sharp brown eyes. Sir Henry Baskerville opened the door.

"Sir Henry." Holmes entered brusquely past him. "Where is Barrymore?"

"I'm afraid he's . . . *indisposed*."

Holmes frowned and knitted his eyebrows at the stilted tone in the young man's voice. A flash of lightning revealed Sir Henry's face to be gray and drawn, and his eyes pale and unblinking. "Where's Watson?" demanded Holmes.

"Follow me . . . *gentlemen*," said Sir Henry, and he turned towards the dining room.

Yamada and Holmes exchanged nods of caution and followed Sir Henry. The dining hall was black as a pit and heavy with smoke. The only light came from the crimson cinders smoldering in the fireplace.

Two streams of smoke billowed from the darkness accompanied by a strident laughter. An emerald muzzle emerged from the shadows, smoke curling from the two distended nostrils. The snakish maw spread wide revealing sharp white fangs and a flicking forked tongue. Behind the maw lurked two contracted glowing red eyes.

"Welcome, Misster Holmess." Serpentine rubbed his front claws together in front of his long body, coiled in massive, scaled folds and loops around the room. "Welcome to Sserpentine Hall."

"Where is Dr. Watson?"

"Your . . . *friend*?" asked the dragon. "There." He waved one talon towards the far corner of the room. The lightning flashed through the window, revealing Watson chained and gagged in an old iron-wrought chair.

"Watson!" Holmes sprang towards his friend. Yamada clamped a hand on Holmes' shoulder and held him back. He pointed. Before Watson were two baby vipers coiled and ready to strike. They reared and hissed at Holmes.

Holmes' eyes darted about the room.

"The *wisse* Misster Yamada," acknowledged Serpentine with a sarcastic bow. "You sseee, Misster Holmess, I have your . . . ahem . . . *friend* and *colleague* as my prissoner. He cannot move without aroussing my offsspring." He stroked the heads of the vipers.

Watson struggled against his bonds and gestured urgently with his head for his friend to get out while he could.

Holmes remained fixed. "What do you want, Serpentine?"

"What do I want?" The dragon emitted a trill of high-pitched laughter accompanied by sniggering bursts of smoke from his nostrils. "I don't want Watsson. I don't even want *you*. Jusst ssummmon Beatrisse Talbin here, and I will gladly releasse your friend."

Watson moaned his protest through his gag.

Holmes was processing every possible move and calculating the chain of events that would result. As he did, the lightning flashed again, revealing two large rectangular silhouettes behind the drawn drapes hanging on each side of the dining room window.

"Ahh." Serpentine's fangs glinted with flecks of venom. "You've sspied my treassure, I sseee." Serpentine jutted his head towards Sir Henry as a signal. Sir Henry drew back first one side of the drapes and then the other. The silhouettes belonged to two glass caskets with tubes running from one to the other connected to electric wires that sparked and sputtered all across the floorboards around the dining room walls. Within the caskets were two inanimate bodies staring lifelessly straight ahead, Mr. and Mrs. Barrymore.

"Do you like my contraption, Misster Holmess?" asked Serpentine. "The two worthlesss humanss serve as the conductorss of energy. Their ssouulss, Misster Holmess, their soulss. They feeed my little oness, and onsse they have drained their ssouuulss, they will be as big and sstrong as their father! Then they will devour your friend and colleague and prosseed acrosss England to bring your countrymen to their kneeess before me!"

"And if I summon Betty?"

"Then," Serpentine gleamed, tapping his foreclaws together, "we can negotiate."

Yamada leaned in close to Holmes' ear. "The wires run up the walls to the roof."

"Don't try it, Yamada," said Serpentine. "You will never get passt me!"

"How much time do we have?" Holmes checked his pocket watch with one hand while his other hand detached the two miniature books from his watch chain.

"I am a creature of the cossmoss. Time is irrelevant. But, if you inssisst on monitoring your friendss' capacity to ssuffer, note the gauge on the side of the cassketss. Onsse the emerald light reaches the top, your friend diess."

Holmes tensed. The emerald light was already three fourths of the way to the top of the gauge. An idea leapt to his mind. "What is it you want from Betty?" He slowly sidestepped towards the large mirror as he spoke.

"Beatrisse Talbin is the mosst powerful intercesssor of all! She knowss the ssecretss of the portalss! She commandss the Golden Dragon! If I can desstroy her, I will be the mosst powerful being in the cosmoss."

"So it's power, then? What of the other dragons? What do you have that they do not?"

"Mee? I have mysself. Sself is everything."

"What is self without orbits?" asked Holmes. "I, too, am a rather isolated creature. I thought all I needed was my brain and a problem to keep it absorbed, but I found that self without admirers or sympathizers was as empty as a dried up syringe."

"You are only human. Therefore, it is natural you should have this weaknesss. I do not. I am my own admirer. I am my own ssympathizzer."

Holmes placed his hand on the mirror. "So this is all the friend you need." His hidden palm inserted one of the books, *The Picture of Dorian Gray*, into the mirror, and the mirror absorbed it. "I hardly blame you. I have never set eyes on anything so magnificent as yourself, except . . ."

Serpentine scowled. "Exssept what?"

Holmes glanced at his fingernails. "Except a swamp adder I met once. Something so small, but clever. You know, it could enter its victim's chamber without a sound. And when it struck, no one would be the wiser. And it got the best of its master in a matter of seconds."

Yamada slipped further into the shadows of the room.

"You call *that* magnificent?" Serpentine raised an incredulous brow.

"What about the blue carbuncle, fit in the palm of my hand, and glowed with such beauty it could tempt a man to murder just for the privilege of holding the bauble to the light." Holmes folded one arm behind his back and slipped the second miniature book, *Crime and Punishment*, into Yamada's palm as the Intercessor stole past him.

Serpentine uncoiled and slinked closer to Holmes. "I am ssubtle but sseductive." He glimpsed his reflection in the mirror. "Sseee how *I* ssparkle in the flicker of the flamess."

Holmes shrugged lightly. "Every star can twinkle."

Yamada crept towards the stairs. He checked the gauges. Just a few slivers left before the gauges were full.

Serpentine shot his opened maw at Holmes and hissed. Holmes deftly avoided the fangs. "You compare Sserpentine to the tiny ssunss that populate thiss pathetic universse? I outshine a thoussand ssunss." The dragon returned his gaze to his own reflection, twisting and weaving his snaky neck to admire himself from all angles.

"I suppose there *are* people who think youth and beauty are everything. Beauty is truth, they say, though I have not always found it so," remarked Holmes.

Mesmeric circles spiraled within the mirror, exaggerating the features of the dragon.

"But beauty *iss* truth, Misster Holmess," replied Serpentine. "I am truth. I am beauty. Therefore, we are the cumulative value of both factorss."

"The argument is an apocryphal one. Easily shattered. If it were to hold, the problem would need to be commutative, but while beauty may have an element of truth, often the bared truth is ugly, very ugly."

Serpentine's eyes were fixed on the circles in the mirror and could not resist sidling even closer up to the glass. "That'ss why the universse neeedss me. No more ugliness. Only me." He rolled over on his back, drooping his heavy head backwards so he could continue to loll at himself with satisfaction.

Watson noted the gauges and looked anxiously from the growing snakelings to their distracted progenitor. Sir Henry stood still, staring blankly at nothing. Watson's muffled cries did not even phase him.

When Yamada reached the middle of the winding staircase, the wires sparked, sizzled, and came to life like lashing vipers, striking out at him. They wrapped themselves tightly around his wrists, ankles, and neck. He clutched the miniature book in his hand, Dostoyevsky's novel about a young man who sought to prove a point by axing a greedy pawnbroker. As he envisioned the grotesque shadow of the young man heaving the large axe over his head, the tiny book expanded. It became long and round like the handle of an axe, and it grew a sharp, deadly blade that sang and crackled as it cut through the tangle of wires. The wires dropped into a lifeless heap, and Yamada shuffled off their coils and sprang on up the stairs.

Holmes noted Yamada's progress out of his peripheral vision and turned his attention to Serpentine who was drawing closer to the mirror as if pulled by an unseen force.

"Ssoo." Serpentine's forked tongue hung lazily out the side of his mouth as he drooled venom, absorbed with self-admiration. "You only have a few ssecondss to call your beloved Beatrisse and ssave your dear Watsson. Will you ssummon her?"

"But you see," Holmes' hands in his pockets were tense, but his demeanor remained calm, "I don't need to summon her. She is already here."

"If she is here, where iss shee?"

"There, in the mirror, look."

Serpentine stared deep into the mirror, searching the spinning and expanding circles for a glimpse of the young female Intercessor.

"She is beauty," declared Holmes, "not just beautiful in appearance but beautiful of soul. And she stands for truth. Not some vague abstraction, but for the truth of compassion, of setting aside self for the sake of others, concepts your greedy heart could never fathom, no matter how many worlds you swallow up or how many lives you trample underfoot!"

Yamada reached the roof. He held the axe with both hands and heaved it high above his head. The lightning converged upon the blade, and the axe flew out of his hands. Guided by the lightning, it struck the conductor, slicing through the main power source.

The emerald in the gauges sunk as they refilled with red, restoring the souls of the Barrymores. The snakelings, no longer receiving sustenance, shriveled up into empty, dried-up shells. Sir Henry blinked and shook his head to clear it. "I say, Watson!" He moved to release the Dr..

"Don't you touch him!" screamed Serpentine. "He's my prissoner! You *all* are my prissoners. I am Sserpentine, and I am gloriouss!" Continuing to project the self-absorption that had seduced Dorian Gray, the mirror now slurped the dragon into its glass with unrelenting suction and fingers of paint sprang out and wrapped themselves around the dragon's neck in an unyielding embrace, pulling the dragon into the mirror. He screamed in a high, piercing hiss, until his entire body was absorbed by the mirror.

Holmes exhaled and wiped his forehead. Sir Henry freed Watson. "My dear chap, that was magnificent!" Watson took Holmes by the hand and wrung it effusively.

"I think, my dear fellow," Holmes adjusted his collar and cufflinks, "our stay in the country has been quite long enough."

CHAPTER 37
THE DIAMOND-HOARDER

Diamond-Hoarder shook his mane and roared at the sun that beat in waves against his diamond encrusted body and baked the plains with its reflected heat. The Diamond-Hoarder dug his front claws into the dust and sat erect as he watched with white gleaming eyes the hordes of onrushing Kukuana warriors, spears raised, flanking him to the right and left, pinning him in.

The dragon lowered his rumpled brow and his curly beard brushed the hilltops. He roared at the warriors, and out of his mouth discharged a violent wind whirling with stinging grains of sand. The force of the sandstorm thrust the warriors back.

Ignosi braced himself against the powerful winds. He raised his cowhide shield to ward off the onslaught and surveyed his men. His men, too, were bracing themselves, but among the violent billows of sand were swirling figures, humanoid figures, made of accumulated grains of sand, taking shape and dispersing like specters. The winds flung the sand ghosts against the warriors, and once one of these humanoid clouds of sand caught hold of a warrior, it pulled him down and buried him alive under the sand.

One such sand ghost screamed towards Ignosi. He thrust his spear through the middle of its granulated form, and the sands splatted out in multiple directions, dissipating the sand ghost. *They are not immortal!*

Once the warriors saw that their shields and spears offered an adequate defense against the sand ghosts, they pressed forward through the melee, towards the dragon. Every second they kept the dragon's attention away from the mountains provided valuable time for the Intercessors to set their trap.

Through the crater in the top of the mountain, the Intercessors could see the whipping sands alternately dulling and revealing the glare of the sun. Far below, in the treasure cave, Foulata and Captain Good stood with Khumalo and Quatermain among the glittering mounds of diamonds, piles of ivory, and towers of gold, as they prepared their trap. The dragon was made of diamonds, the hardest substance in the world. Nothing could destroy a diamond. Except, Khumalo pointed out, another diamond. Now that they were in a chamber crammed with diamonds, all they needed was a means to direct those diamonds forcefully against the dragon's scales and to wait for the warriors to drive the dragon towards the mountain crater.

The crashing footfalls of the approaching menace sent spasmodic tremors throughout the mountain. The Intercessors held anxious breaths as the enormous rock pillars supporting the vaulted ceiling just outside the treasure chamber wobbled precariously. "He's coming," said Quatermain, loading his rifle. "Time is running out."

Foulata nudged Captain Good with her shoulder. "The books, darling."

"Oh, yes, quite," said Good as he un-pocketed the two miniature books. "Which will it be? *War of the Worlds* or *Don Quixote?*"

Khumalo had read both books several times, and he could foresee advantages to both. He preferred the philosophical ponderings of Cervantes to the dismal existentialism of Wells, but for shooting a giant mound of diamonds at a dragon with enough pressure to disintegrate it, the prospect of the Martian ray guns of *War of the Worlds* sounded more promising than a sword and suit of armor. Khumalo was about to open the miniature book to a specific passage when Captain Good grabbed his wrist. "Wait. How do we know we'll get the ray gun? For all we know we'll get the Martians instead."

Quatermain harrumphed and leaned against his rifle. "A stalwart soldier like yourself is not afraid of a few human-devouring beasties from another planet, surely!"

Foulata slammed her fists on her hips and bent a scowl at Quatermain. "My man is not afraid of anything."

Good fogged his monocle with his breath and wiped the glass against his sleeve. "True, my dear, but there is a difference between fearlessness and foolishness." He adjusted the monocle back in his eye and tucked the copy of *Don Quixote* in his breast pocket.

A moon-shaped shadow spread across the treasure cave. The Intercessors looked up to see the glare of the sun eclipsed by the Diamond-Hoarder's head covering half of the crater's opening. He clutched the sides of the crater with greedy claws and lapped a long eager tongue across his teeth as he peered down at the Intercessors below. "I smell diamonds. They are my diamonds. You dare to take my diamonds? I will bury you with my treasure!" He scraped with his sharp claws about the sides of the mountain, digging up a landslide of heavy rocks and dirt that came crashing down upon them.

Quatermain pushed the others into a crevice in the wall to avoid the cascading rocks. Foulata shot a glare up at the creature as she was jostled back by the shoulder of Captain Good. "Let me pass! I have waited long enough." Foulata unsnapped a pouch on her belt and withdrew the bottle labeled "drink me." She raised the bottle to her lips.

"No!" Good snatched the bottle from her. "If anyone is going to fight that monster, it's me!" He tipped the bottle back over his mouth and tapped the bottom of the bottle. Foulata reached for the bottle to snatch it back, but one tiny drop had already trickled into his mouth. He grew.

Good grew to gigantic proportions. Foulata clung to his thumb as he shot upward, and she held on for dear life, for in seconds, she was no bigger than that thumb. She sprang from his thumb across to the cord that hung from his monocle. She landed on his shoulder and held onto the cord as a sailor clings to the ropes for ballast.

The dragon reeled back as Good's head surpassed his own out of the top of the mountain. The titanic beast pounced at him, but the sun glinted off the glass in Good's monocle and struck the Diamond-Hoarder's eyes. Unable to see, the dragon attacked aimlessly.

The dragon roared again, once more exhaling out the gale force winds and billows of stinging sand. As Good jerked back to avoid a blast of sand in his face, his monocle fell from his eye and Foulata let out a long cry as she clung to the cord, plummeting with the falling monocle and landing with a bouncy thump in the bottom of his breast pocket next to the miniature book.

"My darling," called Foulata in a tiny voice.

However tiny her voice, Good's ears were ever attuned to its music. "Yes, my dearest one?"

"What is *Don Quixote*?"

"*Don Quixote*?" repeated Good, readying himself for the oncoming fury of the Diamond-Hoarder. "It's a book about an idealist who fought against windmills and things."

"Windmills!" Foulata loosed the belt from around her middle and used it to strap the miniature book to her back. Hands freed, she climbed up the canvas-like fabric of Good's pocket, clutching the folds and threading as if they were clefts and rope. Reaching the top, she held to the flap of Good's breast pocket. She loosed the belt and, heaving her arm back to gain momentum, she hurled the miniature book out towards the Diamond-Hoarder.

The book in flight assumed the shape of a windmill of extraordinary proportions. The blades on the windmill whirled furiously, cutting through the sand-ghosts as if they were papier-mâché. The windmill high-powered forward, shifting the direction of the blowing sand, propelling it back into the eyes of the Diamond-Hoarder. Ignosi's warriors sent up a loud cheer as the Diamond-Hoarder cried out in pain.

In the treasure cave within the mountain, Khumalo read from *War of the Worlds*.

"Forthwith flashes of actual flame, a bright glare leaping from one to another, sprang from the scattered group of men. It was as if some invisible jet impinged upon them and flashed into white flame."

From the book's pages leapt a huge metallic cone-shaped heat ray balanced on a tripod. Khumalo grinned, impressed, and springing at the tripod, he swung the cone's point around on its turret and aimed the ray upward at the crater in the mountain. But Captain Good now stood where the Diamond-Hoarder had been, right in the sights of the heat ray.

"Say!" called Quatermain up to Captain Good. "Get Diamond-Hoarder back here. We need his face dead center of the crater."

With one hand, Khumalo held the cone steady, and with his other, he sought along the cold, metal mechanisms on the side of the weapon, and settled on a raised lever. He watched the crater and waited.

"Any ideas, Foulata?" asked Good.

"Fight him," she told him. "Make him come back."

"By Jove, I will!" Good climbed up out of the mountain and bounded after the Diamond-Hoarder, who was wrestling with the whipping blades of the windmill.

Good tapped the dragon on the shoulder. The Diamond-Hoarder had just torn off the last blade from the windmill with his powerful teeth and spat it out. He snarled and whirled around to face Captain Good. Good put up his fists in a professional fighter stance. "All right, you overgrown toad! Pick . . ."

Foulata called up, "Don't tell him to pick on someone his own size! Tell him to pick on *me*!"

"What?" asked Good.

Foulata yanked up the cord from which dangled Good's monocle and, catching hold of the lens in both of her hands, she aimed it to reflect the rays of the sun into the dragon's diamond-colored eyes. The sun pierced his eye, and the Diamond-Hoarder howled in pain and swatted at the sun. He ducked to the side to avoid the glare, but Foulata kept adjusting the angle of the lens until she had backed the dragon to the mountain crater.

"There he is!" Quatermain pointed upward. "Right in your sights!"

Khumalo gritted his teeth and slammed the lever forward. The ray gun made a loud humming sound that increased in pitch and volume until it sang out with a loud *Ulla!* And a fiery blast shot into the mounds of diamonds in the mine bursting them to dust. The combustion whirled into a cometing pillar of diamond dust that smashed right into the face of the dragon. The Diamond-Hoarder shattered into a dazzling hail of fragments and was no more.

Chapter 38
THE DEATH-GUARDIAN

The bonfires had died into black smoke spiraling up from charred and crumbling nests, drifting across the deserted village and blotting out the bleak white dawn. The drums were silent. When the sun had first risen over the mountains and shot out its bright rays, the werewolves had vanished into the abandoned buildings.

Holed up in the cellar of the inn, the Intercessors waited in guarded silence. After the thunderous rumble of the Death-Guardian's impending approach, there was a prolonged stillness. Even the rats in the walls of the cellar had stopped squealing and only an occasional scrape and scuffle broke the quiet.

Leslie slouched on an overturned crate and wiggled a stray piece of string about on the floor for Portia to swat. "What are they waiting for? It's been hours."

Hamberdeen slipped the key in and out between his fingers as a sort of puzzle game to keep himself calm. "We've been in worse situations," he reminded Leslie. "There's always a way out."

Betty joined Edmond at the far end of the cellar where he had yanked a brick out of the wall to keep watch. "Do you remember when we were children out on the streets?"

Edmond looked away from her. "It hasn't gotten any better, has it?"

"It is better," replied Betty, "now that *you're* here." She took his paw in her hand. "You were always there for me."

Edmond met her eyes in surprise. He opened his mouth, but his emotions stifled his words.

"Look!" said Hamberdeen, gesturing their attention to the chart. The places on the chart marked Neverland, Baskerville Hall, and Kukuanaland all now bore the triumphant gold letters spelling "Victory!" Betty closed her eyes in relief.

A beam of sunlight broke through the gloom and struck Edmond's eyes. With a brusque snarl, he recoiled and threw his claws across his eyes to shield them from the light.

Leslie glanced up from Portia to Edmond. "I thought the sunlight was supposed to turn a werewolf back to his human form."

Edmond spun around and shot a glare at Leslie. "Go on. Say it. You've been wanting to say it ever since I got back. Tell me how I was just a stable boy who would never amount to anything. Tell me how you knew I'd always end up like this, a groveling, cringing beast, hiding away from the sun."

Leslie gaped at Edmond, for a moment speechless. The string dropped from his hand. "I don't think that. I don't think that at all. I only wish I could do more, that's all." His voice trailed off, and he leaned forward with his arms on his knees and pondered the grimy floor. Portia waved her paw at the limp string, wondering why it had stopped moving.

Death-Guardian leaned in contemplation against the side of the mountain facing the village. He had read the stars like an ancient seer before they vanished into the white dawn. The stars did not bode well, so he waited. Avian perched on the broad onyx shoulder of the Anubian dragon. She crouched low and grinned with her head tucked under her wings, her ruby eyes gleaming amidst the hooded shadow.

Death-Guardian firmed his mouth and narrowed his kohl-lined eyes at the sun breaking past the drifting pillars of smoke.

"The light of dawn has come, and the powers of darkness abate." He spoke in a rolling baritone. "This will never do. Let us have night once more." The Death-Guardian waved his staff across the sky, and the black night once more obscured the light of morning. The white hemisphere of the full moon peered up from behind the mountains in the east. The rising moon called to the werewolf huntsmen, and they lumbered out from their hiding places, stretching their claws, flexing their shoulders, shuffling forward, and calling to the moon as it renewed their brutish strength.

Death-Guardian reared to his full height and gestured to the werewolves with his staff. "Followers of Czerny, fall in behind me. Followers of Dmitri, take the left flank and prepare your crossbows. Followers of Mikhail, take the right flank, and do the same." He used his staff to support his thunderous steps as he strode towards the remnants of the derelict inn. The werewolves took up their positions and fell in behind him. Before the inn, they all stopped. The dragon raised his canine nose to sniff the smoky air. "The traitor is among them. The one they called *Davidson*. And . . . something else . . . Vorever. I sense *Vorever*."

"Yes, great one, yes!" squawked Avian.

Death-Guardian reached towards his left shoulder and coaxed the talons of the smaller dragon to creep upon his curved finger and, once she had clamped her claws around the middle joint, he moved his finger up before his face. "Avian, offspring of Ordog, be our eyes, ears, and voice. Fly as my emissary. Make a reconnaissance. Tell them to send out Davidson and the girl. Tell them, if they surrender, we will spare the others."

"Yes, yes!" Avian stretched out her wings, sprang from his finger, and sailed through the crisp air towards the inn.

"Why is it night again?" Puzzled, Leslie turned from the opening in the wall to the other Intercessors. Betty retrieved the code book from within her vest and flipped through the pages to research the phenomenon.

"Get back!" Edmond pushed Leslie clear of the opening just as Avian's head thrust through, sidelong, with one bulging ruby eye aimed forward, wandering the floor, the walls, the ceiling, to spy out the residents hiding inside.

Edmond shrank into the shadows and gestured for the others to do the same. Leslie ducked behind the crates. Hamberdeen hid between the wine racks and the back wall. Betty slipped the codebook into her vest and buried her diadem under a pile of coals in a wooden bin to conceal its glow. She scooped up Portia and sank behind the coal bin.

No sooner had the Intercessors secured their hiding places than a long conical beam of crimson light exuded from Avian's eye. The light from her eye cut through the dank shadows of the cellar. It scanned the path in front of the opening and lashed to the right just skimming the coal bin, and to the left towards the crates. Just as the light approached his hand, Leslie pulled it back behind the crate and held his breath.

The light snapped off, and Hamberdeen exhaled a long grateful breath and crossed himself, with eyes raised upward.

But the next moment, Avian broke through the loose bricks, and squeezed her body through the breach. Edmond grabbed up a lead pipe and held it ready to crash over the dragon's head. Betty gestured for him to stay back. Leslie reached cautiously, silently around the back of the crates for the crossbow he had dropped.

Avian fluttered to the floor and inched sideways. She craned her neck towards the hatchway then around at the shadows where Edmond skulked. She gave her wings a fluttery shake and spun about in a circle of fire. When she stopped spinning, the fire tapered away and she had transformed into her human form, adorned in silks, tassels, and feathers. She arched a seductive eyebrow. "What's this? Hiding in fear? I am but the emissary. I request a parlay."

She cocked her head as she stepped lightly forward on satin slippers. She paused on tip toes and called, "Davidson! Professor Davidson, my love!" Edmond cringed. She did not see him but leered as one who knows. "Ah, yes, you are here. If you want to spare your friends, give yourself up. It's the right thing to do."

Edmond looked to where Betty was hiding. Their eyes locked. Betty shook her head. Edmond opened his mouth to retort against Avian. Betty put her finger over her lips and shook her head once more. With difficulty, Edmond stifled his outburst.

Avian whirled about and flitted in the direction of the coal bin. "Beatrice Talbin. As long as you are with your friends, they will never be safe. The dragon lords sense the power within you. It draws them like a magnet to wherever you are. I heard the followers of the golden dragon were eager to lay down their lives for their friends. Will you continue to endanger your friends? Or will you cast aside your pride?"

This time Betty was about to respond, but Portia tapped Betty's mouth with her paw. Betty nodded her thanks to the kitten and remained silent.

Avian frowned at not receiving an answer. "It won't do any good. Death-Guardian commands the skies and serves as the gateway between the living and the dead. No one gets past him alive. Leslie Mallowan, Thomas Hamberdeen, curse your comrades, for they are clearly no friends of yours." She lifted her arms on either side of her. Her tasseled shawl, draped over each arm, rose behind her until the sheer silk fluttered into dragon wings. She scrabbled over the crumbling bricks surrounding the breach and flapped away into the sky.

Edmond exhaled his frustration and returned to the opening to watch. Avian disappeared against the monumental shadow of the dragon that leered down upon the village. Edmond's shoulders drooped as he scanned the towering height of the Death-Guardian. Betty joined him.

Leslie climbed out from behind the crates and tested the crossbow. "Wish I had some arrows."

"Don't forget, we still have these." Betty detached the box from her belt and revealed the two miniature books that remained.

"*Christmas Carol* and *Treasure Island?*" Mr. Hamberdeen adjusted his spectacles and blinked at the two books. "A story of redemption and a tale of adventure. But will a treasure chest fly down from the sky and brain the dragon? Or will old Ebenezer himself pop out of the book and stare the dragon down with his relentless bah humbug?"

"Or maybe," suggested Leslie, "we could use the books to maroon the dragon on a deserted island. Or we could summon the ghosts of Christmas Past, Present and Future?"

"Back!" snapped Edmond, for at that moment a red flood-light swung in through the breach. Edmond pushed the others out of range of the light, making a shield of his outstretched arms. Avian had returned and was circling above the inn, her ruby eyes casting down a searchlight to detect any escaping Intercessors.

The ceiling rattled and the cellar floor heaved. A crack fissured across the floor. Leslie hopped clear of the crack as it zigzagged past his feet. Rats squealed and scrambled out of the walls, and broken pipes snaked up through the crumbling foundation, hissing out steam and sludge. The quake shook the box with the miniature books out of Betty's hand. Betty's eyes widened as she snatched at the box in vain. It tipped over in the air and the two miniature books fell into one of the mud-filled crevices in the floor.

A chorus of wolven howls shot through the chaos. The Death-Guardian crashed his staff across the top of the inn, slashing away the roof, top floor, and ceiling, exposing the four Intercessors at the bottom of the steep crater that remained. The moon was fully obliterated by the black form towering on his hind legs over the dismantled inn. Two enormous parallel carmine eyes in the sky broke open, twin demonic slits glaring down upon the tiny Intercessors. His onyx hide gleamed like black silk, his muscular, gold-banded arms akimbo, fists planted on the sides of his belted linen kilt.

Hamberdeen whispered to the others with him. "Find the two books. Meanwhile, I'll distract this oversized hieroglyphic." Before Betty could stop him, Hamberdeen climbed to the top of the wine racks to confront the titanic foe. The Death-Guardian's short-pointed ears pricked up and he lifted his canine muzzle, glaring haughtily down with eyes lined like those of the Egyptian god Horus.

"So! You are the one called Hamberdeen." Death-Guardian bent over to get a closer look at the specimen. "What kind of name is Hamberdeen?"

Leslie gulped at the enormity of the dragon overshadowing them. He wanted to duck behind the overturned crates, but he reminded himself that Inspector Farnesworth of Scotland Yard would never allow himself to be intimidated by any evildoer, no matter how monstrous. Leslie took a trembling step forward and shook his fist at the dragon. "You should talk about names! What about a name like Death?"

Hamberdeen rolled his eyes at Leslie and gestured urgently with both his hands for him to keep out of it. The Death-Guardian threw his head back and roared with laughter. The werewolves clambered up on the peaks of the prominence that surrounded the cratered remains of the inn, snickering and exchanging cruel looks with one another. Their weapons were readied and aimed down at the four Intercessors. "Yes!" boomed the Death-Guardian. "I am Death, and there is no power greater than me."

Betty whispered something into Portia's ear and released her onto the floor. Portia prowled around, sniffing and flapping her paw cautiously at the cracks in the floors and walls, searching for the missing books.

Betty stepped forward. Her mouth bowed up in a placid smile. Her eyelids flicked open, revealing two black orbs steeled upon the onyx dragon and his minions. "So," she said, the red searchlight from Avian hovering about her, "you think Death is all powerful?"

"Shall we put my power to the test?" Death-Guardian shook his staff. "I have slain many before you, insolent human. My spirit was there with Pharaoh when he sent out his decree to kill all the first born of the Hebrews. My will awoke Mount Vesuvius, and an entire city was buried under ash and flame. I am the final barrier, the mystery, the end. To reach Alsó-Világ, you must pass me. And none who enters the realm of shadows ever returns to the land of the living. Now! Fire!" The werewolves stationed around the perimeter opened fire upon the cellar, bombarding the humans with a thick barrage of arrows. Betty calmly lifted her sword and a shield of gold light spread out from its tip. The shield blocked the arrows, and they bounced off harmlessly.

Death-Guardian snarled his anger and smashed his staff against the shield of light. The shield sputtered and failed. Death-Guardian scooped down his mighty claw towards Betty.

Leslie threw himself in front of Betty and raised his unarmed crossbow. "You'll have to go through me!"

Death-Guardian tossed his head back with thunderous laughter. "Amusing, little flea, but I do not have time for your charades. Go nip another dog!" He readied his finger to flick Leslie and Betty like marbles.

The fur on the back of Edmond's neck rose, his ears flattened, and he bared his teeth in a fierce growl. "You will not touch them!" With his eyes burning with rage, Edmond lunged for the Death-Guardian's front talon, sinking his teeth into the scales. The Death-Guardian brushed Edmond away, sending him sprawling across the cellar floor. Edmond's claws scraped the dirt as he caught himself.

Betty looked back at Edmond with concern and whirled to face the onyx dragon. Portia hissed and spat up at the dragon. Dmitri heaved up a broken rafter and tossed it down at Betty while Czerny flung down a large chunk of the wall. Betty instinctively flipped around in the air to avoid the missiles and landed with perfect balance upon her feet. "Well done!" exclaimed Hamberdeen. Betty nodded, surprised and impressed by her own agility. Portia prrowed her approval.

Death-Guardian snorted and clapped his hands together in front of his chest, rotating and pressing the hands around a flaming orb that was forming within his grasp. As he concocted his weapon, he leered as one conjuring a force of evil.

Dmitri waved his pack forward and they vaulted over the perimeter, skidding down the sides towards the cellar below.

"Look out!" cried Hamberdeen. "The wolf brigade is back!"

Edmond raised himself on his back legs, preparing to take on the pack one at a time. Betty drew her sword across the sky from east to west, and as she did, the moon dipped in the west, the sun rose in the east, and the darkness huddled once more below the mountains. The werewolves fell back and shrieked in agony as the full force of the sun's rays blinded them. They squirmed upon the rubble, reaching their arms outward to block the light with their outstretched claws. Edmond sank back into the shadows of the cellar to avoid the sun.

Furious at seeing his handiwork undone, Death-Guardian stomped his foot, shaking the foundations of the earth. The impact sent Leslie falling face forward onto the muddy floor. Hamberdeen tumbled down from the racks. The fissures in the cellar floor ruptured into a yawning pit, plunging Edmond and Betty into the darkness below. Leslie shot his hand towards Betty, but he could not reach her in time. Leslie splatted a puddle in vexation. He felt something hard in the puddle. He raised his hand, and the two miniature books came up with it. Portia and Leslie both looked at the miniature books, then looked at each other in surprise.

But before Leslie could think of how to use the two books, Death-Guardian unleashed the fireballs he had been conjuring. A hail of fiery meteors flew in a steady storm down into the crater. Hamberdeen yanked Leslie back under an overhanging part of the inn, providing some feeble protection. Portia pressed up against Leslie's legs and clenched the floor with her claws.

As they plummeted into the pit, Edmond caught Betty's middle in the crook of his arm. Betty's sword scraped down the side of the crater and caught in a fissure along the wall. Edmond swung his legs around and, balancing himself on the side of the wall while holding onto Betty, he pulled her into a rugged alcove that had cracked open amid the fragmented foundation and disrupted roots. No sooner had Edmond seen that Betty was safe in the cave than the earth around them quaked once more. Betty lifted her hands palms upward to hold the roof of the little cave in place while Edmond balanced on the thin ledge at the narrow opening of the alcove.

Then came the torrenting shower of meteors. Edmond arched his back and gritted his teeth as the hot fireballs pelted and seared his back. Even so, he remained in the breach, shielding Betty from the onslaught, much as he had done once before on the streets of London to protect her from the icy rain when they were children. Betty wanted to reach out to him, but she could not let go of the roof without it collapsing and burying them both.

Edmond clenched his eyes shut in pain as the fiery hail scorched his back. "I've got to get you out of here," he said through his teeth.

"The book. In my vest," Betty cried. "Take it!"

Holding to the ledge with his back claws, Edmond strained his freed arm towards her vest. Betty moved her body closer to him, while maintaining her hold on the roof. He clasped the top of the book.

"Davidson!" roared the Death-Guardian, swooping down to leer at the werewolf guarding Betty with his own life. "Stand aside!"

Edmond wheeled about to face the dragon, his fur burnt and tattered, one ear nearly singed off, his eyes glazed over. He swallowed hard and glared defiance into the black glossy scales of the Death-Guardian. "Betty is my charge. You won't have her."

The Death-Guardian roared in fury. He inhaled long and deep then released a blast of flames full upon Edmond. Edmond raised his arms before his face to block the barrage. In seconds, he was a cloud of ash. The Death-Guardian snuffed his nostrils and the ashes dispersed like a trail of smoke from a burnt-out wick.

An anguished shriek erupted from Betty's core and echoed throughout the pit that surrounded her. She collapsed to her knees in the alcove and covered her horrified face with shaking hands. The earth tumbled down around her. The Death-Guardian dug into the dirt and clutched hold of Betty, dragging her out. He lifted her up as he unbent his frame, once more filling the horizon with his immensity. His werewolf huntsmen sent up a unified cry of victory at seeing the dirt-encrusted hostage in the dragon's claws.

"Edmond Davidson is no more! Thus shall all who oppose me perish!" declared the Death-Guardian. "I am the mighty destroyer! All are subject to my will! Even you, tiny, pathetic girl!" Betty shot a glare at the Death-Guardian, pushing against the pressure of the talon joints to free herself from their grip. Gleams of golden light pulsated in the veins of her forehead, neck, and forearms as she strained against her captivity.

The dragon lord inhaled long and deep, re-stoking the fires of destruction to pour out upon Betty. He tossed Betty down in a heap, and the werewolves formed a circle around her, sending up taunting howls, ecstatic to see their enemy so humbled.

Betty pushed back the strand from across her eyes and glared up at the dragon as his mouth opened to release the flames. She reached into her vest for her book, but the book was no longer there. She froze in panic. But the next moment a wave of peace, like the warm wings of a mother bird, enfolded her.

She closed her eyes and focused on the Golden Dragon. She sensed his presence. *Edmond is safe*, his voice was telling her. *You have not lost him.* She could taste the herbal tea and honey. She could feel the rhythm of the rocking chair and the comfort of the hearth. She could see the joy in the Golden Dragon's eyes. When she opened her own eyes, she found herself in the cozy room in Vandor with the Golden Dragon resting the tip of his chin gently on the top of her head and breathing warm puffs of air upon her, infusing her with strength. They communed in nearly instantaneous thought.

Edmond is not gone.

But I saw him perish!

The tormented werewolf is no more. His soul awaits you.

I must go to him!

Not yet, Daughter of Vandor. To reach Edmond, you must put a stop to the Death-Guardian. Only he stands between you and the land of shadows.

How can I fight him?

We shall fight him together!

Betty lowered her eyes to her hands folded before her. A tug in her senses and she knew she had returned to the rubble of the inn, confronting the looming horror. When she looked up, her eyes were blue like the serene summer sky. Fearless, she rose to face the mighty dragon lord, unafraid.

The surge of fire burst from the dragon's mouth. Betty threw out her palms in front of her. Her palms glowed with a golden aura and absorbed the full force of the fiery blast.

Behind Death-Guardian, Hamberdeen helped Leslie up over the prominence surrounding the crater, and Portia, carrying the two miniature books in her mouth, scampered up over Leslie's back onto the rubble.

The Death-Guardian snarled a curse at Betty and raised his staff to crush her.

"Yes, my lord, yes!" cawed Avian. "Finish her at last!"

Portia tossed the two books up in the air and Leslie caught them in his hand. He placed the first miniature book in the retention spring of the crossbow and held the crossbow on his shoulder. Measuring the distance to the target with his eyes, he aimed at the Death-Guardian's neck.

"That's it," said Hamberdeen. "Steady now. Fire!"

Leslie pulled the trigger and the book hurled towards the Dragon like an arrow. The book unraveled into a giant, heavy chain that wrapped around the dragon's muzzle. Leslie yanked on the chain like a cowboy with a lasso. Hamberdeen lent his strength to Leslie and the two dragged the dragon downward and the weight of Jacob Marley's chains sent Death-Guardian hurtling towards the ground. The werewolves scrambled out of his rapidly spreading shadow to avoid being crushed. Leslie leapt out of the way just in time to escape the weight of the dragon as his titanic body crashed to the ground, radiating out a splay of cracks in the earth.

"Good work, Leslie!" Betty set her hand upon one of the giant links in the chain, spreading a golden light across each of the links, and the links tightened around the Death-Guardian's body. "Now for *Treasure Island!*" she told her cousin.

Leslie tossed the miniature *Treasure Island* to Hamberdeen. He opened it and squinted at the tiny letters through his spectacles. It was Chapter 3 "The Black Spot." From the middle of the book oozed something black, like a great blob of spilt treacle, that splatted near the dragon and formed a giant black spot on the ground. The golden chains of their own accord heaved the Death-Guardian to the black spot. Waves of the black ooze rose towards the dragon, as if he were a magnet attracting its internal ores. The dragon moaned and struggled against the chains, to no avail.

The werewolves saw the imminent demise of their leader and fell back in terror, clambering over one another and scampering off into the woods and up the mountain.

Avian, eyes bulging in alarm, flapped away.

The chains yanked Death-Guardian down into the black spot, and the black spot wrapped its ooze around him. His roar echoed as he fell into the bottomless depths of the hole.

"*Death! Thou shalt die!*" declared Hamberdeen as the ooze overlapped upon itself over and over, sealing itself shut until all that was left on the ground was a small black door with gold metal work around the molded panels and keyhole. A golden plaque in the middle of the door read, "Herein lies the land of shadow, the land of Alsó-Világ. The living cannot enter and none may e'er return."

Betty closed her eyes and released her pent-up breath. A flurry of soft snow dusted down from the sky, the white flakes mingling with the gold specks of light that had settled on Betty's hair, hands, and face. She walked away from Hamberdeen and Leslie. Leslie was about to stop her, but Hamberdeen caught him by the arm and shook his head somberly, his eyes informing Leslie to let Betty be alone for a little while.

Betty found a makeshift ladder and climbed up to the roof of a barn. She sat on the roof, blinking up into the snowflakes. Tears burned her eyes, and her mouth tugged on the sides. Portia snuggled beside her and rested her chin on Betty's lap. She stroked the kitten's fur and managed to choke, "We've got to get him back."

CHAPTER 39
LAND OF SHADOW

Ordog watched his titans fall one by one, a four-act tragedy staged within the sphere hovering in the creased palm of his talon. The furrow across the dragon lord's brow deepened as even the mightiest, the Death-Guardian, failed against the weapons of his enemies. Energy seeped from Ordog's being as all he had conspired over past eons was snatched from him in a matter of hours.

Heaving a throaty groan, he burrowed himself within the mountain. There, he settled with a thunderous rumble in the midst of a hollow cavern enclosed by pillars of rock and surrounded by a spiral of glass casings that glowed in a green spectral mist. His eyelids closed as he inhaled through his nostrils, drawing in the mist, absorbing the energy from the souls trapped within the casings. As his organs quivered with new life with each infusion, Ordog mused to himself.

Vorever has not won. I, Ordog, have existed since the beginning of time. I can wait. Fragments of the scales still exist, even if but the merest splinters, and, in time, I shall gather them all, and they, in turn, will produce even more and even greater titans than their progenitors. The door, left by the Death-Guardian is shut. There is no danger of the Intercessors invading my rest.

Once I return to my full strength, I shall summon the soulless legions of the deep, and they will serve me in my quest!

Vorever watched Ordog in a white-orange flame that danced an inch from his uplifted palm. The golden dragon crouched on the ledge of the cliff overlooking the wide green-gray sea that surrounded the island of Vandor. The waves rolled in towards the island, surged upward, and crashed against the white face of the cliff, shooting out a spray of salty foam. Vorever closed his foreclaw around the flame, and the flame absorbed into his gold-scaled flesh. His blue eyes sharpened and a serene smile rested on his lips. He gazed out across the roaring sea and breathed, "Now is the time."

The spar, halyards, and bowsprit of the *Jolly Roger* were strung with a rainbow of pixie lanterns glowing in the star-hazed night. On deck, the celebration of the victory over Water-Ghoul was in full swing. Pixies flitted around the sails, piping their flutes, squeezing their accordions, and strumming their harps.

Frieda was flushed with joy as Peter swept Hook's broad hat off his head and dipped into an exaggerated bow. Frieda laughed and curtsied. Then, her breath was nearly swept away as Peter playfully pulled her along the deck in a lively mixture of a polka and Irish jig. The layers of skirts and petticoats on Frieda and Captain Hook's topcoat and cravat on Peter swirled about as the two danced. Peter's shadow kept up with the dance as best as he could but had to stoop and spin to avoid Peter's waving arms and kicking feet. Frieda threw her head back to watch as the mermaids flew up from the water into the sky, arched over the ship, and dived back into the waves with a splash. The two children laughed in the momentary shower the splash had precipitated.

Frieda paused to catch her breath and wipe her glasses near the railing where Spinderbeck and Verne were clanking their tankards of frothy hot chocolate in toasts to one another.

"I could never have done it without you, ol' chap," Spinderbeck told Verne.

"No, no, mon ami, *you* were the brave one," said Verne to Spinderbeck.

Tondor stopped plucking her harp and raised a hand to her pixie ear, straining to listen past the ruckus. She perched in an attentive stance on the railing with one booted leg bent in front of her and the other pulled back with the toe just barely touching the railing. She motioned the other pixies to silence and pointed towards the bowsprit. Frieda noted the pixie's watchful stance and brought it to Peter's attention. Peter whistled shrilly past his fingers, and the merriment paused.

A gold cluster of stars spiraled into a portal on deck, and through it stepped Foulata. She lowered herself a little to clear the portal and peered out into this strange, new world with dazzled wonder. "So *this* is Neverland," she breathed in awe as a flock of pixies danced about her hair like curious butterflies. She giggled and reached her slender fingers towards their soft, colorful wings. Tondor landed on Foulata's outstretched finger and bowed reverently, "Welcome, Warrior Maid of Kukuanaland, Dragon-slayer and loyal friend."

Foulata smiled upon the pixie and glanced back over her shoulder at the portal. She reached her free hand in and clasped the hand of Captain Good who soon joined her on deck, followed by Daniel Khumalo.

"It's Daniel!" cried Frieda in delight.

Spinderbeck poured a tankard for Khumalo, insisting he tell them all about the battle against the Diamond-Hoarder.

But another golden portal opened on the other side of the ship, and Sherlock Holmes, Dr. Watson, and Akira Yamada emerged. Watson knitted his eyebrows as he took in the passengers aboard the eighteenth-century ship. He raised a hand beside his face to shield himself from a splash of water from the mermaids diving into the sea. "I say, Holmes! Where the deuce are we *now*?"

Frieda pulled Peter by the hand up to Holmes and Watson. "Welcome to Neverland!" Then, her eyes twinkled at the detective. "I daresay you don't recognize me."

Holmes took a moment to study the small girl who stood before him, but her glasses and ruddy complexion gave her away. "Not Miss Fernsby, surely!" he laughed.

"One and the same," replied Frieda with a proper nod of her head.

"And why not," said Watson to the detective. "With spectral hounds and evil dragons, I'll wager if we stay in Neverland long enough, we'll both be in knickerbockers again with catapults in our back pockets."

Holmes was about to denounce Watson's lapse in logic, when another circle of golden light opened, and Betty entered their world, a gray kitten in her arms. She was followed by Mr. Hamberdeen and Leslie.

Frieda at once sensed the sorrow that weighed on Betty's heart, and she pushed past the others up to her young friend. She took Betty's two hands in hers and was distraught at how clammy they felt. She peered up at her friend with concern. "Edmond?"

"Yes," Betty said, meeting Frieda's eyes. "His soul is trapped in Alsó-Világ, and they say no soul has ever returned from the land of shadows and no living being can ever cross into that realm." Betty turned and looked along the gleaming path the moon had cast across the sea. "Vorever assures me there is a way to get him back, but I don't see how." She raised her chin, but her shoulders trembled and tears formed against her will. "He . . ."

Frieda unwrapped her own shawl and draped it over Betty's shoulders. "If Vorever says there's a way," Frieda nudged her spectacles back up to the bridge of her nose, "then there's a way."

Khumalo set aside his undrunk tankard and rested a hand of sympathy upon Betty's shoulder. "Yes, trust in the wisdom of Vorever."

Holmes felt in his pocket for his handkerchief to lend to Betty, but as the handkerchief unfolded, the residue he had preserved from the Carpathian inn sifted out from the folds. He caught the blue, black, green, and white sprinkles in the palm of his gloved hand. At the same time, the little brown bottle he had retrieved fell from his pocket and rolled into a corner near the door to the captain's cabin. Portia scampered after the bottle, stopping it with her outstretched paw and batting it about the deck.

Tondor sensed something strange about the bottle. She crinkled her nose in curiosity and flit over to where Portia had the bottle cornered against the bulkhead. Tondor tugged on a strand of Portia's fur, and the kitten hopped in surprise, prrowed when she spotted the tiny warrior maid, and sniffed at her. "Greetings, magnificent beast," said Tondor, gazing up into Portia's large green eyes. "May I inspect your quarry?" Portia hesitated but Tondor's warm smile reassured her, and she moved out of the pixie's way. Making a visor of one hand, Tondor peered in through the bottle.

"What is it?" asked Peter.

The glass was fogged, so Tondor blew on it and wiped her hand around in a circular motion. She blinked into the bottle. She could see a wisp of mist clinging to the base of the bottle inside. She put her hand behind her ear and listened. "There's something in the bottle. It wants to be set free."

"Is it alive?" asked Peter, picking up the bottle, and squeezing one eye shut while looking into the mouth of the bottle with his open eye.

"I found it in the kitchen back at the inn, along with this." Holmes indicated the residue in his hand. "The bottle's contents exuded a bitter odor, an alkaloid . . ." Peter brought the bottle close to his mouth to taste when Holmes added, ". . . possibly *poisonous*."

Peter dropped the bottle, but Khumalo caught it before it hit the planking. Betty held his arm with bated breath as he studied the bottle with interest. "This looks like the type of bottle described in folklore," he noted. "Sometimes they are used to trap demons, sometimes they hold the elixir of life, and sometimes they contain the one thing most prized in exchange for some reward, like the mermaid's voice in the Danish tale. The bitterness you detected, Mr. Holmes, is not the bitterness of poison, but that of sorrow and regret. It is the natural chemical reaction when all hope is forsaken. Much of the substance has already been used up, but just a drop remains there at the bottom of the bottle."

Betty squeezed the ends of her shawl tight in her hands, hardly daring to believe what her heart was sensing in the words of Khumalo, that there was indeed still a way to save Edmond.

"I heard it calling," said Tondor Char.

"What did it sound like?" asked Hamberdeen.

"Like a werewolf's mournful howl."

"Ah," said Yamada, closing his eyes as he reflected on the ancient texts he had memorized over the years. "Then it is a werewolf's last hope. And one drop still remains."

Betty's breath caught in her throat. "But how to get the hope to Edmond!" said Betty. "He's in the land of shadows. They say no one can go there."

"Land of shadows, eh?" Peter Pan scratched his head, then snapped his fingers. He turned to his shadow so fast the shadow backstepped quickly in surprise.

"Well, old friend," said Peter, "It's the land of shadows, right? And you're a shadow, right? So, you understand what you must do?"

The shadow nodded.

"No, Peter, not your shadow," gasped Frieda, but Peter put up his hand to gesture her back. He pivoted towards his shadow like a commanding officer sending his best soldier to the front.

"You know what it means, now? Once you go in, you may never come out."

The shadow nodded with confidence and saluted.

"Well, goodbye, then." Peter thrust out his hand and the shadow gave his hand a firm shake. Peter's frown deepened as he fought to suppress his sorrow. "Goodbye forever. And off you go. Get on! Go away! You always got me into trouble anyway!" Peter stalked away, wiped a hand across his nose, and curled up in a corner to sulk.

Betty smiled sadly at Peter, then turned to the shadow. "Thank you, shadow, for volunteering for this mission."

The shadow waved his hand as if to say it was nothing at all and adjusted his hat to a jaunty tilt.

"But how does he get in?" asked Foulata.

"With this key, of course," said Hamberdeen, flourishing the magical key.

"And I have the lantern that will light the way," said Frieda, taking the lantern from a hook near the captain's cabin.

"Then, it will be up to us," said Jules Verne, "to draw Ordog out. We must clear the way for Peter's shadow to reach Edmond."

"And this," added Holmes, stirring the residue in his palm with his index finger, "no doubt scraped from the dragon scales, *this* is what will draw the fiend out of his lair." He clenched his fist around the residue.

Betty placed one hand in the crook of Holmes' arm and one hand on the shoulder of Frieda. "I cannot ask this of you," she said to her friends. "You have all fought well and gallantly, but this may be the hardest battle of them all."

"Just find me some arrows," said Leslie. "I'm starting to get the hang of this crossbow."

Deep within Alsó-Világ, Ordog's chin nestled against his folded talons. The torches set in their sconces around the sepulcher cast a play of shadow and light against his crimson scales. One of his nostrils twitched as a familiar infusion wafted down to him from the world above. *The scales!* One eyelid popped open, and his flaming orb rolled around, scanning his cave for the source of that aroma.

His left ear pricked up as he caught the faintest hum of a high-pitched radiation. *The scales do not wait to be found! The scales come to me!*

A tantalized grin stretched across his lips, and he smacked them greedily. "So, it begins already." He detached his concentration from the souls he had been absorbing and focused rather on tracking down that scent and that sound. *Up there! Up there in the village!*

Ordog's fist smashed out of the side of the mountain, and his talons extended towards a small steaming pot hung on a hob over a burning pile of wood. From the boiling water in the pot rose the steam, carrying to him the scent of the infused dragon scale particles. The rest of Ordog's body ploughed out of the mountain, large lahars of burnt earth and rock crumbling from his shoulders as he exalted himself against the frosty dusk sky. He spread his red and orange wings, and the deafening shudder sent shockwaves rippling across the air.

He reared over the village, and his eyes zeroed in on the steam rising from the iron pot. He rubbed his fore-talons together in front of his lighter-colored underbelly and let his tongue slide along his drooling mouth. His fiery orbs roamed the village, over the onyx door fixed in the ground, over the cratered remains of the demolished inn, over the deserted homes, the large village barn, the tavern, and the church, alert for the presence of the Intercessors, but the village was forsaken and still. *They are here. They are here.*

The church, near the center of the village, was the color of a soft sunset, with three wooden gables, and a central tower that peaked in a large onion-shaped dome of forest green topped by a spire. Inside the sanctuary, on the pulpit, curled up in a nap, was Portia, the kitten. Before the altar on a wide Persian rug, seated in a circle, were the Intercessors. Betty's chart was spread out before them.

In the center of the chart was a gold circle around the words "Alsó-Világ." Above the circle was set Hamberdeen's key. To the left was the brown bottle with a cork to keep the last drop of hope safe until needed. To the right was Frieda's lantern, the white candle within shining upon the faces of the Intercessors.

The code book lay open in Betty's lap. She sat with her chin cupped in her hand, puzzling over the page Yamada had recommended. She read the passage aloud.

When that which is no more reveals that which is
The evil will rise and forever will be there within
The darkness when hope enlightens the shadow the fallen will return
The fallen shake the earth and the soul may be restored beyond the gate

Betty looked to her friends. "What does it mean?"

Tondor marched across the chart and stood with her hands on her hips looking over the passage. "The evil will rise and forever will be there within?" She frowned. "Doesn't sound promising."

"Wait," said Khumalo. "Read the first line again."

Spinderbeck read it aloud. "When that which is no more reveals that which is . . ."

"I wonder." Khumalo withdrew his handkerchief from his breast pocket, the handkerchief he had cut a hole out of to illustrate his point about the universe to Betty. "That which is no more . . ." He indicated the handkerchief. Next, he set the handkerchief over the page. Now the hole cut out of the handkerchief encircled the following parts of the passage. "Forever will be there / when hope enlightens the shadow/ and the soul may be restored."

Hamberdeen's face brightened. "That's it, Daniel. You've found it. Peter's shadow will take the bottle of hope and Frieda's lantern through the doorway, and, when the hope reveals Edmond, the shadow can bring his soul back to the land of the living."

"Ordog is here now," noted Yamada, frowning as he leaned on the handle of Raskolnikov's axe.

"We know what to do." Leslie adjusted the strap of his quiver filled with arrows gifted to him by Tiger Lily's tribe.

"That's right," agreed Foulata as Verne helped her make some adjustments to the firing mechanism of the Martian ray gun. She glanced at Good, and Good returned an affirming nod as he readied his rifle. Watson took the cue and checked to make sure his revolver was loaded. Holmes stood and assisted Betty to her feet. "The game is afoot then."

"Or . . . a paw," replied Betty, her eyes twinkling. She looked to where the kitten was napping. "Are you ready, Portia?"

Portia yawned and blinked from one Intercessor's expectant face to the next.

Ordog overturned the pot, irritated that the residue of the scales had all but evaporated. Infuriated, he slinked towards the center of the village, but stopped when something approached. A shadow stretched across the length of ground between the village and Ordog. It had long sharp claws and long pointed ears. Startled, Ordog followed the shadow with his eyes up to the source.

A tiny kitten approached, backlit by a warm glow. Portia halted before Ordog, a speck of gray fluff against the immensity of Ordog's front talons. She glared up at the dragon. The fur on her back rose as she squeaked out a spit, hiss, and mrrrrow.

The furrow in Ordog's brow lifted in surprise, and he shook with laughter. Portia snorted, plopped down on her haunches, and licked her front paw. The light behind Portia grew brighter, and the little girl holding the lantern approached, accompanied by a young boy in a broad hat and frock coat that were much too big for him.

"Greetings from Neverland, mighty Ordog," said Frieda. "We come to make a bargain with *you*."

Ordog drew one talon across his chin in disbelief. "I can crush you both with one stomp of my foot. Why should I bargain with you?"

Peter tipped back his hat with an indignant frown. "You are addressing *the* Peter Pan, slayer of the Water-Ghoul and out-witter of your pet crocodile."

"That's right," said Frieda. "The tribes, pixies, and mermaids cry out for vengeance. But we are willing to spare you on one condition. Give us the soul of Edmond Davidson."

Ordog's laughter was punctuated by puffs of smoke from his nostrils. "Spare *me*? Your bargain is groundless. I, Ordog, will soon rise up and conquer not only this world, but all the worlds in every story ever written! Do you have something better? What about the source of that delicious infusion I smelled in that pot? Do you have more fragments?" He tapped his talons together before his greedy eyes.

A voice rang out from behind Peter and Frieda. "They do not need fragments. They have me." Betty advanced towards the mountainous dragon, her arms outstretched symmetrically on either side of her body, palms face up.

Ordog's amusement ceased at once, for superimposed over Betty was the colossal spirit of Vorever, glowing with such an overwhelming aura that the evening was as bright as day, and her arms maneuvered his great golden wings as if they were attached to her wrists and shoulders.

"I have faced you before." Ordog tried to pierce the eyes of the Golden Dragon shining through the eyes of the young woman who approached, but the light from those eyes was too much for Ordog. He had to look away.

"You *will* grant my friend safe passage into Alsó-Világ," declared Betty.

"The door is locked," returned Ordog. "He who enters must first get past me!" Head lowered and neck arched, his eyes burned as he crouched before the onyx door like a cornered, snarling mongrel.

"So be it." Betty lifted one arm, and as she did the immense golden wing to her right rose like a theatrical curtain, revealing the loft of the village barn, and within the loft were Foulata, Captain Good, and Khumalo aiming the Martian ray gun directly at Ordog's neck.

This was Hamberdeen's signal. He hurried out from the side door of the church and ushered Peter and Frieda past the distracted Ordog towards the onyx door.

Ordog narrowed his eyes in disdain at the ray gun manned by the three tiny humans. Smoke whooshed from his nostrils as he flexed his ready talons and lifted his fist to crush the barn. Before he could bring down his fist, however, a cloud of sparkles hove into view. It was a regiment of pixies, led by Tondor Char. Her auburn hair was tied up behind her pixie ears with a few loose swirls of hair dancing about her face as she stung the dragon with her determined eyes and blew the charge on her trumpet.

The pixies gale-forced their way to the dragon. Ordog watched the Neverlanders flit past his nose with narrowed eyes and chortled in amusement at these tiny specks who imagined they were anything more than annoying insects to him. He readied his front claws on either side of the flying group, preparing to clap his claws shut upon them.

Tondor drew a gleaming dagger from the sheath on the side of her knee-high velveteen boots and skidded down the air current towards the neck of the crimson dragon. She threw the dagger at an orange tuft between the crimson scales. The dragon howled in pain and swatted at Tondor. The blow sent Tondor somersaulting backward in the air. Portia's eyes widened in alarm at the sight of Tondor and pounced up, catching Tondor on her back, and arched down towards the ground. "Thank you, mighty friend of Vorever," said Tondor, astride the kitten, hanging onto tufts of fur like reins to safely guide her. Portia prrowed and landed gracefully on all four paws not far from where Ordog stood. Ordog inhaled through his nostrils, stoking the flames within. He aimed his open maw at Tondor and the kitten.

Seeing the two in danger, Leslie whipped an arrow from his quiver and set it in the groove of his crossbow. He scrambled up a slope and dropped forward, his crossbow shouldered. He squeezed one eye shut while he aimed and fired a direct hit at the middle of Ordog's forehead. The arrow bore a hole in the dragon's head, but the wound healed quickly, and Ordog turned on Leslie with deadly purpose.

The dragon raised his left talon to stomp Leslie, but Tondor's pixie troop dive-bombed the dragon from both sides and jabbed into the flesh of his ankles with their swords. Green smoke hissed out of the wounds, energy escaping from his being. Ordog snapped his jaws at the attacking pixies, but before he could devour them, the full force of the Martian heat ray hit him in his throat.

"Well done, my dear!" Captain Good jabbed the air with a triumphant fist as Foulata and Khumalo swiveled the tripod around to re-aim.

Ordog reeled back, roaring in ear-splitting agony. The gaping hole in his throat oozed with green slime and he gnashed his teeth in fury. He grimaced back towards his underground cave, eager to retreat and recharge his energy by devouring the souls waiting there, especially that of Edmond Davidson. That soul possessed a strength of will and rebellion that would serve him well against the Intercessors. He was distracted, however, by a blinding light of gold, and he whipped his head back around to center on Betty.

Betty lifted the great golden wing to her left to reveal Yamada in warrior ready stance on the spired dome of the village church. With a powerful shout, Yamada leapt from the dome towards the dragon, swinging the handle of Raskolnikov's axe like a ninja's staff in a series of dexterous circles to the side and above his head. He landed on his feet, body bent forward, eyes raised towards the enemy, and axe poised in both hands before him. The gaping, smoking hole in Ordog's throat prevented the dragon from breathing fire. To compensate, the dragon raised his claws to strike Yamada, but Yamada threw the axe with an expert's aim and it sliced through the air and clipped through each one of Ordog's talons before whipping about and returning like a boomerang to Yamada who adroitly caught the handle. Ordog sucked on his sore toes to staunch the green ooze.

Ordog, once large enough to eclipse the sunlight, was shrinking bit by bit as he lost energy and was now the size of a large building. He screeched in the ancient tongue of the dragons, and a flock of gray miniature dragons erupted from the open crevices in the mountain with a deafening flutter of leathery wings. The miniature dragons swooped down upon the Intercessors, like seagulls hunting wayward fish in the crests of the waves. Orpheus, one of the pixie warriors, was scooped up into the maw of a miniature dragon, who tossed him up into the air, and caught him in its mouth, swallowing the young pixie before he had a chance to call for help.

Leslie loaded and fired his crossbow as fast as he could to drive off the swarm of dragons. Spinderbeck drew his sword and powered up to Betty, who with her own sword, was plowing through the flock of dragons, warding off their grasping claws, as she made her way straight to the source. Ordog.

Foulata pulled the lever on the ray gun, but it only sputtered and droned down into a helpless silence. Verne climbed up into the loft to see if he could help.

The miniature dragons slammed one after another against the loft, and Good fired his rifle into the swarm while Verne repaired the ray gun. At last, there was a promising click within the mechanism of the heat ray followed by a crescendoing hum. Khumalo aimed the barrel in the direction of the dragon swarm and fired. One by one, the miniature dragons disintegrated into a hail of ash. Through this rippling curtain of ash, Ordog thrust his furious head with a long, loud roar of rage.

Betty and Spinderbeck were upon the dragon with their swords. Ordog grasped Betty up into his fist and clenched his claws to squeeze the life out of her as he grinned with sadistic pleasure. Green dust billowed out from between his fingers, choking Betty, and the golden aura slipped from her like an unfastened cloak. *To come so far*, she thought as she blinked past the dust into the darkening skies above Ordog. *Edmond. I only wish I could have saved you before I* . . . She barely managed a weak cough. The wings superimposed on Betty's arms went limp, her face turned pale, and her head dropped backward. "Betty!" called out Spinderbeck in desperation, his sword frozen in his hands.

Holmes and Watson, crouched in the doorway of the church, had been awaiting their signal from Betty. Seeing her caught in the clutches of Ordog, Holmes' face drained of color and his white-knuckled fingers tightened on the door frame. His eyes darted about for all possible methods to free her. He noted a boulder on the edge of the mountain held in place by the long-bowed trunk of a Carpathian pine. His mind worked like quicksilver to calculate the trajectory of the boulder in conjunction to the head of the leering dragon.

Watson started when Holmes clamped his hand on his comrade's shoulder. "Watson. Do you see that twig on that pine? The one close to the boulder?"

Watson stood, shoulder pressed against the side of the church door, his army revolver raised before his face with his finger ready on the trigger. He scowled and squinted past the clouds of ash to the pine his friend was pointing towards. "I see it."

"I want you to shoot that twig . . . now . . . and, for God's sake, don't miss!"

Watson took careful aim and fired at the twig. The twig splintered. The trunk of the tall pine twanged, releasing the boulder like a catapult. The bolder flew in a parabolic path, bounced against the side of the mountain, rumbled down the slope, and crashed against the head of the crimson dragon with a resounding thud. Upon impact, Ordog's claws instinctively splayed open, dropping Betty. The sparkling cloud of pixies buoyed Betty up on their wings as the rush of the wintry winds revived her. The golden aura enveloped her once more, and the superimposed wings spread out from her two arms.

The bolder cracked in two upon the crimson dragon's skull and Ordog jerked his glare at Watson. He scuffled with murderous intent towards Watson. Holmes calmly interposed himself between Ordog and Watson, his fists raised and rounded like a Victorian boxer, his eyes glinting with determination. Yamada joined him, his own hands held karate style. Holmes noted the stance, nodded in appreciation of its effectiveness, and, thus, shifted his position, opening his clenched fists to imitate the style displayed by Yamada.

Ordog laughed at the two puny humans and their feeble attempts at self-defense. Tondor landed on Holmes' shoulder and whispered in his ear. Holmes raised a knowing eyebrow towards Yamada. Yamada smiled and nodded. They pivoted to the side and revealed behind them the golden dragon superimposed over Betty, fixing Ordog with serene blue eyes.

Ordog's panicked eyes darted in all directions, the ray gun, the arrows, the pixies, the Golden Dragon. With nowhere else to turn, Ordog flapped his wings and took to the sky. Betty, emanating the form of the Golden Dragon, soared upward to confront Ordog in a battlefield of stars.

CHAPTER 40
ESCAPE FROM THE LAND OF SHADOW

Mr. Hamberdeen, Frieda, and Peter, accompanied by his shadow, slipped behind the village shops. They stopped, their backs flat against the side of the first building, until Hamberdeen confirmed Ordog was distracted and waved them across the open area to the next shop. In this manner, they reached the onyx door unnoticed.

They hunched over the door while Peter kept an eye on the dragon. Hamberdeen slid his key into the lock. The lock clattered loose and the door pushed open with a suctioning intake of air.

Peter's shadow hung back, but Peter gave him a stern scowl and pushed him towards the door. The shadow swallowed hard, set his broad-brimmed hat on his head, and crept forward. Frieda stopped him, the light of her lantern glimmering in her spectacles, revealing concern as she handed him the lantern. "A light for the darkest places, the mermaid said."

The shadow wrapped his fingers around the brass handle and the light from the candle left him nearly invisible, revealing only a vague outline of his Pannish form.

"And don't forget this." Peter tossed the shadow the bottle with the one last drop of hope.

"And this," added Hamberdeen, pushing the key into the shadow's coat pocket. "So you can open all doors. Remember, the code book says hope will enlighten the shadow. Mind those words, and you will succeed."

The shadow waved a salute and plunged into the doorway, using the lantern to light the rock-hewn steps that led down into the heart of the mountain.

The steps were stained with clots of mud and crustings of rust. The shadow whistled to dispel waves of fear. It was a lullaby once sung by Wendy's mother long ago. The whistle died into forced puffs of voiceless air as he arrived at the dungeons, a labyrinth of passages lined with countless old, rotting doors. Skeletons hung from shackles on the walls, and the skulls of humans, dragons, vampires, and wolves were strewn along the floor.

The shadow's way was blocked by a wooden door with wrought iron hinges. He shined the lantern on the door handle, but it was chained, and the padlock was on the opposite side. He set down the lantern and bottle, shoved the key under the crack at the bottom of the door, and melted into a tar-like puddle on the ground. As such, he was able to slip under the crack. Once on the other side of the door, he reconstituted his Pannish shape, picked up the key, and unlocked the door and retrieved the bottle and lantern.

The door led to a stalactite-dripped chamber that groaned and rumbled with echoes. Here the large stone table stood atop the iron grating from which rose twists of smoke and flakes of ash. The shadow lay flat on the grating and peered down past it to a round inner chamber lit by torchlight. Below a greenish glow emitted from glass casings spiraled around the room. A turn of the key, and the shadow swung open a square of the grating and dropped down.

He landed on the gray tiles conjoined to form a four-pointed compass upon the floor. The torches were set in iron sconces around the wall, and between the torches were glass casings filled with the green mist of the souls trapped within. The gauges on the sides of the casings were half red and half green, indicating the souls were half digested.

The shadow crooked a finger over his mouth as he rounded the room, studying the casings. Each one had a bronze plaque engraved with ancient symbols. The shadow, who barely knew how to read English, scratched his head, wondering how to determine which casing belonged to the soul of Edmond Davidson. He lifted the lantern to read the symbols, and the flame within the lantern guttered in the direction of one casing in particular, leaning towards it as if to reach the soul within.

He shined the lantern up and down the casing, searching for a way to open it. The mist within the casket tapered into a long ghoulish finger that scraped out the words "Tuo em tel" on the glass. The shadow reeled back and clamped a hand over his pounding heart. Swallowing his fear, he set Hamberdeen's key upon the glass pane, and the key flew from his hand and hovered around the glass like a moth around a porch lamp. The key left a golden thread of light in its wake as it formed the gold outline of a door in the glass. The glass within the outline melted and the mist escaped.

With a sinking groan, the mist hung low upon the ground, disappearing by degrees beneath the tiles, like a ghost returning to its grave. Desperate to salvage the soul, the shadow used his hat to scoop it up, but to no avail.

Then he remembered Hamberdeen's words. "Hope will enlighten the shadow." The shadow pulled out the stopper on the bottle.

A howl soughed out from the bottle's mouth accompanied by a glittering steam, but instead of drawing towards the mist, the hope clung to the shadow, wrapping about him like a cast around black plaster. As it did, the hope molded the shadow, like hands about a lump of clay on a potter's wheel, shaping him into a three-dimensional form, a form taller and broader and more concrete.

The shadow breathed in deep, his lungs filling with oxygen, and he rolled back his broadening shoulders, stretched his sinewy arms, and rotated his wrists to accustom himself to his material shape. He took the candle from the lantern to search for the last traces of the disappearing wisps of mist. The mist was drawn to the candle's flame as if in desperate need of the light. The mist whirled around the wick in a vortex of light and shadow, spinning like string about a spindle, winding about the candle, growing larger until it wound about the shadow as well.

The vortex diminished. The soul, the wick, the flame, the hope, the shadow all merged into one being, his face a black mask of shadows, with two glints of light burning through slits where the eyes would be. Instead of flesh, the being was sheathed in a gleaming black mixture of wax, cinder, and shadow. The man-shape was wrapped in a flowing cape of cinder and black shiny wax and wore a black broad hat and black riding boots. The glints of golden light in the eye slits softened as he became aware of who he was. The being had the physique and memories of Edmond Davidson, but retained the lithe, flexible, carefree nature of youth. At the same time, his heart raged and his instincts sang with the driving power of the wolf.

And he knew. He was the conglomerate of all three. He was Blackwick.

Up in the stratosphere, flecks of snow speckled the two titanic combatants, Vorever and Ordog, as they collided across the sky. Vorever, superimposed over Betty, blocked Ordog's thrashing head with a mighty golden wing. Ordog's head clanged against the metallic wing, and he jolted with the concussion. His throat had healed by now, and he exhaled a blast of flame at Betty. Vorever swiveled his long, broad neck around and opened his mouth to swallow the flames. The flames flared back out of Vorever's maw and encircled Ordog in strands of golden light, strapping shut the crimson dragon's jaws.

Ordog snorted angry bursts of smoke as he struggled to free his jaws. He raised his talons to swipe at Betty, but she threw out her palms and shot forth golden lightning, which struck Ordog in the eye, sizzling and burning it out of its socket.

Ordog lowered his head and shrieked in agony, his wings drooping. He plunged from the sky, crashing into the valley below.

The army of Intercessors gathered around the fallen dragon. Betty glided back to earth, and with the Golden Dragon still superimposed about her, she gazed down upon Ordog with severe blue eyes. She planted her hand, with the ghost of the Golden Dragon's foreclaw, upon Ordog's chest, in a gesture of submission. "You will cause harm no more!"

Betty closed her eyes and felt the force of darkness ooze from Ordog, all the energy he had ingested from the countless souls he had stolen throughout the ages. And as his power drained, he shrank.

Ordog grew smaller and smaller, until he was a tiny mouse of a dragon that yiped in fear and tried to scramble away, but Portia prrowed and pounced, batting at it with her paws to ensure it did not escape.

Betty swirled her hands in the air, creating out of the golden light streaming from her fingertips a gilded cage. She scooped Ordog into the cage. Portia stood watchful guard over the minute creature, which, like a panicked mouse, squealed and scampered about in its cage.

Holmes and Watson stood on the outskirts of the village. Holmes retrieved his deerstalker cap from the ground where the commotion had tossed it. He adjusted the cap on his head and glanced out of the corner of his eye at Betty, surrounded by the Intercessors all hugging her and shaking her hand in congratulations. No longer superimposed by the Golden Dragon, Betty stood as herself, humble and amazed at what had happened.

"She's come quite a way from that poor orphan who wrote me those letters," Holmes commented partly to Watson, but mostly to himself. He was proud of Betty, but also, though he would not admit it to Watson, a little sad, the kind of sadness one feels when a perfectly played concerto reaches a moving finale.

The Golden Dragon circled the sky, glowing like a nebula in the light of the moon. Vorever spiraled in graceful loops towards the ground and landed upon all four feet beside Holmes. "Your role in her life is concluded . . . for now," he told the detective. "Your world needs you, your sense of justice and mercy."

Holmes gazed in Betty's direction, his eyes misty at what might have been. To Vorever, he tapped his index finger to the bill of his cap in acknowledgement.

He cleared his throat and turned to his colleague. "Watson, I wonder if Mrs. Hudson will have something nice for us for dinner. If not, there's always Romano's, and perhaps a concert? A little music, something by Chopin, I think."

"Yes," agreed Watson. "Chopin would be just about right."

Holmes, humming the *Heroic Polonaise*, strolled with Watson into the mist of the portal that led back to Baker Street.

CHAPTER 41
VANDOR

Beatrice Talbin, Keeper of the Golden Vigil, spent the warm summer mornings, rainy spring afternoons, stormy autumn evenings, and cold winter nights in the library at Vandor. Every story that ever was or ever could be was housed in the vast shelves. She spent much of the day curled up in the window seat, backdropped by a view of the island's rugged terrain, lulled by the whooshing ocean waves. A cup of steaming tea in her hand and her fluffy gray kitten snuggled in her lap, she reread the books she loved the best.

The Tales of Neverland told the adventures of Peter Pan and Frieda Fernsby, youthful guardians of all the lost and lonely children. *The Adventures of Perlgate Manor* told of Leslie, working his way up in the ranks of Scotland Yard to become Inspector Mallowan, bent on thwarting evildoers. There was the epic poem celebrating the beautiful Kukuana marriage ceremony of Captain Good and Foulata. And the journals of Daniel Khumalo, pursuing a clue he found in *The Book of Ancestors*, following a trail to the pyramids of Egypt. Her favorite was *The Return of Sherlock Holmes*, which told how the detective defeated the evil Professor Moriarty.

The bell on the door to the library jangled.

"Come in." Betty picked up her diadem from underneath a pile of books. She used the shining lid of a teapot as a mirror as she adjusted her long dark locks around the golden band.

Akira Yamada entered, the chart tucked under one arm. He steadied one of the stacks of books piled up around Betty. Portia opened one sleepy green eye, yawned, and stretched. Yamada gave Portia a scratch behind her ears and smiled at Betty. "You are happy here."

"Yes," said Betty. "I love my long talks with Vorever. I love reading about my friends and all their adventures. If it weren't for that," she pointed towards a small, empty cage, the bars seared open and its inmate flown, "everything would be perfect."

"Yes, Ordog grows stronger every day, and once more the Accusers are a force to be reckoned with." Yamada unrolled the chart. In eighteenth-century calligraphy, the words *"Come at once!"* appeared over the outline of France.

Betty nodded, and, carrying Portia in the crook of her arm, she mounted the winding stairs, up into the chamber within the cupola at the top of the tower. In the center of the room was a large gold candle. She set Portia on a gold-tasseled cushion and unlocked a cabinet. She took a long white candle and lit it against the flame of the gold candle. She tilted the white candle so that seven drips of wax dropped into the pool of melted golden wax surrounding the wick of the larger candle. With a long stick she flicked the blackened tip of the wick into the candle's basin.

The wind rushed in through the eye-shaped window, billowing her long black hair and flailing her white cashmere scarf about her shoulders and her neck. She stretched out her palms over the rippling wax and spoke the words of the ritual, in a voice like patchouli escaping from alabaster.

"Seven drips, from the wick, and from the thick, will come Blackwick."

From the black of the burnt wick emerged a shadow. The shadow took shape, wearing a shiny black cape and a black broad-brimmed hat, with tall black riding boots over his long legs. He bent the amber gleams on either side of his shadow-masked face upon Betty. He doffed his hat and dropped on one knee before her.

"I am yours, my lady," said Blackwick, bowing his face over her hand.

"You will use this book as your portal." She handed him A *Tale of Two Cities* by Charles Dickens. "It will take you to France where many lives are at stake. Summon any Intercessor you deem necessary to help you."

"Yes, my lady." Blackwick rose, brushed Betty's hand with a kiss. She rested her hand upon the back of his head, smiling serenely. "God speed, Edmond."

It was not long before Blackwick was seated on the box of a royal blue eighteenth century carriage, shaking the reins of a team of gallant milk white steeds, racing into the misty twilight, on the winding road to Paris.

LITERATURE REFERENCED

Intercessor Challenge: Locate all the literary references throughout Forever Is Eternity. If you are unfamiliar with any of the titles listed here, look them up online or check them out at your library to learn more about these magical portals.

Alighieri, Dante (c. 1265 – 1321)
Divine Comedy

Andersen, Hans Christian (1805 – 1875)
"The Littlest Mermaid"
"The Snow Queen"

Austen, Jane (1775 – 1817)
Mansfield Park
Pride and Prejudice

Barrie, J. M. (1860 – 1937)
Peter Pan

Brontë, Charlotte (1816 – 1855)
Jane Eyre

Brontë, Emily (1818 – 1848)
Wuthering Heights

Burnett, Frances Hodgson (1849 – 1924)
The Secret Garden
A Little Princess

Carroll, Lewis (1832 – 1898)
Alice in Wonderland
Through the Looking Glass (And What Alice Found There)

Coleridge, Samuel Taylor (1772 – 1834)
The Rime of the Ancient Mariner

Dickens, Charles (1812 – 1870)
A Christmas Carol
A Tale of Two Cities
Hard Times

Donne, John (1572 – 1631)
Holy Sonnet 10 "Death, be not proud"

Dostoyevsky, Fyodor (1821 – 1881)
Crime and Punishment

Doyle, Sir Arthur Conan (1859 – 1930)
The Adventures of Sherlock Holmes
The Memoirs of Sherlock Holmes
The Hound of the Baskervilles
The Return of Sherlock Holmes

Dumas, Alexandre (1824 – 1895)
The Three Musketeers

Grimm, Jacob (1785 – 1863) and Wilhelm (1786 – 1859)
"Little Snow White"

Haggard, H. Rider (1856 – 1925)
King Solomon's Mines

Hawthorne, Nathaniel (1804 – 1864)
The Scarlet Letter

Stevenson, Robert Louis (1850 – 1894)
Treasure Island

Stoker, Bram (1847 – 1912)
Dracula

Lord Tennyson, Alfred (1809 – 1892)
"The Charge of the Light Brigade"
"The Lady of Shalott"

Verne, Jules (1828 – 1905)
20,000 Leagues Under the Sea
Around the World in 80 Days
Carpathian Castle
Journey to the Center of the Earth
Michael Strogoff

Wells, H. G. (1866 – 1946)
The Time Machine
War of the Worlds

Wren, P. C. (1875 – 1941)
Beau Geste

Acknowledgements

Forever Is Eternity began as an escape from the stress and anxiety life brings us sometimes. Two special students of mine, due to the pandemic of 2020, were meeting with me through video conferencing. Discovering our shared love of werewolves, vampires, fairies, and goblins, they encouraged me to complete and publish this book. I kept these two in mind as I wrote, and they both agreed to be my first beta readers. For this reason, a large helping of gratitude goes to Cassie Cruz and Amber Martin, who learned that every time they identified passive voice a fairy grew its wings and every time they corrected a nominalization, a goblin found its gold.

A huge bouquet of gratitude goes to another former student and now published poet, Mel Finefrock, author of Patchwork Poetry. She beta read my book with the thoroughness of a content editor and gave me invaluable feedback. Beyond her editing prowess, our shared love of mermaids, candles, and a good cup of tea helped inspire many moments in this book.

To my sisters, who are not only my best friends but also my role models, thank you. Without Tirzah Darnell, author of the Sci-Fi novel Planet of Darkness, I would never have started writing in the first place.

Thanks also belongs to Anna Hazelrigg, who gave me feedback on the cover art as I reviewed the striking designs of Cangxxx Graphics, and to Jody Dyer of Crippled Beagle Publishing, whose guidance in the publishing process enabled me to reach my publishing goals.

Finally, I wish to acknowledge Jolene Scheepers from Story-First Marketing, whose creative art brought the characters in this novel visually to life. Visit enchantedinkaistudio.com to discover more creative fantasy art.

About the Author

Kathleen R. Cuyler graduated with her Master of Arts in English from the University of North Texas. She currently lives in Beeville, Texas, where she teaches English at the local community college. She has authored the textbook Diving into the World of Literature through Kona Publishing and Media Group. Forever Is Eternity is her debut fantasy novel and the first of a series of five books. When Kathleen is not teaching or writing, she loves reading, drinking coffee, and spending time with her pets.

Visit www.mochawavepublishing.com to visit the bookshop, follow her blog, and sign up for her newsletter.

About the Blackwick Series

The Blackwick Series follows Beatrice Talbin, a teenaged girl in 1930s England, who discovers her love of reading is more than an escape from the drudgery of her daily life. It's a gift that gains her admittance to the Society of the Inter-Story Intercessors. Traveling into the books she loves, she and her fellow Intercessors are caught up in a war between the Golden Dragon, Vorever, and his ancient nemesis Ordog, the Crimson Dragon Lord.

🐉 Dragon Lineage 🐉

From the cosmos came the celestial dragons

Vorever   Zed-Cyphrr   Abyssmalith

Neverbird   Labyrinthius

From Vorever came the dragon titans

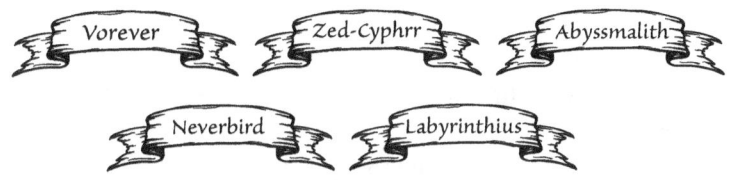

Ordog   Water-Ghoul   Serpentine

Death-Guardian   Diamond-Hoarder

From Ordog came the subdragons

Avian   Moriarty   Milverton   Esmé

The Marquis   Silver Boot   Lord Henry

Dragon Language Glossary:

Arunt: Are
Athana: Beginning
Avadni: Reward
Avanti: Go, Away
Aventiss: Come
Aya: Yes
Ba: Sing
Beethen: To exist, to be
Celvarin: Celestial Dragon
Corseesh: Beautiful
Deveethan: Defy, eliminate
Dirthic: North
Dothan: Does (used as a verb for questions)
Dom: Doom
Een, Eenan, Eenam: One (used for all personal pronouns)
Ēge: Fear (noun), Egen To fear (verb)
Eraath: Epoch
Fa: Find
Feelan: Forward
Feggintar: War
Feggin: Fire
Finetae: Epilogues or an epilogue of a book
Finnen: Find
Fithu: To breathe
Fortunan: Sold one's soul
Furnathar: Leader, master
Gaivarin: Entire universe
Gangen: Go
Gefulen: To feel or to fulfill
Gevehthen: Sacrifice (verb)
Grufen: Command (verb of command)
Ghulantan: East
Gudhan: Good

Hathan: Has
Hordin: West
Hunathane: Henchman
Infantis: Human
Inthum: Into; Inthem: Within
Ishata: Term of endearment; "my beauty"
Konnen: Can do something
Lathan: Let
Loklok: Slave
Malvaren: Corruption
Malwissan: Lie
Margina: Marginalia (like in a book)
Mithem: With
Modor: Mother
Mussen: Must
Nae: No one
Naewissen: Impossible
Nimmen: Take
Norsish: Deed
Nuthan: Now
Onsem: One / All of them
Pfash: Where (question word)
Portag: Portal
Portag nimmen: Take what is in the portal
Portag vunen: Open the portal
Rinthem: Beyond
Sangen: Endure
Saa: Lives
Scriffan: Book
Scriffvarin: A world within worlds
Shlekt: Bad
Sovool: Blood
Sovoolan: Tasted blood
Sullen: Dragon scale
Subvarin: Subdragon
Suthen: South

Thaa: There; over there
Thonen: Those / An article of some kind
Titanvarin: Dragon Titan
Tramen: Nightmare
Varin: Dragon
Verwand: Transformation
Vereeth: True; Vereethan: Truth
Vishin: Potion
Voreev: Time
Vorever: To live all for all time
Vunen: Open
Wissan: To know
Wollen: Will (verb)
Wyrmkin: Child of a subdragon

The adventure continues!
Read the next book in the Blackwick Series!

Follow Kathleen R. Cuyler at
www.mochawavepublishing.com
TikTok @mochawavepub
Instagram @kathycuyler
Facebook Mocha Wave Publishing.

For more information reach out to Kathleen on
info@mochawavepublishing.com

Scan the code and join the "Let's Talk"
newsletter to stay up to date on series news!